The

NIGH~~~~~~

After teaching at the Catholic University of Lublin and the University of Lodz, both in Poland, at the University of Tokyo and at Smith College in the United States, Michael Irwin moved to the University of Kent, in Canterbury, where he became Professor of English, specialising in eighteenth and nineteenth-century literature. His published eighteenth-century work includes a full-length study of Fielding and essays that take in Defoe, Richardson, Sterne, Smollett, Johnson and Pope.

The
SKULL
and the
NIGHTINGALE

Michael Irwin

blue door

Blue Door
An imprint of HarperCollins*Publishers*
77–85 Fulham Palace Road,
Hammersmith, London W6 8JB

www.harpercollins.co.uk

This paperback edition 2014
1

First published in Great Britain by Blue Door 2013

Copyright © Michael Irwin 2013

Michael Irwin asserts the moral right to
be identified as the author of this work

A catalogue record for this book is
available from the British Library

ISBN: 978-0-00-747635-0

Set in Caslon by Palimpsest Book Production Limited,
Falkirk, Stirlingshire

Printed and bound in Great Britain by
Clays Ltd, St Ives plc

For Stella

There is no difference to be found between the skull of King Philip and that of another man.

Samuel Richardson, *Clarissa*

1

It was a breezy day in March when I returned to London from two years of travel, my age twenty-three, my prospects uncertain. I refreshed myself with coffee at the Roebuck before making my way to Fetter Lane, and the office of my godfather's agent, Mr Ward. Conceivably, this gentleman might be about to determine the future course of my life in twenty words. I paused at the entrance to his premises to assume unconcern.

He lurched up from behind his desk as ungainly as ever, a big fellow, with a head like a horse, and a gloomy eye.

'Good afternoon, Mr Ward. I am glad to see you well.'

'Good afternoon, Mr Fenwick. I have been expecting you.'

When we sat down there was a silence. I looked to him for more, but his large face was expressionless. Apparently it was for me to lead the way.

'I hope that my godfather is in good health.'

'I have heard nothing to the contrary.'

Mr Ward had ever been a sparse talker. I tried again.

1

'Have you instructions for me?'

'I have. Your former lodging with Mrs Deacon has been prepared for you. I will send to Mr Gilbert tomorrow to let him know that you have returned.'

'You have nothing further to tell me?'

'Not at this time.'

It seemed that the uncertainty was to continue.

'I shall, of course, be writing to him myself.'

'I had assumed as much, Mr Fenwick.'

Old long-chops was formal as an undertaker. Determined to strike a spark from him I brightened into affability.

'Tell me, Mr Ward, do you not find me wonderfully improved by my grand tour?'

He surveyed me grudgingly till a brief gleam lit his glum face.

'I see you are elegantly dressed, Mr Fenwick. The other improvements may require a little more time to take in.'

It was a slight enough stroke, but it gratified him to the tune of a quarter-smile. I felt sufficiently rewarded: but for my question he might not have tasted such merriment all week.

'You laugh at me, Mr Ward,' said I, ruefully, as though he were a jolly dog. 'If I am to spend much time in London I shall hope to show you the progress I have made.'

He ignored my hinted question.

'You do me too much honour, Mr Fenwick. But if you speak to me in French you will receive no reply.'

This second sally gave rise to the rare full grin, uncovering his big yellow teeth. I chuckled a response to confirm that we were on friendly terms. After all he might one day prove a useful ally. Knowing that I would learn no more, I took my leave.

At least the news had not been bad. There would be a period of suspense as messages went to and from Worcestershire: meanwhile all my possible futures still lay open. The lodgings in Cathcart Street would suit me well enough: I had stayed with Mrs Deacon before leaving for France, and found her courteous and discreet. I could lie low in her house until I heard from my godfather, adjusting myself to English ways again and tuning my tongue to my native language.

❧

When I had exchanged courtesies with Mrs Deacon and sent for my luggage, I sat down in my parlour to write a letter.

My dear Godfather,

I returned to London this afternoon from the travels which you so generously enabled. Mr Ward advised me that I should take my former lodgings with Mrs Deacon and await your further instructions.

The last communication I received from you found me in Rouen, on the final stage of my journey home. You were at that time, you reported, in good health, and were kind enough to say that you looked forward to seeing me on my return. When we meet you will find me, I hope, better informed and a little less awkward. Your generosity would have been ill rewarded if that were not the case.

In my letters to you I have attempted to convey something of what I have acquired. I can now converse fluently in French and tolerably well in German and Italian. My knowledge of the history, politics and arts of the great European countries has been greatly enhanced.

When last in London I was still something of a young country colt. I had exuberance without discipline, curiosity without direction. I hope my two years of travel have made me more reflective and purposeful. At the very least I am improved in deportment and address.

These claims may seem idle boasts. I would hope to make them good in conversation when I have the pleasure of seeing you – the godfather whose generosity to an orphan has done so much to improve his lot and widen his prospects.

I will remain in London and await further directions. Since a defined period of education has now come to an end, you may imagine that I look forward with eagerness and some little anxiety to hearing what advice you now have for me.

I remain, &c.

The composition of this grave epistle was accompanied by a facetious mental commentary. Much of the knowledge I had acquired related to activities that I would not have cared to discuss with my godfather. I was mimicking the cadences of respectability.

But I was dissatisfied with the letter even as I wrote it. It was too priggish, too fulsome: it lacked the playful touches that I fancied Mr Gilbert relished. The two-year absence had put me out of practice: I looked to recover the appropriate tone when I saw my patron again and could adapt my conversation to his responses. Perhaps it had been advisable, at this stage, to err on the side of seriousness. He was a formidable old gentleman in his way, not to be taken for granted.

☙

Perversely pleased to be breathing smoky London air once more, I refused Mrs Deacon's offer to prepare me dinner and strode out through the teeming, noisy streets. The wind had strengthened, and the big shop signs were swinging and creaking overhead. My destination was Keeble's steakhouse near the Strand, which in former days I had often visited with my friend Matt Cullen. With a nod of greeting I took a seat at a table three-quarters full. It quickly struck me that my fellow-diners were talking with particular animation and vigour. I concluded, rightly as I later learned, that this was one of the regular meetings of a Conversation Club. Without attending to what was said I was content to be, once more, sitting in a haze of English words and phrases. I let the talk wash over me and fancied myself linguistically refreshed.

Whatever my future course, for the time being it was comfortable to be home. Weary from travel I drank some wine to feed my reflections, and became pleasantly bemused. What would my godfather have to say to me? Where would I be two weeks hence? Was I to be condemned to rural life? The previous morning I had been conducting my business in French: would I ever have reason to speak that language again? Hereabouts my idle stream of thought circled into an eddy. I wondered in what corner of my skull the unspoken language would be stored. How could such multifarious knowledge, such haystacks of nouns and verbs, such ladders and bridges of number and gender, be folded away into an unseen space? I pondered the paradox until my head swam – indeed I must have been grinning at my own bewilderment, for a voice cried: 'To judge by the smile this young fellow is happy in his meditations.'

I came out of my reverie to see a dozen faces around me, chewing, drinking, talking and laughing.

'Gentlemen,' I said, 'you must excuse me. I was lost in thoughts about the mysterious operations of the human brain.'

'Beware!' cried one of the number, 'I smell a virtuoso. Keep your headpiece out of his hands, or he'll be at it with microscope and scalpel.'

'Never fear,' said I. 'I am an idle speculator under the influence of wine.'

'Then fill your glass,' said another, 'and take us with you.'

I had no great desire to converse, but it seemed churlish to stay silent.

'My thoughts were of this nature. If any one of our company were now to attempt to write down all the words he knew, he could spend the entire night in the undertaking. By the morning, with his task far from complete, the fruit of his labour would already be a thick wedge of manuscript. Yet his brain would need no replenishment. Where has he been storing this copious knowledge, now translated into a material mass? And how can he dispense it yet still retain it?'

The company seemed pleased by the problem. After a pause, someone said: 'As to the former question one might proceed by a course of elimination. To begin facetiously: my poor uncle lost three limbs at the battle of Blenheim, yet his memory was unimpaired. It seems that the storage place you seek is to be found in the head or the torso.'

'There is no need for such questions or such reasoning,' cried another. 'We already know that the mind is the seat of reason and memory.'

'Indeed we do,' said I. 'But although I am no anatomist I believe that the contents of the skull are as unmistakably material as the limbs the gentleman referred to. How are we to account for the unique receptivity of this particular physical organ, its sponge-like capacity to contain words, concepts and images?'

Several tried to speak, but were overridden by a bony fellow with a big voice.

'We discussed such matters a year ago. I posed questions similar to your own – and was denounced as a materialist and an atheist for my pains. But I refuted the charge very simply. The Almighty works miracles with material substance. If an acorn can contain a future tree, surely a human head can contain the contents of a dictionary?'

Fired up by now I struck back: 'You explain one mystery by appealing to another. If the unfathomable powers of omnipotence are to be invoked there is an end to all debate.'

These words produced uproar, and during the heated exchanges that ensued I paid for my entertainment and slipped away.

It was a dark, boisterous night. I made my way back

towards Holborn along busy thoroughfares, clutching my hat whenever I turned a corner into a gust of breeze. North of Lincoln's Inn Fields the streets were quieter and but feebly lit. I was brought up short when a haggard girl stepped out suddenly from the end of an alley, crying: 'Come this way, sir!'

'Not tonight, I thank you,' said I, affably enough.

'No, no' – in a frantic voice – 'I need help. My child . . .'

She turned hurriedly into the alley, and I followed, willing to be of assistance if I could. But after a few yards she turned about, clutched my greatcoat and shouted 'Rape! Rape!' At once a heavy brute of a man sprang from a doorway brandishing a cudgel. Startled as I was I found myself protected, as in certain previous physical encounters, by an instant blaze of animal rage. Half avoiding the bully's blow I seized his coat and rammed him back against the wall. He raised his club again, but I checked him with a punch to the belly, and then struck him a dowse to the chops that smacked his head back against the brickwork. The intending robber staggered sideways and stumbled to his knees. The girl leaped at me, scratching with both hands, but I wrenched her away and threw her on top of her fallen protector. Without waiting for more I hastened away.

Such a fury had surged in me that I walked an extra mile, at top pace, to allow my pounding heart to settle. It had been a sordid episode, but before I reached Mrs Deacon's house I found myself recovered from it and not unsatisfied. The first evening of my return to England had called into play some of the aptitudes fostered by my travels. I had taken a lively part in impromptu discussion and then shown that I could hold my own in a street fight. It seemed that I was resourceful, a young man of parts.

⸎

Next morning I winced a little on rising. There was a stiffness in my shoulder and a handsome purple bruise on my ribs. It would take me a day or two to shake off these effects. Through the window I saw rain, which suited my mood well enough. Here was a stasis in my life, an interlude between the acts: I could make it a time for recuperation and reflection. I knew where I would be likely to find some of my former Oxford companions, but felt no inclination to seek them out. How could I answer the questions that would greet me until I knew what was purposed for my future and what sort of figure I was likely to cut? Matt Cullen I would have been glad to see, for he was a man I could laugh with, but our correspondence had lapsed, and I knew nothing of his whereabouts.

All morning I stayed within doors, completing the journal that I had kept during my travels. The parlour in which I was writing had a mirror at one end in which I several times caught my reflection. At length I rose to study myself more minutely and at full length. In figure I would pass muster, being above the common height, vigorous and well-knit, but my face seemed to me too open, too youthful, redeemed from blandness only by strong brown eyes. Given the common belief that a man's character can be deduced from the front portion of his head, this could be a disadvantage. I practised certain expressions – attentive, amused, eager

– and found the case somewhat improved. I could assume a variety of responses that might make me appear an agreeable companion. In repose, however, my face seemed a *tabula rasa*, awaiting the imprint of further experience.

The rain continuing, I worked diligently at my journal, bringing the record to a conclusion with my arrival in Dover. It was convenient that the combination of vacant time, rough weather, a bottle of ink and the wing-feathers of a goose had enabled me to capture my recollections before they were lost – I had always been quick to forget. My life being thus far in order, I was ready for what was to come.

Cathcart Street was in a quiet neighbourhood, but there was noise enough from it to bring me to the window more than once. The kennel down the middle of the road was swollen by the rain into a thick black stream, lumpy with refuse. Pedestrians in sodden clothes struggled sullenly along its edges, forced close to the walls. It was a dismal sight: there was much to be said for loitering within, warm and dry.

Later in the day, tiring of my own company, I made occasion to take tea with Mrs Deacon. Although I had lodged in the house before, I knew nothing of her beyond the fact that she was a widow, with a young daughter named Charlotte. In conversation she proved civil and shrewd, but maintained a certain reserve. It was this quality, perhaps, that caused me to see her as a handsome woman of forty, looking younger than her age, rather than as indeed a younger woman. Her composure suggested a lack of interest in any physical attraction that she might possess. I was unsure whether to play man of the world or affable young fellow. It was by chance that I found the less formal direction.

'Do you know Mr Gilbert?' I inquired.

'I knew him years ago. If he communicates with me now it is through Mr Ward.'

'Then the messages will be brief. Yesterday he offered me but fifty words.'

She smiled. 'So many? Then you can count yourself a friend.'

'Tell me, Mrs Deacon,' said I, 'how do you think this taciturn gentleman passes his evenings?'

She considered. 'He sits in an arm-chair and reads a big black book. When it grows dark he walks the streets with a big black dog.'

'But what is in the book he reads?'

'Nobody knows. It is one of his secrets.'

This time we both smiled.

I was glad to have hit on this vein of whimsy in my landlady's disposition, and to find myself easy in her company. Later that night, my imagination stirred by wine, I tried to envisage the warm body beneath the long dress. I liked what I saw with my mind's eye, but suppressed the picture as unsuitably distracting in my present situation.

❧

After two or three days of idleness I grew restless. I was in the unsatisfied state produced when the mind teems with questions to which there are no clear answers. Having had no living relatives since the age of ten I was accustomed to a solitary existence. Reserve and self-sufficiency were almost the only qualities I had in common with my godfather. But I fretted at being becalmed. Ambition assured me that Mr Gilbert would not have paid for my education, and sent me to the great cities of Europe unless he had substantial future plans for me. But circumspection reminded me that he was an enigmatic man whose patronage had been conferred from a distance. Although he had rescued me when I was homeless he had scarcely ever spoken of my parents, who had been his friends; and although he had countenanced occasional visits to Fork Hill House he had never encouraged me to stay for more than a few days at a time. At Oxford, therefore, I had been at pains to say nothing of my upbringing, not caring to admit that I had neither family nor home. Appearances had been preserved by bluff and evasion; but the constraint had been wearisome.

It was characteristic of Mr Gilbert to have dropped no hint as to his future intentions. For all I knew he might be planning to buy me a commission in the army or send me to the colonies. I felt no enthusiasm for either prospect. If I was to stay at home the possibilities seemed limited. I could not enter the church: neither my vagrant habits of thought nor my animal spirits would allow it. The law was hardly more inviting.

My favourite hope soared higher: perhaps too high. As far as I knew, my godfather had no living relatives. At his age he was unlikely to attempt marriage; and should he do so his thin loins would be hard put to it to originate an offspring. Surely it was time for him to proclaim me his heir and prepare me for the life of a prosperous landowner? In the country I could walk, ride and perhaps hunt. The more reflective side of my nature would find sustenance in Mr Gilbert's well-stocked library. When I needed younger company and livelier entertainment I would spend a few raucous weeks in London. Satiety achieved, I could again retreat to Worcestershire to read books and view the world philosophically.

This was my preferred narrative: a life I could freely adjust to my personal convenience. Perversely, however, I found even this possibility uninviting as implying a premature acceptance of settled middle age. By a curious paradox my dependent condition had fostered an independence of spirit: I had become accustomed to mingling affability with reserve. It seemed to me that, unlike my Oxford companions, I would be able, if put to it, to live by my wits. I was eager for a challenge that would show me what sort of man I was.

⌀

There had been little in my childhood that I cared to remember. Even my recollections of my mother, now dead for more than ten years, were uncertain. I had turned away from the past, as by instinct, to concentrate my attentions on the present and the future. It suited my disposition to be active: if left too long to brood I tended to lose my good humour and lapse into melancholy. To avert this possibility at the present time I needed a friend in whom I could confide. It was natural, therefore, that my thoughts turned to Sarah Kinsey, the only individual who knew just how I was circumstanced. It was two years since I had last seen her, and not much less than that since she had last written to me. She had faded in my recollection as I found fresh diversion abroad; negligently I had left her letters unanswered. Since my return she was suddenly present again before my mind's eye, shyly pretty, quick to smile. For all the seeming diffidence she had been independent: her tastes and opinions were all her own. We had talked with great freedom.

One night, in sentimental mood, I strolled to Pitman Street where Sarah had been living two years previously. I found the house in darkness, and stood to stare at it. Even as I watched, a light appeared in the window of the upstairs room where I had several times engaged in three-cornered conversation with Sarah and her aunt. Perhaps the two of them were chatting there at that very moment. I lingered for several minutes, indulging the imagined proximity and half tempted to knock at the door.

The matter was resolved when an old man emerged from a neighbouring house.

'Pardon me, friend,' I asked, 'does Mrs Catherine Kinsey live here?'

'She used to,' he said. 'A widow lady. But she left a year ago.'

I thanked him and turned away. Disappointed as I was, I knew that my quest had been an idle one. Even if I could have seen Sarah alone she would surely have reproached me for the breach in our correspondence. And with my future unknown, what had I now to offer? I was downcast as I trudged away: perhaps I would spend my life mourning Sarah as a lost love. Aware that a melancholy so hastily improvised could be of little substance, I savoured it nonetheless.

A week after my arrival in London I received a letter from my godfather:

> My dear Richard,
> I was pleased to receive word of your safe arrival. As you imply, there is much for us to discuss and consider. I would like to see you at Fork Hill House early next week, and hope that you will be able to stay for some few days. However, you may leave the bulk of your effects in the safe hands of Mrs Deacon.
> Your affectionate godfather,
> James Gilbert

It was a characteristically tight-fisted message. I could discern but a single clue concerning my future: it seemed that I was expected to return to London after my visit to Worcestershire. Whether the hint presaged an extended stay in the city or another journey it was impossible to guess.

2

I woke from a dream in which I was fumbling a plump whore in a dark street in Rouen. The impression stayed with me as I lay half insensible: I could smell the horse-dung on the cobbles and feel the girl's damp warmth. Only gradually did I come to myself and recollect that I was in bed in my godfather's house. Even then the idea was so strong upon me that had a maid-servant chanced to enter the room I might have sleepily seized on her, and perhaps derived a flesh and blood child from my fantasy. But the illusion thinned and my intellects began to confront the day. I arose, groped my way to the window and threw back the heavy curtain. On the instant I was myself again, looking out upon green lawns shining with dew below a bright morning sun. It was a sight to fill me with hope and energy. The day might hold revelations, but I felt ready to face them.

Having arrived too late on the preceding evening to see my godfather I had now to impress the man on whom my hopes depended. What manner would be best calculated to

16

win his favour? I concluded that a respectful but easy bearing, quickened with a hint of mischief, should do the business. As I washed and dressed I tried to think myself into this demeanour. Even a hint of importunity concerning my future would be unbecoming. Pleasure at the reunion, gratitude for past kindnesses: these were the emotions to display.

Downstairs I learned that Mr Gilbert had already breakfasted. I was directed to meet him later that morning in the drawing-room at the rear of the house. Arriving before he did I had time to survey, through broad windows, the slopes of Flint Hill fringed, in the distance, by black-branched woodland. On the nearside of those trees everything I could see belonged to my godfather and might one day, conceivably, belong to me. Behind me several family portraits gazed down. I turned to stare back at my adoptive ancestors. In life they might have been formidable: in death they were so many planes of pigment. It could not be many years before my godfather would be similarly reduced. Perhaps he had aged in my absence. Perhaps he would totter in to say, 'Let me be plain with you: I have but one month to live. This estate and all my wealth are to be yours. I wish you joy of them.'

When he did enter, however, it was with no such cadaverous air. He looked as I remembered him, lean, but by no means frail, his face shrewd and thin-lipped. As ever he was neatly groomed: the taut little wig could have been his own hair.

If he was overjoyed to see me he contrived not to show it. I adapted my manner to his, and our first exchanges were courteous rather than familiar. I had brought gifts from

17

abroad, which I formally delivered to my benefactor rather as a visiting English ambassador might present diplomatic offerings to a Chinese potentate. He received them with corresponding decorum. Thoughtful questions were asked concerning people and places, and suitable answers given. The little minuet of civilities was creditably performed by both parties.

Later, in response to his promptings, I told him various tales of my travels, speaking, I thought, gaily and well. He listened with attention, seeming by degrees to relax his customary reserve: I could even fancy that he looked at me with approval. On occasion our dialogue all but quickened into raillery.

'I inferred from your letters,' he said, with lizard-like dryness, 'that throughout your travels you conducted yourself in an exemplary way.'

'It seemed appropriate, sir, to represent myself in a sober light.'

My godfather allowed himself a ghost of a smile: 'I hope this sense of propriety did not circumscribe your pleasures.'

'I was at pains to resist that possibility,' said I, with a reciprocal hint of self-mockery.

He looked me directly in the eye, still faintly smiling.

'I notice a scar on the back of your hand.'

'You embarrass me, sir. It goes back to a small encounter in Florence.'

'A matter of honour?'

'Of intoxication, rather. It was a foolish incident, but no great harm was done.'

He nodded to close the subject, and then turned a sudden conversational corner.

'It is two years since last you were here. Have you perceived any differences?'

'Only that the great oak tree has gone that once stood beside the house.'

'It had become too old and brittle. It reminded me too much of myself.'

Taken by surprise I could fashion no suitably consoling response, but my godfather did not seem to notice. He sat staring at nothing before speaking again: 'I hope you will stay for some few days, and gain a sense of my life here.'

❧

Two evenings later some guests from the neighbourhood came to dinner. I was curious to meet these people, since I might one day have to live on terms with them, and curious, too, to see how my reticent godfather would comport himself in company. But equally it would be my task to rise to whatever the occasion was intended to be. I should think of myself as in some sense on display.

How much the visitors would know of my situation and prospects I could not guess. I would probably be the youngest person present and the one of least social consequence. On the other hand I was educated, gentlemanly, and had recently travelled. It would not do to be ingratiating nor yet forward. I resolved to stay out of general conversation, as far as possible, but to show myself attentive to individuals.

The loudest of the company proved to be Mr Hurlock, a florid squire with a buxom wife. He was a rattling, rallying fellow, aggressive in his manner, with a laugh like the bray of an animal. I saw in him an ageing country bully, coarse and discontented. Mr Quentin, a dark man with a brooding gaze, conveyed more intelligence with greater sobriety of manner. Of a different cast altogether was Mr Yardley, as lean as my godfather, with the stooped shoulders and sallow cheeks of one who devoted many hours to reading. I remembered to have heard him mentioned as a naturalist and collector. There was also Mr Thorpe, a young parson, new to the village. He wore a propitiating smile under an alert eye.

Hurlock greeted me boisterously: 'So you come here from France, young gentleman. Here in Worcestershire we turned against that country in '45, when the Jacobites reached Derby and we felt French breath on the back of our necks.'

I soon diverted him to the subject of hunting, on which he had much to say. Eventually relieved of his company by my godfather I escaped to Thorpe, who proved to be a former Oxford student and quizzed me amiably about university matters.

At dinner I had Mrs Hurlock on my right hand, and found my eye taken more than once by her prominent bosom – a former attraction declined, it seemed, to a feeding apparatus, since she confided that she had borne several children. I could see that twenty years before she must have been a covetable young lady; but time and a coarse husband had diminished her assurance. 'I believe you are a scholar,' she told me, 'and already a man of the world. Alas, I am merely a mother.' To keep her conversing about her surviving offspring was as simple as whipping a top.

On my left sat Mrs Quentin, another dilapidated beauty. I first saw her from behind, and fancied from her slim figure that she was hardly more than thirty. She had merely to turn around to age twenty years, her face being faded and unhappy. When I tried to converse with her over dinner I noticed a reticence and an odd cast of expression apparently attributable to the same cause, namely her desire to keep concealed a set of blackened teeth. I talked to her in a free and lively vein to create the illusion of an exchange, but avoided provoking laughter lest she should feel obliged to join in.

The wider discussion lurched between local and national concerns. Such political comment as I heard was so fanciful that it could have concerned the government of Japan: but after all these folk were a hundred country miles from London – two full days of travel. Hurlock blustered, Thorpe was emollient, Quentin brusque. Yardley spoke but little. My godfather was the best informed of the company, and showed considerable social address. With no attempt to dominate he yet led the conversation, his manner dry and sometimes satirical. He took in all that passed, and had a word for everybody at the table.

Certain fragments of talk stayed in my memory. At one time my attention was caught by a sudden intensity in my godfather's voice.

'We are told,' he said, 'that the Almighty requires praise. I cannot understand why. Is it not as though I should want my dogs to praise me for feeding them?'

'Perhaps, sir,' ventured Thorpe, 'you are interpreting the instruction too literally. Might it not be a figure – a mode of enjoining us to an *active* appreciation of our existence in a miraculous universe?'

'You men of the cloth are all alike,' cried Hurlock, through a mouthful of food. 'If we question any mystery of religion you tell us that it is no more than a damned figure. What do you leave us of substance to believe in?'

His truculence momentarily silenced the table.

'There are the commandments,' said Thorpe, mildly. 'Thou shalt not steal. Thou shalt not kill. Thou shalt not commit adultery.'

Hurlock made to expostulate further, but Mr Gilbert spoke up before him.

'Yes,' said he, with an emphasis that concluded the exchange, 'those would seem to offer us something to steer by – and something to fear.'

When the ladies retired the conversation took a different turn. My godfather, who had drunk frugally, seeming to enjoy his sips more than Hurlock his mouthfuls, proceeded to draw out Mr Yardley, who had hitherto been almost silent. With a little prompting he was induced to address the company on the subject of poisons. He spoke in a high, wavering voice, chuckling from time to time at the curiosities he mentioned:

'We have little understanding of susceptibility. A substance that will gratify one organism may prove fatal to another. You gentlemen drink brandy with pleasure, but it is known that a small amount of that beverage will kill a cat. Heh, heh! Sheep thrive on grass, but clover may prove fatal to them. We know that a snake-bite may kill, but what shall we say when a man dies from the sting of a bee, as has happened in this very parish? Heh, heh! This is the mystery of reaction: the element introduced combines fatally with something in the constitution of the victim.'

My godfather had been listening intently: 'Might not such an external element equally prove advantageous? If brandy can kill a cat, what say you to the possibility that a saucer of burgundy might transform its intelligence?'

Yardley sniggered. 'The example is grotesque, but in principle your hypothesis is just. The world is young: there are a million possibilities still unexplored.'

'What possibilities?' cried Hurlock, crimson with drink, 'I don't follow you, sir.'

'For example,' said my godfather, evenly, 'the possibility that when A is randomly made subject to B – A being a human-being, and B a substance, a situation, or even an idea – some unpredictable outcome may result.'

This proposition being beyond Hurlock in his fuddled state, he flew into a passion.

'Then let us fly to the moon, gentlemen,' he shouted, banging his fist on the table. 'Let us fly to the moon and have done!'

❦

Nothing exceptionable had taken place during the course of the evening; yet I could not rid myself of a sense of oppression. The guests had seemed constrained by Mr Gilbert's presence, as though a little cowed by him. Even Hurlock's outbursts had had a quality of nervous defiance. Might my gentlemanly godfather be intimidating?

The following day he asked my opinion of his guests. Seeking to be diplomatic without insipidity I ventured that Hurlock had seemed not unlike a stage representation of a coarse hunting squire, that Yardley had said a number of interesting things, and that Quentin had something enigmatic about him.

'Your comments are just, as far as they go' said my godfather. 'Hurlock is a fool. Yardley is haphazardly learned.'

'And Mr Quentin?'

My godfather reflected before replying: 'I can understand why you found him enigmatic. To me he is not, because I know the answer to the riddle.' His voice lightened. 'You were properly attentive to the ladies – gallantly so in the case of Mrs Quentin, whose bad teeth, as you must have noticed, foul her breath. Time has been unkind to her: she was comely as a young woman. Mrs Hurlock was the local beauty, eagerly courted; but she made the mistake of marrying Hurlock, who reduced her to a breeding animal. She has now ceased to breed. Perhaps neither woman has a life worth leading.'

Startled by this bluntness, I inclined my head and tried to look sagacious.

'You have now made the acquaintance of my nearest neighbours, such as they are. I contrive to remain on good terms with all of them.'

'I am sure you do, sir,' I hazarded.

Mr Gilbert pursed his thin lips and then spoke reflectively. 'It is in their interest that we should be on good terms.

All of them are in some sense in debt to me. It is remarkable how much influence moderate wealth can buy.'

He spoke without emphasis, but the passage of conversation had shown a greater astringency in him than I had ever previously witnessed. It had also reminded me of the precariousness of my own position. Perhaps that had been the intention.

Over the succeeding days I had a good deal of time to myself. Much of it I passed in the library, where a great fire was kept burning. I found there many publications of recent date, including the two volumes of Dr Johnson's great *Dictionary*, and a number of works concerning philosophy, medicine and astronomy. It was a pleasure to meet also my old friends Tom Jones and Roderick Random. Their presence surprised me. Did this solitary country gentleman sit peacefully by the fire, lost in tales of assignations and boisterous pranks? That possibility seemed the more remote in that here and in other rooms I saw evidence of Mr Gilbert's speculative curiosity: a terrestrial globe, a microscope, a brass telescope, a great magnet, and an articulated human skeleton.

When weary of reading I explored the house. Everywhere there were paintings, hangings and furnishings to admire. Even to my inexperienced eye it was apparent that the Gilbert family, about which I knew next to nothing, had been distinguished not merely by wealth, but by taste and connoisseurship.

I traced back the family line through a series of portraits. There were similarities of feature across the generations, but more striking was a cast of expression that suggested an inherited family temperament. Repeatedly a composed, even severe, countenance implied lurking passions controlled by force of will. I concluded that any one of these gentlemen would have proved a shrewd antagonist in argument or business or a court of law.

As viewed from the drive that led from the main gates the house was an imposing, wide-fronted building. The main rooms, spacious and lofty, answered to that external appearance. For some reason, however, I found myself particularly intrigued when quitting these apartments to venture down narrow staircases and stone-flagged passages into the domestic quarters. Here, like a colony of rabbits, dwelt the servants, far outnumbering those they served, even when there was company in the house. I reflected that such a mansion must necessarily have such a team to run it, as an ocean-going vessel must have men hoisting sails and manning pumps. These servants were my godfather's crew, his prosperity affording shelter and wages for footmen, housemaids, cooks, grooms and gardeners.

When the weather brightened I explored the estate. Hungry for fresh air and exertion I walked at a good pace, breathing deep. One fine morning I found myself running from sheer excess of energy. My furthest excursion was to the woods I had seen from the drawing-room window. In these first days of spring they offered little promise that they could ever resemble the shady groves of pastoral poetry. They were dense, leafless and dark – even menacing – in

aspect, as though ready, at a signal, to advance like Birnam
wood and overwhelm the cultivated land.

I was curious as to my godfather's daily doings. It seemed
that he spent much of each morning talking to attorneys,
tenants or tradesmen and attending to business of various
kinds. I began to infer that he was no passive landowner
but an efficient and industrious overseer of an estate, a master
of practices and responsibilities of which I knew nothing.
Might he wish to groom me to take an active part in the
conduct of these affairs? And would I be content to settle,
at so early an age, into the role of a rural administrator? I
hoped the question would not arise, while hoping also that
it would.

When in his company I observed him closely, looking
for signs that I might read. He was controlled in manner as
in speech, moving unhurriedly. His clothes, impeccably neat,
seemed to be an expression of his being. There was nothing
of the animal about him. It was impossible to imagine him
so much as sweating, still less rutting or at stool. Even in
his eating and drinking he expressed connoisseurship rather
than appetite. His disposition seemed to be the achievement
of years of self-command.

I assumed that there was a purpose to my seemingly purposeless stay, although I could not be sure what it was. Was it

to give me an opportunity to learn, indirectly, more about my godfather, or was it rather that he wished to learn more about me? What did I indeed feel about him, if anything? Grateful, in a formal sense, I certainly was, but my gratitude had no tincture of warmth. I could not feel myself to be blamably deficient in affection when Mr Gilbert himself displayed so little. There was no hint that he regarded me in any sense as the son he had not had. His detachment had evoked in me a similar coolness. He was my benefactor, and therefore to be propitiated. He was clever yet aloof and therefore an object of interest. If for some reason he should turn against me I suspected that he would sever the link between us without a qualm. I was therefore responsive to his moods, and ever on my guard. It had often been remarked of me that I had the capacity to please. At school, at Oxford and on my travels I had adapted myself to those I met and made friends readily. Mr Gilbert would hardly have carried his patronage so far had he not found something agreeable in my disposition. Such kindliness as I had elicited I hoped I could sustain.

I was further encouraged by a deeper and perhaps darker reflection. In several ways, after all, I had the advantage of the old gentleman. I was young and free-spirited, physically strong. If Mr Gilbert was quick-witted then so, I flattered myself, was I. Moreover by virtue of my youth, my education and my travels I might be open to modes of thought that he could not anticipate. If he chose to continue in his course of benevolence he would find me tractable and appreciative. If, for whatever reason, he was planning to dispose of my life in a manner at odds with my disposition we would be commencing a chess-game in which I would hope to hold my own.

We dined together every night, pretty comfortably as it seemed to me, but with no discernible progress towards greater intimacy. Our talk was easy and even lively, but Mr Gilbert said little that was personal. For my part I endeavoured to be entertaining, but was watchful for any hints of inquisition or irony and quick to deflect them with inconsequence, or with ironies of my own. Though nothing of moment passed between us I was satisfied that this time spent together would not lower my godfather's estimation of my abilities.

An aspect of his conversation with which I found myself in instinctive harmony was his habit of moving unexpectedly from civil commonplaces to eccentric speculation. There was an instance of this kind when he asked me what impressions I had formed concerning his estate. Wishing to please I remarked that within its boundaries there seemed to be order, cultivation and contentment. If other landlords were similarly capable and benign, I asked, might we flatter ourselves that in the course of time the whole country might come to enjoy this state of harmony?

'I think that unlikely,' he said. 'We strive for progress, but even our best attempts produce consequences at odds with our intention.'

'But surely, sir,' I urged, 'the building of this great house could be seen as an absolute gain. Here is an outpost of civilized life. Within its walls certain standards of conduct and taste are upheld.'

I strove to speak in the grave manner of one who would maintain such standards.

My godfather, in an habitual gesture, paused, glass in hand, to consider my observation, and then savoured a sip of wine before replying.

'Every building is under siege, this house not excepted. In providing privacy and protection for yourself you offer lodging-space for intruders. Mice have made their home beneath the floorboards. To control them we introduced cats. In summer you will see flies buzzing about the food, and moths blundering into lamps. Spiders lurk in corners. Birds nest in the chimneys. Moss takes root in the walls.'

Absorbed in these reflections he paused, sipped again, and then continued.

'Similar effects are everywhere observable. Even a beggar's shirt provides a tenement for fleas.'

I recalled my reflections about the servants below stairs, but thought it graceless to pursue the analogy.

'You are a philosopher, sir.'

'I have no such pretensions. I improvise. I make do.'

'You may say so; but I have seen optical instruments, shelves of learned books . . .'

'I have dabbled in this and that. I know a little about the flora and fauna of the county. Here my interests intersect with those of Yardley, though he is better informed than I. His concern is for the particular, for narrow observation and classification. Mine is for the general. I look for analogies and patterns. Lately I have taken an interest in meteorology and in the workings of the human body. The two subjects are surely connected, if only at the level of metaphor. The theory of the four humours has been abandoned, but I see why it came into being. We can have storms and droughts within.'

Then, with a sudden smile: 'But we must replenish your glass.'

I soon had reason to recall his words. When I drew the curtains next morning the sun was shining so brightly that I had to close my dazzled eyes. I leaned from a casement and inhaled a sweet, fresh breeze that on the instant filled me with energy. This was surely to be accounted the first day of spring. When I glanced in the mirror I was surprised to see myself smiling broadly. I stripped off my nightshirt and flung my arms wide. Within the glass stood my counterpart, looking young and impudent, his black hair in disarray, his privy member standing out like a staff, and pulsing with a life of its own. I found myself in a divided state: rampant with venereal need I retained wit enough to see the absurdity of such abject submission to physical tides. I broke into a loud laugh at the expense of my animal self, and saw in the mirror my head chuckling as my tail throbbed.

Later in the morning I went striding across the sunlit lawns and fields to release some of my newly-stirred vitality. I was craving youthful company – more particularly female company. The youthfulness I might have waived in my predatory mood. If Mrs Quentin herself had crossed my path her breath might not have saved her honour. When I reached the woods I found that they were as visibly altered as I had been on rising: twigs and branches were flecked with minute spots of green. An unseen bird was singing with passion, proclaiming his feelings or needs to the whole forest.

Touched by this elevated strain I drifted into romantic thoughts of Sarah Kinsey, but thence, by brute declension, into recollections of carnal pleasures in Rome. As memory induced sensation I yielded to the spring, and made shift – with a loud cry – to discharge my seed over a clump of budding primroses. Walking back to the house, with the primacy of the intellect sheepishly restored, I found myself unable to decide whether I had defiled the bright energies of nature or simply partaken of them.

⁓

The following afternoon the sun was yet warmer, and at my godfather's suggestion we strolled out onto the terrace. Our talk having been thus far no more than desultory trifling I was not surprised when he fell silent altogether and stood gazing out at the garden, one hand on the warm stone balustrade.

He spoke again without looking at me.

'Your years of travel have left their mark. You are bolder, more self-assured.'

I bowed, uncertain whether this was pure compliment.

'You have no recollection of your father, I believe?'

'Sadly I have not.'

'You have something of him in your appearance and disposition: the dark eyes, the affable address. Your visit has brought him vividly into my recollection.'

Here, surely, was the moment. Ten words would clinch the matter: 'I have therefore decided to make you my sole heir.' Unaccountably he let the opportunity slip.

'I have been observing you. You are robust and well-made. You have the gift of pleasing in casual conversation. You smile readily, and can make people smile in return. These are not talents that I share.'

'You do yourself an injustice, sir,' I said, beginning my sentence before I could see the end of it. Fortunately he raised a hand to interrupt.

'I speak without false modesty. Such capacities are rooted in temperament. For my part I can attract attention and respect.'

'So I have observed, sir.'

Ignoring this feeble compliment, he sat himself down on a stone bench and motioned me to join him. There was a silence, during which I fancied he was preparing a statement. At length he continued, musingly: 'I enjoyed your letters from Paris and Rome. In this house you have met some of the people with whom I commonly consort. They are a poor crew who live narrow lives. I was therefore refreshed to enjoy a tour of more exotic places, as seen through younger eyes and experienced by livelier senses.'

He turned to me: 'How different my life here has been. In Fork Hill the successive days are all but indistinguishable. Cumulatively they distil a kind of essence, or perfume, which gives pleasure but has left me dulled. National events scarcely impinge upon me. When King George died I felt nothing. By the time I hear that a new ministry has been formed it may be on the verge of collapse.'

'Is not that a peaceful state of affairs?'

'It is. But it resembles the peace of the grave. I need fresh life.'

'It would surely be open to you, sir, to spend some time in London?'

Mr Gilbert turned his face directly towards the sun and was silent for a moment, as though savouring the warmth on his thin cheeks.

'I was once a regular visitor to the capital. But it is five years since I last was there, and I did not enjoy the experience. I found the din and the stench repellent and the social life artificial. Yes, yes, there was more to it than that, of course. But my recollections are of dirt, disorder and foolish gossip. I will not go to London again. Yet I need diversion, I need stimulation.'

With sudden earnestness Mr Gilbert placed a hand on my sleeve.

'In consequence – in consequence I have devised an odd plan. Here I am, out of touch with London and life. The town demands a young man's constitution, and a young man's appetites. My proposal is that you should explore it on my behalf.'

I was floundering. 'How so, sir? In what capacity?'

'In the capacity of a young gentleman. You will stay in your present lodgings, and I will maintain you with a sufficient income. Your task will be to sample the life of the capital and convey to me your sense of it by regular letters.'

My spirits were rising. Was I really to live as I pleased and to be paid for doing so?

'This is a most generous offer, sir. But what in particular—'

He silenced me with a gesture.

'I leave the matter in your hands. When abroad you naturally felt obliged to see certain famous buildings and monuments; and you reported on them fittingly enough. Now I ask something different. Go where your own inclinations lead you. But write down what you see and hear and feel.'

I nodded, knew not what to say, so nodded once more.

'Although I no longer care to visit London it interests me more than I can say. It is a mighty experiment – or assemblage of experiments. I want you to report on the resulting pleasures, oddities and extremities as you experience them.'

He stopped, but I remained silent, seeing that he was still ordering his thoughts. When he spoke again it was in the tone of one summing up an argument: 'My hope is to be able to live two lives simultaneously – the familiar quiet existence here and, by proxy, a young man's life in the town. But is my proposal agreeable to you?'

I took a deep breath. 'How could it fail to be so?'

Mr Gilbert looked at me sharply: 'So you have no misgivings?'

'None, sir.'

'I am glad to hear it.' His face relaxed into a grim little smile. 'I have some myself. It may be that we will lead one another into dark territory.'

3

It is a strange fact that a mere idea can alter one's physical capacities. I am certain that in the excitement elicited by Mr Gilbert's proposition I could have run faster or sprung higher than at other times. Cramped within a coach for the return journey to London I had no scope for physical exertion of any kind, and the confined energy heated my brain till it simmered like a kettle. Fortunately my fellow-travellers were taciturn, leaving me to occupy the two slow, jolting days in thought.

The effect was to modify my exultation. I began to think my task less simple than I had assumed. What topics would find favour with my godfather? Wherever I looked there were doubts. It seemed unlikely that he would derive much entertainment from drawing-room chatter: indeed he had positively implied an interest in livelier activities. I could undertake escapades of one sort or another; but my descriptions of such doings would require tact. Drunken pranks might be seen as doltish. I would not wish to play the carousing clown; yet if I were too squeamish my letters might prove tepid.

There was also dignity at stake. I was not so craven as to be willing to prostitute my entire waking life to Mr Gilbert's requirements. If I was now to become a London gentleman I should do so on my own terms, and have interests of my own to pursue.

This line of thought led me to the notion that I could explore the town at more than one level. The modest dignity to which I aspired was not of a kind to prevent my enjoying mischief and carousal. Part of the time, however, I could wander the streets as a mere observer, sketching the singular, and often ugly, sights of London. There was much to be seen. I had long taken a passing interest in the work of builders, carpenters, glaziers, watermen and other such skilled artisans. The city teemed also with vendors, vagabonds, thieves and performers. Recording their doings would be an entertainment for me, and might provide material to divert my godfather. His responses would show me which of my activities he found most intriguing, and I would be guided accordingly.

A visit to Mr Ward gave me further encouragement. My godfather – who never went into such details in person – had handsomely adjusted my allowance to provide all the freedom I could wish for. Before commencing on my duties I could allow myself some pleasure. Needing to assuage my animal desires, which had by now become clamorous, I visited Mrs Traill's admirable establishment in York Street, where the young ladies were warranted to be free of contamination. But although I was pleasured with efficiency my imagination was left sadly unengaged. I concluded, with some disgust, that I had merely relieved a physical need in a species of public privy. During my travels I had enjoyed some extended intrigues. Now settled in London I would need to look beyond Mrs Traill.

It was not surprising, therefore, that I thought again of Sarah Kinsey. My desire for her person had always been compounded with admiration for her intelligence, good sense and underlying spirit. Unless she and her aunt had left the town I might hope to find her out and revive our old intimacy. I looked forward to telling her about my changed situation. With her, if all went well, I could contrive a private life of which my godfather would be told nothing.

Meanwhile, to equip myself for the parts I had decided to play I made immediate appointments with hairdresser, tailor, hosier and shoe-maker. My revised wardrobe included two new frock suits and as many waistcoats, one scarlet and one blue. Resolved also to appear sufficiently formidable, I purchased a sword of a quality proper to the wounding of the highest gentleman in the land, should the occasion unluckily arise. In appearance, at least, I was now equipped to mingle in the best company.

Pursuing my plan I procured also a number of plain garments that might enable me to pass muster as merchant, traveller, or skilled workman. To master my new terrain I obtained the latest map of London, and carefully perused it. With a little simplification it could be seen as a rectangle, perhaps five miles wide by three miles deep. At the western extremity lay Hyde Park, at the eastern were Wapping and Mile End. To the north the thoroughfares seemed to trail into open country beyond Old Street and Great Ormond Street. The southern limit was a series of irregular clusterings along the further shore of the Thames. This tract of land had somehow become home to half a million people. What similar tract on the face of the globe could match it for variety of interest? There would surely be much to see and hear.

My dear Godfather,

How would the town now strike you? Perhaps as bewilderingly frantic. At Fork Hill all is tranquillity. Here the senses are ceaselessly assailed. To enter any of the main streets is to be thrust into competition: wagons, coaches, carriages, chaises, chairs and pedestrians vie for space and priority. All too easily the traffic thickens to a standstill. How it was kept in motion before the opening of Westminster Bridge I cannot guess. At the busier times of day even walking is a struggle that can too easily become a scuffle. The air is clouded with vapours, and there is an incessant rattling, clattering, rumbling and banging, diversified by shouts and curses.

Night brings an additional strangeness. Can there ever before, in the history of the world, have been such a concentration of artificial light? Birds and insects must be bewildered by it. Yet on either side of the illuminated thoroughfares lie courtyards and alleys of Stygian darkness. The robber or pickpocket may strike boldly, confident that in seconds he can be lost to sight in a lightless labyrinth of side streets.

Within the houses of the wealthy, of course, life can be as sedately ordered as one could wish. It strikes me, however, that the law of complementarity you mentioned in relation to your own house, is visibly at work in London at large. The agglomeration, within a confined space, of the tradesmen, vendors, vehicles and goods needed to sustain this fashionable elegance must simultaneously engender dirt, disease and crime. Your perfumed fine lady, in her silks and satins, is as remote from such enabling ugliness as a flower from its muddy roots.

I fancy you would find the smell of the streets little changed, being compounded still of chimney-smoke, assorted refuse, and excrement, animal and human. Certain districts have their own speciality: thus Covent Garden stinks of rotten vegetables, Billingsgate of fish, and Smithfield of blood and offal. Why should vegetable and animal matter cause such olfactory offence as it decays? Death is given a bad name.

In the few days since my return the height of my achievement has been to see Mr Garrick perform upon the stage and Lord Chesterfield ride past me in a coach. I have, however, hit upon a general plan of action which I hope you will approve. Cram half a million people together and there will surely be collisions, grindings, smoulderings, combustion and explosions. Among the outcomes of this process, this mighty human experiment,

*as you called it, will surely be fresh discoveries, new ways
of looking at the world.*

*Where are these observations tending? I wish to suggest
that a mere social diary could not fairly represent the
multifarious doings of this metropolis. If you do not object
I will try to move between the strata of London life. The
whole city shall be my arena.*

*This by way of preface: I hope soon to be reporting in
more particular terms.*

Yours, &c.

I wrote those words within a week of returning to the city,
and went through three drafts before constructing my fair
copy. My letters needed to appear spontaneous – an effect
not to be achieved without labour. I had puzzled as to how
much and how often to write, but concluded that in either
case the best course was irregularity. My next offering was
deliberately more diverse.

My dear Godfather,

*I have now visited a number of fashionable
drawing-rooms. As you suggested, I used your name as an
introduction to Lord Vincent. You asked me to give my
opinion of that gentleman. He cuts a fine figure, tall and
erect. I found him civil but almost insipidly courteous,
averse to any expression of personal opinion. He asked me
to send you his good wishes and spoke of his cousin,
Mrs Jennings, apparently an old friend of yours.*

*Since Mr Pitt was present – although I did not speak
with him – there was naturally talk of foreign wars and*

unstable ministries, but as elsewhere in such gatherings I have as yet heard little of consequence. The prevailing gossip is concerned with petty feuds and scandals. I must wonder whether you would find such stuff worth your attention.

More rewardingly, I have sampled other levels of London life, attending theatres and auctions, dallying in coffee-houses, listening to mountebanks and ballad-singers. We have been enjoying some brisk spring weather: the April breezes blow, the dust swirls and the shop-signs swing and creak overhead.

On Tuesday last, near Charing Cross, I was one of a gathering held in thrall by a street-performer. He stood beside a cart, a fat fellow with a hanging belly. His nationality I could not guess, but he knew little English. He claimed attention by a bold presence and a big voice.

'Three Acts!' he cried. 'Three Acts!' – and brandished as many fingers in the air.

'One: I drink!'

He produced from his cart a bucket, filled with water. Holding it aloft with both hands he put his lips to the brim and began to drink, at first – amid some shouts of derision – quite cautiously, but then with greater confidence. Several times he broke off to draw breath, but always resumed to gulp more mightily, his audience watching with growing respect as it became plain that he would imbibe the entire contents. The contours of his body were visibly altered as the water filled it.

There was some applause when he finished, but he silenced it with a gesture.

'Two: I eat!'

Turning the bucket upside-down he placed on it a glass bowl containing several bright green frogs. He took one out and raised it in his fist, squirming and struggling. To the accompaniment of a groan from the spectators, he placed it in his mouth. With a frightful grimace he somehow contrived that two of the legs protruded, twitching, from the corners of his lips. Then he swallowed it. With less flamboyance, but at a stately pace, he proceeded to gulp down four more.

Having done so he stood for a moment with closed eyes, taking several deep breaths, as though adjusting the contents of his stomach more commodiously. His audience was now watching intently.

'Three,' he cried, 'I bring back! I bring back! Pay, pay! Please pay!'

He held out his hat, and such was his ascendancy that many a spectator tossed in a coin. Having collected what he could, he motioned us to move back and create a space, within which he remained for some moments stock still. After drawing several deep breaths he opened his mouth wide and with one hand twisted his right ear. At once a great jet of water came from his throat, as though from a fireman's hose, splashing on the cobbles. Checking it, he extricated from his mouth, alive and flailing, one of the frogs he had swallowed, and dropped the poor Jonah back in the bowl. He repeated the process four more times, so that all five were safely retrieved. There being loud applause he attempted a second collection, but it proved less successful than the first since the performance was complete.

On an impulse I gave him a crown. After all, the poor devil, adrift in a foreign land, was somehow contriving to make an honest living through exercise of a meagre range of personal talents. I could not but wonder about his daily life. He looked weary, and his clothes were well splashed. What refreshment could he enjoy, having swallowed and regurgitated a gallon of water? What woman would consort with this dank mound? Where, if anywhere, does he live?

I have renewed acquaintanceship with two of my Oxford companions, Ralph Latimer and Nick Horn. Latimer is fashionably languid, but harbours serious ambitions. As a relative of the Grenvilles he hopes soon to turn his back on his present freedoms and prepare for a higher role. It is less likely that Horn will seek respectability. He is a small, restless, nimble fellow, who will attempt anything by way of diversion. I have seen him climb a cathedral tower, half drunk, and on another occasion, for a five-shilling wager, wrestle with a pig.

The conversation I enjoy with such friends is livelier than drawing-room chatter, but too often deformed by liquor. Let me offer you a recent specimen, chosen because it recalled to me a discussion at your own table. The hour was late, and we had attained the melancholy mode. Latimer pronounced, with great emphasis: 'Believe me, friends, there is much in this life to make a man uneasy.'

This gloomy sentiment made us confoundedly grave. The conversation had been raised to a formidable altitude, but one or two of us tried our wings.

'I am of much the same opinion,' said a heavy fellow. 'Can even the best of us survive long enough to learn how to live?'

I myself ventured, with solemnity: 'Who knows but that one of us, even before the month is out, may be standing before his Maker? Is not that a tremendous thought?'

Latimer, unimpressed, was disposed to be argumentative.

'You say "standing", but the word is prejudicial. Can we so confidently assume the existence of legs in the life to come?'

To keep the shuttlecock aloft I improvised: 'At the moment of Judgement might we not be mercifully permitted some temporary sense of perpen-perpendicularity?'

'To be followed by what?' asked Horn.

Intimidated by this dark prospect, we all stared into vacancy, and our speculations expired.

It occurs to me that most people seem to shrink from contemplation of the after-life. Even those who are most earnest during divine service, as though glimpsing eternity, promptly revert to their workaday, unconcerned selves at the final blessing.

I conclude with a further note on the life of the streets. Within five minutes of leaving a polite assembly last evening I saw a man stumbling along with blood streaming from a wound to his head. London life is everywhere precarious. Even when walking to a steakhouse one may be under challenge.

Should that shove be reciprocated? Might that urchin be a thief? How remote from the rural life of reflection. Who can philosophize about swimming while compelled to swim? Last week, feeling a tattered pedestrian press too close I flung him from me. On the instant I regretted my reaction, for the wretch went staggering into the dirt. However, his rags falling open and disclosing two fine watches he was seized as a thief and mauled by the mob. My aggression had been justified by the event, but I might as easily have been wrong.

Daily I immerse myself further in the life of the city: I look about, listen and explore. You will soon hear further from me.

I remain, &c.

In adjusting myself to London life I was greatly influenced by a conversation with Latimer. I had asked him whether he knew the whereabouts of our friend Matt Cullen.

'I do not,' said he, frowning. 'But I fear he is a lost man.'

'Lost?'

'His prospects have taken a turn for the worse. He was in London last year, but was rarely seen. Then he vanished. Horn heard that he had returned to his native village to contrive a marriage. It seems that he is gone from us – condemned to rural nonentity.'

'Whereas we who remain . . .'

Latimer over-rode my hint of satire: 'I can speak only for

myself. I look to become a man of consequence. I cultivate men of standing. I make myself agreeable.'

'That is candidly said.'

'So it is. Observe how I speak with a trace of self-mockery to render my complacency acceptable. But truly, young gentlemen such as ourselves are on a slippery slope. We must feel for every foothold.'

'How will Nick Horn fare in this slippery predicament?'

'Horn will enjoy himself for a year or two longer and then fall away.'

'Like Cullen?'

'Like Cullen, but not as fast or as far. His family has greater means.'

Though he spoke airily it was manifest that he meant what he said. Partly to embarrass him I asked: 'And what say you to my own prospects?'

I was glad to see that the question made him pause.

'There I am in doubt. You were always a reserved fellow, Dick, not easily sifted.'

'I am in your debt to the tune of half a compliment. But tell me, Mr Latimer: does not your ambition deflect you from the pleasures of the moment?'

'It does not. Strip away my gentlemanly apparel and you would behold in me a satyr-like creature. One day the wise head will be obliged to disown the goatish tail – but not quite yet. There is still some discreet sport ahead.'

I found much to ponder in this exchange. If Cullen and even Horn could fall back so easily then I could plummet out of sight. But there was comfort in the realization that, after all, I did not envy Latimer his security. While he was obliged to fill his days with social visits and petty attempts at ingratiation I was free to roam the foulest streets and drink with porter or pedlar.

❦

My dear Godfather,

Last night, in company with Latimer and Horn, I visited the Seven Stars, in Coventry Street, the resort of some of our lustier men of fashion. To enter its doors was to plunge into cacophony; a herd of young bucks was in full cry, and punch flowed freely. The prevailing mirth had its tart London tang, suggesting that at any moment merriment might become aggression. In particular I happened to recognize among the roisterers Captain Derby, whom I had met briefly in Rome, a tall bully with some reputation as a duellist.

Horn, a seasoned visitor, led us boldly through to a back room, somewhat less crowded and noisy. It was here that I was to make the acquaintance of Mr Thomas Crocker.

How can I convey the appearance of this gentleman? If you saw a painting of his head alone you would think him handsome. He has an open countenance, inclining to plumpness, and an air of animation and quick intelligence. As I came into the room this face took my attention, occupying, as it did, a gap on the far side of the room, as though he were sitting slightly apart from his neighbours. Only at a second glance did I understand the source of this isolation: his body is of a bulk quite extraordinary, even freakish. I have since learned that he is nearly thirty stone in weight. When he is seated on a bench his thighs spread wide, so that he fills the space of two men. Had he not been heir to a notable estate he could have made a living as a prodigy in a fair-ground, along with my friend the frog-swallower.

Despite his physical appearance, however, it was soon clear that his companions regard him as their leader. Without exertion he commanded the room.

I sat quiet, observing the company and contributing little. My attention was caught by a silent man who seemed to be an attendant on the party rather than a participant. He was a lean fellow of middle height, with a pale, bony face and a watchful eye. I exchanged some sentences with him and learned that his name was Francis Pike.

The entertainment took a turn I could not have anticipated. When we joined the company and Horn introduced me, Crocker had been cordial enough but said little. Later he called out to me: 'Mr Fenwick, I am informed by Mr Latimer that you sing.'

'After a fashion,' I replied, somewhat taken aback.

(I have been told that I sing tolerably well, though this is not, I think, a talent that I have ever had occasion to mention to you.)

'Then this shall be our cue,' he cried out, 'for an interlude of music.'

He lunged to his feet, and with a shove thrust back the table, creating space to accommodate a mighty belly. His face seemed slightly swollen now, and shone with

49

perspiration, but in manner he was perfectly controlled.
Silence fell, and he launched into song, in a baritone voice
that would have graced a public stage:

No nightingale now haunts the grove,
No western breezes sweetly moan,
For Phyllida forswears her love,
And leaves me here to mourn alone . . .

Here was a strange interlude in a tipsy gathering.
The lament, a pastoral nullity, was heard with a respect
that the execution indeed deserved. It was an incongruous
performance from that huge body, as though an elephant
should tread a minuet. Hardly had the applause died
down than I was summoned to his side and invited to
change the mood by joining him in the edifying ballad
that begins:

I'm wedded to a waspish wife
Who shames the name of woman:
She's sharper than a surgeon's knife
And sourer than a lemon.

The duet being warmly received, Crocker saluted me
with a slap on the shoulders that all but knocked me
down, convincing me that his physical strength is
proportioned to his size. We chatted for some minutes, and
I found him as nimble in mind as he is ponderous in
body. He asked me about myself with seemingly unfeigned
interest, and once or twice I surprised him into a loud

laugh. I was pleased to have won his favour this far, since it seemed that here was a man whose eccentricity might put me in the way of some odd experiences. That expectation was to be gratified sooner than I could have anticipated.

Perhaps half an hour after our duet the door crashed open with a suddenness that checked all conversation. In strode the tall Captain Derby, his cheeks now crimson and his wig awry. It seemed that this invasion was a freak of conduct prompted by drink, because he had broken free of a knot of companions who stopped short in the doorway. Derby took up a stance facing Crocker, and spoke out in an insolent voice: 'Mr Crocker, I come to admire your person. I am told that you have the biggest belly in London.'

There was silence for a moment, before Crocker gave a cool reply.

'That may be so, sir. And I take it that you have the smallest brain.'

Whether Derby's reputation was current in London I had no idea: perhaps Crocker took him to be merely an oaf; but I knew what must follow. The intruder grinned, as in a situation familiar to him.

'It seems that you do not know me, Mr Blubber. I brook no such impudence.'

He crashed his fist on the table. 'I shall require satisfaction.'

Mr Crocker, undisturbed, responded affably: 'Surely, sir, a duel could afford you very little satisfaction, since my body offers so large a target to ball or blade.'

The captain's reddened face twisted into a sneer. 'Since you are too fat to conduct yourself like a gentleman—'

As he spoke, his hand reached for a glass of punch. I knew on the instant that he meant to throw the contents over Crocker; but in that same instant the intention was forestalled. Francis Pike, the lean gentleman mentioned above, leaped upon Derby. He moved with such speed that I could not see exactly what he did; but it seemed that he simultaneously dashed his head into Derby's face and felled him. In a trice he was astride the man, and holding a knife to his nostrils. Several hands went to a sword-hilt, but no further move was made since Pike was so clearly master of the situation. He addressed Derby, who appeared to be half dazed, in a level, even polite, voice: 'I recommend that you withdraw, sir. If you cause further disturbance I shall alter your face with this knife.'

He stood up and stepped back, quite imperturbable, although with some of his antagonist's blood on his wig. Derby could hardly have had another such experience in his career as rake and bully, and I did not know what his reaction would be. He clambered slowly to his feet, uncertain in balance and bleeding from nose and mouth. No one moved to help him. Amid a general silence he limped from the room without a word, avoiding every eye. Hardly had conversation burst out once more than it was stilled a second time as one of Derby's earlier companions marched in and, although clearly drunk, made a creditable bow in the general direction of Crocker.

'I apologize to you, sir,' he said, 'and to the company, for the conduct of Captain Derby. He is lately returned from abroad and does not know the customs of this house.'

'Thank you, sir,' replied Crocker, who had not turned a hair during the entire proceeding. 'I will regard the episode as closed.'

With that we returned to our punch and our chatter. Pike became as unobtrusive as he had been before and no one made reference to his intervention.

I was eager to learn more about the conventions governing these events. In particular I wished to know how it was that the resourceful Mr Pike had licence to disable a gentleman whose conduct was objectionable. Little Horn was convulsed by what had occurred; but I could draw nothing from him or Latimer beyond the statement that Mr Crocker's entourage was governed by its own laws.

Soon that entourage rose to take its leave. Mr Crocker paused by me to say that he hoped we would become better acquainted and sing together again.

I will be happy to maintain the contact. There is striking singularity and force in this huge gentleman. I am sure that he will feature again in our correspondence.

I remain, &c.

4

Having written three times to my godfather I was anxious
for a reply. During my years abroad he had sent me no
more than occasional acknowledgements of the long letters
I had written. He said enough to show that he had read my
words attentively, but offered no news of his own. This
practice had suited me at the time, but I now looked for
something more. I had offered Mr Gilbert several kinds of
matter, and needed to know where I had come closest to
meeting his expectations. I resolved to send one further
message of safely general description and then remain silent
until I had received a response:

> *My dear Godfather,*
> *Here is a brief epistle on a single theme. On Monday*
> *last, in the garb of a tradesman, I undertook my longest*
> *expedition so far, beyond Tower Hill and the rotting-fish*
> *stench of Billingsgate to the docks, wharves and warehouses*
> *of Wapping. Hereabouts one sees an astonishing sight:*

the Thames bristles with the masts of a thousand merchant ships of every size and condition. How the movements of these vessels and the unloading of their cargo are overseen and controlled I cannot conceive. Yet somehow order is derived from this chaos.

The riverside quarter seethes, correspondingly, with activity as relentlessly purposeful as that of bees or ants. To walk and watch here is to apprehend by instant conviction what everyone knows as a general truth – that the Thames is the vital tap-root of our capital city. If the mouth of the river were to be blockaded London would shrivel and decay like a dying tree. Through this channel the city takes in the produce of the whole known world – foodstuffs, fabrics, gold, diamonds, timber and stone – to be adapted and dispersed in accordance with its own needs and practices.

In the country – in your own Worcestershire – there is a familiar annual progress as nature's energies erupt from the earth – for example in the form of grass to be translated by farm animals into meat, milk, wool and leather. In London such rhythms are half forgotten: an insatiable city gulps down an unending variety of goods from the ends of the earth.

It is a mighty undertaking and a mighty spectacle. However, this trading has a darker side. The river is no longer the silver ribbon of poetry, but a turbid black-brown stream, the water thickened with filth. It is to be hoped, but also to be doubted, that the copious sewage of the city flows out to the open sea as surely and regularly as the merchant ships sail in. When the tide retreats the river-banks are seen to be strewn with every sort of civic detritus from sodden rags, bottles and wood-fragments to animal carcases.

On shore, in the warehouses and counting-houses, commerce is visible as a living thing. Goods are translated into guineas, and guineas into goods – a reciprocal exchange with the life-sustaining regularity of a heartbeat. Regrettably, however, the corporal metaphor does not end there. The vitalizing activity generates refuse as the river itself does. One sees rats and beggars searching through the rubbish for leavings to devour. But more dangerous creatures haunt these streets and alleys, parasites on trade: smugglers, pilferers and robbers. The district is a world in itself, and a perilous world, where one must be perpetually on guard. But it excited me: I must learn more about it.

Yours, &c.

～

There intervened an encounter that was for a time to distract my attention from my dealings with Mr Gilbert. I was in Piccadilly, near Hyde Park. Wrapped about in a drab great-coat I could have been taken for a merchant of the middling sort. No doubt it was for that reason that Catherine Kinsey, Sarah's aunt, was able to pass within two feet of me without so much as a second glance. Pulling my hat over my brows I turned about and followed her at a small distance. If she had been alone I would have greeted her, but she was walking, and conversing, with another woman of similar age

56

and respectability. They turned left, and left again, into Alcott Street, where they parted. Mrs Kinsey's companion continued on her way; she herself entered the front door of a house on the corner with Margaret Street.

I lingered outside it with a pounding heart: surely I had tracked Sarah down. Yet my exhilaration was tempered by curiosity. This was a fine street of handsome new buildings. If the Kinseys lived here they had dramatically risen in the world. Might they have inherited money? It was perhaps as well that, dressed as I was, I could make no further approach at this time: I needed to present myself to better advantage.

Next morning I came to the house in gentlemanly guise. To the maid who answered my knock I said that an old acquaintance of Mrs Kinsey, Richard Fenwick, newly returned to London, had called to pay his respects. I was left on the doorstep for some little time before a carefully rehearsed reply was brought to me. Mrs Kinsey sent her compliments. She would be very pleased to see Mr Fenwick, but particular circumstances prevented her from doing so that morning. She hoped that I might be able to call at the same time on the following day.

So it came about that I was duly ushered into her presence twenty-four hours later. Even before we spoke I had observed that the interior of the house, its curtains and furnishings, confirmed the impression conveyed by its exterior: it seemed that Mrs Kinsey had prospered extraordinarily since I had last spoken to her.

She had always been an affable lady. Our exchanges were warm but brief, speedily resolving into the very situation for which I had scarcely dared to hope. Mrs Kinsey informed me that she was unexpectedly called away, but was sure that I would be pleased to meet her niece once more. After bows and courtesies the lady departed, and Sarah came in.

I felt an instant sense of shock. Here was the Sarah I had known, but changed in every way for the better. She was more expensively and elegantly dressed, she moved more gracefully. What seemed to be a slight thinning of the cheeks and an enhanced brightness of the eyes elevated her face from its former prettiness into positive beauty. Above all there was a confidence in her manner that lent her a striking animation. In the past she had been subject to an instinctive diffidence, although capable of sudden directness and rebellious wit. Now these underlying traits were in the ascendancy. As we exchanged greetings and sat down she looked me in the eye and seemed to be suppressing a smile.

I had some airy opening remarks prepared: '. . . regretted loss of contact . . . my own fault . . . warm memories . . . would hope to renew . . .'

Her reply was concise: 'I am pleased to see you again, Mr Fenwick. I was here yesterday when you called, but the circumstances were a little awkward. So I arranged to visit again this morning when I knew you would be here.'

'To visit?'

'Why yes. This is my aunt's house.'

'Then you—?'

'I live in Margaret Street. I am married, Mr Fenwick.'

'Married?' I was trapped in the interrogative mode.

'I was married last September to Mr Walter Ogden.'

She was easy and terse, in full command. It was necessary

to rally a little: 'I have known you well enough to forego formalities. How did this come about?'

'I met Mr Ogden last July, through the merest chance.'

I tried, with indifferent success, to sound quizzical rather than sour: 'A swift courtship. Mr Ogden must be a man of considerable charm.'

'Determination was the decisive quality. Mr Ogden is a man of strong will.'

'Would I like him?'

'I hardly think so. Two men could hardly be more different.'

'In what respect?'

'In most respects. He is a particularly serious man.'

'A solemn one?' I ventured.

She considered the suggestion serenely, and then smiled.

'Perhaps a little.'

'Are you laughing at him?'

'I do laugh at him sometimes – but only behind his back. I do not care to vex him.'

'You make him sound formidable.'

'And so he is.' She paused, before adding lightly: 'He deals in diamonds. For that reason he was untroubled by my own lack of means.'

'Indeed.' I sought a new direction: 'Did you ever mention me to him?'

'I mentioned that I had been visited at one time by a genteel young man of uncertain prospects.'

'Did that disclosure disturb him?'

'Not the least in the world.'

Disappointed and obscurely resentful in several ways at

once I could find nothing further to say. It was left to Sarah to resume the conversation: 'Since we are being so unfashionably plain with one another, may I ask about your own situation. I take it that your Grand Tour is at an end?'

'It is. I returned last month. Thanks to the generosity of my godfather I am now a licensed man about town – at least for a year or two.'

'Then it would seem that we are both provided for.'

Was there a hint of bitterness in her voice – the faintest of hints?

It was my turn to look her in the eyes. 'This has become a particularly candid conversation.'

She held my gaze. 'Each of us now knows how the other is placed.'

'You have been able to marry into prosperity. Perhaps it was as well that our correspondence had lapsed.'

'It must be in some such way that most friendships fade.'

I stood up. 'I must congratulate you on your good fortune – and leave you.'

She rose in her turn, with a slight flush, and spoke in an altered voice: 'I should not like us to part in this vein.'

'In what vein, Mrs Ogden?'

'Cold, bright, false. I would not wish to seem unfeeling. We have been close, you and I . . .' Her voice quickened: 'But we were both left ill-provided for, and so have had to make our way in the world as best we can.'

On the way home, and indeed for several days following, I found myself discomposed. Who could have foreseen that Sarah would already have a husband, and a rich one, and that marriage would have given her such assurance. My feelings were oddly diverse. It had been disconcerting to be thrown on to the defence by a woman I had once patronized. I was stung by the instant dissolution of what had become a gratifying fantasy compounding tender feeling and ruthless seduction. And I felt that I had undervalued this handsome, cool young lady. Mr Ogden had shown himself a shrewd judge, and captured a wife who would do him credit, even if, as I was determined must be the case, she had married him merely to secure her future. Common sense told me that Sarah must be happier as the wife of a wealthy man than as the lover of an adventurer with uncertain prospects, but I was unwilling to be persuaded. The best bargain I could make with myself was to see this lost chance as a source of half-pleasing melancholy. I made shift with this notion since I had much else to occupy me, but it was clouded with resentment and unease: I had lost a point of moral anchorage.

Since April showers were frequent I was often indoors, where I did a good deal of writing. In addition to drafting of letters I was keeping a new journal as a quarry of possible epistolary material. Sometimes I would sing, and sometimes write facetious verses – a diversion I had enjoyed during my travels. I remained on friendly but formal terms with my landlady. Only gradually had I learned that her husband had been Mr Gilbert's tailor, and had died of a fever when she was expecting their first child, her daughter, Charlotte. Through the agency of Mr Ward my godfather had intervened on her behalf, securing the house in which she lived on condition that he could make use of it from time to time.

I had regular conversations with her, and found her agreeable company. If I asked a blunt question she would give a direct reply. When I inquired, perhaps impertinently: 'What are your pleasures, Mrs Deacon – what do you live for?' she thought for a moment before saying: 'Charlotte; reading; thinking; friends; coffee; and conversation.' She had a quietly assured manner, and would sometimes quiz me in her turn: 'If circumstances had been different, Mr Fenwick, what profession would have suited you?' 'Are you of my opinion, that men can be as vain as women?' 'Could you make shift on a desert island, like Robinson Crusoe?'

I had scarcely noticed Charlotte during my previous stay in the house; she was now some twelve years of age, a shy girl with dark hair. I cannot recall how it came about, but one wet afternoon I played chess with her. Knowing myself to be a moderately skilful performer, and thinking to be indulgent, I was so negligent that she defeated me with ease. By way of compliment to her prowess I was more serious in a return match, only to be a second time defeated. We had yet one more game. By now on my mettle I tried my hardest, but was beaten yet a third time. Charlotte showed no exultation at these triumphs, but thanked me for playing with her, and retired. Despite the humiliation I was glad to have stumbled upon this unexpected show of talent: it had always pleased me to find people unpredictable. Mrs Deacon later told me that, although an indifferent player herself, she had taught Charlotte the game and had been astonished by her aptitude for it.

It occurred to me that I could simply spend more time in Cathcart Street, inventing stories for my godfather – spinning a false life from my own brain – rather than walking the streets to grub out scraps of entertainment for him. But physical restlessness denied me that possibility. Although my rooms were well enough the ceilings were low, causing me to feel large and caged. It was a relief to go out.

My nether limbs were well exercised by these prowlings. When indoors I would at intervals strengthen my arms by lifting my desk or pulling myself up to a beam. The room must so often have been shaken by these exertions that I wondered whether Mrs Deacon might not feel some apprehension – perhaps even pleasurable apprehension – at being reminded of the presence of a vigorous male beast in her respectable house. She was still a handsome woman, and had manifestly lain with at least one man.

One evening, on impulse, I again went to dine at Keeble's steakhouse. The talking fraternity being absent on this occasion, I was glad to sit at an empty table and think in peace. It was with slight irritation, therefore, that I became aware of another solitary fellow taking a seat opposite my own. To postpone conversation I kept my eyes on my plate. When I at last looked up it was to find myself confronted by the grinning face of Matt Cullen.

My immediate reaction was to burst into an immoderate fit of laughter, in which Matt joined me. Our fellow-diners looked around, puzzled and smiling, at the spectacle of two young gentlemen unaccountably helpless with mirth. I was delighted to encounter Matt once more, and to find him just as I remembered, long-limbed, an awkward mover, with an expression of sleepy good-nature, always on the brink of a smile.

'I am the more surprised to see you,' said I, 'because Latimer told me that you had retreated to the country to undergo marriage.'

'There was that possibility.' He drew a slow sigh. 'Both families favoured the union. But there was a fatal flaw in the scheme.'

'That being?'

'That being the absence of any spark of animal inclination in either of the parties principally concerned. Each could see the lack of desire so heartily reciprocated that we retreated by mutual consent, leaving our families incensed.'

'Then what fresh hope has brought you back to town?'

'A forlorn one. You see in Cullen a farcical parody of our old companion Ralph Latimer. I seek the patronage of the Duke of Dorset.'

'On what grounds?'

'On the grounds that I am a distant cousin and that I have played cricket with his son.'

The absurdity of it set us laughing again.

'But what of your own case?' asked Matt, as we resumed eating. 'What have you been doing?'

'I wrote to you from abroad.'

'Two letters only, concerned with the exertions of a single bodily member. And here you are in London, apparently embarking on a new life.'

'So my godfather has decreed.'

'You may recollect that I know the gentleman's name, having been brought up within forty miles of his estate. Mr Gilbert, is it not?'

'It is.'

Suddenly feeling easy and reckless I cast aside my scruples.

'You shall hear my story,' said I, 'and you will be only the second person to do so.'

I broached it along with a second bottle of wine. Matt leaned forward to listen, his face as nearly serious as I had ever seen it. I traversed the whole ground, from my first meeting with Mr Gilbert, following the death of my mother, through the years when I had divided my time between boarding school and my aunt's house in York; thence to Oxford, my Grand Tour and the arrangement now agreed. When I had finished Matt shook his head.

'A singular history,' he said. 'Mr Gilbert has been generous, yet you seem to describe a benefactor devoid of warmth.'

'That is how he strikes me. He is studiously guarded in all he does. He sips at life.'

'Has he no vices to make him human?'

'None that I have observed. His daily life is as smooth as an egg. It affords the Evil One no hand-hold.'

'Has he always been so cool? Did he never think of marriage?'

'Not that I have heard. But I know little of his past.'

'He must care for you to have done as much as he has.'

'I would like to think so. But his kindness may derive solely from his friendship with my parents. I cannot tell.

This is my problem, Matt: I must divert a man whose disposition I do not understand. I am locked into a strange game.'

Cullen washed down these observations with a gulp of wine, and pondered them for a moment or two, his features pursed up around his half-smile.

'Might not this be a game with no loser? Mr Gilbert is pleased to give money to a promising young gentleman, and the young gentleman is pleased to receive it.'

'I hope it may prove so simple. My godfather fancied that we might be led into "dark territory". That was his phrase. Should I feel concerned?'

Matt smirked.

'How gladly, Dick, I would take the same risks for the same money.'

My dear Richard,

I have read with interest the experiences you have described and your observations thereon. You have plainly been to no small trouble to record a variety of activities that might entertain me. I was surprised, however, to notice that you have apparently encountered no members of the opposite sex since your return to London.

Your general strategy I am happy to endorse. Indeed I will go further. I suspect that your account of polite society is likely to hold few surprises for me. To speak in general, I would rather hear more of Mr Crocker, who would appear to be something of an original, than of Lord Vincent and his coterie. It has become a matter of *regret to me that, through some pressure of chance or temperament, my own youthful years in the capital were passed largely at that more respectable, and less entertaining, social level. For that reason I will tend to have a greater interest in the excesses, the follies, and even the shady underside of the town. Without leaving my comfortable country estate I look forward to being escorted to regions of experience that I could never have visited on my own. I hope that I will soon be hearing from you again.*

I remain, &c.

I studied this letter with minute attention. Surely it was not merely confirming, but modifying, what amounted to my contract of employment? My respectable godfather wanted spicier tales than I had so far offered him. And was there not a hint that my role should be that of participant rather than mere observer?

Here was an appealing invitation to hedonism. Perhaps I should have warmed him with an account of my visit to Mrs Traill . . . But I was immediately aware that the fat worm that had been proffered might contain a fatal hook. It was scarcely to be expected that at some future date Mr Gilbert would say: 'You have been so wholeheartedly lewd and dissolute that I am resolved to leave you every penny I possess.' I needed a clearer understanding as to how far I might safely venture. But my general plan had been approved: there was some reassurance in that. And as it happened I was enabled to respond to my godfather's fresh challenge almost immediately.

My dear Godfather,

I was very pleased to receive your letter. Your mention of Mr Crocker came opportunely: it is not two days since I learned more about that gentleman from Horn and Latimer, who have been acquainted with him for some little time.

He comes from the west of England. His late father, comparably huge, was a wealthy landowner. While a boy, Crocker was kept at home because of his unusual appearance, and was educated by private tutors. However he showed intelligence and spirit. When his father died, the young heir to the estate introduced a number of surprising features, including an aviary and an outdoor theatre. He hosted parties which became legendary in the county. Soon he was making sorties to London, where his wit and physical strength forestalled any attempt to treat him as an object of ridicule.

Latimer remains a little wary of him. 'He is so much a physical oddity,' said he, 'as to have no clear place in society. His eccentricity may overflow into some excess of a dangerous kind. To know him is very well; but it would not do to be implicated in folly. There is tattle wherever he goes.'

Horn's observations were more physical: 'That great belly is a fantastical depository: they say he can piss a quart at a single discharge. Concerning the operation of his bowels I prefer not to speculate.'

'That is a rare show of delicacy, Mr Horn,' said Latimer. 'I do know for a fact that he rarely stands upright for long – the strain is too great. If he falls he

cannot easily rise without aid. Nor can he so much as pull on his own stockings, being unable to reach his feet. If one of them itches he must scratch it with the other.'

'Worse than that,' cries Horn. 'I hear the poor devil has been unable to see his own pintle these five years, unless by means of a mirror. Yet it is known that he has appetites in that region also. He purchases the attentions of discreet and adept ladies.'

That night, at Latimer's instigation, I attended Drury Lane Theatre. Our interest was less in the main piece, an insipid comedy, than in an accompanying pastoral interlude. The part of Ceres was taken by the actress Jane Page, whom Latimer has lately been cultivating. He invited my compliments, which were duly vouchsafed, for she is a stately creature, who can command the stage. To be frank, however, I had found my attention elsewhere engaged. The young lady who played the part of Celia, a shepherdess, was so graceful in her movements, so artless in her manner that I was quite transported by her. My imagination could even accommodate the absurd notion of serenading this rustic maiden on a green hillside in some lost world of innocence.

Afterwards Latimer played host to several of the performers, in hope of furthering his friendship with the goddess of plenty. It seemed to me that he enjoyed only moderate success in this enterprise. Miss Page acknowledged his compliments prettily, but conceded no more than trifling hints of encouragement. Also present, however, was Celia, the shepherdess, in the person of a young actress named Kitty Brindley. I enjoyed some decorous

conversation with her. The air of pastoral innocence was
now, of course, largely dissipated, but something of the
illusion survived, because she proved to be indeed a young
country girl, new to London and the stage. Might she
have been artlessly enacting no other role than that of
herself? I was so beguiled by the simultaneous claims of
poetical imaginings and eager warmth below the waist,
that I happily prolonged the self-deception. Indeed I came
to feel that our encounter might be the prelude to others
of a more-intimate kind. If this proves to be the case, you
will receive a full account of what ensues.

I was lately cheered by a chance reunion with Matt
Cullen, an Oxford friend. You may recall that I
mentioned him, as coming from Malvern. In his company
I can be comfortable.

Yours, &c

Everything I had written was true: there had been no need
for embellishment. The attractions of Kitty Brindley now
served a double purpose: they distracted me from my regrets
concerning Sarah and they promised to provide the kind of
entertainment that Mr Gilbert seemed to have in mind.

❧

I was enjoying my survey of London independently of its
possible usefulness to my correspondence with Mr Gilbert.
I was glad to have an occupation, instead of trifling away
the time in the mode of Horn and Latimer. Already I knew
far more of the town than they did. Everywhere I found

fresh cause for curiosity. New houses, new shops, whole new streets, were coming into being. I would linger to watch builders at work and see houses rise from the earth with the slow persistence of plants. Properly considered, I told myself, the exertions involved were extraordinary. Ground plans were marked out with pegs and string. Cartload upon cartload of new-minted bricks were hauled in from distant manufactories by straining horses. Somehow a team of illiterate labourers, under minimal supervision, could raise walls straight and true, accommodating door or window, portico or chimney, as the architect had ordained. Everywhere I looked innumerable skills were collaboratively in operation – carpentry, tiling, plastering, the mixing of mortar, the laying of bricks, the cutting of glass – of which no Gentleman could claim the smallest knowledge.

The case was the same whatever professional activity I considered. From somewhere there came an endless supply of young men who could climb a mast, furl a sail, carve the corpses of sheep or pigs, forge metal, shape a carriage-wheel, bind a book, make a chair, a greatcoat or a wig. The class of Gentleman, in which I maintained a tenuous foothold, was dependent on all these skills yet serenely ignorant of them. How would I be placed if I should suddenly find myself penniless? My reassurance was that if the uneducated and often stunted labourers whom I had seen could learn a craft or a trade then no doubt I myself could do as much, if compelled by necessity. Perhaps there lurked within my still unformed personality a potential carpenter, architect or sea-captain. Although I hoped never to be put to the test, it was agreeable to fancy myself Protean.

5

When Cullen next called, I showed him Gilbert's letter. He shook his head in envy.

'Your very patron urges you to sin. Satan has smiled upon you.'

He was yet more envious when I told him of my planned pleasures with Kitty Brindley.

'But I love the girl myself. I have seen her perform, and was ravished. How tragic that she should yield to your puny attributes of money and person.'

Our conversation took a fresh turn when Matt happened to ask after Sarah, whom he had met once or twice in the weeks before I left for France. I told him of my encounter with her and my feelings after it. Matt, as ever, listened with attention, frowning or grinning. When I had done he gave his opinion that here was fresh meat for Mr Gilbert.

'Your dealings with Kitty are for today and tomorrow,' said he. 'Here is a narrative with longer life in it, and spiced with wickedness. I say to you: renew your pursuit of this lady. Cuckold the merchant. Your godfather will revel in such a conquest.'

It was to my credit, I think, that I chose to demur.

'Am I to understand that my friend is urging me to commit adultery?'

'Yes,' said Cullen. 'I believe that this would not be your first transgression of the kind. And consider the balance of pleasure in the case. You, Mrs Ogden and your godfather could achieve gratification: only Mr Ogden stands to be discommoded.'

'But Mr Ogden may be a gentleman of great merit and tenderness.'

'He may, however, be nothing of the sort. And he need suffer only if he comes to learn of the transaction.'

We left the house, embarking on a walk that took us down to the Strand and thence along the busy river in an easterly direction. The sun was shining on crowded streets and dirty water. Cullen and I conversed in snatches, laughing often. He described a recent meeting with the Duke, who had said to him only: 'I have not forgot you, Mr Collins.' Matt felt that the small twig on which his hopes were perched had shrunk.

On a whim we hired a boat to take us across the river to Southwark. Our Charon, a scrawny old fellow, sang after a fashion as he rowed.

'I cannot but notice that you have no teeth, friend,' observed Matt, who would converse with anybody. 'Do you not find difficulty in eating?'

The boatman further exhibited his deficiency in a hearty laugh.

'Why, no sir, for the gums are grown harder. 'Tis a blessing, for I am freed of toothache and can whistle as I never could before.'

'You are a philosopher,' said I, and added a shilling to his fare.

Once disembarked we continued to stroll by the Thames, and paused to make a modest contribution to it.

'The truth is,' I observed as we pissed, 'that our oarsman was in the wrong. Cheerful as he is he would be happier with teeth. If he could have them again, he would.'

'I am not so sure,' said Matt. 'We should not take our losses too seriously.'

'So will you undertake not to hang yourself if the Duke fails you?'

'Certainly.' Matt folded away his member. 'The first duty of human-kind is to stay alive; the second is to be as merry as circumstances permit. Such is my philosophy.'

Wandering on, we talked of our uncertain prospects.

'Your future is more promising than mine,' said Matt. 'Mr Gilbert has invested too much in you to cast you aside.'

We walked back across Westminster Bridge and on to Keeble's for a steak. I was hailed by the tall fellow from the Conversation Club.

'Last week,' said he, 'we returned to your theme and considered the case of the nightingale. Anatomize the bird and you will find lungs and membranes. There is the instrument, but where is the song? And where is the composer?'

'You have killed him,' cried Cullen, 'for the sake of your experiment.'

After a glass or two of wine he and I returned to the

subject of women. We agreed, with shared self-pity, that the venereal adventure was fraught with difficulty and mystery. Somehow we lurched into bar' aric Latin banter.

'Magnum est gratificatio sen ualis,' improvised Matt, who had never been a zealous student, 'sed si filius natus est, gravis est responsibilitas.'

'Et si infectio venerealis contractus est,' I added, on the basis of an unfortunate Italian experience, 'magna est poena, magnum est dolor.'

In such ways we sniggered away the rest of the afternoon like two schoolboys. Mr Gilbert could never have comprehended these trifling, companionable pleasures.

~

My dear Godfather,

I have attended another of Mr Crocker's gatherings at the Seven Stars. Latimer and Horn went with me as before. The company seemed to be much as I remembered it, with Crocker presiding from his great chair in the centre of the crescent of drinking men. By the time we entered the talk was already vociferous. I took a seat by the one silent man in the room, who happened to be Francis Pike, the gaunt fellow who had silenced Captain Derby. Having learned from Horn that this individual was in regular attendance on Crocker, I was curious to find out more about him.

Concerning the encounter with Captain Derby he spoke with detachment.

'In such cases, sir, I have the advantage over most

opponents. I know what must be done. Stun your man, bring him to the ground, and he's no longer a threat.'

'Yours must be a dangerous profession,' I suggested.

'That may be so, sir. Fortunately I seem to feel pain less than most men. Perhaps I have grown accustomed to it. I have had bones broke, and shed blood.' He paused, before adding, with the faintest of smiles: 'Above all, sir, not being a gentleman, I am considered to be outside the rules of honourable conduct, and therefore see no need to be bound by 'em.'

I felt confident enough to inquire, with delicacy, whether he might not be regarded by some as a bully. He rejected the insinuation very calmly.

'No, sir, because I never start a quarrel. Your practised duellist who calls out a harmless fellow man for sport – he's the bully.'

'To talk to,' I said, 'you seem a polite, composed sort of man.'

'And so I hope I am, sir. But that is also my professional manner. I find it has a concentrating effect, like the barrel of a musket.'

These exchanges were cut short when I was summoned to take a chair beside our host. To be seated by him was to be immediately reminded of his bulk. His thigh is double the thickness of my own. By contrast his face, well-formed and bright-eyed, is no more than plump, but it perspired freely, causing him to dab at it with a handkerchief.

'I am pleased to see you, Mr Fenwick,' said he. 'I hope you will sing with me again.'

'With great pleasure.'

'By the way, I am acquainted with Lord Vincent, whom I believe you know.'

'Very slightly.'

'I have been observing you. You yourself I see to be watchful, eager to take in everything about you.'

'I hope I am,' said I, by now embarrassed.

'You were deep in conversation with Mr Pike, who is often taciturn.'

'I found him most interesting.'

'That shows judgement. He may be the most interesting man in the room.'

He turned away and rapped for silence: 'Gentlemen, if you will indulge me, I feel disposed to sing.'

Amid applause he got himself to his feet. I could see that he was immersed in his performance, half jocose though it was. While he sang no one would have thought of his unwieldy body – he lived through his voice:

Come, friends, and bear me company:
I dare not go to bed.
I've drunk too little or drunk too much,
And my heart is heavy as lead.
Although this life is all too short
The nights can last too long,
So help me pass the lingering hours,
And join me in a song.

The whole company did indeed join lustily in the chorus:

In an hour, in a week, in a month, in a year,
Where shall we be? No man can say.
If we drink, if we fight, if we whore while we're here,
Then sooner or later the devil's to pay.
So sing through the night,
Sing while we may,
Till a new dawn reminds us to live for the day.

*Crocker lowered his great rump amid much cheering
and stamping of feet. By now the room was very warm
and we were all in a tipsy sweat. Invited by our host to
perform, I offered 'The soaring lark salutes the morn'.
When I had concluded, Crocker and I were persuaded
to sing an indecorous duet:*

A tippler's throat is a conduit pipe:
Pour, landlord, pour.
We drink to piss, and piss our drink, and drink to piss
once more.
A man don't leak till a man has drunk,
So let the liquor flow:
We take it in and shake it down, and then we let it go.

*The assembled tipplers sang with us till the windows
shook and our ears rang.*

*It seems to be the custom at these gatherings to drink
and talk at large until Crocker takes the lead in some
way. When the singing was done the former general
carousal was resumed. Voices rose and laughter rang out.
Somewhat elevated myself, I noticed the prudent Latimer*

slip away. I was sitting with Horn, who was by now very loud, at one point laughing so hard that he fell to the floor.

At length Crocker again forced himself upright.

'Gentlemen!' he cried, 'there is work to be done. Let us withdraw.'

I confess that, owing to the influence of wine, my recollections of what followed are less than distinct. Crocker's table was pulled aside, and he stalked ponderously from the room. The rest of us rose – with a crashing of chairs, bottles and glasses – and followed him into the night air. Crocker ensconced himself in what was apparently his private chair, to be borne away by four men, with the company trooping at their heels. I wondered if we were to be plunged into some violence of the Mohock kind – though in truth I had never heard that Crocker was associated with such doings. We made a strange procession: an obese, chair-borne Achilles followed by a rabble of drunken Myrmidons. There was no show of provocation or aggression, although I fancy anyone standing in our way might have been thrown aside. Perhaps Crocker himself and Pike, who stayed close to his chair, were the only individuals among us still in a condition to think clearly. At some point we turned from the main thoroughfare and followed a link-boy through a maze of unlighted alleys.

At length we were motioned to a halt. The moon, emerging from a cloud, showed us to be standing beside a long wall. It seemed an unpromising destination. I was aware of Crocker alighting from his chariot and, *through the agency of Pike, getting us, his foot soldiers, positioned at short intervals along the wall. He himself took a central place. His stentorian command, ringing through the night air, enjoined us to set our shoulders to the brickwork and then push rhythmically against it in response to his further shouts, as though trying to budge a great wagon. All concerned fell uncomplainingly to this apparently futile task. We strained in unison, strained repeatedly – and strained to no effect. But after a number of such lunges there seemed, to my surprise, to be some slight sense of motion in the brickwork. We maintained our efforts till a distinct swaying ensued and eventually, to the accompaniment of a ragged cheer, an indeterminate length of the wall gave way completely, collapsing inwards with a rumbling crash.*

Like many others, I went down with the wall, and had to stumble to my feet among broken bricks. There was a confusion of curses and a loud barking of dogs. The moon was now hidden by a cloud of dust. All present hastily dispersed as best they could, given the darkness, their drunken state and the shock of the fall. I found my way to Cathcart Street I know not how, my clothes filthy, my wig full of dirt, and one stocking soaked with blood.

Next morning I wondered at the course the evening had taken, and asked myself whose wall we had destroyed, and why. I also felt some astonishment that the wall had indeed collapsed. My uncertain conclusion was that the cause had to do with vibration, the faint

movement communicated to the brickwork engendering a
counter-movement.

Why Crocker should have organized this assault
I cannot imagine. He appeared to be fairly sober
throughout the evening, his freakish size perhaps
rendering him resistant to the inebriating power of punch.
Nor would I take him to be a belligerent man. I look
forward to finding out more about him, and about the
strange doings of the past night.

Yours, &c.

This escapade had left me rather the worse for wear. Not until the afternoon was I washed, dressed and restored to rights. A feeble explanation to Mrs Deacon concerning the state of my laundry – I had suffered an 'unfortunate mishap' – was received civilly, but with the hint of amusement that it deserved. It would not do for me to appear ridiculous again. I wished my landlady to think me a spirited gentleman of fashion, not a lout.

After taking a dish of tea I felt a little better. It seemed to me that the doings of the previous night, discreetly edited, might entertain my godfather. Lacking the energy to go out of doors, I settled down to compose what eventually became the letter here transcribed.

While doing so I conceived the idea of keeping a record of my entire correspondence with Mr Gilbert. My recollections being already somewhat misty, it seemed important that I should at least be clear as to what I had reported. I could not risk falling into self-contradiction. Fortunately I had preserved fragmentary drafts of my earlier epistles;

now I pieced them together and re-wrote them as fair copies. Henceforward I would keep this archive up to date, as constituting my official memory.

Latimer and I had tacitly chosen to consider our pursuit of Kitty Brindley and Jane Page a joint enterprise. We returned to the theatre to see again the interlude that had pleased us and afterwards to dine once more with the principal performers. I enjoyed the little pastoral as much as before – in fact more, given my interest in the young shepherdess. There ensued, however, a distraction that I could not have foreseen.

We stayed to see the comedy that followed the interlude. In the course of it I happened to look from our box above the stage towards the audience at large, and noticed, in the second row, Sarah Ogden, sitting beside a man I could only assume to be her husband. I leaned back, out of their line of vision, but could not resist further glances in their direction. The top quarter of Ogden – all that was visible – suggested a thick-set, impassive man. Sarah was more responsive to the performance, but to me there seemed some constraint in her manner. I wondered if she had seen me and was discomfited by my proximity.

Our engagement after the performance – at which, as it seemed to me, Kitty was once more encouraging and Jane Page once more elusive – pushed this episode to the back of my mind. The following morning, however, it returned with vexing vividness. I found myself recalling my warmest interlude with Sarah, nearly three years previously, when she had been visibly stirred, perhaps even drawn a few steps along the path toward capitulation. Could the dull Ogden elicit such responses? I resolved that at some future time I would indeed resume my pursuit of her. The affair with Kitty Brindley I was willing to expose to my godfather's curiosity. Here was a second narrative, a private one, of which I would tell him nothing.

My dear Godfather,

I continue pertinacious in the pursuit of pleasure. This afternoon I took tea with Miss Brindley, tête-à-tête, at her lodgings in Rose Street.

It seems to me that in the negotiation that ensued we were both to be commended for the art with which we translated into euphemism what we knew to be a business transaction. I represented myself as a young fellow still making my way in the world, well provided for but (alas!) in no position to commit myself to a settled way of life. Miss Kitty's sketch of her past was the stuff of a country ballad. She had left her native village for love of a soldier who had promised marriage but then deserted her. It would have gone hard for her had she not fallen in with Jane Page, who had secured her some trifling employment in the theatre. Since then she had advanced in her profession, and had hopes of rising further.

You may wish to know something of her appearance. In person she inclines to be slightly plump, but in that pleasing way that seems to be the effect of youthfulness only. She has large blue eyes, a clear complexion and a ready smile often followed, however, by a lowering of her eyes, as though she is in doubt that she may have been too forward. In manner she is open and candid, a quality in the fair sex that has always attracted me.

When considering her career in London she was thankful, she said, for her good fortune, because she could have fared far worse. On the other hand she had broken all ties with her parents, her prospects in the theatre were uncertain, and she could not but feel anxiety concerning her future. (When I referred, in studiously general terms, to the most notorious perils of her profession, she replied 'What would I know of those, sir?')

It was perhaps droll that we each affected simplicity while signalling to one another as directly as circling animals. Our attempted deceptions (and self-deceptions) were mutually apprehended and tolerated. The common ground to which we tiptoed our way was the fiction that we were like-minded innocents from the country, ill at ease in this unfeeling town. What Miss Brindley wants, of course, though she cannot say as much, is a wealthy husband, or failing that, as will most probably be the eventual case, a sufficiently wealthy protector. There are members of her profession who have achieved as much. My hope, and in effect my offer, was that at this early point in her career I could offer her a companionable and moderately remunerative apprenticeship for the future to which she aspires.

I have written more glibly than I feel, representing Miss Brindley, her charms and little stratagems, as also my own pursuit of her, with irony and a hint of derision. However, I have another perception of a warmer and more generous kind. After all there is a natural charm and even innocence in her disposition. I am surely not the first man to have had a conversation of this kind with her but, equally surely, I am by no means the twenty-first.

By the time we parted we had reached, as it seemed to me, an understanding as to the immediate future course of our relationship, and this with no hint of a leer, a smirk or a double entendre. The young lady will surely have observed that I was powerfully aroused by her; yet on quitting her apartment I ventured only to kiss her small hand.

When I come to do more you will hear further from Yours, &c.

Mr Gilbert's reply must have been written very soon after he had received my letter:

My dear Richard,
It would appear that you have been living a full and varied life in London, very much along the lines I would have hoped.

However I now feel the need to discuss with you directly certain issues arising from our project. I would be obliged, therefore, if at your earliest convenience you could arrange to pass a few days here at Fork Hill.

I remain, &c.

I took the coach the following morning.

6

So it was that I returned to Fork Hill House some six weeks after my previous visit. When I had shaken off the stupefaction of the journey, and washed the odours of it from my person, I felt flushed with vigour and ready to face any challenge that might lie in store. I was no mere supplicant, but a young man of some little consequence, Mr Gilbert's personal emissary from the capital. The bedroom I had occupied in March had been prepared exactly as before, as though it were now reserved for my exclusive use. The servants greeted me with smiles of recognition, pleased that I remembered their names. Even the great dogs licked my hand and waved their tails in welcome. I was encouraged to have become, to this small extent, an accepted member of the household.

Mr Gilbert was, as ever, politely formal, but I sensed a suppressed excitement underlying the courtesies. His glance was more restless, his words came more quickly.

'We must talk,' he said, 'and at some little length – but not for a day or two.'

The change I felt in myself was mirrored in my godfather's estate. The garden in front of the house was a blaze of spring flowers, golden and red. At the rear the expanse of his land was no longer held at bay by a palisade of black branches but merged into a surrounding sea of green leaves. I wandered out, as before, towards those woods, exulting in the clean air and warm sunshine. In the fields there were scores of white lambs, cropping the grass alongside their dams. Here was a true pastoral scene, where my Kitty would have been at home as shepherdess. Bird songs trilled around and above me, a sound I had scarcely heard in London, and I was inhaling the sweet scents of growth rather than the stench of refuse. If this was the healthy life, as I felt it to be, then surely London, with its din and stink, might threaten illness, mental if not physical. My mind seemed clearer here.

Borrowing a horse from my godfather's stable I rode out to explore the surrounding countryside, something I had never attempted before. It was a fertile, secluded region, the nearest town being five miles away. To ride again was a release – how much more pleasing to be in partnership with a horse than to have it haul your carriage like a slave.

I was happy to amble at random, thinking about the days ahead. What conversational manner should I adopt when talking to my godfather? My former style – deference with an occasional glint of spirit – seemed inadequate to the changed situation. Too much in that vein and he might conclude that I lacked the mischief to be a bold participant in London life. Should I speak more freely, even suggestively? I would need to stay alert and be guided by Mr Gilbert's response.

I rode through Fork Hill itself, a straggling hamlet a mile from my godfather's house. Passing the churchyard I heard my name called, and looked around to see Mr Thorpe, the clergyman I had met on my previous visit. I dismounted to shake his hand, and we stood conversing in the shade of a huge oak tree, while my horse grazed the verge.

In the open air, fresh from hauling a fallen gravestone upright – his task when he had seen me – he looked younger and more vigorous than I had previously taken him to be. And so I told him, emboldened by the fact that he seemed a friendly fellow, pleased to enjoy the distraction of a chat. When I asked him whether he did not find life in a secluded parsonage a little dull, he gave the question thought.

'I would once have done so. At Oxford I was considered a lively spark. But since coming here I have been at pains to accept my destined place.'

I pursued the point, perhaps in tactless terms: 'Is that not rather as though a butterfly should become a caterpillar?'

Thorpe did not take offence: 'Better a healthy caterpillar than a bedraggled butterfly. I hope to marry one day. My wife will be a parson's wife, and my children will be a parson's children. Then the transformation will be complete.'

When he hinted a question concerning my own prospects I said something to the effect that these were at the mercy of my godfather.

Thorpe nodded. 'I understand you. In these parts we are all beholden to Mr Gilbert, and must study to deserve his good opinion.'

We smiled, in mutual understanding, and I parted from him cordially, pleased to have found a possible ally in this unknown territory.

⌇

Within three days of my arrival my godfather again hosted a dinner. To my surprise the guests were as before, save only that Thorpe was absent. Although bored by the prospect of the evening ahead I was on balance not displeased: if I came to be seen by Mr Gilbert's neighbours as a familiar member of the household he could not easily cast me aside.

I had hoped to play the courteous listener, but found myself more than once thrust into prominence. Mr Hurlock, as witlessly noisy as before, assailed me with his raillery. He questioned me about the pleasures of London life, brushing aside my demurrals.

'Don't believe the boy!' he cried out. 'I say don't believe him! Does he look like a monk? He does not! There he sits, a handsome enough piece of young flesh. Never tell me there haven't been women in the case. The town teems with 'em. Covent Garden, Drury Lane: there the ladies gather, and there the young men swarm about 'em like lice in a wig. Don't tell us you haven't been there, young man!'

My godfather made an ill-judged attempt to turn the current of the rant: 'I believe you may have visited such places yourself, in your time.'

Spluttering wine, Hurlock exploded into a laugh.

'You may believe it, Mr Gilbert. You may well believe it, sir! I've gone belly to belly in many a London garret.'

By now the embarrassment around the table, particularly in the countenance of his wife, was such as to be perceived even by Hurlock. He extricated himself as best he could: 'That was in my plundering days, before I was married. *Long* before I was married!'

He let out his bark of laughter, but laughed alone. My godfather changed the topic.

'Mr Quentin, I hear that you may be contemplating a visit to London?'

There was a silence, and I saw that Mrs Quentin, who was sitting opposite me, had flushed. With an effort, her husband spoke out: 'I have been obliged to plan such a visit. It is not what I want or can afford, but it must be undertaken. My wife requires the services of a skilful dentist, such as cannot be found in these parts. We must seek help in London.'

There were murmurs of sympathy, but I could see that the unfortunate Mrs Quentin was on the verge of tears, whether at the prospect of the dental ordeal or from the mortification of hearing her plight publicly discussed. To ease the situation I launched into a lively monologue about recent advances in dental knowledge, and new devices that had become available. I spoke with knowledge, because the previous month Latimer's uncle had had the last of his teeth extracted and a set of false ones installed. I did not, of course, allude to the discomfort he had suffered, nor to the resulting unnaturalness of his facial expression. Mr Quentin seemed interested in what I had said, asking a number of questions, and his wife recovered her composure.

As the talk became general I hoped to subside into the

background, but was again thwarted. Mr Gilbert asked me to repeat, for Mr Yardley's benefit, my account of the London frog-swallower. I obliged the company as best I could. The ladies grimaced but Yardley nodded and clicked his tongue. He gave it as his opinion that a bellyful of water would be no very forbidding environment for a frog, save only in respect of its warmth, uncomfortable for a cold-blooded amphibian.

Towards the end of the meal my godfather engaged with Mrs Hurlock on the subject of music, reminding her that in years gone by he had sometimes heard her sing. To my surprise the buxom lady became positively animated on this theme, recalling the names of several of her favourite pieces. When, in a polite show of interest, I seconded her admiration for Handel's 'Say not to me I am unkind', Mr Gilbert promptly proposed that she and I should sing it together. Having no desire to perform in this company, and little confidence in the abilities of Mrs Hurlock, I would gladly have refused, but she responded eagerly, and the Quentins politely supported the proposal. It would have seemed churlish in me not to oblige. I was influenced also by the reaction of Mr Hurlock, whose over-fed face expressed blank disgust. It would be a pleasure to irritate him further.

To my surprise our impromptu duet proved creditable. Mrs Hurlock's voice, although not strong, was sweet and true, and I was able to adapt my own performance to it. We were warmly applauded, particularly by my godfather. Mrs Hurlock, redeemed from anonymity, quite blushed with pleasure, in what must once have been her girlish manner.

Her husband was the one person present who listened with hostility and clapped perfunctorily. Plainly he would have been happier at a cock-fight. When the ladies had left us he emptied two large bumpers in brisk succession and lapsed into a doze. Quentin remained subdued, but Yardley, prompted by my godfather, talked about the ingenious construction of birds' nests, claiming that certain instinctive animal capacities might amount to something akin to human thought. He was interrupted by Hurlock, who woke from his sleep crying out at random: 'Say nothing of Spain! The only enemy we need fear is the Pope of Rome!'

When our party dispersed my godfather and I went out upon the terrace to bid farewell to the guests. Mrs Quentin shyly thanked me for providing her a little reassurance concerning her forthcoming trials. Mrs Hurlock expressed the hope that we might sing together once more on some future occasion. Her husband, half asleep, was muttering and stumbling. A bright moon turned the lawns to silver and gleamed on the roofs of the carriages as they rattled away along the drive. Mr Gilbert and I watched them till they were out of sight and we were alone together on the silent terrace.

'The night is mild,' said he. 'And the time has come for us to talk. I think we might sit out here for a while. Would you be so good as to fetch the port.'

I did so without a word, my heart beating faster. Mr Gilbert and I sat on either side of a small table. He took a sip of port and stared out across the moonlit garden. When he spoke it was with the air of a man embarking on a difficult topic.

'I should have said either less or more in my letter. I am now resolved to say more.'

I drank a little port myself, to give him space.

He continued, with his eyes still looking into the distance: 'You have known me only as the person I am at present. I have been several others. Some with a sturdier figure. They are now gone.'

He turned to me, his voice suddenly sharp.

'You have met my neighbours, and no doubt think them, as I do, a pitiful crew. Mrs Quentin with her rotting teeth; the sottish Hurlock, who has all but lost the power of thought.'

I half-heartedly made to demur, but he over-rode me.

'Yet such people were the local beauties, the local blades. Mrs Hurlock in particular – Anna Halliday, as she was – attracted much admiration. She is greatly altered. You may not now believe that I admired her myself.' He smiled thinly. 'Hurlock was in pursuit of her – Hurlock, the great buck of the county, but a fool. I might easily have won her – she preferred my company. What, you may ask, was the stumbling block?'

I shook my head.

'Let me tell you. I looked past what she was, and saw what she would be – saw the matron in the maid. It was wisdom of a kind, but of the wrong kind – that of an older man. This was not the only such opportunity that I missed. I was confident that my time would come, but it never did. In terms of marriage, in terms of *passion*, it never did.'

Unexpectedly Mr Gilbert changed his tone, surprising me with a compliment: 'You conducted yourself with credit this evening. I observed you closely. You were polite to Hurlock, attentive to Yardley, good-natured in your concern for Mrs Quentin. You sang pleasingly. Yet you were detached. You were forming judgements. The young man I saw was the young man who writes me letters.'

He turned to interrogate me.

'How would you describe yourself? I see that you are courteous, shrewd, amiable. What other qualities would you claim?'

I knew that my answer should be no less forthright than the question.

'Let me set aside false modesty. I am physically vigorous. I cannot claim to be a scholar, but I am reflective and read quite widely. I can adapt myself to most kinds of company. I am sensual, probably to a fault. By temperament I am cheerful and amiably disposed, but I can have darker moods – even fits of rage.'

Mr Gilbert nodded, as though I had said nothing to surprise him.

'You are not afraid to take risks?'

'No.'

'You have a relish for unusual situations?'

'Yes.'

'Can you be ruthless?'

This question called for a little thought.

'I believe I can.'

I wondered at these questions. Was I to be asked to stage a robbery, or an assassination? But Mr Gilbert let the matter drop as suddenly as he had broached it, and poured more port. One of his great black dogs padded silently from the house and laid his head on my godfather's knee. I felt at ease – even exhilarated. What a singular exchange this was, under the stars, our words punctuated by stirrings of twigs in the breeze or the occasional scuttling of a rabbit. Where would it take us next? In the moonlight my godfather, with his pale face and small wig, had a ghostly luminosity that seemed to render him more dominant. Fondling the dog's ears he spoke again, this time ruminatively: 'I lost another neighbour, Squire Warhurst, last year. By all accounts he died a good death, praying to the last. He was confident of admission to Heaven, and Parson Thorpe endorsed that expectation. His soul may be there as we speak. Yet the man was a bully, a glutton and a hell-bent whoremonger till mending his ways at fifty, following a stroke. If Warhurst has been saved I can feel guardedly optimistic as to my own prospects.'

He broke off: 'You suspect that I am facetious?'

'To be candid, sir, I was not sure.'

My godfather smiled faintly. 'I am not sure myself. But seriously, or half-seriously, I reflect that the years and capacities I have left are insufficient for me to emulate this man's sinfulness, even if I wished to do so. May I not, then, indulge myself a little? A very little?'

After a hesitation he continued, as though lost in soliloquy: 'A man may avoid the sin he is too timid to commit. In such a case, surely, the professed belief is mere faint-heartedness. Might not the Almighty deem that the fellow has been cowardly rather than virtuous? Might not the eternal reward be curtailed accordingly? If so, the poor devil would be twice deprived – in this life and again in the next.'

I tried to meet the challenge: 'Then you believe in an after-life?'

'Of course.' A pause. 'From time to time.'

Somewhat baffled by now, I tried to exert myself: 'Sir, I am not sure where your remarks are tending.'

'Then I must make myself clear.' My godfather drew a breath and spoke out with decision. 'The case is this. I have preserved appearances for so long that none of my neighbours know – indeed, I scarcely know myself – what lies below the surface of my character. Caution and good fortune have protected me, but they have protected me too far – protected me from life itself. I have never married, never fathered a child, never broken a bone, or so much as seen a corpse, save on a gibbet. I live in a great house defended by servants and dogs. The price I pay for my safety is imprisonment of a kind. I need a window in this confinement, a window through which to see a wider life.'

'Were you not saying as much to me on my last visit?'

'I was, but I wish to go further. *There* lies the point – I wish to go further.'

He took a full mouthful of port. By now he was agitated, his breathing quicker.

'I invited you to describe the life of London. But as I read your letters I came to recognize that I seek something more particular – the recklessness of personal doings. Do you follow me?'

'I think so, sir.'

'I wonder if you do . . .' His tone changed. 'Let me say that I like the sound of your friend Mr Crocker. I have a taste for situations where normal conduct breaks down

– where there is excess and abnormality. Perhaps you inferred as much.'

'I did.'

'Where Yardley is interested in plants and animals, my study is human conduct, the Passions: Vanity, Greed, Avarice, Rage, Lust . . .'

Mr Gilbert enumerated these qualities with emphasis, speaking so fervidly as seeming to reveal a passion of his own. He leaned towards me across the table.

'I propose an experiment. Life has slipped past me half unnoticed. I am tormented by a restlessness that I cannot subdue. I would wish my final years to be more vivid, more diversified, more – pungent. In short' – he rapped the table – 'my project is in some sense to live again. I would hope to live differently and *dangerously* – through you and *through your exploits*. I am not so old that reports of mischief and gallantry will fail to warm my blood.'

He checked himself, and resumed in more measured tones: 'I may no longer be robust but I am far from frail. The connoisseur who cannot paint may yet enjoy a picture. I aspire to be a connoisseur of experience – but the experiences will be yours.'

He sat back and looked at me. 'I await your response.'

'I must consider, sir.'

I spoke mechanically, but was incapable of considering anything, being lost in the situation. The moon shone down on us still. There were servants asleep in the dark house, birds and animals at rest all around us in their lairs. And here in the sweet-scented night air we were meditating the most eccentric of transactions. Was there, at that moment, any man in England engaged in a stranger conversation?

'Why do you smile?' asked Mr Gilbert.

I found myself laughing aloud with real gaiety, as I might have laughed with Matt Cullen – something I had never previously done in the presence of my godfather.

'I beg your pardon, sir: I was not aware that I was smiling. The reaction was involuntary. It means that I welcome your proposition.'

'I am glad to hear it. But you will no doubt wish to ask me questions.'

Indeed I did; but the most obvious inquiry – 'How am I to be rewarded?' – seemed below the dignity of these intimate exchanges. I tried to think.

'How far will I be expected to go?'

'As far as you see fit.'

'Then I may, for example, go further in my pursuit of Miss Brindley?'

'Much further.' Mr Gilbert leaned forward again. 'Your first account of this lady, in her pastoral guise, spoke directly to me. As a young man I found myself *plagued*: – the word is not too strong – by the pastoral. Art, poetry, drama insisted that love should be idyllic, Arcadian. The reality fell far short. The physical encounter could not match the rhetoric.'

He glanced at me wryly: 'If you ever feel such qualms I fancy that your physical appetites can usually over-ride them.'

'I have found that to be the case.'

The port had had its effect. We were smiling now, positively conspiratorial.

'At the other extreme from pastoral fancy,' said my godfather, 'it seemed to me that after your duet Mrs Hurlock was looking at you with a kindly eye.'

'I had a fleeting impression to that effect myself.'

'Tell me, as a matter of hypothesis only: would your animal spirits render you capable of congress with that faded beauty?'

I realized, with astonishment, that his question was seriously meant. I sought for an answer that would gratify him.

'I am sure they would – given darkness and wine.' The port prompted a blunter phrase. 'I fancy I could make her squeal.'

I feared I had gone too far, but the words elicited an unexpected grin of appreciation. Here was a new frankness: the boundaries of our relationship had been widened by a chance phrase.

'I am impressed to hear it. Perhaps such an opportunity may one day arise.'

I laughed with him, but was disconcerted. For years Mr Gilbert had comported himself with authority and even severity; yet he must all the while have carried these secret appetites in his mind, like maggots within an apple. I began to wonder whether he might be a rather wicked old man.

Moonlight and port stirred me to further recklessness: 'Then if I set about seducing a married woman?'

'I would hope to receive a full account of the campaign – and the conquest.'

We sat silent for a moment. The big dog shook himself and walked away into the shadows. After he had vanished Mr Gilbert resumed in an altered voice: 'I have spoken frivolously. I must not allow myself to be misunderstood.

Yes, I would be intrigued to enter a bedroom with you; but I do not look *merely* for carnal details. Your scruples and disappointments would be of equal moment to me.'

He was very serious now. 'I cannot easily explain myself. All my life I have mused on such matters, have debated them in my mind. But the debate was false, because one-sided. I could marshal the arguments from reason and morality: these were available in books. But the arguments from the other side, the arguments from passion, went unheard, because I never indulged my passions, never took moral risks. I was like a man who denounces wine having never tasted it. I look for a fairer disputation between passion and conscience, and I look to you to provide me the evidence I failed to gather for myself.'

And again he asked: 'Do you follow me?'

'I do,' I replied, and meant what I said.

Mr Gilbert emptied his glass.

'This is likely to prove a strange adventure for us – perhaps as much so as a voyage to the Indies.'

'Where will our project end, sir?'

'I cannot say. That uncertainty is part of the experiment.'

He stood up, holding the table a moment to steady himself. I rose with him.

'We have had an intriguing conversation. But it is late, and I must go to my bed. I think we now understand one another better. Give me your hand, Richard.'

I did so, again looking him in the eyes, and our compact was sealed.

The night was cooler now, but I went up to my bedroom still warmed by the port I had drunk, and by my crowding thoughts. More of substance had passed between Mr Gilbert and me in that hour on the terrace than in all our previous conversations combined. There was excitement and uncertainty ahead. Drawing back the curtain I stared out of my window at the moon, wondering what fantasies might be seething in my godfather's head as he pulled on his nightshirt. What did he now think of me? Would he be able to sleep?

There were doubts to tease me. My godfather was encouraging me to run risks on his behalf, moral and physical: yet what had he offered in return? Nothing: the compact had been entirely one-sided. But were we not now collaborators? Surely the moral scruples he had mentioned would ensure that his partner in sin would receive an adequate reward? I would have to be content with these insubstantial reassurances.

⚬⁓⚬

By the time I had risen the following morning my godfather was already occupied. I was glad of the opportunity to regain my equanimity, being fairly certain that he would expect us to behave as though nothing significant had passed between us. Presumably he was eager for me to return to London to commence upon my new duties. On the other hand it could seem indecorous in me to scuttle away forthwith to embark on debauchery.

I wandered out into the sweet-scented, brightly-flowering gardens. I neither knew nor cared to know the names of the plants that were pleasuring my eyes and nose. Here was sensuality of a kind nicely adjusted to my godfather's elderly capacities. It struck me now that his proposal might prove as challenging to himself as to me. He had mentioned the danger to his posthumous prospects – a danger likely to loom larger in his eyes as time went on. Might there not also be a physical risk in tasting red meat after years of living on pulse? Perhaps his heart might be over-strained. Perhaps the old gentleman would expire in a spasm of vicarious excitement as he read of a defloration. Might not that be a happy outcome for both of us, I asked myself. Provided, of course, that he had made an appropriate will.

Strolling to the rear of the house I came upon two or three peacocks, which were flourishing their mighty tail-feathers in glittering patterns of blue and green. I was delighted to see these strutting avian beaux – kindred spirits, celebrating the carnal impulses of spring. Yet on closer inspection they offered food for philosophy. Supporting each great arc of splendour was a corsetry of struts; a mechanical apparatus rooted around the privy parts, the inglorious bum. The proximity of luminous beauty and crude function was the pastoral paradox reduced to visual aphorism. Fortunately for these preening, small-brained birds they could display and breed, display and breed, untroubled by reflection.

I encountered Mr Gilbert late that afternoon. He was a little freer and more affable than I had usually seen him, but he made no allusion to our nocturnal conversation. It appeared that he had been sitting for his portrait, a project on which the painter, a Worcester man, had been engaged for some time. When I expressed interest my godfather took me to see the incomplete picture. It showed him on the terrace, leaning upon the balustrade and looking out across the green fields of his estate. I offered compliments appropriate to the intermediate state of the portrait, which promised to be a sufficiently accomplished piece of work. It preserved some aspects of my godfather's personality very accurately – but others had vanished through the strainer of the artist's observation. Posterity would gain from it no glimpse of the man I had spoken with the night before.

'You have visited much of the house, I believe,' said Mr Gilbert, 'but I would like to show you a corner you will not have seen.'

He led me up a narrow, winding staircase that took us past all three storeys and eventually to a door opening on to a flat portion of the roof. We emerged into airy vacancy, with clouds blowing across the blue sky overhead and a wide green landscape spread out all around us. For the first time I could see my godfather's estate – perhaps to be my future inheritance – as a whole. It seemed to me a vast expanse, but he pointed out its limits.

'There where the woodland begins,' he said, 'lies Mr Hurlock's property. If it were combined with my own I might be the greatest landowner in the county.'

At dinner that evening he made no explicit reference to our nocturnal conversation, although one or two remarks showed it was very much alive in his mind. Only at one point did he say something unexpected: 'By the bye, you have made mention of your friend Matt Cullen. I have heard a little about that young man from an acquaintance in Malvern who knows the family. You might do well to avoid confiding too far in him. I will say no more than that.'

Since he had closed the matter I did not expostulate, but I was both puzzled and amused by the warning.

Two days later I was again in the coach to London, rattling along wet roads amid falling white petals that mingled with the spring showers.

7

Once again optimism was modified by second thoughts. To be sure I should easily find matter enough to please my godfather in the new mode now proposed. My dealings with Kitty could hardly fail to supply salacious or comic entertainment. With Horn and Latimer I could continue to sample the heartier pleasures of the town, perhaps even an occasional brawl or debauch. Through Crocker I had hopes of less commonplace diversions. My explorations of London at large could continue as before.

Yet I was wary of possible pitfalls. It seemed to me that Mr Gilbert, perhaps under the influence of moonlight and port, had been inconsistent. He wanted a taste of the sensual pleasures he had missed, but he might not welcome the inference that his caution had been timorous. I should never seem to hint: 'Such are the joys your faint-heartedness has denied you'. Perhaps I should even imply that there had been wisdom in his doubts: my amorous joys could be seasoned with disappointment.

But there were deeper issues. It had seemed no great matter to offer Gilbert an account of my lighter pleasures. Now he seemed to be demanding an intimacy, between us that might prove positively contaminating. Had I not promised myself that my attempt upon Sarah would be a private narrative of which he would hear nothing? Yet had I not all but broached the topic to him? Unless I exerted myself I might be corrupted before I knew it.

I looked forward to discussing these issues with Matt Cullen. The warning from my godfather I would of course disregard: given the delicacy – or indelicacy – of our compact I could see why he would not wish me to have a confidant with connections in the county. I had no such concern, and was in urgent need of a sympathetic ear.

Such solace, however, was to be denied me. Waiting in Cathcart Street was a letter:

Dear Dick,

We may be about to pass one another on a country road in our respective stage coaches. I have been summoned to Malvern by my father, who has been laid low by the gout. Knowing that condition to be a painful one I am not unsympathetic; but I suspect that my presence will afford him little relief.

I hope that my visit to the country will prove a brief one, and that I will be conversing with you again in the near future. Meanwhile pray offer such succour as you can to my kinsman the Duke, who will be all but inconsolable at my absence.

Yours, &c.

P.S. I recently fell in with a quiet fellow named Gow who proved to work for the diamond merchant of whom we have spoken. It seems Mr Ogden conducts his business from premises in Duke Street, near the coffee-house. You may wish to stroll there to appraise your rival.

I scarcely took in the postscript at the time in my disappointment at Matt's absence. But I was cheered by a second note, delivered only hours before my arrival:

If you should be free to pay him a visit around noon tomorrow Tom Crocker would be pleased to see you.

My dear Godfather,

I was pleased to find at my lodgings an invitation to visit Thomas Crocker, although surprised to see that the address given was not that of the house he had formerly occupied. He is now to be found in Wyvern Street.

There were to be further surprises. Assuming that the occasion would be a formal one I dressed accordingly. When I arrived, however, I was admitted to a large house, in which were to be seen no guests and very little furniture. I was left to wait in a high drawing-room, containing no more than a single table and a few chairs. The walls were bare and the windows uncurtained. To increase my confusion my host shuffled in wearing no wig and clad in a loose coat and slippers. However, he greeted me with a smile.

'Mr Fenwick, I must apologize: you will think my invitation misleading. It was sent on impulse, without sufficient thought. I hoped to welcome you informally and get to know you better. I should have made my purpose clearer.'

It was curious to see Mr Crocker in this altered guise, like an actor who has stripped off the trappings of the dramatic role you have just seen him playing. He had shambled in inelegantly, but was serene in his own domain. Even his gestures and facial expressions were altered: he could almost have been a huge schoolboy. I infer that his public appearances require contrivance. The large legs must be constrained by tight stockings, the loose bulk strapped into a corset, so that he can preside and move with a show of dignity.

Crocker sent for some coffee.

'You see the place three-quarters empty.' he said. 'I am at present moving house. Here – let me show you something that may amuse you.'

He led me to the far side of the great room. Leaning against a shuttered window were a number of paintings, loosely wrapped with paper, and apparently to be hung on the bare walls. Crocker tore the paper from one of the smaller ones.

'Thanks to my excessive wealth,' said he, 'I have been enabled to have my features recorded by the ingenious Mr Hogarth.'

It was a fine portrait of Crocker's face, full of wit and intelligence.

'Would you not say, Mr Fenwick, that here is a · handsome man?'

'I would indeed,' I replied, surprised by the self-regarding question.

'Then what say you to this?'

He ripped the paper from a larger work, over six foot in height. Looking out from it, all but identically, was the same face, but in this case providing merely a summit to a bulging pyramid that filled the frame – Crocker's body, finely dressed, but grotesquely abundant.

'I fancy Mr Hogarth enjoyed the joke of this double commission,' said he, 'though he was too courteous to say as much. Which of the pictures would you call the truer?'

I hesitated. 'They are equally true. But they tell different truths.'

'That is justly said. I know which of those truths I find the more flattering, but I am obliged to inhabit both of them. I had it in mind to hang these pictures here side by side, by way of a satire; but I think the gesture might make my visitors uncomfortable.'

Coffee being brought, we sat down to it – or in Crocker's case sprawled back at ease in an over-sized chair. He launched companionably into conversation: 'This year I decided to re-arrange my life. I came to London and looked about for a large property. You see me in the course of migration.'

'And your country estate?'

Crocker blew out his cheeks and then drank some coffee. 'I think to sell it. Lately I found that the countryside lowered my spirits. I would trudge round my land and return to the house despondent. The sheep and the cattle, grazing the fields year after year after year filled me with melancholy. I am glad to be away from them.'

'Was that a sufficient reason for migration to the capital?'

'It was but part of the reason. The chief motive was a desire for diversion.'

'Diversion from what?'

'From monotony. From cows and sheep. From thought. From myself.'

'Does the remedy work?'

'It has kept my mind busy. Here is a mansion with many rooms. I am having it painted, and have chosen the colours to be used. I have brought in some furnishings and carpets and curtains and ordered many more. When all is in place I must host a great party to declare the house open. But there is also work to be done outside. Let me show you.'

He drained his cup and led me to a great window at the rear of the room.

'As you can see,' he said, 'we have hardly begun.'

Here was a large space, apparently a courtyard. What chiefly took my eye was a broken wall at the far end, where some workmen were busy.

'Surely,' said I, 'that was the wall we pushed down the other week?'

'Of course,' he replied. 'Thomas Crocker is a gentleman, and would push down no wall but his own. As you see, it is being re-built with a wide gateway, to admit carriages.'

'Might not your workmen have taken it down more efficiently?'

'Much more efficiently. But I had read that a wall

*could be demolished by the method we attempted, and it
tickled me to try the experiment by moonlight.'*

'Another exercise in diversion?'

*'It was.' He was suddenly rueful. 'But such pleasures
are short-lived. I felt a pang of glee as the wall began to
yield; then in the morning all I had for our pains was a
mound of dirt and broken brickwork. No matter'* – *he
brightened once more* – *'the men are at work and elegance
will be retrieved from chaos.'*

*'Was there not some pleasure in recruiting your friends
to perform this task?'*

*'Certainly. And it was healthy exertion for a band of
tipplers and tattlers* – *the most useful work they had done
in months.'*

*He broke into a chuckle at this, his stomach shaking,
but then apologized: 'You must excuse me, Mr Fenwick: I
laugh too easily. My life is often ridiculous* – *and like
Laurence Sterne I believe that laughter does us good.'*

*As we wandered back towards the coffee he broke into
song, his voice echoing through the hollow room:*

Now to sweeten the night
Let the bow sweep the string.
Hear the music take flight
As the violins sing—

I chimed in for the chorus:

Sing, sing, sing—
As the violins sing.

111

Catching one another's eye we launched with spirit into the topers' second verse:

Let horse-hair scrape gut
Till the cat mews away,
And we caper and strut,
As we hear the horse neigh—
Neigh, neigh, neigh—
As we hear the horse neigh.

'I observe, Mr Crocker,' said I, 'that you do not care to be confined by formalities.'

'I have made the same observation regarding yourself, Mr Fenwick. It was one of my reasons for inviting you here this morning.'

We proceeded to converse with great freedom. I felt flattered when he remarked that he is rarely so open: he has many drinking companions but few friends. He frankly disclosed his view of his own situation: fate has been hard on him with regard to physical appearance, but correspondingly generous in terms of wealth. He will use this asset to minimize his disadvantages and make his life as agreeable as it can be.

One aspect of his philosophy would, I think, particularly interest you. Speaking again of the party he would hold when his house was ready he declared that it would be not merely a lavish but a provocative affair.

'It has been my practice,' he said, 'to host entertainments that surprise and bewilder the guests. Since life is short I try to make it richer by brewing up

extravagant mixtures of sensations. I hope you will
partake of them.'

And I will. I feel drawn to Mr Crocker, and pleased
to be accounted his friend.

Later that day I paid a second visit, this time to Miss
Brindley. Over tea we embarked on a negotiation as
delicate as the construction of a house of cards. Without
an indecorous word being said it was somehow agreed:

> *that it was in our power to contrive a pleasure that*
> *both of us might welcome;*
> *that the necessary arrangements and expense should*
> *fall to my charge;*
> *that though the pleasure might be equal the potential*
> *sacrifices were not;*
> *that the female party should therefore receive financial*
> *compensation;*
> *that in the event of unsought consequences the female*
> *party should be provided for.*

All this, and more, was satisfactorily communicated with
the lightness and sweetness of the chirruping of spring birds.
The pleasing prose of the matter is that late next week we
will be spending an evening and a night together.

I am, &c.

❧

Although I had enjoyed both these encounters, the need
to describe them was irksome to me: my social life had

become my profession. Perhaps for that reason a venture still outside Mr Gilbert's knowledge assumed greater importance for me. My mind returning to Matt's postscript, I several times walked down Duke Street during working hours. Not until my third such excursion did I see the gentleman I was seeking. Mr Ogden was standing outside his own premises, my conjecture as to his identity being confirmed when a passer-by addressed him by name. I was able to observe him unremarked as he engaged in a brief conversation. He was a thick-set, short-necked fellow who would have been credited with brawn and vigour had it not appeared that his physical solidity might be compacted fat. His face was pasty and serious, suggestive of the determination Sarah had mentioned. He might have been a dozen years my senior, but it was hard to judge, since he looked to be one of those stolid, under-spirited fellows who resign youth for middle age at fifteen. His stockings showed a weighty calf, but not a shapely one. During the short colloquy he spoke little and displayed no change of expression. Yet this dull merchant had seen what I had not seen and been where I had not been. The thought induced such a spurt of rage that I could have dashed my fist into his big face. As it was, I stalked back to Cathcart Street hot with disgust.

That evening, still unsettled, I rifled through a packet of correspondence to find a letter Sarah had sent me soon after I went to France – a letter I had left unanswered.

Dear Mr Fenwick,
Following your advice I shall direct this communication
to Paris; but I cannot rid myself of a superstitious fear
that I am sending it into thin air – that it will prove no

communication at all, because it will never reach you. It will seem wonderful to me if that fear proves unjustified, and somehow by coach and by boat and by coach again my letter will be conveyed from England to France and left where your hands will take it up and open it, and your eyes peruse it.

I hope that you will write soon and tell me about your travels. Having experienced only York and a little of London I cannot imagine what you are seeing or doing, or how you have been faring. Take me with you through your letters, so that I may feel I am beside you in Paris or Rome as an unseen fellow traveller.

Nothing of note has happened to me since I bade you good-bye. You know enough about my life in London to imagine every one of my days. I have not enjoyed a serious conversation – I mean a conversation about anything other than small social matters – in all these weeks. My aunt, of course, continues kind: I live comfortably enough at the level to which I am accustomed, and know that I have nothing to complain of. Yet in my mind there is a very great alteration. You were the one person who opened windows through which I could glimpse a wider world of learning, wit, and discovery. It hardly needs to be said that I read still, and read eagerly, but I feel that I am cut off, like one in prison, from the life that books reveal and the life you now inhabit.

I suspect you may not realize how greatly the partial similarity of our lives has influenced my disposition. If I had never known you I think I might have been sufficiently contented with the life I now lead, rather as a *caged bird may flutter and sing without apparent envy of his free-flying cousins beyond the confining wires. But I have seen you, like myself an orphan, like myself left to the care of an aunt, find your way into that outside world and flourish in the liberty it affords. Even when we were both in York you seemed to me destined for such freedom. I need not refer to the prospects that may arise from your godfather's generosity: whatever happens you will remain a free man. I have seen you flower. You are educated and accomplished, and converse with educated and accomplished men. I cannot help wondering whether, with my far more limited abilities I might not myself have made shift to survive and modestly prosper in that richer, more diverse life.*

Now I am ashamed of what I have written, for it seems selfish and envious. Pray interpret my message as what I intended it to be, a means of conveying, with strong feeling, if with all due decorum, how much I have missed your company and your conversation, and how much I long to hear from you.

I remain, &c.

What right had I to thrust myself upon Sarah again, having failed to reply to this appeal – failed to send an answer of any kind? Why had I not written? At the time I had been caught up with a young Parisian lady, but it was an affair of no great consequence to either of us. The truth was that I had been unable to respond in kind to Sarah's candour and intimacy. Her words drew me back towards a past I was trying to escape. Immersed in the present and in my possible future I shrank from the passing reference to my aunt as a cat shrinks from water.

My father I scarcely remembered; my mother, and my Aunt Mary, at whose house I had for several years passed my school holidays, I could recall indistinctly – but I rarely chose to do so. My aunt's death, during my first year at university, had closed off that past conveniently and completely. In leaving Sarah's letter unanswered I was confirming my rejection of our shared experiences. Why then, was I now so eager to see her, to claim her?

I could not say; but I knew that the emotions concerned lay too deep to be admitted to Mr Gilbert. Once more I resolved that Sarah would not feature in my letters to him.

My dear Godfather,

I invite you to accompany me through the several stages of a carousal. The occasion was the twenty-fifth birthday of Robert Eckersley, a tall, blustering fellow I knew when at Oxford. The place was the Black Lion tavern in Holland Street. The organizers of the party were Nick Horn and a sportive gentleman named Talbot.

The building, an old one, with blackened beams, is said to be haunted by the spirit of a merchant stabbed to death there in Shakespeare's day. Owing to this circumstance, much of our early conversation was concerned with ghosts. One faction claimed that they believed in them; the other protested their scepticism – Nick Horn being one of their number.

117

'If ever I fancied I was seeing a ghost,' said he, 'I would know that I was drunk.'

This dispute led our landlord to observe that he knew a gypsy-woman who had supernatural powers and could read the future. By popular acclaim she was sent for, and a villainous old body she proved to be, stooped and furtive. She was nonetheless invited, for a fee of a crown, to exercise her arts on Eckersley, the subject of our celebrations.

She begged leave to look at his palm, which she scrutinized closely, tracing out the main lines upon it with a black fingernail. Despite her unprepossessing appearance there was a concentration in her demeanour that impressed us all, reducing us to near silence. She spoke at last in a monotone, with her eyes still closed.

'Your name,' she said, 'begins with an "E". It is Eglington – no: Eckersley. You have a sister, Alice. Your father's name is – is Samuel. I think he may be in France.'

Knowing these claims to be true, we were astonished and uneasy. Eckersley, who had grinned at first, was now impressed. Horn, however, remained a sceptic.

'Ask her,' he said, 'the name of your cat.'

We all knew the name, since we had been joking about the creature earlier in the evening. When Eckersley put the question the old woman hid her face in her hands. There was a silence. Horn grinned triumphantly. At length she sat upright and spoke out clearly.

'His name is Milton,' she said.

There was a gasp at this – even some applause.

Eckersley wore a look of comical stupefaction. Horn was the first to speak.

'This old crone is uncanny,' he said. 'Ask her to foretell your future.'

Talbot intervened at once: 'No, no, Nick. This has gone far enough.'

There were expostulations on both sides of the case, but Eckersley overrode them:

'Why should I fear the future? Old woman: what will I be doing this day next year?'

The gypsy gazed into his face in a prolonged silence. Her verdict came in a hoarse whisper: 'I can see nothing. This day next year you will not be here.'

'Why not? Why not?' asked Eckersley, much excited.

The old woman turned to him with great solemnity:

'Because – because on your twenty-fifth birthday you will die.'

Poor Eckersley looked thunder-struck. 'But today—'

He got no further, for Horn and Talbot broke into howls of mirth. After a moment's blankness Eckersley threw himself upon them in fury, punching and kicking with all his might. Fortunately there were enough of us sufficiently sober to pull the combatants apart. Eckersley, confused by being condemned to death and then reprieved within a quarter of a minute, was consoled by a fresh glass of wine and the damage he had inflicted on Horn before being dragged away. Horn laughed still, though blood was streaming from his nose.

The next stage of our party was heralded by a bawled announcement from Talbot:

'Gentlemen: it is my pleasure to introduce the famous Belinda Cartwright.'

I had heard of this personage and her performance, but never previously seen her. She entered to applause, dressed like a lady of fashion, and stepping to the music of an old fiddler. So elegantly and completely was she accoutred, from high wig to satin shoes that there was scarcely an inch of her person not concealed by paint or fabric. It soon became apparent that the very object and essence of her performance would be gradually to lay bare the female form thus concealed. To do her justice she was an accomplished artist in her way: she moved with easy grace. Her garments had been so fashioned that most came away at a touch or a twist – to cries of approval from her rapt audience. Even her white stockings she seemed somehow to peel away with a mere gesture. At the last, doffing a light slip, she displayed that strangely erotic incongruity: the painted and coiffured head of a young lady at a formal gathering above a voluptuous naked form. She curtsied deep as we young bucks, stirred alike in imagination and in blood, rose in riotous applause.

By way of encore she took up a series of extravagant postures and poses that frankly disclosed the few intimate areas which she had not already had occasion to reveal. All this time the old fiddler, who must know the lady's body in rather more detail than that of his own wife, sawed out a witty accompaniment.

Later Miss Cartwright, now loosely clud, joined the company for conversation and a glass of wine. While she could by no means be bribed to give the last favour, she was willing to use her deft fingers to snuff out some of the flames she had ignited. I observed that she several times complacently received the tribute of a guinea slipped, not into her hand, but into the dainty monosyllable itself.

These pleasures had taken us to what might have been the dispersal of our party. All had drunk too much; one or two had been obliged to relieve the pressures within by a hearty cascade. In truth the room was now in a disgusting condition. The landlord, although he had profited well from the evening, was eager to see the back of us. Several gentlemen had already slipped away when it was proposed by Horn and Talbot that we should conclude our revel by escorting our guest of honour, Mr Eckersley, who was in no very promising condition for walking, back to his lodgings in Bank Street. This suggestion being warmly received, the survivors of the party stumbled downstairs and out into blank darkness.

Even in our sorry state it seemed likely that we could deliver Mr Eckersley and disband without further complication. The landlord procured a link-boy to light our way. It happened, however, that the night breeze and the effort to walk revived our raucousness, so that we blundered along making the devil of a din, laughing, singing, shouting and cursing. Our diminutive torch-bearer had not led us far before a window was flung open above and we heard a furious householder bawling abuse at us. Many voices threw instant defiance at the poor devil we had awakened but it was little Horn, who has a stentorian shout and a bottomless reserve of invective, who led the attack, yelling into the darkness:

'You pox-rotten, louse-ridden, bastard son of a Hockley whore! Clamp your stinking chops before I kick your door in and stuff your tongue down your windpipe—'

As the link-boy flourished his torch we could see other windows opening, and heads poking out to add fresh shouts of protest. The decisive intervention, however, came from the original complainant. He leaned from his casement and, with some dexterity, discharged the contents of a Jordan souse over Nick Horn, who was still in full cry. In a moment Nick had grubbed up a loose cobblestone and hurled it up at his foe. When it struck the wall and fell back he snatched it again and in a mad fit of fury flung it through a lower window.

We were at once under siege, amid cries of outrage, with substances of all kinds raining upon us. Crockery, eggs and urine were the least disagreeable of them. A couple of broken chairs came down, and I glimpsed a cat hitting the cobbles with a squeal and limping away. It was the last thing I saw before the link-boy wisely doused his torch and took to his heels. Our disorderly band had scattered under this aerial assault, and I had just enough self-possession to retire and make my way back to Cathcart Street.

This was a sorry end to what had been a lively evening. It is a pity that high spirits can so easily decline into doltishness.

I remain, &c.

8

It occurred to me to wonder whether my godfather had dropped a hint to Mr Ward concerning my new responsibilities – or irresponsibilities – in London. I found the thought a disagreeable one. How close these two gentlemen were I had never known, but it was clear that there was regular communication between them, and that Ward was more than a mere agent and adviser. I had always hoped to look well in his eyes.

To test the situation I walked to Fetter Lane one morning to visit him. He was correct as ever in his demeanour: if he had been given reasons to view me in a new light he disguised the fact. I noticed, however, that this normally imperturbable gentleman seemed a little distressed. His long face was pale, and his eyes wandered.

'Pardon me, Mr Ward,' said I. 'Is there something amiss?'

He hesitated for a moment, disconcerted by my directness, but then muttered that his wife had been ill with a fever. I expressed my condolences, although surprised to learn that this cautious fellow had ever risked matrimony. His suppressed misery remaining vivid in my mind I returned to the office later in the day, bringing some fruit, honey and other things that I thought might be of benefit to the invalid. As Mr Ward received this trifling gift I saw him, for a second time, distinctly discomposed.

'I thank you, Mr Fenwick,' said he. 'This shows a good nature in you.'

It was pleasing to find myself considered good-natured, even if the compliment had cost little in the way of exertion. Perhaps I had more virtue in my disposition than I had given myself credit for. Touched by the glimmer of warmth I made further inquiries a day or two later, and was pleased to learn that Mrs Ward was much recovered.

❧

My dear Godfather,

On Friday last Miss Brindley and I took a hackney coach to the Full Moon in Gowling Street, an inn recommended to me by Latimer as ideally suited to the kind of transaction in view. It lived up to his description in that all guests would seem to be granted both the courtesy due to respectable married couples and the privacy required by the unmarried. Miss Brindley responded to the minor luxuries of the place as though she had never seen such wonders.

'How genteelly they treat us,' she said. 'I feel I must be at my best.'

'I'm sure my Kitty will be equal to the occasion,' said I.

'I shall try to perform like a lady,' she replied, 'but I hope you will make allowance for my lack of experience.'

We indulged in such mildly indelicate exchanges over the supper provided in our room. Even here Miss Brindley managed to reprise her pastoral role. She ate and drank with a charming exhibition of simple enjoyment, and a bashful lowering of her eyelids. Thickly heated in my nether parts I yet found it civilized that such hints and blandishments should preface the physical act.

Afterwards I proceeded with decorum, sitting beside her on the edge of the bed and taking her hand. She broke away from our first kiss as though overcome by timidity, but permitted the second to be more prolonged. At the third her passion broke its bounds, and she clung to me tightly when I gently pushed her across the bed and unlaced her garments to release her breasts to my hands and lips. As I grew more demanding she twisted beneath me, with sounds of protest and pleasure.

Some little time later she broke from me again, and sat up panting, her hair and her clothing greatly disarranged. At her request I extinguished all the lights but one, while she went away to undress in a small ante-room. When she returned there was still but a single candle burning, and its soft glow set off her unclad form to great advantage. I had myself remained dressed, relishing the notion that she should be nakedly exposed to the gaze of a fully clad man, as though she were a captured slave to be appraised by a fastidious despot. Placing my hands upon her shoulders I turned her slowly around to survey her at leisure, enjoying the play of light and shadow on her smooth skin. Current fashions are such that we men can infer very little about a woman's body until we undress her, or she undresses herself. Kitty was as plumply well-formed as I could have hoped; the one surprise, to me a pleasing one, being the uncommonly thick thatch of black hair below her white belly, made yet darker by the candle-shadow. Pressing close behind her I ran my hand down over her breasts, and down again among those dense curls and through them, thrusting my fingers into her. She cried aloud, already hot and wet.

It has struck me before now as strange that the excitement of physical love, like the seemingly antithetical tedium of a stage coach journey, intensifies the immediate experience, yet in retrospect shrinks it to mere generalization. So it was on this occasion. Once I had torn off my own clothes and snuffed the last candle, being almost burnt by the hot wax on my fingers, the night became a compound of physical exertions and sensations, shifting shadows, groans and cries, caresses and clutches, a mingling of perfumes and rank animal odours. What I can recall with certainty is the moment of scalding pleasure when the ravening bird first plunged into the bush, and later Kitty's scream as the eager spasm made me buck and rear like the victim of an electrical shock.

My mistress proved herself a demurely deft practitioner in all the amorous arts. After she had twice spent, with an ardour that seemed to leave her in a swoon, it was her skilful manipulation that roused me to a further and prolonged encounter.

I awoke in the small hours with a full bladder and a headache, still closely clasping my sleeping Dulcinea. Our bodies were slippery with mingled sweat. The amorous excitement that had exalted me the night before was entirely dissipated. It seemed to me that I was incongruously sharing a bed with a stranger. Becoming aware that my now shrunken member was gummed to her thigh by the dried residuum of vital fluids, I cautiously detached it. She did not stir, and we remained locked in a posture of intimacy no longer agreeable to me. With stealth I extricated myself till I could lie on my back, staring up towards the ceiling. Hot, itching and calmly dispirited, I was unable to sleep again until I had resolved my disillusion into the following couplets:

The pleasures that in prospect shone so fair
Dissolve and vanish in the morning air.

How slight, how brief, the spell desire can cast:
The goal once gained, the rapture cannot last.

Th' ethereal maid, who cost so many a sigh –
Alas, I view her with a literal eye.

Though goddess-like she seemed while yet half-known,
She squeaks like Moll, she sweats like greasy Joan;

While I, self-cheated, bilked of heav'nly bliss,
Must plunge, forlorn, from that world back to this.

The lines have little merit, but they faithfully record my sense of weary discontent as I lay beside the sleeping Miss Brindley at dawn.

When we rose next morning I found little to cheer me. Where love is in the case it may be that the closeness of minds and hearts overcomes all other considerations; but where it is not, and desire ceases to activate the imagination, the intimacies of toilet and chamber-pot must be fatal to the fading ideal. I could still glimpse in Kitty, as in an altered perspective, the qualities that had fed my fantasy, but they now seemed to constitute but a trivial proportion of her personality.

Of course I contrived that we breakfasted and parted on amicable terms. I am not always kind, but I hope that, more often than not, I can behave kindly.

I record these reactions as I experienced them at the time, since I know from past encounters that a day or two of recuperation may alter my feelings and even my opinions. It is nonetheless the case that, though physically appeased, I returned to my lodgings disturbed by what seemed to me another application of the treacherous laws of compensation, satisfaction of the body conducing to dissatisfaction in the mind.

I will confide further as time passes and my animal spirits revive.

Yours, &c.

❧

My dear Godfather,

Yesterday, acting upon impulse, I headed westward to join the crowds gathering for the latest round of executions at Tyburn.

128

Grim though the experience proved to be, it gave much food for thought. The throng that lined the route was animated by passions hard to interpret. There was exhilaration, made morbid by its presiding cause – the lust to witness death. There was gratification at seeing criminals suffer for their crimes: notorious malefactors are roundly jeered as they depart for Hades. In some cases, by contrast, a condemned man may be so popular, with parts of the crowd at least, as to be cheered to the echo.

Among the five prisoners to be executed today was the highwayman Jack Gardiner, who has won the hearts of the public through rumoured acts of magnanimity and an escape from prison to rival that of Jack Sheppard. There was resounding applause for him, and his name was shouted out, as though in celebration. I had secured a station close to the scaffold where not long ago Lord Ferrers arrived in his own coach to be hanged in a suit of satin. On this occasion there was nothing but squalor.

The condemned men in their cart passed within a few feet of me, each with a noose already about his neck. It was hard to comprehend that shortly they would be men no more, but swinging carcases. Gardiner sat erect, with a bold smile, waving to his admirers like a hero returning from war. As he drew opposite, he looked me directly in the eye and nodded, still smiling, as though tipping the wink to an old friend. It was uncanny to be in direct communication with a man about to leap off the edge of the world.

In contrast two or three of his companions appeared so drunk as scarcely to know where they were. It was as though the celebrated Jack Gardiner were the leading actor in a theatrical event. The other condemned men, and even the chaplain and the hangman himself, were no more than the minor performers needed to fill out the scene. There was a crescendo of cheering and jeering as the last formalities were completed at the scaffold. The ropes dangling from the victims' throats were fastened to the gallows, prayers were gabbled, and a few parting words were spoken by each of the prisoners, inaudible in the hubbub. There came a defiant wave from Gardiner, who had the heroism to play out his role to the end, before the cart pulled away, amid a clamour of enthusiasm and lamentation, and the men were left dancing in air. At once their friends rushed forward to shorten their ordeal by dragging at their legs to break their necks. The men who had passed me but a few minutes earlier had been extinguished, and their souls, if any, dispersed.

Twenty-four hours later I am still shaken by what I saw. I find consolation in the thought that it is better to be shocked by such scenes than to remain unmoved by them.

I remain, &c.

~

I continued uneasy at the extent to which my compact with Mr Gilbert was encroaching upon my daily doings, my thoughts and even my feelings. I had attended the party for Eckersley solely in search of epistolary topics and then found difficulty in concluding my account of it. It seemed that I was obliged to play oaf or prig. It was with misgivings that I had settled on the latter role.

The emotions I experienced at Tyburn had been similarly falsified by my intention to write about them. I had felt what I described myself as feeling, but in a dulled way, as at one remove, and had been in any case somewhat stupefied by the clamour and squalor around me.

There had been downright omissions from my description of the visit to Crocker. In conversation with him I had come to reveal more about my relations with my godfather than I had disclosed to anyone else save Sarah and more recently Cullen. I had spoken the more freely in that he had himself made admissions which I would have felt it a breach of confidence to pass on to my godfather.

'My habits of life,' he told me, 'are shaped by a single determining consideration – namely that I am unlikely to live as long as a further ten years. So physicians have assured me. My father, whom I somewhat resemble in figure and constitution, died in his thirty-eighth year. The carcase that I am confined in, or consist of – depending upon your view of such matters – will soon overtax the pump that moves it – and so good night. This is an unfortunate circumstance, but all is not gloom. Labouring under such disadvantages I conclude that I deserve consolation, and therefore feel free to indulge my tastes and curiosities, and enjoy my life as long as it lasts.'

But it was in writing of my night with Kitty Brindley that I had experienced my greatest difficulties. Here was matter, I had thought, perfectly suited to my godfather's tastes and curiosities – and after all it was only fair to give him what he was paying for. In truth I had performed and responded pretty much as I said. But I had been distracted, even in the heat of carnal acts, by the need to be aware of my own sensations. Later it had occurred to me to respond also to Mr Gilbert's stated uneasiness with the delusions of pastoral: only when I had returned to Cathcart Street did I cobble together my couplets of disillusion.

My conquest of Kitty had indeed left me with a sense of discomfort. The source of it, however, was by no means merely physical. My knowledge that I was to lay the transaction open to my godfather's prurience somehow tainted it. It was now clearer to me than ever that I could not endure to have my whole existence exposed to him in this way. I was confirmed in my resolve to inhabit two distinct narratives. The more superficial one, available to Gilbert, and manipulated as necessary, could include Horn, Latimer, Crocker, in his public guise and, for all my reluctance, Kitty. A second life, of which he would know nothing, would take in my friendship with Matt Cullen, the private face of Tom Crocker and my pursuit of Sarah Kinsey. In *that* narrative I could be truly myself.

❧

My dear Godfather,

Horn and I were strolling in St James's Park when we happened to pass Latimer and Lord Ashton, who were walking the other way. The trivial incident was pleasing to me for the intricacy of the responses it elicited. Lord Ashton looked quite properly blank, for neither Horn nor I have ever spoken to him. Latimer contrived to intimate, through the slightest of inclinations of the head and the ghost of a simper, that he knew us, and was not too proud to acknowledge that he knew us, but that he was too preoccupied in serious conversation with a Minister of State to vouchsafe more than that. Horn and I correspondingly conveyed that we were gratified to see a friend of ours in such exalted company, but that we were, of course, too conscious of our own lack of consequence to think of addressing him. To our credit we were able to walk on till we were hidden behind a large tree before bursting into loud laughter at the absurd solemnity of the exchange. Later that same day we mocked Latimer unmercifully for his affectation. Serene as ever, he took our taunts in good part; the truth is that, thanks to family connections, he is a rising man. It may well be that in a year or two none of us will find anything in the least surprising or comical in such an encounter.

I myself mingled with the modestly mighty when paying a further visit to Lord Vincent. The best of my conversation, however, was with his cousin, Mrs Jennings, a witty lady of mature years. She told me that she knew you well some decades ago, and thought you a talented fellow, bound for a career in government. She was surprised, she said, that you were eventually content to withdraw into the country. You will, I am sure, remember her: she is the aunt of Mr Thorpe, whom I have met at your house.

Today being fine I paid my sixpence to be ferried once more across the crowded Thames – on this occasion to

133

visit Greenwich. I was curious to see a remarkable invention of which you will no doubt have heard – the 'camera obscura'. Let me describe it, in case you have not seen it in operation. In a dark chamber the spectator looks down at the surface of a small round table upon which is thrown, in miniature – through some contrivance of mirrors, lenses and prisms – a reflected picture of some portion of the surrounding countryside. By the adjustment of a lever the scene may be shifted, so that, in the course of a visit, one may successively see everything within the landscape that surrounds the building: the streets and houses, the open fields with their trees, windmills and sheep, the river with its busy traffic. Every movement is visible: the progress of a boat or a wagon, the swaying of branches, the fluttering of a flag. Here is reality transformed into a series of living pictures for your contemplation. The material world seems tamed by diminution. It is even possible to put one's hand upon the table and, as it were, pick up one of the moving ships.

Yet this magical device is subject to a limitation, being dependent upon the brightness of the sky. As I was watching, half entranced at seeing the countryside of Greenwich spread out before me, it happened that the sun was covered by a cloud, with the result that the pictured scene subsided into greyness.

I ate at the Anchor, down by the river, and found myself reflecting about food in general. We human-beings, together with cats, dogs, foxes, ferrets and birds, are among the limited number of carnivorous creatures in these islands. Horses, cows, sheep, goats and rabbits seem

to manage very well without devouring the carcases of
their fellow-creatures; but it does not appear that this
dietary habit is associated with any discernible benevolence
in their disposition. I would like this observation to lead
me to some deep moral truth but, like most of my incidental
speculations, it takes me nowhere. Perhaps Mr Yardley
could shed further light on the subject.

After the meal, urgently needing to make water,
I found myself obliged to do so directly into the Thames.
It struck me that under such extreme pressure a physical
sensation was produced disquietingly similar to the
amorous spasm. On the other hand, being somewhat
intoxicated, I also found aesthetic pleasure in the
innumerable sparkles of light in the arc of urine. There is
beauty in all things, I piously concluded.

Horn, Latimer and I plan to attend a masquerade.
This species of entertainment is familiar to them, but will
be new to me. I look forward to describing it to you.

I am, &c.

I had several reasons for sending Mr Gilbert this more sedate letter. As yet I had received no reply to my earlier communications: once again I needed to mark time until I had confirmation that I was writing what he wanted to read. Nor would it do for him to expect bloodshed and maidenheads from every epistle: at that rate I would soon debauch myself into imbecility. To do him justice I suspected that, despite the bias of our recent conversation, he would still prefer our correspondence to be leavened with some little show of urbanity and reflection – as I would myself.

Even this subdued letter had had to be composed with care. Having written a paragraph about the possible usefulness of a camera obscura to an invalid who craved a glimpse of the outside world, I eliminated it, as seeming to offer a metaphor too awkwardly apt to our own contrivances.

I had touched upon my encounter with Mrs Jennings because it seemed likely that my godfather would in any case learn that I had met her. The truth was that our conversation had been long and frank, and had begun from her recollections of my father. Gaudy in pink silk, she was a droll old creature with a humorous eye.

'I see at a glance,' she said, 'that you are the son of Roger Fenwick, once a famous breaker of hearts. Are you not? I was sure of it. You have the same smile, the same dark eyes, the same turn of the head. I must warn you, young man, that if you hint at elopement I shall immediately take you at your word. We can enjoy a life of gaiety, you and I, and my husband will never miss me: he has scarcely heard a word I have said these five years. I once hoped that your father would make me such an offer, but the cruel creature never did.'

When I mentioned my godfather she smiled and tapped my arm with her fan: 'Mr Gilbert knew my family well at that time, and I met him often. He was a friend of your father, and forever at his elbow, watching and listening as though trying to learn the secrets of charm. To do him justice he was a pretty fellow himself in his thin way, and by all accounts clever; but he was so cautious, so circumspect. His reserve made him dull company: he sought out the ladies, but had nothing to say to them. Imagine a vast bottle of wine with an orifice no bigger than the eye of a needle: you could taste no more than a drip or two of his thoughts and feelings. I expected that such a calculating, close-knit gentleman would find political preferment. Instead he settled for rural life. But who knows – perhaps his talents are more healthily occupied in overseeing an estate and a parish?'

When she asked me for my opinion of him as he now was I tried to be circumspect; but she listened to my observations with a satirical smile.

'You are loyal, Mr Fenwick, as you should be,' she said. 'I will say only that it is my personal belief that most men who fail to marry go a little mad.'

I further learned from Mrs Jennings that it is no mere chance that her nephew is employed at Fork Hill: 'I hear from several sources that Mr Gilbert sees his relatives and friends as constituting a web, with himself at the centre. One may apply to him Mr Pope's words:

The spider's touch, how exquisitely fine!
Feels at each thread, and lives along the line.

The living held by my nephew is in Mr Gilbert's gift, and you may be sure that he remembered the family connection. He enjoys exercising patronage, and perhaps sometimes withholding it.'

Mrs Jennings and I viewed my godfather's life from opposite ends: she had seen the young man and could only surmise the older; I was in the converse position. Having encountered him solely in his own domain, austere and authoritative, I had now been enabled to glance back thirty years or more to see a diffident prig. Was the personality I was familiar with a transformation of that former self or a mere protective shell – or perhaps something of both? At least it had become clearer to me why he might want me to re-enact his youth for him in lustier terms.

As regards myself I was reminded again of a deficiency. When Mrs Jennings spoke of my father and his charm she plainly, and reasonably, felt that I would be gratified and would wish to hear more about him. I felt no such curiosity. If there was music in that forgotten past, I was deaf to it: I lived in the present.

9

One morning I was surprised by a visit from Crocker, who climbed up to my rooms with difficulty, huffing and puffing, his hips pressed against the wall on either side. He emerged from the staircase, as he himself said, like a cork from a bottle. If I had fed him a hearty meal I fancy he might have been unable to descend.

Subsiding into a settee he told me that he had called because his spirits were low and he needed distraction. He looked so hugely disconsolate that I could hardly suppress a smile.

'Shall we sing?' I ventured.

He heaved a monstrous sigh, but launched into 'The gentle doe that lurks unseen'. I chimed in, both of us warbling rather sweetly. No sooner were we done than he struck up 'The Kitchen Maid'. My ceiling being low our combining voices fairly shook the windows. We concluded with great vigour:

You find my ways too easy, sir,
But I care not a fig.
And if my hands are greasy, sir,
I'll wipe them on your wig—
I'll wipe them, I'll wipe them,
I'll wipe them on your wig.

The silence that followed made us conscious of the din we had created.

'That was intolerable,' said Crocker. He toppled himself upright. 'I must apologize to your landlady.'

He spoke heartily, as though taken with the idea. Seconding his whim I followed him down the stairs. He found descending them simpler, his method being to press his bulk against the walls for stability and let his feet stumble rapidly from step to step.

When Mrs Deacon greeted us in her own parlour, Crocker vouchsafed her one of his minimal bows, delivered by the head alone.

'Madam,' he said, 'I am here to apologize for the disgraceful noise that has disturbed you. The blame is entirely mine. Feeling melancholy, I began to sing, and Mr Fenwick joined in to humour me. Please pardon our discourtesy.'

My admirable landlady responded in kind.

'No apology is needed: I enjoyed the performance.'

She and Crocker exchanged a humorous glance that showed them aware of the absurd element in these formal courtesies. I was pleased to see Crocker cheerful again: he had found the diversion he sought. Almost at once he hit on a way of prolonging it.

'I am told that your daughter has an extraordinary talent for the game of chess.'

I had made some such comment in passing, but would not have expected Crocker to remember it. Mrs Deacon was plainly gratified to hear her daughter praised. After further conversation Charlotte was sent for, and introduced to our guest. She was too shy to venture more than a few words, but proved willing to be drawn into a game.

The chessboard was set out on a low table between Crocker, whose haunches filled most of a settee, and Charlotte, whose slender form was perched on a stool. To the eye they were comically mismatched. Mrs Deacon and I sat side by side watching, and exchanging occasional remarks. I found the scene pleasing, partly for its peacefulness, partly because it held four such contrasting individuals in unlikely equilibrium.

Crocker was probably a more skilled player than I, but he fared as badly: a brisk defeat, which took him by surprise, was followed by a longer, more considered game in which he was again the loser. He had tried his best (as he later confirmed to me), but was delighted to be beaten, shaking his head in bewildered admiration for his opponent's skill. Before leaving the house he took Mrs Deacon aside and insisted, despite her protests, that she accept five guineas to be put towards the education of her daughter.

'You have produced a young prodigy, madam,' said he. 'I feel honoured to be able to offer this small gesture of further encouragement.'

Crocker's cheerfulness was by now entirely restored. He

and my landlady parted on excellent terms, pleased with one another.

'You are fortunate,' he told me. 'Female company is a fine thing: it civilizes a man.'

I described this interlude in my Journal as an odd fragment of London life agreeable to me but quite outside my godfather's range of interest.

⁊

My dear Richard,

I have read your recent letters with close attention. Your life has become interestingly turbulent. The nocturnal entertainment that you describe would seem to have been the kind of revelry I shunned as a young man. But I was glad of the chance to glimpse it through the window of your narrative. If I had been present Miss Cartwright's excesses would have put me out of countenance, yet I found pleasure in reading about them. As to the brawl that ended the evening, it may be that a powerful nation needs to tolerate such aggression in its day-to-day doings as a resource it can turn to account in time of war.

Mrs Jennings I remember well. She was Arabella Thorpe when I knew her in London, a lively coquette admired and courted in fashionable circles. She married Ben Jennings, a bluff soldier, and had several children.

The highwayman, Gardiner, whom you mention, is well-known in these parts. He was born in Worcester, and commenced his career within the county. Rumour has it that he has left more than one local girl with child.

You have been frank in your communications; let me reciprocate by admitting to a certain envy as I read of your doings. Given that I myself had these desires and capacities why was it that I could not achieve the satisfactions you have achieved? How mysterious and devious I always found the negotiations needed to bridge the great gap between the social proprieties on the one hand, and shared animal nakedness on the other. Where is a young man to learn – where did you yourself learn? – the art of these transactions? Starting from mere conversational exchanges, somehow the deed is brought about, somehow the genitals are brought into conjunction. One day you must explain the transition to me. Those like Miss Cartwright would seem to offer a welcome short-cut through these complications: so much money is to be paid for so much in the way of intimate display. Here, it would appear, is a clean bargain, well understood on all sides. Such performances suggest the nature and the extent of the furtive hungers in our society – I mean among men, for I cannot imagine that a Mr Cartwright would be in request to reveal his body to an audience of ladies.

To particularize further: I am in some admiration at your conquest of Miss Brindley. She would surely have wanted far more than you were ready to give. Yet there was something sufficiently appealing in your advances to persuade her to accept an arrangement both precarious and temporary. I assume that a decisive element in such a case must be the woman's gratified awareness that she has excited the desires of an eligible man. But could she be sufficiently inflamed if the man in question behaved with the respect that polite conduct dictates? Somehow animal responses must be signalled from both sides. It seems that, like your father, you have mastered the secret language that resolves this dilemma.

I look forward to hearing more about Miss Brindley. You must let me know whether your desire for her person has been dissipated by that one night of copulation, or whether hot blood and imagination may in time revive it.

In the course of our moonlit conversation, however, you mentioned your interest in a married woman. I would be glad to learn more, since such a pursuit would surely provide a greater challenge, and therefore shed a stronger light on the strange operations of lust.

I remain interested in your unusual friend Mr Crocker, and would even infer that there might be an improbable element of affinity between him and myself. The eccentric man who has resources without responsibilities is equipped to experiment with life.

I have told you of my interest in the working of the Passions. It has traditionally been argued that a man's character is defined by the predominance of some single Passion, such as Pride, Avarice or Ambition. My own belief is that the determining impulse derives from a combination of Passions. Thus we see in Shakespeare's Moor a fatal blending of Pride and Jealousy. It may be that Mr Crocker is doubly driven – it is to be hoped to less deadly effect – by his love of novelty and a need to be distracted from his physical condition.

I look forward to hearing more from you.

I remain, &c.

This was by far the longest and frankest letter I had ever received from my godfather. I read it repeatedly, anxious to grasp everything that was implied. At first sight I thought it a pitiable production: Mrs Jennings' opinions about him were proved to be well-founded: it seemed that his habitual correctness was indeed a mask for timidity. Yet here he was, so hungry to glimpse what he had been too hen-hearted to experience, that he was willing to set aside his hard-won dignity and show himself envious and inquisitive. Was it not demeaning to be the partner in prurience of such a man? Yet there was an underlying wistfulness in these admissions. I could almost find it in me to be sorry for the old fellow.

It occurred to me that these disclosures could strengthen my position. After the years of formality my godfather and I were sharing an exchange of confidences. When I next met him how would he be able to retreat into his distant, authoritative manner? Had he not put himself, at least to some small extent, in *my* power?

Unfortunately it was easy to turn these arguments about. Would he have taken such risks unless he knew me to be inescapably a dependant? All my hopes remained vested in him: he had nothing to fear from me. Nor did I doubt that his remarks concerning the Passions were seriously intended. I had seen ample evidence of his speculative bent. His fastidious mind could readily set aside his own erotic appetites to enable disinterested speculation on the workings of the Passions at large. There could be a clue in his suggestion that such Passions might work in combination. Perhaps in his own case Lust was awkwardly allied with Circumspection, or – as he had shrewdly hinted concerning Crocker – with a growing awareness of his own mortality.

The worst of his letter was his eager sniffing after an adulterous affair. How had the old hound picked up so faint a scent? I would need to head him off.

My dear Godfather,

Nothing is more expressive of the monstrous energy of London than the continuous process of building and unbuilding. Construction, of course, is everywhere visible, perhaps most admirably in the vicinity of Grosvenor Square and Berkeley Square, where I often pause to watch the workmen at their task. The phenomenon I have called 'unbuilding' I had witnessed only in its consequences until yesterday, when by chance I saw it in action.

I was walking northwards from Leicester Fields, near the district of St Giles, when I heard, somewhere to my right, a loud rumbling, followed by a more general commotion of shouting and screaming. Hurrying in the direction of the noise I turned a corner and saw a remarkable sight: an old house, four storeys high, in the very process of collapse. There was a widening crack almost from top to bottom. Part of the upper front wall had already fallen and smashed to pieces, producing the sound I had heard. Even as I watched, another great slab of brickwork broke away and came thundering down to the cobbles, raising a cloud of dust, as the spectators leaped back, shrieking. The portion of roof above the lost wall then sagged and crumbled, spewing out a shower of splintering tiles.

The din from this avalanche gradually subsided. When the air cleared somewhat we could see the rooms of the upper storeys thrown open to view, with the floors sloping towards us and broken staircases leading out into vacancy. At intervals a bed, a table or a chair would slither forwards and drop onto the broken brickwork piled below.

One could judge from the appearance of the interior that this was a building in a wretched state of dirt and disrepair, destined to founder. I learned from those around me that it was the third house in the district to fall this year. This particular street is one of the last resorts of the destitute, and should no doubt be razed in its entirety in the interests of public safety; but the power and will to take such radical measures seem to be lacking. In consequence one sees many houses such as this dying from old age and decrepitude, the crooked window frames sustained by wedges and the broken panes stopped up with rags.

I was told that on this occasion, by good fortune, those within had seen or felt the early signs of disintegration and saved their lives by rushing out before the walls began to crack. In other such cases there have been deaths, particularly among small children and the old. I went on my way somewhat discomposed. Such a collapse seems to take on emblematic force in this time of changing beliefs and toppling Ministries.

It also serves as a reminder of the provisional nature of all buildings. It comes naturally to us to accept our houses as so many settled facts of existence, when they are truly no more than accumulations of convention and contrivance. We glue our bricks together with mortar, nail down slices of tree-trunk for a floor, build into our walls brittle sheets of glass, to admit light but shut out wind and rain. Then we have curtains to exclude the very light that the glass admits, and candles or lamps to restore the light that has been excluded. It is perhaps less wonderful that some of these structures should collapse than that the great majority remain stoutly upright and protect us from wind and weather.

When Crocker's platoon of inebriates pushed down his wall it appeared that vibration might have been the crucial element in their success. Might it not be the case that the seemingly solid streets of London are so abused by continual traffic as on occasion to impart an accumulating tremor sufficient to unsettle foundations from below?

I have received your long letter, and studied it with care. It is gratifying to me that some of my anecdotes have stirred your interest. You may look to hear more in subsequent communications. Your hint that 'hot blood and imagination' might revive my flagging desire for Miss Brindley's person has already proved prophetic. Those lively partners have once more been working in collaboration. When I was physically replenished my mind quickly generated a strategy, which I will later describe to you, for recuperating the lady in my eyes.

The other campaign to which you distantly allude will
proceed but slowly, if it proceeds at all.

You broached a number of personal and general
issues of great interest to me. Aware of my youth and
inexperience I will not presume to comment upon them
at this early stage; but I shall be returning to them in
subsequent letters.

Yours, &c.

I was relieved to have completed this composition: several
days had elapsed since I had heard from my godfather, and
a reply seemed necessary. Lacking suitable subject-matter I
had invented the falling house, having occasionally, like most
Londoners, seen the aftermath of such a collapse. Once
more I had secured myself a respite: but I knew that my
next letter would have to provide livelier reading. My hope
was that the masquerade at Vauxhall would supply what I
needed, particularly given that Kitty was to be present.

There was another matter that I had deliberately omitted
to mention: namely an entirely unexpected visit from Mr
Quentin. I had forgotten his existence, and recalled only
when he was in front of me the likely reason for his journey
to London.

He proved an awkward guest, refusing refreshment and
offering no clue as to the motive for his visit. His manner
was nervous, his dark eyes constantly glancing about the
room, as though he feared that there might be a spy in
hiding in a cupboard or behind a chair. When I asked
about Mrs Quentin's dental treatment he shook his head
gloomily.

'It has been a protracted business,' he said. 'Yes, and a painful business. The teeth were worn and brittle, Mr Fenwick. Several of them broke – broke in the course of extraction, making it hard to remove the root. My wife was distressed – greatly distressed. She bled profusely. Her mouth is much swollen, but we are told that it will settle – gradually settle. Meanwhile she is reduced to a liquid diet until she has sufficiently recovered to allow for the provision of artificial teeth.'

Not greatly exhilarated by this information I said what I could to express sympathy and convey good wishes. For some time thereafter we continued to make conversation of a strained and desultory kind. Having disposed of his wife's misfortunes, Mr Quentin seemed to have little more to say. If I asked a question he offered no more than a brief reply. Only rarely did he volunteer a remark of his own; the several silences between us being such as to make me think either that he was about to announce his departure or that there was some topic he secretly wished to raise – as, for example, when a man means to ask for a loan but cannot nerve himself to blurt out his request. If that had indeed been the case I would gladly have offered him the loan – or a gift, for that matter – to be rid of his oppressive company.

When eventually my improbable guest did take his leave, suitable courtesies were of course exchanged, but they rang hollow. The seemingly purposeless visit could not but seem strange to me, and it was plain that Quentin knew it.

Later I wondered whether he had been sent by Mr Gilbert

himself to see me in my quarters and report on anything exceptionable. But even if he had, there was nothing to fear: I had been as sober and courteous as my godfather could have wished. It would be interesting to see whether word of this encounter reached Mr Gilbert.

I soon received a more welcome visitor in the shape of Matt Cullen, newly returned from Worcestershire. I sent out for wine, Mrs Deacon had a meal cooked for us, and Matt and I sat talking till late in the night. I was immediately in better heart merely for seeing him. As always, there was something in his comfortable manner, and habitual half-smile, that made life in general seem a more light-hearted affair. He spoke cheerfully even about his father's gout, although it became clear that the attack had been severe, and that Matt himself had been at pains to provide necessary comfort and assistance.

When I told him how matters now stood between myself and Mr Gilbert he listened intently, even while grinning as though there were something droll about the entire situation. I showed him my godfather's recent letter, drawing attention to the curiosity expressed concerning Sarah. Matt sat musing for some few moments and then chuckled aloud.

'You find yourself in a strange pickle, Master Fenwick,' said he. 'I heard Mr Gilbert's name mentioned several times in Malvern, and always to the same effect. It seems that his influence has extended throughout the county. He has earned the respect conferred on those who are owed money. Some of our best-known landowners are said to be in his debt. Whether he is liked I cannot say; but he is feared. This is a patron well worth pleasing, Dick – even at the price of kissing his withered arse.'

'I could wish that that was the extent of the problem,' I said. 'He's a dainty old fellow: I'd as lief kiss his arse as yours. The case is more serious. I ask myself whether my godfather may not be corrupting me.'

'Is he not asking you to enjoy the very pleasures you prefer?'

'Yes, but he now goes further. He transgresses boundaries. You know that my feeling towards Sarah is a solemn matter. If I pursue her it will be in deadly earnest. I cannot lay the matter open for my godfather's entertainment.'

'Have you not already done so?'

'I have hinted – no more. But I seem to have whetted his appetite.'

'You should whet it further. In that direction lies prosperity.'

'Am I to be allowed no life of my own? Am I to be my godfather's performing dog?'

'You put the case prejudicially,' said Matt. 'But why not? Provided that the performance guarantees you a sufficiently fat lamb chop.'

How seriously he was speaking it was hard to judge: we had both drunk well.

'Cullen,' I said, 'you are a man without principles.'

'I have *numerous* principles. But I resort to them only in emergencies, for fear I should wear them out.'

When I told him how Gilbert had warned me against him, he feigned offence.

'Here I am, pleading his cause. This is a dotard blind to true merit.'

'Then my case is hopeless,' said I.

10

I called on Tom Crocker to see what progress he had made in furnishing his house. He and Francis Pike were engaged in unpacking a number of objects purchased at an auction. These were miscellaneous goods indeed, including a large mirror, a tiger skin, a fat smiling Buddha (purchased, said Crocker, because it reminded him of himself) and a huge carving, in dark wood, of a snarling wild boar. Crocker expressed himself particularly pleased with this latter purchase, which he said he proposed to use as a seat. When with some effort he straddled it, animal and rider did indeed look oddly comfortable together.

Being hard at work Pike was not wearing a wig. I was therefore able to see, for the first time, that his right ear was badly torn. When he was out of the room I asked Crocker about it, and, to my embarrassment, he called Pike back to give me an account of what had happened. He did so with his habitual composure: 'That damage, sir, was done when I was a boy, living in the country. When my family had no food I turned to poaching, and on one occasion I was caught by the gamekeepers. Wanting to make an example of me they nailed my ear to a tree. When they had gone I was able to tear myself free.'

'Were you not in agony?' I asked, shuddering.

Pike paused, his bony face thoughtful. 'It *was* painful, sir; and there was quite considerable loss of blood. But I don't consider the ear a serious part of the body – only a flap of gristle. I've had worse things happen to me.'

'Mr Pike is a practical philosopher,' said Crocker. 'However bad the situation, he hits on the best course he can find, and goes on with life.'

I was taken around the house on a tour of inspection. Considerable progress had been made since my previous visit: there were carpets, curtains and furnishings in place, and some of the pictures had been hung. Through a window I saw that the wall of the rear garden had been completed.

I was quite unprepared for the shock that awaited me. We had moved upstairs to see a room destined to be a library. A stocky man was standing there, looking intently from window to doorway and back again, as though calculating distances.

'Ah!' said Crocker to me, 'you must meet Mr Ogden. Mr Ogden, this is my friend Mr Fenwick, come to admire our progress.'

Ogden turned absently, as though our entry had interrupted a train of thought, and offered a token bow.

'I am pleased to meet you, Mr Ogden,' I said, in some little confusion. 'Your name is already known to me. I was acquainted with your wife when we both lived in York.'

'Yes, yes, I believe she has mentioned you,' he replied, inattentively.

Ogden was staring directly at me, but with no sign of interest. He was just as I recollected him, heavy and drab, if not without a certain force. Somehow he woke in me an instant sense of physical aversion: I could not easily have brought myself to shake his hand.

'London is smaller than we think,' said Crocker, unaware of such tensions. 'Mr Ogden lives in Margaret Street, just along the way. He is giving me valuable advice on the refurbishment of this house.'

'I understood that you dealt in diamonds, Mr Ogden,' said I, surprised.

'I did, sir – I do. But my interests have reached outwards towards glass, mirrors, crystal, chandeliers . . .'

He spoke politely, but let his sentence trail away. Crocker intervened on his behalf: 'To get the measure of Mr Ogden you must see his work. His great interest is in the disposition of light within a house. The source may be a window, a doorway, a mirror or a chandelier. He can direct your eye and double the illumination. But he is making his survey and we must leave him to it.'

Ogden and I exchanged the briefest of bows and he turned away, plainly glad to return to his labours. I walked on with my host, making conversation to hide any trace of discomfiture. Asked about my acquaintanceship with Mrs Ogden I put the matter to rest lightly enough. Crocker said that he had met someone else who knew of me: the actress Jane Page. 'A handsome woman and a talented performer,' said I. I could not tell from his manner whether he had heard of my doings with Kitty Brindley. Soon afterwards I took my leave.

As I made my way down Wyvern Street I was surprised to see, forty yards ahead of me, the broad back and square shoulders of Ogden. I could have caught up with him as he stumped along, but preferred to follow and keep him in view. He turned the corner into Margaret Street and entered a fine new mansion. The man who owned this house and could buy another, along the road, for Mrs Kinsey must be rich indeed.

Walking on I admitted to myself that I had been shaken by my exchange with Ogden. It would have better become the fellow to remain a stranger to me until I had duly ploughed his wife. Nor had I been pleased to learn that there was more to him than I had supposed: Crocker had spoken of him, and to him, not as a tradesman but as a professional adviser.

Could I still think to cuckold such a man – perhaps now to be seen as the friend of a friend? Indeed I could. I was resentful that Ogden had acknowledged me so casually, that an encounter that had discomposed me had made so little impression on him – and this even though he knew that I had been a friend of his wife. It was, of course, convenient for my purposes that he should be devoid of suspicion, but still his self-absorption rankled.

I knew the reaction was absurd. What would I have had him say? Perhaps, ideally: 'Mr Fenwick, your reputation precedes you. For Sarah's satisfaction and your own I will put her at your disposal at any time you wish.'

Yet even that would not have sufficed. I wanted to plague

this impassive lump of a man with agonies of jealousy. Was I unreasonable? Of course, and grotesquely so. But love is unreasonable, lust more so. It could not be that this Ogden was equipped to gratify Sarah's body or her mind. If he was indeed something a little more than a merchant, his interest in the disposition of light, or whatnot, seemed to have done nothing to brighten his manner or his conversation. He was irredeemably a dullard, a trader, a clod.

My resentment had hardly subsided when it was accidentally re-awakened. That very evening Matt Cullen burst in to see me, brimming with good spirits.

'I was walking in the Park this morning,' said he, 'and was rewarded with an unexpected sight: Mrs Ogden, unmistakably Sarah Ogden, walking with her aunt. She did not see me, but I observed her boldly, from behind a tree. Dick, you were right. Since last I saw her she has become a beauty. Having done the carnal deed she is a woman transformed.'

'So I told you,' I replied peevishly. 'And today I met her pasty-faced proprietor.'

I described what had passed, trying, but failing, to restrain my vexation. Matt regarded me with a satirical eye.

'Why so peevish, Master Fenwick? Sweet Kitty Brindley is at your disposal. As for Mrs Ogden, you have resolved to enjoy her in due course. Restrain your animosity and set about the task.'

'You are right,' I conceded. 'But the animosity becomes an incentive in itself.'

'As I have told you,' said Matt, 'this is just the story to beguile Mr Gilbert.'

The following morning, over a dish of tea, I reviewed the case once more and gave way to an abrupt blaze of fury. I was quite literally shaken: the tea-cup was trembling in my hand. 'Why so peevish, Master Fenwick?' Cullen's question had been a reasonable one. My rage was absurdly misplaced and disproportionate. If Sarah had married a dolt, then surely so much the more hopeful for my purpose? I could not justify, or even make sense of, my anger. All I could muster was a confused sense that Sarah represented my past – or all of it that I cared to remember – and that she and it had been commandeered by a vulgarian.

Here was a strange tale – strange even to myself. After all I would take Matt's advice and relate it to Gilbert as it unfolded. The fact of beginning to tell it would coerce me into enacting it.

> *My dear Godfather,*
>
> *Two nights ago I again met Horn and Latimer at the Black Lion. Latimer had news for us: he is to become personal secretary to Lord Ashton, a statesman of rising power. Horn and I were derisive, knowing that this advancement owes everything to family connection.*
>
> *'Tell us,' said Horn, 'what do you take to be the personal qualities that have won the favour of his lordship?'*
>
> *'Where is one to begin?' replied Latimer. 'Courtesy, composure, urbanity . . .'*

'My friend,' cried Horn, 'you are talking to men who have eaten with you, drunk with you and vomited with you. We know these seeming virtues for what they are – namely a pitiful lack of animal spirits, scarcely to be distinguished from torpor.'

'What Horn and I must consider,' said I, 'is whether we should prevent the appointment by exposing your shortcomings to the world.'

'The case is so strong,' said Horn, 'that, speaking personally, I can think of but one consideration that might silence me. You could find an old friend the well-paid sinecure he so richly deserves.'

We were joined by Talbot and others, who drank toasts to Latimer's good fortune. The conversation turned from luck to chance, perhaps because we had several members of White's among our number. There was comparison between wagers involving judgement or daring, and those based upon chance alone, as with a race between two rain-drops down a window, or the number of grains of wheat that can be held in a spoon.

A few more bottles sufficing to lure us from theory to practice, there was a wager between Scales and Winterton to establish how many empty glasses might be balanced one upon another. The man whose attempt brought the tower down would lose his money. Given their elevated condition the contestants performed well: the fragile column rose steadily. When it began to sway they were insistent that no spectator should affect the outcome by motion, breath or even sound. You must picture a dozen intoxicated youths, sweating under their wigs yet frozen into an agony of immobility as the last three glasses were added to the tottering pillar. There was a mighty cheer when it swayed, broke, and crashed to the floor.

After paying his debt Winterton, the loser, looked for a broom with which to sweep up the broken glass. As Chance would have it, he found in the cupboard a coil of rope, which he brought back as a possible source of further mischief. Our room being on the second floor someone wagered Horn a guinea that he would not slither down the rope to the street below. Horn, who can climb like a monkey, not only did so but immediately climbed back up again, a feat then emulated, if less nimbly, by two or three others, amid roars of encouragement.

There the matter might have ended had not some rash fool suggested a further challenge – that the rope should be suspended between our window and the corresponding one in the building opposite, so that those sufficiently venturesome might use it to cross the road. There followed a period of negotiation and manoeuvre. Those living opposite were bribed into assent to our plan, but our fuddled brains had difficulty in organizing the conveyance of the rope's end to the appropriate window. When the connection was pronounced secure, the question arose as to who should first make use of it. On an impulse I volunteered, and swung myself across hand over hand.

Horn readily completed the same crossing. Eckersley embarked more nervously, wrapping his legs around the rope, struggling to move himself along and once or twice yelping in fright. However he, too, reached the far window, where friendly hands hauled him in. Then

Winterton, by now quite drunk, gave a great yell, as though to lift his spirits, and swung himself out, clinging with hands alone, as I had done. Our cheers faded when we saw that he was floundering. He lurched halfway across, kicking out wildly, but then lost his hold and fell, with a cry, scattering the crowd that had gathered to watch.

We clattered down in some disarray. Poor Winterton, betrayed by Chance for the second time that night, lay sprawled on the cobbles, cursing and whimpering, surrounded by curious onlookers, some diverted by the spectacle of this fallen Icarus, others concerned, but unsure how to assist. We broke up a tavern table to improvise a litter and carried the wounded warrior within. A surgeon being sent for it appeared that our friend has a broken ankle, but should make a good recovery.

My next letter will provide a full account of the masquerade. Miss Brindley is to be present. As you anticipated, the passing of time has done much to revive my desire for this lady. My hope is that the fantastical nature of the masquerade will revive it still further.

You inquired about 'the married woman'. Let me sketch a background.

When, as a schoolboy, I spent part of the year in York I knew a girl named Sarah Kinsey, like me an orphan living with an aunt. Before leaving for France I met her again in London, where she and the aunt were then resident. Partly, perhaps, because of the similarity of our circumstances, we were warm friends – almost something more. She wrote to me while I was away, but I am ashamed to say that at the time I was too agreeably distracted to reply. When I returned to London I visited the house in which she and her aunt had lived, but found that they had moved away. Some weeks later, however, and purely by chance, I did encounter her, and learned that she is now married to a wealthy merchant.

I should have accepted the situation, particularly since it was my own negligence that had brought it about. Two considerations made this difficult. One was that Sarah – now Sarah Ogden – seemed to me remarkably improved: wittier, more handsome, more assured. So much the better, you might say, for the man who had married her. However, I have since seen her husband and learned a little about him. He is a merchant, a dealer in diamonds, heavy, slow and morose. Sarah's new character I take to derive from the confidence that wealth confers. This Ogden can in no wise be worthy of her. He will make nothing of her intelligence, her wit. In his company she cannot but dwindle.

Let me be blunt: I am offended that this dull fellow enjoys favours that I could have had and am now denied. I look to seduce this woman away from him and into my bed. How the matter will end I know not. There are a thousand such affairs in London now, developing and resolving themselves in the limited number of possible ways – most commonly, I suppose, in satiety and separation. But I cannot think of conclusions at present. It is in the nature of such an enterprise that the conquest is seen as everything and the consequence as nothing.

I have been led to confide so bluntly by the
coincidence that yesterday, when visiting Crocker,
I found myself being introduced to Ogden himself. It
appears that he is advising on certain aspects of the
embellishment of the new house, he having ventured
beyond his trade in diamonds to deal in decorative arts
of a more general kind. My conversation with him was
brief, but it fed my distaste for him, and has whetted
my purpose.

I remain, &c.

I read through my letter with misgivings. Was I as ugly a human-being as this summary suggested? I had purposed no more than to drop certain teasing hints, but jealous rage had taken charge of the quill and committed me before I was aware, in defiance of calculation or propriety. I could have torn up the sheet and started again, but had not the heart. My emotions in this matter were such that to describe them at all was to falsify. Yet these intricacies were contained within a simplicity. Either I accepted that Sarah was lost to me, and so avoided her, or I set out to seduce her: there was no middle course.

At the Black Lion the rash fool who had proposed suspending the rope across the road had been I, eager to create further possibilities of diversion for my godfather. I justified my recklessness by volunteering to be the first to try the experiment. When sober I felt this defence to be a poor one: I had little fear of high places and was proficient at climbing of this sort. Winterton had become my victim – and at one remove a victim of Mr Gilbert.

My dear Godfather,

Here is my promised account of the masquerade at Vauxhall.

Horn and Latimer had spoken slightingly of public masquerades, whether at Vauxhall or at Ranelagh, claiming that visitors of any social standing collude in a pretence – since they commonly recognize one another even in costume – while the rest are a motley crew of drinkers, lechers, prostitutes, and nobodies. These cavils notwithstanding they seemed very ready to try the experiment again. As for myself, I admit to feeling some little excitement when preparing for the evening. You will know, I am sure, that these masquerades are uniquely open and unceremonious: anyone is admitted who can pay for a ticket; unescorted women frequently attend. I had heard on several sides that the resort to disguise, even when little more than a formality, tends to dissolve the restraints governing ordinary life.

I enjoyed some slight foretaste of this freedom while dressing for the evening. From a shop catering solely to masqueraders I had purchased a costume to translate me into a falcon. I was to be clad in black from head to knee; my stockings would suggest the scaliness of the bird's legs, there were claws covering my feet, and when I raised my arms it would be to unfold dark wings, fringed with feathers. Standing before a tall mirror I donned this apparel garment by garment, by no means impressed: I

saw only my everyday self, rendered ridiculous. When I
added the final item, however, a black mask with
glittering false eyes and a sharp curving beak, the case
was changed. His face now gone, Richard Fenwick had
become a pitiless predator. At once I was enacting my
new role, jerking my head from side to side, as though in
quest of prey, the eyes alert, the beak jutting menacingly; I
raised and flapped my wings of cloth, half believing that
I might fly. The sense of metamorphosis was bewilderingly
strong. I felt that if my case were typical there would be
strange impulses of attraction and repulsion in the air.

I travelled to Vauxhall in a hackney-coach along with
Latimer, now a foppish Spanish grandee, and Horn, who
had become an Indian chieftain, with painted face and a
head-dress of feathers. Already I could feel my expectations
confirmed. Our conversation was halting: well as we knew
one another we were no longer ourselves.

As we entered the Gardens we were by chance caught
up in a great swirl of movement that separated me from
my companions. I was swept along one of the wide alleys
amid a noisy throng of grotesque beings. Here were a
witch, a pirate, a walking tree; there was Father Time
with his scythe, one arm around a skeleton. Over us all,
comprising one man on the shoulders of another, towered
a Cyclops, with a single great eye below a false forehead.

There seemed to be a general liberty, even between the
sexes, to accost, jeer, jostle or clutch. Among the couplings
were some lewd conjunctions: a scarlet-clad cardinal
fondled the breasts of a milkmaid, and a young nun was
warmly reciprocating the embraces of a gorilla. I could

not even be confident as to gender: a princess who ogled me had the physique of a man. Many behaved as I had done before the mirror, adapting their actions to their assumed characters. A highwayman swaggered and cocked a wooden pistol; a bear lumbered along pawing at passers-by. I myself, with no conscious intention to do so, was threatening strangers with my beak, and sometimes opening out my wings with a sharp cry.

The music from a bandstand was all but drowned by the hubbub of high-pitched voices. All around me I heard the shrill squeak affected by masquers as a further gesture of disguise: 'Who am I?' 'I know you, madam!' I was more than once hailed myself: 'Who are you, sir?' 'Who are you, Mr Falcon?' It should be said that some visitors wore merely a loose, enveloping domino and a plain mask, or a hood. Yet this seemed to me as great a dissimulation as any other, in falsely proclaiming 'I am nobody!'

The crowd surged on, past a great arcade where there was eating and copious drinking. I could see much that was foolish or even sordid, but I could not share my friends' detached view of such entertainment. There was something truly a little disturbing in being leered at, mocked or seized upon by strangers. In the real world Mr Fenwick is forbidden to embrace a lady he has never seen before, but here a bird of prey was free to throw his wings around a passing princess.

Looking out for Kitty I more than once squeaked a greeting to a possible manifestation of her, only to be derided by a stranger. Horn waved to me on one occasion, by now hand in hand with a Moorish slave-girl: he was hurrying her on towards the darker avenues beyond the arcades. From every side came extravagant gestures and screeched challenges.

I began to be aware of a deeper level of disorder. However absurd the costumes, most of those present seemed eager, even feverishly eager, to escape from their habitual selves in hope of adventure. It must surely be that there are energies and desires swimming below the surface of society like fish below ice. In the course of the evening I glimpsed several carnal engagements in the darker corners of the park; but for each individual so occupied I would hazard that a score were tantalized by faint intimations of such a possibility. After all it would not be one's 'self' that was sinning but the temporary usurper – a harlequin, an animal or a demon.

Moving past the arcades in the direction taken by Horn, I found the crowd thinner. On either side of the main avenue ran narrower ones, illuminated only intermittently by pools of greenish light diffused by lamps set among the trees. Looking about I spied a slim figure, clad in white, that I fancied might be Kitty. She saw me, and at once slipped down a side path. I could make out that this was a water-nymph, in a single clinging garment, her face half concealed by the long straight hair provided by a head-dress of thin reeds. Surely this must be Kitty – yet I still could not be certain; and when I was within a dozen paces of her she slipped aside once more. Spreading my wings I hastened after my prey.

In pursuing her I re-joined the main path where the crowd was thicker. A hand clutched my arm, as a voice squeaked, 'Hold, Falcon!' I turned to see a pregnant woman of enormous size, with prodigious false breasts and a red wig. She squeaked again: 'Sir, you are responsible for my condition.'

'Perhaps so,' I squawked. 'But I acted under compulsion. You ravished me!'

'Impudent fellow!' roared the large lady. 'Do you dare insult me?'

Only then did I recognize Crocker, his big belly moulded into false pregnancy and cushions of bosom wedged into his bodice.

'I know you, madam!' I squeaked, pecking at Tom's breasts with my falcon beak.

We talked for a few minutes. I had never seen Crocker in better spirits: he seemed delighted to have been able to lose himself so completely in his hideous disguise. It was a fine night, completely dark by now, but still warm, with a faint breeze blowing. I enjoyed the moment: a monstrous pregnant woman and a bird of prey in amicable conversation under the trees. As we stood there I noticed, from the corner of an eye, a Roman legionnaire hovering near us, one hand on the hilt of his short sword. A second glance translated him into Francis Pike, presumably present as escort and protector to the pregnant maiden.

When I moved on I again caught sight of my water-nymph, peering at me from behind a tree. Renewing the chase I was at last able to fold my wings about her, gasping, 'I know you, madam! I have you madam!', while she squeaked, 'Spare me, spare me, god of the skies!' Having thus secured my victim I bore her away for supper and a glass of wine in one of the arcades. Even here she preserved her character, peeping from behind her water-weed hair and then averting her gaze, as if in fright, or starting up, as though she might fly from me once more. Pleasingly warmed by this show of unwilling submission I was glad, at last, to take her hand and lead her out of the gardens, pushing our way through the leering masqueraders. Before we left I saw the full-breasted Crocker once more, conversing with a red-coated soldier, whom I recognized as Jane Page when Kitty waved a greeting.

She and I retreated to a chamber I had reserved in a nearby hostelry accustomed to guests of exotic appearance. The success of my experiment was already manifest. Miss Brindley was no longer the simple girl with whose body I had become familiar, but an elusive, almost ethereal creature. She maintained her performance to the very last, so that I could half believe that I was about to violate a naiad, and experienced almost a shock as I flung up the skirts of her costume and saw again the dark bush of hair. As I forced myself upon her, Kitty was still in character, crying out piteously for mercy as she thrust her loins against me to deepen the intrusion. Lost in the fantasy I was masterful and cruel. Never have I more keenly relished the ridiculous game of joining giblets. Kitty later told me that even during the act she had almost thought herself a water-nymph, pitilessly despoiled but unable to resist the physical joy of surrender.

Recovering ourselves we drank more wine and fell to

talking, still in excellent humour and a warm frame of
mind. Kitty spoke of her early life in the country, and
recalled a particular afternoon when she and several
others gathered to watch a b̶ . brought to a cow. She
vividly described how the passion and scale of the act,
the sight of the great shaft being steered to the cleft
and then forced home again and again fired the blood of
all those watching, including herself, so that in imitation
of the performance she lost her maidenhead to a young
farm-hand an hour later. She instanced that experience as
persuading her of the raw animal impulses behind desire,
and the contagion of those impulses even between one
species and another. I so far justified her words as to fall
an instant prey to this contagion, even at second hand,
ploughing Kitty with farm-yard vigour till she cried out
again and again that yes, yes and yes, I was a better
man than her rustic first love.

As on the previous occasion I woke up after some hours
and lay thinking amid the fading odours of lust. This
time I could not flatter myself with illusions of objectivity
regained. It seems that a man's body is so thoroughly
animal as always to be capable of renewed desire and
hence renewed susceptibility to illusion.

There was a little more to the letter, but nothing of note. The
paragraphs last quoted, which I had hoped would tickle
my godfather into fantasies of his own, were a calculated
misrepresentation. Kitty had indeed described the scene with
the bull – but in a very different spirit. The recollection, so
far from exciting her, made her laugh so helplessly that she

rolled off the bed on to the floor, with a loud thump. When I helped her back and asked what she found so amusing she could say only that the proceedings necessary to the creation of new life struck her as ludicrous. I was, as I truly wrote, seized by a contagion, but it was the contagion of laughter. Kitty and I made love again, and very pleasantly, none the less so for giggling so persistently that we could barely complete the act.

Thinking that I had, for the time being, fired off all my ammunition, I was resolved not to write again to Mr Gilbert until I had received a reply. Within days came a letter saying that he had urgent reasons for requiring my presence at Fork Hill as soon as I could get there.

11

'I am sorry that you could not occupy your usual room. There are reasons for the change – reasons which may, perhaps, emerge. But I hope you slept well.'

'I slept very well.'

We were sitting in the drawing-room, the morning following my return to Fork Hill. Once more I was impressed by the silence of the house in contrast to the incessant noise of London, and relieved to be sitting on a solid chair after two days of being flung about in a coach. As yet there had been no explanation for the urgency of my godfather's summons: I had an irritated suspicion that he enjoyed sending me to and fro at his bidding. A little dulled by the journey I listened to him warily, trying to follow the drift of his thinking. He seemed particularly animated and free.

'We will have a great deal to discuss while you are here – a great deal. To begin at random: I was interested to hear that you met Mrs Jennings. Thirty-five years ago – more – I was well acquainted with that lady, and so was your father.

We were all three in London together, all three of us young. In those days, of course, she was Miss Bella Thorpe. Was her husband present when you met her?'

'He was physically present, but rarely spoke: it appears that he is stone deaf.'

'Ben Jennings stone deaf?' My godfather seemed pleased. 'Who could have foretold it? But bodies are frail: there are so many parts to go amiss: I hear that Yardley has twisted his knee, and can scarcely walk. Which reminds me – indirectly reminds me: I believe that you also saw Mr Quentin?'

'He paid me a brief visit, but very little passed between us. He seemed preoccupied. I gathered that his wife's treatment had proved painful.'

'That does not surprise me: it had been delayed too long. I have yet to meet her since her return, but Quentin tells me that she has all but recovered. We will see for ourselves, for they are to be guests here soon.'

He mused for a moment, with pursed lips, his immobility at one with the stillness of the room. 'Miss Thorpe was a spirited, humorous lady, as I recollect her.'

'She is so still.'

'It was plain to me that she was drawn to your father, who was her match in both qualities. Unhappily for her the flame was not mutual, though he liked her well enough. Perhaps she married too carelessly in her disappointment. Ben Jennings had but two virtues: an affable disposition and a great deal of money. He laughed easily but was as dull as a sheep. He must have been astonished to capture the vivacious Miss Thorpe. It was a match between chalk and cheese: she will often have puzzled him over the years.'

174

He smiled at the thought. 'That time remains vivid in my mind. Yet it must be twenty years since last we spoke. You say she remembered me clearly?'

'She did indeed. She spoke of you as witty and shrewd, but circumspect.'

'Circumspect I was – perhaps too much the observer. But I have remained aware of Mrs Jennings from a distance. When I heard that her nephew was destined for the church I was pleased to be able to help him. Thorpe seems comfortable in Fork Hill, and is well liked by his parishioners. But he has rarely mentioned his aunt.'

Here was my godfather positively loquacious, happy to jump from topic to topic. He jumped again: 'The portrait that you saw has been completed. A few guests are coming to see it, and I wanted you to be one of them. Needless to say, this little ceremony is not for my benefit but for that of the artist. Mr Rowley came to me well recommended, and would seem to be an accomplished portrait painter – perhaps a rival for Gainsborough. But you must judge for yourself when the picture is laid bare. Rowley will be here for the occasion.'

He suddenly rose and crossed the room to reach into a drawer. I had a moment to reflect upon the reference to Quentin. My godfather knew of the visit that I had chosen not to mention. Was this a hint to me that I had been under observation? Even if it was, I had no way of knowing whether he had asked Quentin to report on me or Quentin had himself elected to do so. Mr Gilbert returned with what proved to be a song-book.

'Look this through at your leisure. After the success of

your last performance I hope that you will sing again with Mrs Hurlock for the pleasure of our guests.'

I murmured polite assent, while glancing through the pages. Most of the songs were fortunately already familiar to me.

'You will see that they are pastoral and sentimental pieces – calculated, I hope, to appeal to Mrs Hurlock. She has been sent a copy of the book, as has Mrs Quentin, who has kindly agreed to play the harpsichord.'

'I am glad that she feels ready to venture into company again.'

I spoke decorously enough, while wondering whether the lady would by now be equipped with teeth of some sort.

Mr Gilbert changed direction once more, smiling before he spoke: 'After your exertions in London you will find Fork Hill very quiet. We have not had a skirmish or a naked dancer in the house in all my years here. The little gathering to view the portrait will take place in two days' time. If, before then, you would care to ride down to the village, I am told that Mr Thorpe would be pleased to see you.'

The following afternoon I duly knocked on the door of the vicarage, a substantial, high-windowed house near the church. Thorpe welcomed me warmly.

As we exchanged courtesies I was reminded that this was an individual in whose company I felt slightly uncertain. Although he was some few years older than me I held the advantage in several respects. I lived in London, had travelled in Europe and was likely to be heir to his very patron; he had been consigned to village life and the role of clergyman. On the other hand he seemed a man of sense, was in a position to know a good deal about my godfather, and could perhaps look forward to a future more assured than my own. I was pleased to be able to converse with him again, and sound him out.

His rooms were large, the furnishings plain but comfortable.

'You have space enough in your house for a wife and family,' I suggested.

'And space enough in my life, also,' he said, smiling. 'I am looking about.'

As I stood in his tranquil parlour I had a sudden perception of his existence as something utterly different from anything I myself could now tolerate. Here was a man educated as I had been, and to all appearances not markedly dissimilar in temperament. Yet for him in this vicarage quiet day must follow quiet day. The seasons would change around him, there would be sermons to write, occasional weddings, christenings and burials over which to preside – but what else? How would he pass his evenings unless in walking or reading? What friends could he find? Had he a maid-servant to debauch? What had he to look forward to, unless the after-life?

'Do you hunt?' I asked, perhaps too abruptly.

'Occasionally. It is not a favourite occupation of mine.'

He answered the question I had not put: 'You wonder whether my life is intolerably dull. One adjusts one's expectations. In London you live in the present: all is haste and change. In the country we inhabit the past: life is slow and prompts contemplation.'

We wandered out into a rear garden, where there was a cherry tree bearing fruit as yet little bigger than peas. A white cloud drifted away from the sun, and we were suddenly warm and pleasantly dazzled.

'I had the pleasure of meeting your aunt in London,' I said.

'So she told me in one of her rare letters. I saw her quite often as a boy, but now we live in different worlds. It must be eighteen months since we last met.'

'She would seem to have known Mr Gilbert rather well in their younger days.'

'Indeed. The connection has been of service to me.'

There was a pause during which we were both, I think, wondering whether we could safely take the topic further.

'She hinted that she found him a reserved young man,' I ventured.

'So she told me also. Of course she knew the man he was rather than the man he has become.'

'Since those days he must have gained in authority . . .'

'Very considerably,' said Thorpe. 'He has the confidence that comes from being a leading figure in the county.'

'Has he so much influence?'

'Oh yes.'

Thorpe turned and led the way back to the house.

'My own living, of course, was in his gift . . .' He hesitated. 'But there are others who are dependent on him. Without his patronage, many lives would falter.'

Unsure of his drift, I nodded, and ventured a blunt question: 'Were you content to enter the church?'

Thorpe laughed. 'There were few alternatives. But yes, I was happy enough as regards a choice of professional occupation. I hope to make a tolerable village parson. Country life suits me well enough, and I can make myself useful at births, weddings, sick-beds and funerals.'

Pleased by his frank manner I took a further step: 'You emphasize the practical aspect of your work rather than the doctrinal one . . .'

'Yes, because that aspect suits me better. A bishop once told me: "One can be a good soldier without being a patriot." I try to be a good soldier.'

'Then you have a purpose in life?'

'I hope I have. A sufficient purpose.' He changed his tone: 'Mr Fenwick, the afternoon being fine, I have a suggestion – namely that we should call on the unfortunate Mr Yardley, who is confined to his house by an injury.'

I consented readily, intrigued at the prospect of seeing Yardley at home.

Since he lived but half a mile from the vicarage we made the journey on foot, at first along the quiet village street and then down a narrow lane, choked with summer grass and weeds. The cottage, a small one, proved to be well hidden, lost in a garden of sorts that seemed hardly less wild than the lane. Creeping plants reached up around the walls on all sides, hiding some of the windows with their foliage.

We were admitted by a withered old housekeeper whom Thorpe had mentioned as being Yardley's only domestic servant and companion. Without a word she ushered us into a dark den, so crammed with cupboards and chests of drawers as to be effectively reduced to less than half its size. If Thorpe's house seemed too large for his immediate requirements, Yardley's was its antithesis.

The old man was sitting hunched in a chair, with one heavily bandaged leg propped up on a low stool. He looked leaner and more lugubrious than I remembered him, and showed little sign of being gratified by our visit.

'I cannot get up,' he said, regarding us almost belligerently. 'The doctor tells me I should stand as little as possible.'

'Is the injury healing?' asked Thorpe.

'I cannot say – and no more can the doctor: the damage is all internal. The fool binds up the affected part and hopes that it will heal itself. If it does, of course, he will claim the credit; if not he will accept no responsibility. But sit down, sit down.'

Thorpe and I made shift to extricate chairs from the confusion of furniture.

'How did this accident come about?' I asked.

'Absurdly – quite absurdly. I had my eyes on a kingfisher and caught my foot under the root of a tree. Down I went, twisted my knee and could not get up again. I was left to crawl my way home like a snake.'

He sniggered unexpectedly at this recollection, and became more cheerful.

'You must excuse me, Mr Fenwick, for being less than welcoming. Thorpe here is used to my ways. I have so few visitors that I scarcely remember how to behave. I pass my days in the company of insects and mammals. There is no cause to speak.'

'But you must speak with your housekeeper,' said Thorpe.

'Why do you think so?' Yardley seemed surprised. 'We

are all but strangers. She lodges here as a jackdaw may make its nest in a rabbit hole. Little passes between us. I have kept count of the words I utter in a week. The total is commonly less than two hundred – sometimes less than one hundred. I write far more words than I speak.'

'Mr Yardley has a singular bias,' said Thorpe. 'His energies go into observing, collecting and classifying. These drawers and shelves are crammed with his specimens.'

'Specimens of what kind?' I asked.

'I am a regular contributor to the *Naturalist's Journal*,' said Yardley. 'I have collected butterflies, moths, beetles, and birds' eggs. In these drawers are dried plants. In the cabinet over there you would find a selection of animal skulls and skeletons. I have also shells, stones and crystals, but they are of less interest to me.'

'Where do your observations take you?' I inquired, hoping to draw him out. 'Are you working on a treatise of some sort?'

'No,' said Yardley. 'I collect, examine, describe. I have no greater end in view.'

The response silenced me, but Thorpe again intervened.

'You must understand,' he said, 'that Mr Yardley thinks in particularities.'

'Exactly so,' said Yardley. 'It may be that some other man, differently constituted, will make use of my work in a theoretical way. I am content with notes and memoranda and the *Naturalist's Journal*: I have no ambition to enter the Royal Society.'

'Your immediate ambition,' said Thorpe, 'must be to get to your feet again. What did the doctor say on that score?'

'Nothing.' Yardley sniggered again. 'He fears to make a forecast that might be proved wrong.'

'Meanwhile you are a prisoner in your own house,' cried Thorpe. 'This is wretched luck. What could I bring you to raise your spirits? Some food? Some wine?'

Yardley shook his head. 'Wine lifts my spirits, so I drink it in company. But I've never cared for the taste. I'm like the cat, which relishes fish but shrinks from water. Hurlock is your otter.'

⁂

Perhaps because his knee was painful Yardley soon became subdued once more, his narrow body drooping. Thorpe and I contrived a little further conversation and then took our leave.

'You may think,' said Thorpe, as we waded through the long grass, 'that Yardley did not welcome our visit; but that is his habitual manner, twisted knee or no twisted knee. If no one visits him, however, he feels aggrieved. I assume you know his history?'

'I know nothing about him, beyond meeting him twice at dinner.'

Thorpe looked surprised. 'He is another of your godfather's pensioners. I know the story only by hearsay, but it seems Mr Gilbert came upon him years ago when he had not long commenced his botanical studies and was living in poverty. He set him up here as you have seen, in a small cottage with a small income.'

'That would seem to be a generous act.'

'I am sure that it was generously intended. But one outcome of it was to turn Mr Yardley in upon himself. Since he had no reason to seek work and no great desire to find friends he gradually became a recluse. If Mr Gilbert did not prise him out of his shell occasionally he might commune with insects alone.'

'A melancholy outcome.'

'Whether it is melancholy for Yardley I cannot say. He seems to enjoy his life, whatever others might think of it. But I fancy there was some disappointment for your godfather. It is said that he hoped to be sponsoring some great work of scholarship. As we have just been told, Yardley has no plans of that kind.'

'But Mr Gilbert has not cast him aside?'

'He has not; but I think he has come to value Mr Yardley purely for himself, a singular specimen in his own right.'

'Then you see Mr Gilbert as a naturalist of sorts?'

Thorpe smiled: 'If you yourself made that suggestion I would not contradict you.'

❧

Only as his guests began to arrive did Mr Gilbert remark to me that Mr Hurlock could not be present. His wife would be coming with her friend, a Mrs Ford. Colonel Stearns together with his wife and two grown-up daughters were the first of the visitors to appear. I conversed for some little time with Stearns, a quiet man, not easily to be associated with blood or battle. Thorpe came with the Quentins, Mrs Quentin being tight-lipped and somewhat pale. There were two or three other elderly guests, whose names I have forgotten. Mrs Hurlock caught my eye and smiled as she entered with her companion. It was a sober gathering, but the mere presence of so many people and voices produced a mild animation that made the big house livelier than I had ever seen it.

At length we were led through to the drawing-room where the painting was to be displayed. It was still upon an easel, and hidden by a cloth. My godfather introduced Mr Rowley, a tall, spindling fellow with a crooked jaw, and it was the painter himself who drew back the cloth, to a small flurry of approbation. For me, who had seen the work at an earlier stage, there were several surprises. To one side of the house you could now see the foliage of the oak tree that had been cut down before the picture was painted. The colouring was altogether richer, bringing out, in particular, the texture of the stonework and the details of my godfather's braided coat. But above all the face was now more interesting and enigmatic than it had been. The landowner still looked with pride on his estate, but there was also, as it seemed to me, a certain detachment and calculation in his gaze: he was viewing his property yet seeing or thinking beyond it.

While Mr Rowley spoke to the colonel, who seemed to be a possible future client, I asked my godfather about the oak tree, and was told that he had described it to the artist so that the painting might reach back to include an element from the past. Later I talked to the painter himself, and was glad to do so: it seemed to me magical that this plain-looking fellow who might have passed for a waiter or a barber, could imprint a face or a scene on his mind and set it down on canvas perfectly miniaturized. When I mentioned the change that I had observed in the depiction of Mr Gilbert he replied that this should not seem surprising: 'I could catch a likeness of sorts in a few strokes, but that is a single aspect, a single mood. As I see more I can add more.'

'Then can you show several moods at once?'

'I would hope so.'

I thought, but did not say, that here was a demonstration of the plurality of the passions.

My godfather brought Mrs Quentin across to consult me about our coming performance. Her manner was as timid as before: she spoke few words, seemingly as ill at ease with her artificial teeth as she had been with her decaying ones. I undertook most of the talking in order to spare her embarrassment. Fortunately she felt comfortable as far as the music was concerned, confident that she could accompany any of the songs in the book.

The size of the gathering meant that the great dining hall was for once to be brought into use. As we made our way to it my godfather appeared at my side: 'Hurlock is in Warwickshire. He has to administer the estate of his brother, who died last month. But this is not the kind of entertainment he would care for. Mrs Hurlock, by the way, is to spend the night here.'

He turned away to speak to the colonel, but his words, as he must have anticipated, had given my mind an electrical shock. I recollected our previous conversation about Mrs Hurlock. Had she been invited to stay in order to put her at my disposal? Would my godfather lose faith in me if I failed to take advantage of this opportunity?

To enhance my confusion I found myself seated at table between Mrs Hurlock and her friend, Mrs Ford. It quickly became apparent that the latter lady, perhaps twenty years the elder, was something of a cipher, content to eat, drink and nod. I could devote my attention to my singing partner and – as now seemed outrageously possible – prospective mistress. An obvious gesture was to offer my commiserations concerning her late brother-in-law; but she seemed little interested in that gentleman, whom she had met, she said, very seldom. She was far readier to talk about the perform- ance to come. My godfather had marked one or two songs as being, in his view, particularly suited to us, and we quickly agreed on those and a few others, and on the order in which we should sing them. Mrs Hurlock confided that she had practised all the songs in the book: 'I was free to do so because my husband has been away. Between ourselves he is no great lover of music.'

This I had no difficulty in believing. It was remarkable to me how much more spirited she seemed on this occasion than in either of our previous meetings, whether because of the prospect of singing, or simply through freedom from the oppressive presence of Mr Hurlock. She did remark that music excited her in rather the same way, she thought, as hunting excited her husband.

I maintained this dialogue while all the time apprehensive as to how the evening might end. It seemed preposterous that my godfather should be inciting me to seduce this older woman, the wife of a friend, in his own house. Yet how else was I to construe the sudden summons when Hurlock was away, and the unusual arrangement that his wife should be passing the night there? I asked myself whether I would be physically capable of coition with this buxom matron, and was relieved to conclude that there should be no difficulty on that score, at least. Whether because she was more vivacious tonight, or because I was rallying to the challenge, I felt potentially roused, even potentially formidable. It stirred me to be making light-hearted conversation with the respectable Mrs Hurlock, while thinking 'In a few hours I may reduce you to a very different state.' I was encouraged in this bravado by noticing that the lady once or twice glanced at me in a manner that in a younger woman could have seemed provocative.

My immersion in this personal drama was so complete that I scarcely observed, and certainly cannot recollect with any clarity, what else was taking place at the table. I have a general sense that my godfather presided with his habitual courtesy, ensuring that no guest was neglected. Mrs Quentin remained reticent, eating with caution. The older guests questioned Mr Rowley, and Thorpe coaxed the colonel's daughters into conversation.

For the performance we retired to the drawing-room, where chairs had been set out in front of the harpsichord. It was a relief to me that Mrs Hurlock and our accompanist were confident in their abilities. I might find this the easiest part of the evening.

We began with a simple duet, 'Now Philomel, in leafy darkness lost', which was greeted warmly. I could see the colonel expressing vigorous approval to my godfather. After a second such piece, 'I mourn the fading rose', was similarly received, Mrs Quentin played Barton's Court Minuet with skill and feeling. It was pleasant to see her blush of gratification, as she acknowledged the applause with a tight little smile.

We now came to the two songs my godfather had marked. Mrs Hurlock, in excellent voice, was quite transformed in singing, and even enacting the first of them, nonsense though it was. I could almost see a trace of Kitty Brindley in her performance:

Let Strephon claim
My heart is cold:
I never wished him ill.
I love him not,
And told him so,
Yet he pursues me still.

Am I to blame
If he had hopes
That I cannot fulfil?
I love him not—
Yet give him leave
To love me if he will.

The song chosen for me could have been a response to this coquettish rejection:

It were too craven to be calm
When she for whom I burn
Will feel no pity for my plight.
She stole my heart without a qualm,

188

May I not steal in turn?
Too cruel still, she scorns my pray'rs
And mocks my piteous sighs.
Say, Cupid, have I not the right
To steal upon her unawares,
And take what she denies?

We concluded in duet once more: a rendition of Mr
Handel's ornate setting of Tennant's couplets:

Conflicting passions vex my troubled soul,
Too bold, too rash for reason to control.
Let hope and doubt, resistance and desire,
Dissolve as one in love's transforming fire.

Our little audience seemed delighted with this performance,
clapping vigorously, to the obvious pleasure of Mrs Quentin
and Mrs Hurlock. I would have been pleased enough myself
had I been less conscious of the possible implications of
the last three songs. We had sung them, as the occasion
seemed to require, with small hints of interplay which for
our listeners would have been mere gestures, but which to
me seemed truly insinuating.

Mr Gilbert having thanked us in a few becoming sentences,
the company reverted to general conversation, of which I
now recall little. The colonel and his wife were complimentary; I spent some time with Mr Quentin, neither of us
mentioning his London visit; Thorpe congratulated me upon
my singing and remarked that he was particularly pleased
to see the two ladies, often overshadowed in company, so

confident and so accomplished. I participated in these exchanges without thought. Like a man about to fight a duel, I felt my mind concentrated, my senses quickened and my heart beating hard. Across the room Mrs Hurlock was talking with my godfather; once or twice she glanced in my direction with what could be seen as a collusive smile. Yet what of that? We had indeed colluded in song.

My task was clear: but where was the attempt to be made? What did my godfather have in mind? The situation was absurd. What little I knew about this lady was powerfully dissuasive: she was married, a mother, twenty years my senior. My very future might be decided by this venture; but if I was successful no reward was guaranteed, and if I failed the consequence could be appalling.

My godfather drew me aside.

'The power of song has been at work,' he said. 'I fancy Mrs Hurlock now sees you quite in a pastoral light.'

I sought for an answer. 'She seems to be enjoying the evening . . .'

'She does indeed. I hope she will find more to enjoy.'

With which words he slipped away, leaving me to engage my tongue in further exchanges with Mrs Ford.

Soon afterwards the first carriages were called: the elderly guests departed, as did the colonel and his family. My moment of trial was coming nearer. The Quentins and Mr Thorpe left together. It appeared that Mr Rowley would be staying the night, but since he was to set out early the next morning he begged leave to retire. My godfather ushered myself, Mrs Ford and Mrs Hurlock through to a smaller drawing-room.

'We must surely talk a little more,' he said, 'before we retire in our turn.'

As we went he murmured to me: 'Mrs Hurlock is to sleep in the room you usually occupy. It would be a strange business if you went to it by mistake, from sheer habit.'

So here was the final hint – or instruction. I was to assail Mrs Hurlock in the bed where I had been accustomed to sleep. If she shrieked and woke the house, my single shred of excuse would be that I had broken in upon her in error.

Mr Gilbert, in exccllent spirits, insisted that we all four, even the ladies, should drink some port. Mrs Hurlock assented readily, but Mrs Ford by now tired, would take only a little.

'Let me observe once more,' said my godfather, 'how much pleasure our musicians gave me tonight. You were both in excellent voice. Mrs Hurlock, I hope you enjoyed the performance as much as I did.'

Mrs Hurlock, bright-eyed and a little flushed, replied: 'I have enjoyed the evening more than I can say. I was transported into another world.'

'I am delighted to hear it,' said Mr Gilbert.

Seizing the moment, I said: 'I could not have wished for a better partner in song.'

The words won me a glance of complaisance, but I could have no idea how things were in the lady's mind and body. Were the intimations I had noticed an instinctive reversion to youthful coquetry? Or might she be feeling merely a maternal impulse of fondness? Most likely of all, was she not simply making the most of an agreeable evening that she now felt had come to its end?

Soon enough Mrs Ford was seen to stifle a small yawn, and plainly wished to retire. A maid-servant was summoned to show her to her room. Mrs Hurlock chose to withdraw at the same time. I fancied I received one last look of complicity from her.

When they had gone my godfather poured some more port: 'In the circumstances I think half a glass should be sufficient.'

He remained standing, but drank unhurriedly, and with his usual air of discriminating enjoyment. To the casual eye he would have seemed absorbed in calm reflection, but I noticed, as once before, a slight tremulousness in the hand that held the glass.

'Now I shall retire,' he said. 'I leave you to your own devices.'

With a nod he was gone, and I was alone with my responsibility.

As I drank the last of the wine I assessed my situation as coolly as I could. I was hot and aroused, my heart by now fairly pounding. My room was directly above the one to which Mrs Hurlock had retired. If my intrusion caused instant outrage I might just be able to plead that, tired and a little intoxicated, I had mistakenly followed an accustomed route. But such a defence would be available for less than half a minute. I would have to make an instant appraisal of Mrs Hurlock's response, and either retreat at once or force the issue.

I left the drawing room and stood still for a moment, aware of the great dark space of the house all about me. Somewhere a maid would be lurking, charged with putting out candles, closing windows and locking doors. But the hall and the staircase were silent. I climbed cautiously to the floor above: silence again. Before me stretched a long passage, illuminated dimly, but sufficiently, by the moonlight that slanted through a single large window at the end. The last door on the right before that window was the one I would have to enter. I crept up to it, listened for a moment, but heard nothing within. The moment had come: I turned the handle, went in swiftly, and closed the door behind me.

My sense of anticipation was so keen that I registered what followed with extreme exactness. The curtain of the window opposite had been drawn back, so that the moon shone directly into the room. The lady, in a white nightgown, had been looking out, but she instantly turned to face me. I walked slowly towards her through the moonlight, but she made no attempt to cry out or to speak. Only as I put my hand on her plump shoulder did I hear a low voice: 'What are you doing?'

I whispered back: 'Have I not the right to take what she denies?'

'But – but I am a married woman.'

She raised a hand as though to push me away, but I set it aside.

'Someone will hear us . . .'

It was all the invitation I needed. I put my arms around her and pressed her to me. The indistinct moonlit lady felt large and warm, and as I kissed her wet mouth she was once more Mrs Hurlock, a plump country matron. What the devil was I about? But the game was afoot now, and there could be no turning back. Still with my mouth on hers I walked her stumblingly towards the bed. She whimpered a little but offered no resistance. I pushed her backwards across the bed and threw up her nightdress: a little effort and the deed would be done. But as Strephon fumbled at his breeches to free his trusty whore-pipe, the wayward Chloe stumbled to her feet and pushed him away.

'No!' she cried, 'No, no, no!'

I made to embrace her again, but she shook herself free. When I seized her shoulders she pushed away my face and then scratched at me. Suddenly I was in a fuddled rage: here I was gallantly endeavouring to pleasure this frump and she was attacking me for my pains. I wrenched her off me, flung her face forward across the bed, lifted her night-dress again and delivered two mighty slaps to her plump buttocks. She squawked and wept and was still: the fight was won. I turned her about and pushed her legs apart. A fumble at her privities, warm and moist, assured me that I would be compelling her to do exactly what her body desired. She yelped again as I forced myself deep into her, and what with the long anticipation, the anxiety, and the incitement of her final struggle I was betrayed, by that one thrust, into the shuddering gushes of completion.

The engagement thus summarily concluded I collapsed upon my new mistress sweating, panting, and horrified. My conquest had become instant ignominy, my stout victim was in tears, and I had laid myself open to a charge of rape.

In the silence my breathing and my heartbeat slowly settled but my mind did not. I was lost for words – lost for so much as a single idea. Why had I ventured on this absurd and shameful assault. No mere apology could meet the situation. 'Forgive me, madam, your charms were too great to resist . . .?' The mere attempt would be grotesque. Yet was I to fasten my breeches and shuffle away without speaking? Whatever I said or did I was a ruined man – the drunken Mohock who had galloped his horse over a cliff. If Mrs Hurlock should now rouse the house, my godfather would have no alternative but to disown me.

Disengaging myself I sat up on the bed, more wretched than I had ever been in my life. I think, though I cannot now be sure, that I was opening my mouth to say something – anything – when my victim sat upright also, clutched my arm, and spoke first.

'Richard,' she said, 'what have we done?'

Those five beautiful words transformed me, producing such a surge of spirits that I was thinking and feeling in a dozen diverse ways at once. This tender-hearted woman was sharing responsibility for the deed: I was saved. The poor old trull had thought I was moved by sentiment. Desperate to couple she had gorged on this mere tit-bit of sensation. She could never tell her husband because she had confessed to complicity. Did not this good soul deserve better service than I had given her? Was not the fat bitch greedy for further action? I would give her a towsing she would not soon forget.

My body was surging with force once more. Without a word I jumped to my feet and stripped off all my clothes, while she sat gawping. I seized her nightgown, pulled it off over her head and fell upon her like an animal, clutching at the wetness between her legs, biting at her great breasts. By now she was nobody, a female thing of flesh and fissure, a voice calling 'Oh! Oh! Oh!' as I bullied her into sensation.

195

At length, when she was limp in my grasp, I turned her about on to her knees, with her face in the pillow and her buttocks in the air, and settled to hearty cock-work, steady and remorseless. Recollections of such performances must be shadowy, but I held my stroke unrelentingly for what seemed a full quarter of an hour. I had told my godfather I would make her squeal, and squeal she did, as frantically and continuously as he could have hoped, the sound only partly muffled by the pillow. When I at last discharged she gave a shrill, prolonged cry, and we collapsed forward, slippery with seed and sweat and so emptied of force as to be barely conscious.

I came to myself thinking: 'Thank God! But how absurd, how absurd . . .' I was exhausted, but I had triumphed, and now had but one task remaining – to leave the room with tolerably good grace. It would be disastrous to be drawn into an exchange of avowals. The best I could hope for would be to emulate the dashing highwayman who wins regard with farewell courtesies. I kissed the lady and murmured in her ear: 'You gave me leave to love'. Even while I spoke, the incongruity between the dainty line of the song and the pungent odours of our copulation all but made me laugh. I would have been lost for a further gesture but for the happy accident, at that very moment, of a creak from the floorboards. It meant nothing – such small sounds were common enough in that house – but I responded to it as to a cue, raising a finger to my lips. Quickly but stealthily I donned my clothes once more. As the plump lady rose from her bed I took her in my arms and whispered: 'Mr Gilbert must never guess. But remember: there is but a strip of woodland between his estate and yours . . .' One more kiss, which she irksomely prolonged, and I was free to slip away from the room.

Outside I stopped to listen, but all was still. I crept up to my room on stockinged feet. Physically so weary that I could barely summon the strength to get into bed, I found my mind still spinning. My whole future had seemed to hang on a hair, yet after all I had saved the day – or the night – and proved myself: surely my godfather would be impressed to hear of this performance. As for the lady – whose very name I could scarcely recall – having enjoyed a good night's singing and a hearty tumble she could have little cause for complaint. When would she last have been ridden, never mind pleasured, by her sot of a husband? She would take away a fond memory of the evening, and would in future sing her pastoral ditties with deeper sentiment. There had been the finest of balances between victory and possible defeat. But no matter – I had prevailed, I had prevailed . . . My thoughts spun the faster, till I slept like a top.

12

In the morning my thoughts were darker. As I nervously washed every trace of Mrs Hurlock from my person I saw pitfall after pitfall ahead. How would she respond to me this morning? She might come downstairs simpering, which would be bad, or whimpering, which would be worse. If she directly accused me, how could I defend myself? If I survived the morning, might she not have a later change of heart, and confess everything to her husband?

I made my way apprehensively to the small dining-room where breakfast would be served. It was empty save for one of the maids, who told me that Mr Rowley had already left the house. I drank a dish of tea unhurriedly, rehearsing an appearance of composure. Mrs Ford, whose existence I had forgotten, was the next person to enter: we conversed about the weather. My godfather joined us, brisk but courtly, without a trace of interrogation in his greeting to me. He ordered more tea and muffins, and told us that the colonel had been impressed by Mr Rowley and was likely to employ him. We were still discussing this topic when Mrs Hurlock came in. I glanced up warily and was relieved to see that she looked serene. When my godfather asked if she had slept well she replied: 'I have never passed a more comfortable night.' My hopes rose. All might yet be well: she had reverted from wanton lover to worthy matron, but showed no trace of regret and seemed in command of the situation. The four of us drank tea, ate muffins, and chattered like civilized beings about painting, music, the colonel's daughters and Mrs Quentin's new teeth.

The two ladies were to be taken to their respective homes in Mr Gilbert's carriage. As we waited for it, on the sunlit terrace, Mrs Hurlock turned to me and mouthed, in mock reproach: 'Cruel . . .'

'Only to be kind,' I murmured in return.

When the carriage emerged and was wheeled around I knew that I should offer a last gesture to my portly paramour: a delicate matter in that I needed to convey warmth while raising no extravagant hopes – and this with due decorum, in the presence of Mrs Ford and my godfather. In the event I acquitted myself with credit. I told Mrs Hurlock how greatly I had enjoyed the previous night's performance, squeezed her hand very slightly as I kissed it in farewell, and concluded: 'We must sing together again one day.'

'We must indeed,' she replied, with an edge of emphasis.

Perhaps the tensions of the night and the morning had tried me too far. As the coach disappeared around a curve in the drive a spasm of laughter broke from me, as sudden as a belch. Noticing that my godfather was watching me with a smile, I laughed the more – so helplessly that I was quite doubled over, and had to clutch the stone balustrade for support.

'When you are recovered,' said Mr Gilbert, 'let us go indoors and talk.'

We went to his study, which was cool and quiet. Ready to give a spirited account of the night's exploits I awaited questions, but there were none.

'The evening was all I could have wished,' said my godfather, with satisfaction. 'The portrait and the music were well received, and Mr Hurlock was comprehensively cuckolded.'

I looked at him, surprised.

'When you were at work on Mrs Hurlock I was in the adjacent room, and could hear what passed. You were most thorough, and the lady was clearly gratified. As a young woman she was thought to be warm-blooded. It seems that the rumours were justified.'

He pursed up his mouth in reflection. 'When I thought of marrying her I wondered how she would comport herself in the bedroom. Thanks to your exertions I now know. You made good your undertaking.'

I was astonished. There were competing retorts at the tip of my tongue, either of them sufficient to annihilate my prospects. One was that the youthful Mr Gilbert might have found the lady something of an over-match. The other was that in eavesdropping on the act he had finally shown himself in his true colours: an impotent old goat, a proxy whoremonger. As I hesitated my godfather regarded me directly, with the slightest of smiles, as though daring me to speak out. Self-respect demanded an expression of outrage – but self-interest warned me, urgently, not to throw away a fortune. Self-interest carried the day. I remained silent, and my godfather resumed: 'You will suspect me of malice towards Hurlock. And rightly. But the experiment was the thing – a most revealing experiment. Here was a sober country matron, a creature of convention, who had lived a blameless married life these twenty years. Yet you subdued her in five minutes. Of course, the ground had been prepared: there were the songs, the compliments, the wine, the moonlight . . . To say nothing of the pastoral prologue . . .'

Seemingly it was my turn to speak. I tried to echo him: 'That is the comical see-saw. The animal act inspires graceful verses and melodies, and these in turn tempt us to the animal act. Our duets entered the lady's ears and persuaded her brain to open the front door to me.'

My godfather nodded. 'Flesh and spirit in collusion. But perhaps Man is not singular in this regard. Yardley might adduce the lark or the nightingale by way of comparison.'

'To speak more prosaically,' said I, 'the lady's husband surely assisted our cause. Who would wish to share a bed with him?'

'Who indeed?'

'That gentleman will hardly be pleased if he guesses what has happened.'

'He will not guess. And were he to do so he would say nothing. He is in my debt.'

The last five words were spoken with peculiar emphasis. 'When will he return?'

'Very shortly. As I told you, he has been disposing of the estate of his brother. The task will be bad for his temper:

he is incompetent in such matters. He had hopes of a bequest, but I believe that none will be forthcoming. He will return home sullen.'

Mr Gilbert rose.

'You acquitted yourself impressively, as Mrs Hurlock would no doubt confirm. We will discuss these matters further. But now you must excuse me: my lawyer is waiting.'

Later in the day I visited the room adjacent to the one in which Mrs Hurlock had passed the night. It was another panelled bedroom, reserved for guests. How close could Gilbert have come to our doings – how thick was the intervening wall? It looked solid enough; but I saw that there was a door built into the panelling. It opened to a deep closet, the far side of which was made of wood – the panelling of the next room. As I inspected this I found that part of one of the panels could be pushed aside. Mr Gilbert could have enjoyed a moonlit view of the coupling of godson and guest. Mrs Hurlock's cries would certainly have been heard loud and clear.

I retired to the library to review my situation. My first thought was that my wretched godfather had schemed a way into proximity to actions he could no longer perform. I had encountered one or two such sad specimens in the brothels of London and Paris. Given the susceptibility of Mrs Hurlock he could surely have attempted to enjoy her himself had he been competent to do so.

Yet once more the simple interpretation seemed to fall short of the whole truth. Mr Gilbert had been in earnest when talking of his interest in the Passions. Perhaps the mainspring of his own conduct was indeed a desire to study the desires of others. The source of that interest might be a temperamental rather than a physical incapacity. I recalled Yardley's remark concerning cats: perhaps my godfather, comparably, had an appetite for sensual fulfilment yet an aversion for the medium in which fulfilment might be found – that medium being surrender to the emotions, willingness to risk rejection or humiliation. The remedy would be to live vicariously. I was the otter to catch fish on his behalf.

If I should complain that this role offended me, my god-father might reasonably object that I had volunteered for it. I had boasted that I could make Mrs Hurlock squeal and, given the chance, had proceeded to do so. It was a little late for me to make a moral protest. On what principle could Mr Gilbert's conduct be judged more reprehensible than my own? Nonetheless I knew, and was sure that my godfather knew, that he had presumed too far. When he told me that he had overheard my engagement with Mrs Hurlock, should I not have indicated, if only by raising an eyebrow, that I was offended? Might not my silence have been taken for acceptance of my standing as an agent, a minion, a jackal?

Perturbed by these misgivings, I found some consolation in recalling my humbling of the respectable Mrs Hurlock. I could feel an objective interest in that achievement almost in the spirit of my godfather. What an odd business it had been. Could music have so potent an effect? Might Yardley, stirred by the call of the nightingale, seek pleasure in the arms of a sixpenny village whore? But if song had indeed warmed my Celia's heart, the fact that her Strephon had been so smitten as to burst into her chamber had also had its influence. Even then it had taken a couple of hard slaps to seal the victory: Strephon had prevailed by showing himself vicious. Yet I seemed to have emerged with honour – in Mrs Hurlock's eyes as well as in my own. Here was a further reminder that Love and Lust – as the abstraction passions Mr Gilbert would consider them – were confused, confusing and dangerous essences. A man with a delicate stomach was right to regard them with suspicion.

At dinner my godfather made no further mention of Mrs Hurlock. Before retiring he expressed the hope that I might stay until the end of the week; he would be busy for the next two or three days, but there were some important matters he wished to discuss with me. I wondered why he had not broached them that very evening, but was in no position to demur.

The following day, again becalmed, I withdrew to the library, where diversion came unexpectedly. Browsing the shelves I chanced upon a narrow volume, *Pictures from Parnassus*, consisting of descriptive passages from Homer and Virgil, translated into heroic couplets in the style of Mr Pope. The name of the author appeared not only on the cover but in a hand-written inscription on the title-page:

To James Gilbert, Esq,
  Although your modesty forbade me the privilege of a
 printed dedication, I must insist upon this record of my

*indebtedness to the patron whose generosity made possible
the publication of these imperfect exercises.*

*It is my earnest hope that I may one day be permitted
to dedicate to you a sustained work more worthy of your
notice.*

Your grateful and obedient servant,
John Quentin

There was a Preface to the effect that, admirable as had
been the exertions of Pope and others, there had not yet
been a translation into verse of the great epics that achieved
the appropriate balance between fidelity to the original texts
and poetic freshness. The Author hoped that the modest
attempts that followed would be seen as steps, however
faltering, in the direction of a more complete rendering. If
they were well received he would be encouraged to attempt
the longer flight that was as yet beyond his youthful powers.

I had never heard previously heard of Quentin's scholarly
or poetic talents. The book I had found was dated some
twenty years previously yet I could see no succeeding volume
on my godfather's shelves. To my eyes the verses seemed
well enough, but I did not greatly value my own judgement
on such matters. I resolved to seek out Mr Quentin that
very afternoon and learn more about his poetic endeavours:
after all I owed him a visit.

The weather being fine I walked into the village. Somewhat
to my embarrassment the first person I saw was Mr Thorpe,
standing in the sunlight outside his own front door. I felt
myself flushing – fantastical though my misgivings were I
half expected him to cry: 'I hear you gave Mrs Hurlock a

hearty pumping.' In the event, of course, he was as civil as ever, and we fell into easy conversation. When I mentioned my errand, however, and asked whether he knew of Quentin's poetic ambitions, he became suddenly serious.

'Let us go indoors,' he said. 'This is a delicate matter.'

We retired to his drawing-room and took some tea.

'I know something of the story,' said Thorpe, 'but only through Mrs Quentin. At the time your godfather first met him, Mr Quentin was a young man, not long down from university, and striving to make his way as a poet. Mr Gilbert recognized him as a man of talent, and gave him a sufficient pension to live in the village and devote his time to writing. His first published work, the one you saw, was well received. Subsequently his ambition was to produce a version of the *Iliad* that would surpass Mr Pope's both in fidelity to the original and in poetic force. But after that first volume nothing came.'

'His muse deserted him?'

'I believe the cause was less simple. He was unluckily torn between scholarship and poetry. He would tear up a draft, either because it was false to the Greek or because, while accurate, it was poetically lifeless. What he approved as a scholar disappointed the poet, and what pleased the poet offended the scholar. So he lost heart, and gradually ceased to try. If he seems saturnine it is because he lives in a quiet anguish of disappointment.'

'Did the poor devil find no other occupation?'

'Unfortunately he did not. He and his wife were beset by misfortunes. She has been ill more than once. They had two children who both died in infancy.'

'And are they still dependent on my godfather?'

'Effectively I fancy they are. Mr Quentin inherited a small annuity, but I doubt if it would be enough to live on.'

'His case seems remarkably similar to that of Mr Yardley.'

Thorpe nodded, as though pleased I had taken this point. 'Indeed. But there are two differences. Yardley has after all continued to pursue his interests: he was and still is a devoted naturalist. By contrast Quentin, or so his wife hints, has lost all interest in both poetry and the classics. The other difference is that Yardley is too absorbed in his studies to worry about material matters. If his income were suddenly to cease he would scarcely notice. Soon he would be found dead among his specimens. But Quentin suffers continual anxiety about money: he did so even before the expenditure on his wife's teeth.'

Something in Thorpe's tone made me catch his eye: 'Has Mr Gilbert ever threatened to withdraw his favours?'

'I think not; but Quentin may fear that possibility – or may simply detest his indebtedness.' Thorpe paused, before adding in an altered tone. 'Mr Gilbert is a reserved man: his intentions are hard to read. Perhaps you as his godson . . .'

It was my turn to pause, but I was willing to be cautiously open with Thorpe.

'I may be little wiser than yourself. My first meeting with Mr Gilbert, or the first I can recall, took place when I was ten years of age. Since then, although he generously provided for my upbringing, I have seldom seen him. I have spent as much time in his company this year as in all the previous years combined.'

'You surprise me, Mr Fenwick. He mentions you quite often, and seems at ease in your company.'

'But, as you suggest, it is hard to read his mind.'

There was silence for a moment. I almost fancied that I could read Thorpe's mind as he adjusted his view of me. I was not, after all, to be seen as a man who had privileged access to Mr Gilbert. On the other hand that very fact might licence further candour.

'You will understand,' said Thorpe, 'that it would not be advisable to mention this book to Quentin: it is something he would gladly forget. Perhaps Mr Gilbert himself might find it a delicate topic . . .'

'He might indeed. I have learned from you this week that he assisted two young scholars, neither of whom succeeded as he hoped. For a proud man this may have been an embarrassment.'

'Exactly so,' said Thorpe. 'But in many another venture he has prospered. Thanks to his help the village school is flourishing. Local farmers have profited from the introduction of new methods that he encouraged them to adopt. He has been shrewd in his buying and selling of land. He may be the most powerful man in the county.'

Shortly thereafter I took my leave. Although I had abandoned the idea of visiting the Quentins I continued my walk in order to reflect on the information I had received. Should I see my godfather as surrounded by pensioners, by bought men? Was I myself no more than such another vassal as the mouldering Yardley or the surly Quentin? If that were true, at least I was fulfilling my undertakings as they had not. An alternative view was that these cases confirmed Mr Gilbert's account of himself as an experimenter of sorts. Given his increased confidence in me, might I not aspire to be a fellow-projector rather than a subject?

✣

Two days later I returned from a walk to find Mr and Mrs Hurlock drinking tea on the terrace with my godfather. Their conversation broke off as I approached, but I inferred that Hurlock was reporting the results of his visit to Warwickshire. I took in a great deal in two seconds. Hurlock looked worse than usual in the afternoon sunlight: his nose was the colour of a ripe plum, and his dirty wig could have been his own hair gone rotten. Mrs Hurlock and my godfather were easy and composed. Perhaps as a result I found myself comfortable in the situation and even amused by it, wondering how it was that the fleeting glances I exchanged with Mrs Hurlock and Mr Gilbert could communicate two quite distinct flickers of insinuation.

Hurlock himself, partly drunk, talked loudly and assertively. He was in ill humour, cursing the state of the roads and the discomfort of travelling in hot weather: 'My shirt was drenched: the carriage stank. I would have sweated less making the journey on foot.'

Later, in his jeering mode, he expressed relief at having missed our concert: 'Your warbling would have meant nothing to me. I have no more ear for music than a tree. Young man, my wife praises your voice. Be thankful you were not born in Italy: the surgeons might have condemned you to a lifetime of singing.'

I smiled complaisantly at this feeble jocosity, thinking: 'Bluster away, poor sot: I have rogered your wife – as all here know, save yourself.'

There seemed to be neither affection nor a common understanding between the Hurlocks. I wondered that they could share the same house, to say nothing of the same bed. Mrs Hurlock, however, impressed me with her composure: no casual observer could have inferred that anything had passed between us. It was impossible to guess her thoughts. I suspected a hint, however, in her casual remark that, with the weather lately so fine, she had taken to walking in the woods of an afternoon.

When his guests departed my godfather remarked: 'It was as I suspected: Hurlock's hopes of relief from his brother's estate have proved groundless. He will be drinking heavily tonight.'

At dinner-time, I was handed a note from Mr Gilbert excusing his absence on the grounds of a slight indisposition. He asked me to be good enough to come to his study at ten the next morning, because there were important topics that we needed to discuss. I ate alone, my appetite diminished by suspense.

❧

Having gestured that I should be seated, my godfather sat motionless: his face was taut and a little pale. When he spoke he spoke hurriedly, avoiding my eyes: 'I must apologize. I hoped to have this conversation last night, with darkness and wine to free the tongue, as once before. But my resolve failed. The indisposition referred to in my note amounted to no more than that – a pitiful weakness.

'However, I used the note to force my own hand, so that now, this morning, we *must* talk. We must talk: but there is too much to say, too much to put into order. Where to begin? Where to begin?' He tapped the desk with his fingertips. 'You laughed the other morning when Mrs Hurlock had left. You seem to laugh often, as your father did. You will have noticed that I do not laugh myself. No more does Quentin. Hurlock laughs loudly and often, but without mirth, as an ass brays. You were laughing with obvious mirth – but why?'

Taken by surprise, I sought for an honest answer.

'It is hard to tell, sir. There was an absurdity in the situation. I think I laughed at that absurdity. But I recall that my mind was producing conflicting thoughts simultaneously – more than it could accommodate. Perhaps the laughter signified that thinking had failed.'

Mr Gilbert digested my explanation. 'You were laughing at disorder; I think I even smiled myself. But I am unaccustomed to disorder: it is what I have always striven to avoid – until now. I am in unfamiliar territory.'

He glanced at me: 'You will not make sense of what I am saying, because I can barely do so myself. I must be clearer. I must be clearer.'

He got to his feet, and began to pace slowly about, tapping his left palm with his right fist, as though to assist his thought.

'You wrote to me of the masquerade, the choice of costume, the playing of a part. Forty years ago I set out to dress up *as myself* and perform *as myself*. It was a deliberate

211

decision. I was in some confusion and needed rules to live by. Gradually I refined costume and conduct until they fitted me perfectly.'

He stopped and turned to me.

'But there was a price to pay. I had other needs, other behaviours, which could not be – which *were not* – accommodated by the person I had elected to become.'

By this time the old fellow was in a state of some excitement: the colour was back in his cheeks and there was a fleck of spittle at one corner of his mouth. Still self-absorbed he went on: 'I know my abilities and limitations. I do not possess the personal charm of yourself or your father. I substitute courtesy. I observe that while I can like or admire this person or that, I am deficient in affection. I see a balance-sheet of good and bad qualities and respond accordingly. No doubt as a consequence of this habit I have no intimates.

'My interest in the Passions derives from the difference between myself and others. I see these differences and try to account for them. But I have come to suspect a falsity in this very habit of observation – a falsity akin to seeing in two dimensions a phenomenon that exists in three dimensions.'

He broke off, and put both palms on his desk, bowing his head as though to collect himself.

'Over the years I attempted experiments of a kind – experiments to make good what I was missing by providing me fresh perspectives. Some succeeded up to a point, but they remained external, something I could grasp but not *inhabit*. I sought to live an alternative life, to see through someone else's eyes. Now you have granted me such an experience. I am grateful for it. But I am disturbed by the conflicting feelings you have evoked.'

He sat down and looked at me attentively.

'You said that it was a mixture of thoughts that made you laugh the other morning. Can you be more particular?'

'I can try to be.'

I thought for a few moments before saying, pausing after each clause: 'Among my thoughts were the following: I was glad to have fulfilled my undertaking; I hoped that there would be no ill consequences; I was gratified that Mrs Hurlock had enjoyed herself; I was incredulous at the improbability of the episode; I was confused by the mixture of abstract ideas and animal appetites that had been at work; and I was amused that the three of us chatted together while unable to mention the topic uppermost in our minds.'

My godfather nodded gravely at this gallimaufry, as though taking in some serious philosophical proposition.

'I think I was aware,' said he, 'of all those sentiments in my vicinity, but additionally of at least three others. One was gratification that the boorish Hurlock, who once lorded it in these shires, had been humbled; the second was that I had belatedly, if vicariously, serviced the woman who had taken my eye five and twenty years ago; the third was complacency at having planned and presided over this thoroughly reprehensible proceeding.'

He had spoken carefully, his voice willed to calmness, but the spark in his eye showed that he knew how singular and incriminating a statement he was making. I remained silent.

Mr Gilbert seemed suddenly more at ease, as though the difficult part of his task had now been done. When he spoke again he spoke comfortably: 'You must understand that these are sentiments that I would never previously have *allowed myself to feel*, still less to disclose. I have passed a private Rubicon and entered the realm of Disorder, with you as my sole companion and guide.'

I heard myself say: 'What quarter of that realm do you next wish to explore?'

'The Ogden territory has a particular interest for me.'

When I said nothing, he resumed: 'Your dealings with Miss Brindley I could easily follow: they confirmed recollections of my own. You saw her in a pastoral light until you enjoyed her body. First the one Passion and then the other: idealized desire succeeded by physical repletion. So much is familiar to me. I wish to learn more about *complication*, about simultaneous and conflicting feelings, as implied in your references to Mrs Ogden.'

I had a sense of suffocation. My godfather might speak as a disinterested philosopher of behaviour; but his abstractions bore directly upon my freedom of action and even of emotion. He had used me to seduce a matron I scarcely knew – hiring my body, so to speak; now it seemed that he planned to encroach on my deepest feelings. If ever I bedded Sarah might this old devil be peering through a keyhole or taking notes in a bedroom cupboard?

Yet I recalled Cullen's comments. Had I not put my personal life at my godfather's disposal? It was too late to resort to dignified reproach.

'That is a delicate affair,' I said at last, hoping to put a dampener on the subject. 'I cannot be optimistic about my chances of success.'

'Then the campaign may be protracted,' replied Gilbert, not in the least put out. 'You implied that Mr Ogden is exploring a new profession. Can you tell me more?'

I described the meeting at Crocker's house, and Ogden's apparent interest in the disposition of light. Gilbert listened attentively, as though registering a point of interest.

'Perhaps we can turn this to advantage,' he said. 'Have you decided what your next move will be?'

'Not yet. Bear in mind, sir, that it will prove difficult for me to achieve so much as a private conversation with the lady in question.'

Gilbert smiled thinly. 'I might find a means to tempt her husband out of town.'

'Thank you,' I replied, but I spoke mechanically. I needed to hint demurral. All I could manage was: 'I hope the affair does not prove a disappointment to you.'

Either Gilbert was oblivious to the shading of irony or he chose to ignore it.

'I will be disappointed,' he said, 'only if nothing happens between you and Mrs Ogden. Her capitulation or her resistance might equally prove to be of interest.'

Here was a crumb of relief: at least I was not to be assessed merely on my success as an instrument of copulation. But even that crumb left a disagreeable after-taste: presumably I would be expected to submit minute reports on matters emotional.

He immediately confirmed that supposition: 'Remember that it is the Passions that are of concern to me – Passions declared, suppressed, conflicting, compounded. These are the demons that determine our conduct.'

Aware how one-sided our conversation had been, I tried to express speculative interest.

'What say you, sir, to the exhibitions of Passion in great works of literature – in Homer's Epics or Shakespeare's Tragedies?'

'They have become deadened by familiarity. Moreover they pertain to a past world. I cannot feel the reality of an emotion unless it relates to the life I know. Your conquest of Mrs Hurlock I could taste on my tongue.'

❦

Later in the day I took a walk across the estate, trying to calculate where the week's visit had taken me. Had I advanced my cause? Surely each fresh appearance at Flint Hill House strengthened my credentials as a prospective heir. Local people and servants now knew me well. Moreover I had done all that my godfather had hoped for, and he had confided in me as never before. The balance of dependency must have shifted in my favour.

Yet Gilbert now appeared darker, more perplexing, more dangerous. He had not suggested how much further our experiment was to proceed, or when it should end. Indeed he did not seem to look *beyond* the experiment at all. He had said nothing concerning my future prospects, and offered no quid pro quo for my new exertions. He might consider, not unreasonably, that he was already rewarding me handsomely enough. If that were the case, however, would I ever be more than a paid employee, a performing rake?

The inquiries concerning the Ogdens I found hateful. It was as though my conflicting feelings towards Sarah were to be reduced to the level of my encounter with Mrs Hurlock – that affair serving as an anticipatory parody or burlesque.

As I continued in this train of thought, my walk took me into the woodland that bordered the estate, and I lost myself among the trees. I had not foreseen, as I might have done, that I would come face to face with Mrs Hurlock.

Without a word (for I could think of nothing to say) I embraced her, and sprawled her down on a patch of grass. The lady reciprocated my attentions with passionate ardour. In minutes our procreative organs were exposed to the afternoon sunshine and we were mating strenuously. When the act was completed – to the evident satisfaction of both parties – Mrs Hurlock hastily disengaged herself saying, to my relief, 'I must go! I must go! I will be late!' She hurried towards her house, having bestowed on me a farewell kiss.

As I rose, with knees somewhat tremulous, to adjust and brush down my breeches, I was conscious of two reactions. One was that I had rarely achieved copulation at so small an expense of words. The other was that I had restored some little dignity to both Mrs Hurlock and myself by ploughing her again without my godfather's knowledge. This had been honest fucking.

I had hitherto had no feelings towards the lady, but as I came away I experienced some *fellow*-feeling: we had both taken refuge from personal plights in the brief distraction of the physical act. Perhaps the woodland setting had sustained

Mrs Hurlock's pastoral fantasies. In any case I fancied she would find it quietly pleasing to talk to her husband with another man's seed inside her. As for me I would dine with my godfather proudly sticky from this unplanned gesture of independence.

13

My journey back to London was such as to recall Hurlock's complaints on his return from Warwickshire. The coach bucked, swayed and shook along roads baked hard as stone by weeks without rain. I and my fellow-passengers sweated intolerably as we were rocked from side to side. We breathed a stifling air, pungent with the odours of damp leather and over-heated horses and men. Too peevish and dispirited to talk, we bounced together for mile upon mile without a word save for a grunt or curse at a particularly harsh jolt.

Throughout the two days of wretched travel I pondered on what had passed at Fork Hill, my mind drifting in and out of brief spells of troubled sleep. Should I feel guilt, I asked myself again, at my conquest of Mrs Hurlock? It seemed that three people had been gratified in their different ways by what had passed, and nobody harmed. But there had been something repugnant about displaying Mrs Hurlock's animal responses to Gilbert's lascivious oversight. This had not been my intention, of course, but I *had* assented to do the same thing at second hand. It had been an ugly business. Was there not a danger that my godfather would have a truly tainting effect upon me – that my moral sense, such as it was, would be weakened? Without often considering such matters I liked to think of myself as being in general of an amiable disposition – certainly neither callous nor cruel. But had I not pawned my moral independence to my godfather? Was I not contracted to do his bidding as hedonist and intriguer? To make matters worse he was now intent on presiding over my attempted seduction of Mrs Ogden. Sarah was not in the same category as a Mrs Hurlock or even a Kitty Brindley. Here a deeper morality, a private morality, was at issue. Somehow I would have to draw a line, or to dissemble. Neither her deeper feelings nor my own should be exposed to Mr Gilbert's cold inspection.

For all the discomfort of the journey I was unprepared for what I found on arrival. It appeared that, as in some monstrous chemical experiment, the torrid weather had coated London with foulness. Kennels and gutters were bone-dry and clogged with sewage. There were piles of rubbish everywhere, foetid in the heat and swarming with flies. The stench was scarcely to be endured. Moreover this corrupt air was so warm and lifeless as to seem unsustaining: my lungs strained to take in enough to rouse my body and mind.

It was some relief to get back to Cathcart Street, where Anna, Mrs Deacon's little servant girl, brought me copious supplies of warm water. Having sluiced away the sweat and dirt of the journey and donned fresh clothes I was physically easier, but there remained an underlying discomfort that I could not shake off. London had become repulsive, and I felt that even here I was controlled from Fork Hill, a puppet dangling from a taut string a hundred miles long.

The asphyxiating weather and my heavy mood were to persist for several more days. It was a strange time, by most accounts London's longest spell without rain in thirty years. To witness the effects of this drought I made myself walk abroad, if at a languid pace. It was observable that all the activities of the city had slowed down in the heat like a clock in need of winding. People stayed within doors, and many shops were closed. Few would venture near the over-powering stench of Smithfield or Billingsgate. Horses were patched with white lather and dogs lay panting on the cobbles with protruded tongues. The leaves on the trees hung limply, and the parks were queerly discoloured, the grass parched to the consistency of thin white hair. London and all its inhabitants, human and animal, seemed alike ugly, surly and dyspeptic.

In a similar condition myself I had conceived but a single useful idea – that I would make this spell of extraordinary weather my excuse for doing nothing, and would postpone my next letter to Mr Gilbert accordingly. My performance with Mrs Hurlock had surely entitled me to a respite. The letter when it was written could reasonably consist almost wholly of an account of the inertia suffusing the city. By the time I wrote a second time I would have devised a plan to protect my privacy. The delay might also, perhaps, serve to lower the temperature of my godfather's expectations. If my pursuit of Sarah was to be resumed – an undertaking for which the enervating heat had dulled my enthusiasm – I

221

would report it slowly, in economical instalments, recording overtures, tactics and responses.

My lassitude deepening, I abandoned walking and stayed within doors. The nights were as airless as the days: in bed I would set aside the covers yet remain too hot to sleep for more than a couple of hours – usually towards dawn. I lay sprawled as helpless and wretched as the dogs I had seen in the street. Even the calm Mrs Deacon showed traces of perspiration on her forehead. Lazily reviving a former fancy I reflected that if I was to be constrained to couple with an older woman I would greatly prefer my landlady to Mrs Hurlock. In my state of lethargy, however, even that impulse was no more than a spark.

One afternoon, in a show of exceptional exertion, I succeeded in making an expedition to the house of Mr Crocker. To arrive in a condition of reasonable decorum I made use of a chair, but still felt half suffocated by the journey. The unfortunate wretches who had borne my weight had suffered so badly in the heat that I overpaid them in proportion to their panting.

Conscious as I was of Crocker's physical difficulties I should have anticipated that the visit was unlikely to be a success. As I entered I could see at a glance that progress had been made in the furnishing and decoration of the house, but I was to have little chance to study these changes. In the drawing-room Crocker, sprawled awkwardly astride his wooden boar, looked the more shapeless and dejected for the contrast with his snarling charger. He wore no wig, and had been wiping the perspiration from his face with a large handkerchief, which he waved feebly by way of greeting.

'I am glad to see you, Dick,' he said, in a weary voice. 'At least, I believe so. I am too spent to know exactly what I think or feel – if, indeed, anything. All my energies are trickling away in sweat. But I am a gentleman still and will procure for you a cooling drink made from limes.'

This was brought, and proved refreshing. Crocker himself had a great pitcher of the same beverage at his side, but he waved away my appreciative remarks.

'It is momentarily agreeable on the tongue,' he said, 'but it flows through me as through a great colander of flesh, and emerges again all over my person.'

'It is miserably hot,' I observed. 'but—'

'Stop!' groaned Crocker. 'There can be no "but": this weather is not to be borne. The intolerable heat could kill me.'

I tried to commiserate, but to little effect. Crocker listened moodily, and took a long draught directly from his pitcher.

'If there is a God,' he said, 'He is an unjust and spiteful God. He creates me three times the size of a normal man and then broils me for His sport.'

For some minutes we carried on a conversation of sorts, but then he raised a hand.

'It is ungracious of me, Dick, but I think I must retire. I find myself a trifle giddy.'

I could see that his face had become very white. He made to climb off the boar, but staggered heavily as he did so: I got to my feet just in time to intervene and prevent him from falling. It took all my strength to support his damp, drooping weight. He let out a wordless shout for assistance, and I was relieved to see two sturdy footmen hurry in. With some difficulty they assisted him to stumble across to a large settee, on which he fell back, gasping. One of the footmen loosened his shirt and the other put a wet cloth to his forehead. Crocker sat panting for some moments, his head bowed, but at length looked up and managed a smile.

'You see how it is with me, Dick. I was not designed to live in tropical climes.'

I offered a few consolatory phrases, and then took my leave, dispirited, sorry for Crocker and discontented with myself. My journey in the chair had been so disagreeable that I decided on walking as the lesser evil, and trudged away light-headed. Wyvern Street led me into Margaret Street, and as I passed the Ogdens' house I reflected that in all probability I was now within a few yards of Sarah. The thought detained me but briefly, and stirred not a flicker of lust. I was not myself: the heat had half stifled me, body and brain.

That evening Matt Cullen was shown up and sank gasping into a chair.

'God help me, Dick: I can't recall another such summer. A man cannot breathe.'

We sat looking at one another, emptied of energy, and grinning stupidly at our common impotence. I sent out for a quantity of cold beer, which roused us sufficiently to get us talking, if at but half our customary velocity. Matt said that he had no news to communicate, the town having been so lowered by the heat during the period of my absence that nothing whatsoever had happened. Accordingly it fell to me to provide a detailed account of all that had passed at Fork Hill. As I told the story it sounded strange even to my own ears. Matt listened with his customary intentness, from time to time giving an incredulous shake of the head.

'You should be grateful to Mr Gilbert,' he said. 'It is an indulgent godfather who steers his young charge to the brink of an available notch.'

'An over-ripe one,' I demurred.

'That is ungraciously said. By your own account it was in eminently usable condition. The old fellow did you a favour.'

'Only in order to do himself a favour. Good God, Matt, he wanted Dame Hurlock plundered and her husband cuckolded, and commandeered my member to do the deed.'

'Which it did very willingly and to its own gratification,' cried Matt. 'In any case your patron has been rewarding you handsomely for your labours. All was carried out according to contract.'

'And so I have reluctantly admitted to myself,' I conceded. 'It was in the bond. But what say you to the old devil's interference in my dealings with Sarah Ogden? '

'I deplore this whimpering from a wholehearted whore-monger.' Matt sat up to rally his thoughts. 'Here you are, resolved to lie with Ogden's wife – a reprehensible intention, but let us set that consideration aside. Your tolerant and kindly godfather, so far from objecting, urges you on, pays you, and offers you any assistance in his power. To resent that intervention is to be a strangely fastidious seducer. You are in the absurd position of pleading the exquisite purity of your impure motive. Consider, Mr Fenwick, pray consider. When the dissolute Cullen turns preacher the evil in question must be grave indeed.'

I tried to laugh, but could not. What he had said was near the mark: I was in no position to argue. But somewhere, I still felt sure, there lurked a principle that I would have hoped to retrieve.

'The truth is,' I said, half-truthfully, 'that at the moment I find myself too hot and too weary and too irritable to care very deeply about Gilbert or Sarah or life itself. I am in the soft toils of apathy.'

'I think I may be in the same plight,' said Matt. 'Let us return to these grave topics when the weather has changed.'

For some minutes we sat in unaccustomed silence, drinking beer, each occupied with his own thoughts. When Matt spoke again it was with unexpected seriousness.

'We have drifted into a queer plight, you and I. There is Fenwick, enjoying a life of pleasure, but unhappily aware that he is his godfather's plaything. Here is Cullen, paying court to a weary old nobleman who scarcely knows him. What has become of these promising young gentlemen? Have they no dignity? This cannot be the way to live.'

'I have had such a thought many times,' said I, 'but I could do nothing with it. Have you anything to propose?'

'We could—' said Matt, and hesitated. 'We *could*, if we had the will, leave this tainted island and travel to Virginia or the West Indies to seek our fortune. If we scraped together every guinea we possess . . .'

I replied in the same vein, taking him seriously: 'That would be possible. There are clothes and possessions that we might sell . . .'

'We are young and healthy,' said Matt. 'We are educated.'

'More than that,' I added, with sudden enthusiasm. 'We might prove to have abilities that as yet we have never had a chance to exercise.'

'True,' said Matt. 'It might be that one of us is a natural cattle-breeder.'

It was at this point that we began to laugh.

'What could be more likely?' said I. 'And one of us will surely show a talent for growing sugar or cotton—'

'Or timber,' suggested Matt.

'The timber is already grown. We would have only to chop down the trees, cut them into slices and sell the planks.'

'Given all the building in the new world we would soon be rich men.'

In this way what had been, for a few moments, all but a serious suggestion subsided into fatuities. Cullen and I sniggered away over the last of our beer, offering suggestions increasingly facetious on such topics as gold-mining, cattle, Indians, slave-girls, bear-skins and buffalo. Yet the humour was forced and the laughter was flat. We could not so easily dismiss the qualms we had acknowledged.

❧

A day or two later, feeling that I had procrastinated as long as I reasonably could, I wrote to my godfather, recounting the discomforts of the city, and using the lassitude induced by the heat as my excuse for having nothing of personal interest to report. The letter concluded:

I saw curious evidence, the other day, of the decline in energy that this weather has occasioned. Some poor rogue, in the stocks for I know not what offence, was being but perfunctorily pelted. There was enough in the way of filth and rotten eggs and trickling blood to make him wretched and disfigure his features, but in truth he got off lightly, his assailants showing little relish for the sport and wandering away after a throw or two.

I confess that I have found myself debilitated, physically and mentally. In the hot, noxious air I have experienced the sensation, as never before, of being one of a multitude huddled together, eating, drinking, sleeping, talking, fornicating, defecating . . . I feel myself to be an animal among half a million others in a teeming, stinking warren. Perhaps it is not surprising that the unnatural conditions of these past few weeks should have conduced to unnatural thoughts. I recall your reference to meteorology. In this continual heat the whole body feels dilated, distended. Even one's hands are visibly a little swollen. Is it wholly fanciful, then, to conceive that there may be, correspondingly, some minute temporary deformation of the mind that makes us see things awry or think about them confusedly?

The weather must surely change soon. Look to receive a livelier letter from your godson when at last the city is cooled by a fall of rain.

I am, &c.

When the change did come it proved to be dramatic. One could smell it, or taste it, in advance. The air grew hotter yet, and had a metallic tang to it. There were brief eddies of hot wind, accompanied by indeterminate creaks and shudderings. I was walking along the Strand when I first perceived these signs. They produced an almost instant reaction among pedestrians, street-sellers, and even horses and dogs, as though all were moved to apprehension by a common animal instinct. When the first large drops of warm rain fell the thoroughfares were already all but deserted. In moments the sky darkened dramatically. There came a sudden flicker of dazzling light, followed by a prolonged and rattling peal of thunder. Scurrying along I reached the front door of my lodging just as the rain began to pelt down in earnest.

At the bedroom window I watched and listened to the great downpour. The rain fell vertically and with such force as to shut out the view across our narrow street. It drummed on the roof above me and sent water streaming down the panes so thickly that soon I could scarcely see out at all. Lightning flashed and flashed again, and peal upon peal of thunder broke out, with the crack of a cannon followed by a rumbling echo. I could fancy the whole house shook. In the space of a few minutes the air had become notice-ably cooler, and there crept into the house through chinks or chimneys the delicious clean scent of this liquor from the skies.

Exhilarated beyond description I suddenly stripped off coat and wig, clattered down two flights of stairs and ran out into the street in my shirtsleeves. By now, indeed, it could hardly be called a street, for a dark stream filled the whole breadth of it from wall to wall and was swirling away down the slope. In seconds my garments were saturated, clinging to my body, and the water was over my ankles, filling my shoes. I cared not at all, and laughed at the next flash of lightning in a kind of crazed exaltation. I had an image in my mind of this great flood purging the whole filthy city, laying the dust, sluicing away the accumulations of dirt, decay and stench. It was a joy to breathe the fresh, cooled air.

Half-blinded by the rain I waded my way to the end of the street, where it joined Tanner Hill, and clutched at a post to hold myself upright. What had become the Tanner Hill river – to which the Cathcart Street stream was but a tributary – was flowing away in a torrent destined, around a dozen corners and curves, to pour into the Thames.

I had thought myself the only human-being abroad in the storm, but just beyond the corner I saw a ragged old man, perhaps a beggar, standing with closed eyes, folded arms and a contented smile, delighting to be washed by the rain. As thunder pealed again I greeted my fellow idiot, shook his hand, and on the cheerful impulse of the moment forced two fingers into my soaking pocket to find a guinea for him. He cackled in wonder at the acquisition, as though it had been a gift from the heavens – which in a sense it was.

With some little difficulty I splashed my way back to the

house against the stream, losing a shoe along the way. Only when I reached the front door did I realize that I had left my keys upstairs. Mrs Deacon answered my knock, plainly astonished that anyone should call in the midst of such a storm, and still more astonished to see her tenant in such a plight. She looked at me doubtfully as I stepped into the hall, and seemed at a loss as to what to say. But as I smeared the water from my face with the back of a hand I began to laugh, and I heard her laugh, too, as she hurried away to fetch me a towel.

14

The following morning the sky was clear, but gutters and kennels were still flowing fast, and great ponds of water lay in the streets. Donning stout boots I walked down to the Strand, slithering on the wet stones. A few shop signs had come crashing down in the storm and were lying amid broken bricks, but those in place were legible once more, washed clean by the rain. Shops and stalls were doing a lively trade and the whole town seemed refreshed.

Outside the Pumpkin, in Tyler Street, I was hailed by Nick Horn, comically resplendent in scarlet coat and embroidered waistcoat, and brandishing a cane.

'To judge from your grimace,' he said, 'you think me over-dressed.'

'I do. Your shoes will be sodden and your clothes splashed with mud.'

'No matter,' said Nick. 'I am bound for the park. At last a gentleman can wear a little finery without sweating like a bricklayer. So I play the popinjay for once, and preen a little.'

He postponed his parading, however, till we had taken coffee.

'We have not spoken since the masquerade,' said he. 'Such an interval should spawn two hours of gossip; but the damnable heat so reduced us that nothing has happened: we have all gone to ground.'

'Have you seen Latimer?'

'Only once; but thereabouts lies a crumb of news. Miss Page has rejected him, which does not surprise me – but in favour of Mr Crocker, which does. She must esteem the size of that gentleman's fortune more than she dreads the weight of his body.'

'Perhaps she finds Mr Crocker more interesting company.'

'That may be: Latimer has turned respectable, and respectability makes a man dull. I believe Miss Page's friend Kitty is a lady in whom you take an interest?'

'I do – a lively interest.'

'Did you see her in *The Relapse*?'

'I did not.'

'A sad omission. Take my word, Dick, this was something out of the common run. If the damned heat had not kept people away she would by now be the toast of London.'

❧

A day later I myself visited St James's Park. It had recovered its freshness and colour with remarkable speed and was again a place of aristocratic resort. To stroll along its paths was to engage in a kind of dance, the elegant pedestrians moving at a measured pace, pausing to nod to an acquaintance or stopping to speak to a friend. There was always the chance, of course, of an unexpected social encounter. On this occasion I saw, with a sense of shock, that Mr and Mrs Ogden were approaching me, he heavy in black, she graceful in blue and white. Here was a chance that I had at all costs to seize. They had plainly seen me, and were calculating whether it would be courtesy enough to pass by with no more than a formal acknowledgement. I stepped into their path, bowed and greeted them. Wary courtesies were exchanged. Ogden was dour, but I flattered myself that there was a hint of amusement in Sarah's response. For the moment my only recourse was courteous affability.

I asked Mr Ogden about the progress of Crocker's house.

'I was last there two days ago,' he said. 'The renovation is all but complete.'

I asked Mrs Ogden whether she had seen the house. She said that she had not, but that she hoped one day to do so.

I observed to Mr Ogden that it seemed to me interesting and unusual that through dealing in diamonds he had found a second vocation.

'It *is* perhaps unusual,' said Ogden. 'I know of no other such case. To me the transition seemed a natural one.'

I smilingly asked Mrs Ogden whether her husband had applied his talents to their own home. She replied that he had, and to distinctive effect.

Turning once more to Mr Ogden I inquired whether his work had perhaps derived from, or led him to, a study of the science of optics.

'My knowledge of that subject is superficial. I deal in practicalities.'

'You will have surely visited Greenwich.'

'On several occasions.'

During these drab exchanges I was observing both husband and wife. My opinion of Ogden was confirmed: the man was impermeable. His eyes communicated nothing and his inexpressive face could have been made of clay. He spoke tonelessly, seeming to have no ear for conversation, no taste for pleasantry or humour: I could not imagine him smiling. His responses had a deadening effect, in that he disposed of ideas rather than developing them. It might be that he had little time for social exchanges in general or that he found me personally uninteresting – a possibility I resented. I stifled an impulse to strike him a blow to the guts that would double him over and compel him to take me seriously.

If Ogden was inscrutable his wife was not: the shifting expressions on her face provided a commentary upon our scanty verbal gestures. From old acquaintanceship I knew how to read them. She was by turns amused, mocking or indulgent in her responses to her husband's remarks, but I had had no sense of fondness. How could this mercurial woman endure the company of so sluggish a man?

Nevertheless I was losing heart as our little conference began to flag. It seemed that I would gain no ground. Help came from an unexpected quarter: a smiling Mrs Kinsey appeared, and greeted me most warmly. Ogden immediately made an excuse for departure, claiming that he had a meeting to attend, and I was left with Sarah and her aunt.

This unexpected situation might have produced embarrassment had not Mrs Kinsey's cheerfulness carried all before it. She was as talkative as Ogden had been taciturn, falling into a vein of raillery I had quite forgotten, although it had been familiar to me as a boy: 'Here's a strange situation. When did we three last talk together? It must have been two years ago – two years and more – in our house in Pitman Street. But when did we last talk in the open air? There's a question for you. I say, not since we all lived in York and were walking by the river one Sunday afternoon, with a great wind blowing. You had a cheerful face, Mr Fenwick, because you were soon to leave for the university; and Sarah yours was as long, for the same reason.'

Sarah made to interpose, but her aunt was scampering in a new direction: 'We were interrupted – our conversation was interrupted. Who was it now? I can see his yellow face – that dreary fellow who worked at the Cathedral.'

'Surely not the archbishop?' suggested Sarah.

'No, no, you foolish girl. Perhaps a canon or deacon or some such thing. A yellow face and a big lower lip.'

'Mr Donaldson!' cried Sarah.

'Of course,' said I. 'It comes back to me. The wind blew his wig away, and I had to retrieve it.'

We were all three laughing, attracting curious glances from the passers-by.

'And to see the two of you now—' exclaimed Mrs Kinsey. 'Nay, to see the three of us, passing for elegant gentlefolk. But I know better!'

'My dear aunt, you are talking nonsense,' said Sarah. 'Here is Mr Fenwick with a frilled shirt, a velvet jacket and a sword – every inch a London gentleman.'

'And here you see Mrs Ogden,' said I, 'a picture of

elegance in her white dress and blue cloak. Kings would fall at her feet.'

'They would do so in vain,' said Sarah, 'because Mr Ogden would remove them.'

She and her aunt both laughed at this.

'Mr Ogden would protect you to the last,' said Mrs Kinsey.

'Unless he were in Amsterdam, or immersed in one of his projects.'

Again the two laughed, with shared understanding, while I smiled politely.

We conversed a little longer, in this same affable spirit, until I broke off, on the pretext that I, too, had an appointment. The chance meeting had gone so well that I wished to make the most of it by leaving on warm terms. Sarah gave me a parting glance of such friendliness as almost to confuse me.

I strode away elated. Mrs Kinsey's cheerful garrulity had instantly permitted me the very thing I had wished for, an amicable encounter with Sarah. We had briefly talked just in the old way. Surely I had regained much of the ground lost at our last meeting? She had even made a disparaging remark at her husband's expense. A light-hearted one, certainly, but could she have made *any* such comment in my presence without thinking how it might be construed – especially given that I had just spent ten minutes in the man's torpid company?

Strangely Mrs Kinsey's random reference to that autumn day in York had brought to life some pleasant recollections that I had long suppressed. Sarah and I had a shared past out of which, for good or ill, my present character had grown. I needed to be close to her again. Mr Gilbert's promptings were neither here nor there.

❧

My dear Godfather,

It is some little time since the town was purged of its accumulated dust and dirt by a thunderstorm of Old Testament ferocity. I can breathe deep once more, and my energy returns. I look about me with restored curiosity. As I came out of Grey's Coffee House this morning I found myself staring at a chimney-boy across the street. He was waiting for his master, as I assumed, and seemed listlessly unaware of his surroundings. I could study him, without impertinence, as Mr Yardley might study a beetle. He was so blackened by his labours, from head to foot, that I found it difficult to construe him, even when I crossed the road to examine him more closely. I took him to be eight or nine years of age, but he might have been a stunted twelve-year-old. One sleeve of his soot-caked shirt had been torn away, revealing great calluses on his elbow. I spoke to him, and his eyes turned towards me, white in his black face, but he said nothing. When I offered him a shilling he seized it and hid it in his clothing, but still neither spoke nor smiled. The poor child seemed less alert and intelligent than some dogs I have known, hardly more than a living flue-brush. As I left him his master appeared. No doubt within a few minutes the boy would once more have been embedded in stifling soot. I was haunted by thoughts of him for the rest of the day. How long can this creature have to live? What pleasures, if any, will those few years offer?

I saw Crocker some weeks ago, but found him so distressed by the heat that I resolved not to call again until he had had ample time to recover his spirits. Within a week of the change in the weather I was pleased to receive a note from him:

Mr Thomas Crocker is surprised, if not downright offended, to have seen nothing lately of Mr Richard Fenwick. A visit from that gentleman tomorrow afternoon would go some way towards stemming the rising tide of Mr Crocker's resentment.

When I duly made my way to Wyvern Street I found Crocker at ease once more, resplendently huge in a white silk shirt.

'When last you saw me,' said he, 'I was laid low – a pitiful sight.'

He adopted the declamatory mode:
'Thus some vast whale, once monarch of the seas,
Lies meanly sprawled on Norway's barren shore,
In fatal exile from the element
That lent him life and power.'
'But now you are afloat once more?'
'More than that: I am wallowing and spouting. The builders have gone, and you see me master of a completed house.'

Certainly much had been done since my last visit. In my experience a handsome face and graceful appearance will often disguise a commonplace disposition. Crocker *may be physically an oddity, but in his home an intriguing personality is everywhere displayed, refracted into furnishings and paintings, colours and patterns. I have seen London houses designed to display, like a museum, the owner's numerous possessions; by contrast Crocker has devised a comfortable space to inhabit. Ornaments and pictures are few but – to my untrained eye – of high quality. The walls are pale and plain, curtains and hangings strongly coloured. Sunlight pours in through tall windows to bring everything within to shining life. This is the brightest, least cluttered house I have visited in London.*

I asked Crocker what had become of the Hogarth portraits.

'A gentleman should not seem self-concerned,' he said. 'I have concluded that they are a private joke, and have accordingly banished them upstairs.'

When I remarked upon the light he responded eagerly.

'Being prone to melancholy I dislike gloom of all kinds, and can feel hemmed in by curtains and shadows. Your acquaintance, Mr Ogden, was of great service to me. He has a keen awareness of the times and angles at which light will enter this or that aperture, and the skill to transmit it onwards from room to room, by means of archways, internal windows and artfully-placed mirrors.'

Unwilling as I was to hear the man praised I could not but assent to Crocker's opinion concerning his achievement here. I tried to learn more.

'Did he talk to you about his strange craft?'

'I could scarcely wring a sentence from him on any

topic but the task in hand,' said Crocker. 'He's a queer slab of humanity, quite lost in his work. He paces the floors, squints around corners, calculates angles . . . But he can be insistent: he had me enlarge a window, put in a skylight, and shift my chandeliers. In every case his advice was justified by the result. As a gesture of thanks I not only paid his bill but bought a diamond from him.'

'I assume that each of his trades informs the other?' said I.

'Exactly so. I had scarcely considered the matter before, but diamonds are abjectly dependent on light. In a dungeon a diamond would be useless to you, unless to scratch the Lord's Prayer on a drinking glass.'

'Will you wear this jewel on your person?' I asked.

'My person is striking enough, without such adornment. No, the diamond, now a pendant, was my gift to a young lady whom I believe you have met.'

'That is a handsome present indeed. Do we talk of Jane Page?'

'We do.'

I had heard of this attachment from Nick Horn.

'What drew you together?'

'This is a lady of beauty and character. As for her side of the affair, who can say? She speaks well of my wit. And she may know something of my financial circumstances.'

'And accordingly she has enjoyed lively talk and one of Mr Ogden's diamonds.'

We were both grinning now, but by no means jeering.

*It pleased me to see that his complacency was that of a
man with a new lover rather than a new mistress.*

*'I have made yet another friend,' said Crocker, 'whom
you can meet forthwith.'*

*We went out to the courtyard, where he led me to a
long cage. Perched high in a corner, on a bare tree-branch,
was a diminutive monkey. When Crocker approached it
climbed slowly down and hung opposite his face,
peering out with bright round eyes.*

*'Francis Pike bought it from a sailor at Knott's
Market,' said Crocker. 'He thought it would entertain me,
and so it does.'*

'What was its native country?'

*'Pike could not say: the sailor who sold it was too lost
in liquor to deal in such niceties. I have christened him
Trinculo.'*

*I looked at the little animal intently. 'He is something
of a miniature human-being, especially about the face and
hands.'*

*'You are right; and for that reason I credit him with
thought and feeling. Perhaps fancifully I see him
sorrowful, mischievous or bored.'*

*The creature turned to me, with a derisive grimace
that made me laugh.*

'Do you ever let him out?'

'At least once a day,' said Crocker.

*He opened a small gate, at head height. Trinculo
emerged, and with a deft spring landed on Crocker's
shoulder. He made himself comfortable, with one small
hand clasping the curls of his master's wig.*

'It is a favourite perch of his,' said Crocker. 'As yet, I am glad to say, he has neither bitten me nor pissed upon me.'

When he returned Trinculo to its cage the creature leaped around and around it, jumping and swinging with extraordinary agility. Having completed this performance he sat on a branch and smirked at us.

'The poor wretch has been shipped across oceans,' said Crocker. 'He will never see his home again. The lost Gulliver will live and die in Brobdingnag.'

As we returned to the house he remarked that he had heard from Miss Page that I was acquainted with her friend Kitty Brindley.

'Both she and Jane,' said he, 'are shortly to appear in Love at a Distance, *and I am advised that Miss Brindley will win all hearts as Lydia Lark. We must surely attend on the opening night and dine with the ladies afterwards.'*

I hope these inconsequential recollections may be of some slight interest—

By this point in my letter I felt that I was wading through clay. My godfather would expect substantial news concerning Sarah, yet here was mere chatter. I was hemmed in by symmetrical difficulties. I had nothing new to report but a brief conversation. Less obviously, while I felt that the meeting in the Park had given me fresh hope I was unwilling to tell Gilbert why. I could not do so without disclosing feelings that I wished to keep to myself. Puzzled, I pushed my pen aside.

Distraction was provided by the arrival of Matt Cullen, who walked up and down the room grinning and rubbing his hands.

'What has roused you?' I asked.

'Today,' said he, 'I saw the Duke and at last spoke out. "Enough, dotard!" I told him. "Enough of empty smiles and false promises: I have cringed too long. Strike my name from your list of pitiful petitioners. I will make my own way in life." With that I swept out.'

He stopped his pacing and looked at me. 'How do you like my story?'

'I like it so well,' I said, 'that I wish I could believe it.'

'So do I,' said Matt. 'But one day it may come true: I feel my manhood boiling within, only just below the level of speech. Meanwhile – and hence this visit – I have done you a useful service. I have information concerning the life and character of Walter Ogden.'

I sat up at attention. 'How did this come about?'

'I will tell you.' Matt threw himself into a chair. 'I have again encountered Mr John Gow, who works for Ogden. He is a good witness in that he has no great fault to find with Ogden as an employer, and so has no cause to lie. But he seems to have little liking for him.'

'How did you explain your interest?'

'I said that I was slightly acquainted with the woman Ogden has married – which is literally true. Gow made no further inquiry.'

'And what did you learn?'

'Ogden was the only child of an English diamond merchant and his Dutch wife. He was but twenty when his father died, leaving him to take charge of the business. His mother returned to Amsterdam, where he regularly visits her.'

'Then he has few relatives in this country?'

'I think none.'

'But as to character – what are his tastes, his vices and virtues?'

'There is little to learn, according to Gow. Ogden is esteemed an honest man, but seems to have few friends. No vices were mentioned: he drinks little, and neither gambles nor whores. There was surprise at his sudden marriage.'

'What of his pleasures?'

'He will go to the theatre – sometimes to a concert.'

'Then what, in God's name, keeps the fellow moving and breathing? What prises him out of bed in the morning?'

Matt raised a finger.

'Mr Gow said something on that score. Apparently your friend has become absorbed by the topic of light, and the distribution of light, within doors – a field of endeavour in which there would seem to be little competition. He has an interest also in colour and design. His ambition is to do for the interiors of great houses what Spence and Brown have done for the gardens outside them. There lies his master passion. Three or four men of consequence have already made use of his services. He may have it in him to found a new profession.'

'Meanwhile,' said I. 'Can he satisfy the needs of his wife?'

'A gross question,' said Matt, grinning again. 'Who knows what those needs may be? But I have not done, and I have saved the best till last. Ogden is about to make one of his visits to Amsterdam. And the ingenious Cullen extracted further particulars. Ogden travels on Friday next, and will be away for a week. He will leave for Harwich by the morning coach and then take ship for Rotterdam.'

~~~

The opening performance of *Love at a Distance* amply fulfilled Jane Page's predictions. Johnston's comedy had made little impression when originally presented, but this revival found unexpected life in it, and the audience were soon roaring approval. Miss Page played Miss Melville, the heroine, with her usual elegance, but it was Kitty, as the country girl, Lydia Lark, who presided over the evening. She invested a trite comic role with a humour hard to describe. Speaking artlessly she yet managed to convey, by small drolleries of voice or facial expression, that she knew just what she was about, and was relishing her own ingenuous flourishes – as when composing a letter to her cousin in the country:

> *'You will hardly believe me, dear coz, but yesterday I took tea with a beau whose leg was skinny as a chicken's, and his wig so monstrous great that it would stuff two chairs or a sofa at home in Tapperton . . .*
>
> *I can't but giggle to see how the fine ladies of London paint their faces white as a corpse. If 'tis true, as I have been told, that they do so to hide their blushes they must have great cause to be bashful.'*

There were shouts and whistles at the close, and flowers were flung on to the stage. Given my prior claim to Kitty, I found myself both proud and proprietorial. Who were these impudent fellows making so free with their plaudits?

Crocker had made good his undertaking that after the performance we would meet the leading actresses. The ladies were in the best of spirits, exalted by their triumph. Manifestly they were true friends, Miss Page rejoicing in Kitty's more obvious success. It appeared also that she felt genuine affection for Tom Crocker: the two were very easy together.

I was gratified to find that Kitty still appeared to regard me with favour, although having received little from me for some time, beyond a brief note or two. I did my best to explain away that neglect and seem worthy of a loyalty that I had scarcely earned.

We spoke of the evening at Vauxhall, at which we had all been present, and Crocker announced that he himself planned to host a masquerade to inaugurate his new home. Later, to unanimous approval, he suggested that we four should make an expedition along the Thames to Richmond the following week.

☙

Before concluding the letter to Gilbert I reviewed my situation, heartened by what I had learned from Matt. I could surely turn Ogden's absences in Amsterdam to account.

But doubts remained. Hurlock I could see through, and see around: there was nothing to him but empty bluster and an over-charged stomach. By contrast in Ogden there was something I could not reach: he was as alien to me as Crocker's frisking monkey. I resented his capacity to keep some essential aspect of his nature hidden. But this secret self, if there was one, would in due course be cuckolded along with the rest of him.

In a different vein of thought I wondered how I could reconcile my intentions concerning Sarah with my renewed interest in Miss Brindley. I fell back once more upon the comfortable theory that I was inhabiting two distinct narratives. The affair with Kitty was a sub-plot, a matter of physical pleasure merely. She well understood the limited scope of our unwritten contract. My *essential* undertaking, to lead me who could tell where, was the conquest of Sarah. And *there*, principles would surely come into play.

Yet I felt twinges still. What the devil was I about? Could I lay claim to any sort of morality at all? Which of the ten commandments was I still willing to observe? At least I had no mother or father to honour, felt no interest in false gods, had no need to steal, and no intention to kill. And surely the man – at any rate the young man – who habitually kept all ten of the commandments would be both less and more than human?

Returning to my letter I left the last sentence incomplete and reported, half-truthfully, that I had been interrupted at that point by a visitor. The individual in question (it seemed advisable not to name Matt, given my godfather's curious warning) had proved, by chance, to be an acquaintance of Ogden, and had remarked that he was next week to visit Amsterdam. I would try to use this opportunity to call at the Ogdens' house, talk with Sarah, and learn more about her circumstances and her mood.

Meanwhile I had once more seen Miss Brindley – who had indeed made a great impression in her latest role – and hoped to be able to report in my very next letter on a warm resumption of our former intimacies.

By way of a postscript I remarked that I hoped Mrs Hurlock continued well. I also inquired solicitously about Yardley's leg and Mrs Quentin's teeth. Having been in doubt as to what story to tell in my letters, I found it a relief to instigate a humdrum *dialogue*, however fragmentary, and thereby perhaps regain a foothold in ordinary epistolary commerce.

15

My dear Richard,

It became as intolerably hot here as you say it did in
London. Our streams dried to nothing. The thirsty cattle
were plagued with flies. Nor was it comfortable within
doors: I found myself tetchy, restless, sleeping but fitfully
and puzzled by senseless dreams. It seems that the
weather can influence even a sleeping mind.

Here, too, oppressive heat was followed by mighty
precipitations: rivers burst their banks, and Elstone Lake
doubled in size. Our roads became impassable for a time.
Safe on my hill I did not greatly care: the air was cool
once more, and my spirits revived.

You ask about Mrs Hurlock. I have seen her several
times since your return to London. She has twice
remarked to me how much she enjoyed our musical
evening, on both occasions adding that she hoped it would
not be the last of its kind. I think we may fairly claim, if
only to one another, that the first of our experiments was

a signal success: we concocted perhaps the most vivid experience of the lady's life. I have an impression that she has even gained some slight advantage in her relations with Mr Hurlock. She appears more assured, while he has been uneasy of late, perhaps humbled by financial difficulties.

Mrs Hurlock was in urgent need of what we provided for her. I well understand that in the case of Mrs Ogden no such immediate conquest can be expected. The husband would seem to be both uxorious and forceful. However, I may be able to offer assistance. On a visit to Newbridge I learned that Lord Downs is contemplating renovations to Holbrook Hall. When I repeated your account of the work of Mr Ogden he expressed no little interest. At my suggestion he wrote him a letter of inquiry, which you will find sealed inside this epistle. I assured him that you would pass it on. You therefore have an excuse for visiting Mr Ogden's home. If he pursues the opportunity, of course, he must spend time in Newbridge . . .

Yardley is recovering and can get about a little. I learned this from Thorpe, who also brought me news of a disturbing kind. It seems that Quentin has disappeared. He left his house two days ago, saying that he needed a long walk. Apparently he was accustomed to such solitary excursions. On this occasion, however, he did not return and there has been no further news of him. It is to be hoped that he has not come to harm.

I have been musing again on the extent to which the pastoral ideal, in its various guises, is invoked to dignify our animal appetites. Unwilling to admit that we couple like dogs or horses, we proclaim an artificial iridescence. Do our most exalted invitations to love amount to more than the howling of wolves or the bellowing of bulls? Even the preliminary outcome is an animal one: mouths are pressed together.

Unfortunately reflections of this cast tend towards an all-consuming scepticism or cynicism. Does not the rhetoric of the Christian faith relate to human life at large as does the poetry of love to fornication? In either case a higher significance is boasted, by no means deducible from the physical facts. If my comparison is just, the post-coitus disappointments you experienced with Miss Brindley foreshadow post-mortem annihilation.

I tell myself that I should shun such aridities of thought – such inability, despite all the claims of poets and theologians, to see beyond animal explanations. As yet, inexplicably, but perhaps fortunately, this habit of conjecture has failed to diminish my interest in the human appetites and activities that it belittles. I look forward to further news of your dealings with Miss Brindley and Mrs Ogden. They may tell us something about human nature in general, and the female constitution in particular. Will that at last amount to merely a roguish chapter in Peregrine Pickle *or to a whole novel by Mr Richardson?*

I remain, &c.

My dear Godfather,
You raise certain abstract issues which I may take up at a later date. For the moment I will stay with

practicalities. The letter from Lord Downs may indeed prove useful. I shall put the matter to the test and will let you know the result.

Although I had been confidently assured that yesterday would be the day of Ogden's departure, I was resolved to leave nothing to chance. I made my way to Gracechurch Street and lingered outside the Spread Eagle, near the departure point for Harwich. I was soon rewarded by the sight of Ogden alighting from a chair to join the travellers. To be doubly certain I stayed until the coach rattled away. As it did so I enjoyed a pang of excitement: horses, wheels and wind were kindly combining to waft my rival to another country, leaving the coast clear.

I will wait for a day or two: it might help my case if Sarah becomes a little bored with solitude. But rest assured that I shall soon be knocking at the Ogdens' front door.

I shall write again shortly, with an account of that visit. Meanwhile I must hope that your next letter brings more encouraging news concerning Mr Quentin.

I remain, &c.

I extracted this missive from a longer record in my Journal. It had been written with Gilbert in mind, but in the event I omitted the latter part as being of more interest to myself than to him. It described my doings following Ogden's departure.

I was so dressed (I thought) as to be able to move unnoticeably through mercantile or maritime London. Here was a chance for another exploration: I felt a desire to breathe a different air – even a different stench. Accordingly I made my way through Houndsditch and the Minories towards the warehouses, docks and countless bristling masts of Wapping.

Turning the corner I found myself in a teeming market of a kind I had never seen before. There was a singular contrast between the shabbiness of sellers and customers and the exotic nature of the goods on display. I saw cutlasses and daggers, pelts, masks, fans, ornaments of ivory and stone. One corner offered some unfamiliar livestock, including small birds, parrots, snakes, tortoises, and even a bear-cub in a cage. In its diversity the place was like a fashionable auction house pushed out of doors. It came to me that I was in Knott's Market, where Pike had bought Trinculo.

I drifted from stall to stall, thinking to make a purchase or two. After some desultory bargaining I secured, as a possible gift for Kitty Brindley, a necklace of red stones, said to come from India. I was examining a brass pistol when I heard a murmur from behind: 'Take care of your pockets, sir.' I turned to see Pike himself, in shabby hat and drab clothes.

He led me out of the market and down a narrow alley to the World's End Inn, a shabby wooden construction by the river, and a great resort of sailors. We sat drinking beer by an open window, and I was glad of the air it admitted, for the crowded room was fogged by tobacco smoke. Pike could have passed as a regular customer – which for all I knew he might have been. I am not sure that I can capture the singular quality of our conversation. When he is not talking his face is without expression, showing no trace of response to what has been said. Yet he may then abruptly speak out, sometimes with blunt eloquence.

'I saw you in the market, sir, and thought I should warn you. It can be dangerous.'

'Because of pickpockets?'

'Pickpockets, robberies, skirmishes . . . As for the market, the goods aren't always to be trusted. I once saw a unicorn for sale here.'

'A unicorn?'

'So they called it – a small pony or some such, with a horn grafted into its skull. It would soon have been dead.'

'Did the poor creature find a buyer?'

'Immediately. Folk gladly pay money for magic.'

'But who could devise such a vile thing?'

'Someone wanting money.'

He implied no moral judgement. Here was a man at home in a world of which I knew nothing: he had earned the right to his opinions or lack of them.

'You are a regular visitor to these parts, Mr Pike?'

'I am, sir. There are genuine curiosities to be found here, and I sometimes deal in such things.'

He gestured towards the window, before breaking into the longest speech I had yet heard from him.

'Look behind you, sir. What do you see? That's a second London there on the water – merchant ships for mile upon mile. Goods from every part of the world. So there'll be thefts and bribes and leakages. The spillage runs into Knott's Market.'

'You called it a dangerous place.'

'So it is.' He looked at me appraisingly. 'You're a sturdy

young gentleman; but you could be knocked on the head for your purse. A visitor here is seen as fair game.'

'They would know me as a visitor?'

Pike gestured again, this time towards the crowded room in front of me.

'Faces brown from the weather. Yours is white. You're taller than most here and you walk upright, not like a seaman or a snatch. You have your teeth still. Your clothes are plain, but they don't look used. There's no hiding the fact, sir: you're a gentleman.'

'Is that a compliment?'

'No sir, not in Wapping.'

Amused, if nettled, to learn that my attempts at disguise had been so unconvincing, I glanced at the man's face – battered, watchful, independent.

'Mr Pike, you are an unusual fellow.'

He considered my words. 'In gentlemanly society that may be the case. You would find plenty like me in the army, or at sea.'

'How came it that you met Mr Crocker?'

'I was working in a tavern. Mr Crocker happened to be visiting when I had to put a stop to a little disturbance. We had a conversation, and he took me into his employment.'

I took a risk: 'Might I inquire, Mr Pike – and by all means refuse to answer if you think me impertinent – in what capacity did he employ you?'

'There's no name for what I do. I'm part body-guard, part practical assistant.'

'Do you enjoy the work?'

'Mr Crocker pays me well and treats me well. And I like

to have a foot in a different world. I was interested to see the gentlemanly side of life.'

Intrigued by the hint of derision I asked, 'What other sides of life have you seen?'

'A number,' said Pike, equably. 'I've worked with cattle; I was two years in the army and four on board ship. I was a thief for a time, and a successful one.'

He drank more beer, then leaned forward to address me with a new directness.

'Here we sit, Mr Fenwick, chatting on easy terms in the company of sailors, robbers and receivers. Most of Mr Crocker's friends would find this surprising.'

'I have a taste for fresh experiences.'

'I could guess as much, sir.' He paused, as though deciding whether to say more. 'To me you stood out among Mr Crocker's acquaintances for two reasons. One was that you liked him, and didn't seek his company for the joke of it.'

I met his gaze, nodding to show that I shared the misgivings he had hinted.

'And the other?'

'At your own level you're an adventurer, as I am myself.'

'Then is *that* a compliment, Mr Pike?'

'It's as you take it, sir.'

His tone being studiously neutral I was left to react. I could have laughed off the imputation, or rebuked it as an impertinence. In the event I did neither.

'Compliment or not, Mr Pike, I think your opinion may be just.'

Unexpectedly he offered an interpretation of what he had said: 'The times are changing, in wars and in politics. But

257

most men live in the past – live as they were reared. Only a few move with the changes. Mr Crocker does, and so do you.'

'And you yourself?'

'Oh yes. I've had no choice.'

I raised my glass, and in this dirty riverside tavern we drank a wordless toast in beer. We talked a little longer before my new friend, if such I may consider him, went about his business and I returned to Westminster by way of the Tower, Thames Street and the Strand.

❧

At the Ogdens' house I was informed by a servant that Mr Ogden was away. Affecting disappointment I asked her to tell her mistress that Mr Fenwick had called with a possible commission for her husband. Since he was absent, could she spare me a few moments so that I could pass on my message? My godfather's key duly opened the lock: in three minutes I was received by Sarah in a bright drawing-room.

I knew that the first step towards making a good impression would be to avoid making a bad one. Accordingly I spoke with detached courtesy, as though taking part in a play. My task was the simpler in that I knew Sarah's responses in advance. I had seen her husband's work (I reminded her) in Mr Crocker's house, and mentioned it to my godfather, who had shown great interest – hence the proposition I had been asked to pass on. Would Mr Ogden be here tomorrow? Away for a week? In Amsterdam? So her mother-in-law was Dutch? How interesting. Given the circumstances, might I leave the written inquiry with her, since I had nothing to add to it myself, being no more than an intermediary?

This was easily agreed. As I had hoped, the sealed missive from Lord Downs served as a safe-conduct, clearing me from suspicion. My readiness to hand it over no doubt also served to dispose of any fears of importunity on my part: my task done, I would soon depart.

However, as we exchanged courtesies, a reference to Mr Ogden's work in his own home led Sarah to show me some of the rooms. To prolong the episode I expressed great interest in all I saw, although the truth was that I was uncertain as to my own reaction. The effects I had admired in Crocker's house were here carried further. It seemed to me that the furnishings and decorative materials had all been selected as contributions to patternings of light and colour. Glass was much in evidence, whether formed into windows or mirrors, or fragmented into sparkling prismatic chandeliers. In one or two places a large round lens had been built into a wall or partition, as a window affording a distorted view of the room beyond. There was an absence of gilding, carvings, brackets, pillars, busts, portraits or effusive decorations of any kind. All was plain and transparent, save in two or three places where small lozenges of stained glass shone blue, green or red. It seemed ironic that all this clarity should have been created by a man of a character so closed and windowless.

As we walked from room to room I fancied that Sarah was watching my reactions with a quizzical eye. Her intelligence was not to be under-estimated: I might well lose credit equally by being too critical or too emptily complimentary. I made some little show of looking about appraisingly from a variety of vantage-points.

'The effect is remarkable,' I hazarded. 'It confirms the opinions I formed at Mr Crocker's house. Your husband has a strong, clear taste of an unusual kind.'

'Do you approve it?'

'I do indeed. But I fear it may be ahead of the times. When decoration and disguise are so much in fashion there is a fear of such clarity. It sheds too candid a light on the paint, powder and false hair that we see in fashionable gatherings.' I ventured a compliment: 'But Mr Ogden's wife has nothing to fear in this respect.'

'Nothing as yet,' said Sarah.

She smiled, and I smiled in response, both of us at ease. We had achieved the mood I had hoped for; and I was eager to sustain it. Sarah herself assisted me: 'Will you take tea, Mr Fenwick?'

'That would be most agreeable.'

We returned to the drawing-room that glowed with honey-coloured morning light. I was at pains to observe every formality of deportment as maid-servants came and went. I could not dramatically advance my campaign on this visit, but an ill-judged gesture could undermine it. My immediate aims were merely to further ingratiate myself and to learn something of the Ogdens' daily life. I spoke again as one making polite conversation: 'Do you often entertain here?'

'Very infrequently. Mr Ogden is not fond of large gatherings.' She smiled again. 'Perhaps it is as well: you know that I have had little experience of playing the hostess.'

'But I suspect that you have the necessary skills, as by instinct.'

'Your suggestion is kind, but I am not convinced.'

I made a bolder move: 'Some weeks ago I saw you and your husband at the theatre.'

'I saw you, too – in a box.'

'It did not seem appropriate to bow.'

'And why not, Mr Fenwick?'

I chose my words: 'At your aunt's house your last remarks seemed – dismissive.'

The tea was brought in at that moment, and the interruption gave us both time to consider. When Sarah resumed it was with a new directness and informality: 'I was delivering a prepared speech, like something in a novel. Who can live daily life at that level of formality? And who would want to?'

She spoke as one offering a kind of apology. It seemed necessary to respond with similar directness.

'I was ill at ease myself. I had come to visit an old friend, and found a woman transformed.'

'I *was* a woman transformed. A year previously I had been the Sarah Kinsey whom you knew. Suddenly a new path was laid open before me. I could take it, or continue my gentle stroll to nowhere. In taking it I knew that I had to learn new modes of behaviour.'

Here was an opportunity to seek information. I contrived a tone of casual politeness: 'How did you chance to meet Mr Ogden?'

Sarah hesitated – then laughed and blushed simultaneously. 'You are almost the only person I could tell. We met in the most embarrassing of circumstances. My aunt and I had fallen upon hard times. She felt obliged to sell a diamond ring she had inherited, but knew not how to do so. On her behalf, and quite timorously, as you may imagine, I made inquiries at a shop I had seen in Duke Street, and found myself talking to Mr Ogden. He was very helpful to us.'

'And from that time onwards . . .?'

'From that time onwards Mr Ogden became an acquaintance, a friend – and then a persistent suitor.'

I felt that I could be playful. 'Did he woo you with diamonds?'

'No,' said Sarah, emphatically – but then laughed again, as though enjoying this freedom to be frank. 'Not directly. But Mr Ogden wished to be kind to me, and was wealthy enough to be very kind indeed.'

We exchanged smiles, and then sipped tea, both, I think, wondering where that last remark had taken us. I spoke again at random: 'Have you a new circle of friends?'

'Of acquaintances, rather. My closest friend is still Miss Martin, whom you will remember from our days in York. We regularly correspond.'

'I find it hard to imagine your new life.'

I made the remark without thought, but it produced a sudden silence. When Sarah did respond, she spoke seriously: 'I cannot easily describe it. Mr Ogden's work takes up much of his time. When he is away I read, I write letters – I see my aunt almost daily . . .'

'Do you pay no visits?'

'Very few. Perhaps that situation will change with time.'

She spoke as one closing a topic. 'Let me ask in turn: how is the mysterious Mr Gilbert?'

'He remains mysterious. Perhaps my life is a little like your own in that I am well provided for, but waiting for something more to happen.'

Feeling that I might have taken a step too far I quickly changed course: 'It is taking me some little time to find my bearings in London.'

'Perhaps it seems tame after your continental adventures?'

I was pleased, rather than otherwise, to note an edge of irony in Sarah's words: we were conversing personally rather than formally. Before I could reply she said: 'What does your godfather expect of you?'

'As yet he encourages me simply to report to him on the pleasures of the town.'

'That does not sound an arduous task.' Sarah spoke dryly, but suddenly laughed. 'It is fantastical that you and I should be having such a conversation. Only a few years ago we were living modestly, or even meanly, in York.'

'Fate has been kind to us.'

'Fate in the form of money. We have been floated away to deep waters. Where shall we be heading next?'

She laughed again, but a little nervously. For a second time she was blushing. I could see her with a double eye, at once as the settled wife of a prosperous merchant and as little more than an inexperienced girl from the north who had known in an affectionate way only two men, of whom I was one. And now my presence had brought the blood into her cheeks.

To my surprise, even to my consternation, I was seized

by a pang of lust that altered my body and made me shift in my seat. I had to have this woman, or rather both these women. At one mighty coupling I could re-visit my lost childhood and take revenge on the squat tradesman who had usurped me. The impulse was so strong that I could have seized her there and then. I had just enough mastery of myself to accept that I had achieved enough for one day. Taking her words, fatuously enough, as a cue I said: 'At this moment, I fear, I must hoist sail for the Strand: I am to meet my friend Mr Chalmers.'

We parted with the normal courtesies, but the tone on both sides was of a warmth to imply expectation of another meeting. I went away in high spirits, not to visit the fictitious Mr Chalmers but to return to Cathcart Street.

If a single phrase could have expressed my feelings it would have been a jubilant 'She is vulnerable'. Ogden had provided her with money – but what else? It seemed that she had few friends, or even acquaintances. To whom could she express herself, in whom could she confide? Only, it seemed, her aunt. In the half an hour, or less, that we had spent together she was already speaking to me almost as in former days, already skirting indiscretion. I needed only to proceed as I had begun and she would be mine.

❧

I invited Matt Cullen to dinner so that we could discuss the changing situation. As we devoured chicken pie I showed him the letter from Mr Gilbert and described what had passed between me and Sarah.

264

'Where is the difficulty?' he asked. 'Your desires and opportunities are in equilibrium. You copulate and describe doing
so. Then, as a reward, you inherit an estate.'

'You are a gross animal, Cullen, and cannot see the indelicacy of prostituting one's deepest feelings.'

'Pooh,' said he. 'You are making difficulties where none
exist. Here' (he drew a line on the table with his finger) 'is
your planned ravishment of Mrs Ogden. There' (he drew
another line a few inches away) 'is the account you send to
your godfather. Bar a few names and places the tale you tell
him can be a complete fiction.'

'But the old glutton will expect *regular* reports for his
money.'

'Then make the story last. Slice it thin. Feed it to him in
ounces.'

He took a large forkful of chicken pie, grinning at the
contrast.

'Do you think he will be content with an invalid's diet?'

'You must use your skill as a cook: give him sauce to go
with the meat.'

'What kind of sauce?'

'Several kinds. He will relish physical detail. The lady will
blush, her hand will touch yours, her bosom will heave.
There can be weeks of such morsels before you reach beneath
her skirts.'

'That is well, if crudely, said. You saw that Gilbert
mentioned *Clarissa*?'

'Just so,' cried Matt. 'There is your model. If Lovelace
extracts a blush from his captive virgin he writes a twenty-
page letter. Follow his example.'

'I could do something of that sort. But my difficulty goes deeper.'

'What difficulty?'

'The following contradiction.' I drank some wine to help me pin down the paradox: 'Mr Gilbert wishes to taste, vicariously, the fleshly pleasures he has missed – but in order to be reassured that they would have disappointed him. Does he see himself as inferior, because he was deficient in animal desires, or superior, because he rose above them?'

Matt frowned. 'From what you have told me, I would say both.'

'Exactly. You have it. *There* lies the difficulty.'

'I see a difficulty for Gilbert; but why for you?'

'If I fail to do the deed he may think I have no more potency than himself.'

'So you must succeed.'

'If I do he may think me a slave to appetite – a lecher with no philosophy in him.'

Matt groaned. 'Life is full of contradictions. Your course is clear. Enjoy the woman but tell your godfather you did not. Take Mrs Ogden and take the money.'

&

My dear Godfather,

I had expected to be describing my visit to Mrs Ogden. However I have postponed that meeting for a day since I wish to be at my liveliest when I see her, and this morning finds me depleted following the energetic encounter with Miss Brindley that will provide the main topic for this letter.

As you acknowledge, the case of Sarah Ogden is quite unlike that of Mrs Hurlock. She is young, innocent, newly married and of considerable intelligence – there is a mind to be seduced. Hence the need for patience and contrivance. I must hint at pleasures which (as I believe) the squat Ogden cannot provide her. At the same time I must discern possible causes of irritation, in hope of making infidelity seem a justified reprisal. Seeds of resentment and desire must be planted in the lady's mind, to grow as stealthily as fingernails.

A further consideration is that she and I, acquainted since childhood, have many shared recollections and associations which I will hope to invoke. I should be able to render her more susceptible by reaching back as Mr Ogden cannot.

I must again admit, perhaps ignobly, to a deep distaste for her husband's person and personality. Shackled to this sluggish dog Sarah is condemned to diminution. Her wit will droop, her curiosity subside. It seems a duty to take anticipatory revenge.

These observations perhaps bear upon some of the musings in your recent letter. It may well be that, for Mrs Hurlock, brute appetite is closely adjacent to 'pastoral' pretension. Surely, however, our impulses are often less simple. The rutting of animals cannot involve anticipation, reflection or memory, yet such awareness enhances human desires. When lust is combined with liking, jealousy, anger, curiosity, it becomes something greater. Am I not close, here, to your own views concerning the possibility of *Passions* working in conjunction? In some human couplings, I hope, the pleasure is more than merely physical: several kinds of gratification are simultaneously achieved, the effect being akin to a chord in music.

Your recent 'aridities of thought' perhaps discount these ancillaries as merely enabling the physical act. My hope is that in some liaisons at least they can be celebrated in the physical consummation and even become an aspect of it.

But perhaps I am by now above myself, and writing nonsense. Let me return to the earthier topic of my dealings with Kitty Brindley. Yesterday she and I, together with Crocker and his new mistress, Jane Page, went by river to Richmond. Miss Brindley has become a notable figure on the London stage, flattered and courted wherever she goes. I was intrigued to see how far this change in her reputation might have affected her disposition.

The alteration was marked. There was a new vanity, displayed in countless small ways. Whether standing or sitting she would strike an attitude, as though posing for a portrait. She was imperious with those who assisted her or waited upon her. By her manner she seemed to blame our host, Mr Crocker, for the damp weather that attended our little voyage: when obliged to take shelter from the rain she positively sulked. Over dinner, when the four of us were alone together, she was more agreeable, but still managed to imply obliviousness to the previous intimacies between her and myself. It was as though I were expected to pay court to her over again – and with no clear prospect of success.

I naturally wondered what would follow when evening came and, as arranged, we were to be alone together once more at the Full Moon inn. Perhaps she would seek to exercise her new-found authority by keeping me at arm's length. Perhaps I had already been usurped by some wealthier rival.

Sure enough, when our party broke up she professed herself tired, and demanded to be taken back to her own lodging in Rose Street instead of to the Full Moon. However, in anticipation of some such evasion I had a counter-strategy prepared. Seeming to acquiesce in her change of mind, I hired a hackney carriage and gave loud instructions to the coachman to take us to Rose Street. He set off in that direction, but by prior arrangement with me turned aside after the first mile and proceeded towards the inn. Since it was growing dark, and I had engaged Kitty in conversation, she did not at first realize what had been done. By the time she did so, and loudly protested, I gave a further signal to the coachman, who whipped up his horses and took us pell-mell the rest of the way.

When we arrived it was clearly in her mind to create something of an outcry. I was confident, however, that my determination and greater assurance would carry the day: if she expostulated she would not be believed. My expectation proved justified: I was able to hurry her into the inn, greet the landlord – who had seen us together before – and get her up the stairs to the room we had formerly occupied.

She upbraided me with fury, all but accusing me of

269

rape. I gave a calm reply: 'My dear Kitty, we have enjoyed pleasurable hours in this very bed. Since the last time we did so we have not had so much as a difference of opinion. I naturally assumed that your earlier refusal was no more than an affectation or a caprice.'

She glared – but I continued in equable vein: 'We have passed an agreeable day. I intend to enjoy further pleasures here tonight – pleasures in which I hope you will choose to be a sharer rather than a victim.'

Leaving her to digest my words I unconcernedly poured out some of the wine which I had ordered in advance. When I gave her a glass, however, she dashed it furiously from my hand. With no sign of anger I took a sip or two myself, regarding her with a smile, and then turned to set the glass down on the table.

'Do not dare to touch me!' she hissed, shrinking away.

By instinct I offered exactly the appropriate response. Firmly, but with no show of violence, I grasped her wrists and forced her back across the bed.

'It is time,' I said, holding her down, 'for the animal that is within you to be released.'

With that I wrenched her skirt up above her waist. She struggled and kicked, but in so doing succeeded only in further exposing her procreative parts. I passed my hand down her white belly and thrust it into her bush of black curls. She cried out again, but the cry subsided into a moan, which proved to be the signal of capitulation. When, a little later, I released her wrists she wrapped her arms around me and gave way to pleasure. Our earlier

270

conflict seemed to have inflamed us: we became almost
monstrous in our doings.

    How these exchanges bear upon my earlier
pronouncements in this letter I scarcely know. There is
much for me to explore and discover.

    I remain, &c.

The composition of this letter, which followed my visit to
Sarah but *preceded* the excursion to Richmond, proved a
laborious task. My idea was simply to offer my godfather
some tit-bits to occupy his attention. Whether I was sincere
in some, or any, of my general observations I scarcely knew.
Mr Gilbert seemed to have thought himself into a state of
detached yet prurient impotence mysterious to me. I could
do no more than toss a handful of speculative remarks in
the general direction of his predicament. The later paragraphs
were fabricated with no little self-disgust: I was ashamed to
be demeaning Kitty by these absurd fictions; but felt that I
had no choice.

✑

The weather being fine for our excursion to Richmond we
set out in the best of spirits. We were a party of five –
Crocker, myself, Pike, Jane and Kitty – or perhaps six, since
Pike brought Trinculo in a small cage. As we were proceeding
to the landing stage where the hired vessel was waiting, our
good mood was disrupted by an unfortunate incident. A
raw-boned boatman, one of a ragged group, cried out: 'Never
take the fat fellow – he'll sink you like a stone.' His friends

greeted the remark with raucous laughter. Crocker walked towards him, smiling. 'You're a scarecrow,' he said, 'but I like your humour.' Reaching into a pocket he pulled out a crown and tossed it to one side of the jester. As the rascal stooped eagerly to pick up the coin Crocker, with unexpected nimbleness, stepped forward and planted a great kick on his backside that sent him sprawling face forward in the dirt, with his head striking a post. The action was so sudden and violent as to produce a moment's silence. But as the fallen man struggled to his feet, with blood trickling down his face, there were angry shouts: I feared a skirmish. Pike put down the cage and stepped alongside me as though ready to do battle. Fortunately the injured man turned and slouched away, clutching his coin, while our own boatman came forward to shepherd us to our craft.

As we headed up river Crocker sat silent, his face darkly flushed: we could see that he was ashamed of what he had done. Jane tried to rally him: 'You are formidable,' said she. 'I will take care never to rouse your fury.'

'It was an ugly impulse,' said Crocker, gloomily. 'I am mortified.'

'Then you should not be,' said I. 'Such impudence is not to be borne.'

But it took an unexpected intervention from our boatman to raise Crocker's spirits.

'Never you mind, sir,' he called out. 'Ned Spratt won't bear a grudge. You overpaid him. He'd take two kicks in the breech for a shilling any day.'

These words wrung a smile from Crocker, and from that moment our expedition was an assured success. The sun was shining warmly, but a breeze filled our sail. We soon drew away from the city into cleaner water and clearer air, leaving the London stench behind us. Houses gave way to fields and meadows. There were bird-calls around us and the river chattered under our bows. The ladies raised light parasols to protect their complexions, but seemed enchanted by the blue skies and the gentle swaying of the boat. Moving between languid swans we followed the large curves of the Thames into quieter and quieter country till we were steered smoothly to our destination, a small landing stage near Richmond.

We were in the grounds of a riverside inn secured for our exclusive use. Crocker and I and the ladies, with Pike and Trinculo in attendance, climbed many steps to a high terrace, commanding a view across the Thames.

'I trust that you are all comfortable,' cried Crocker, when we were seated around a large table, 'and that Sol's scorching ray is sufficiently moderated by the soft zephyr that murmurs through the trees.'

Jane quoted drowsily: 'Phoebus is smiling on valley and hill.'

'Phoebus smiles,' said I to my neighbour, 'and so does Miss Brindley.'

Indeed she did: I had never seen her so vivacious. Now she spoke up saucily in her rustic vein: 'And well may I smile, zur – these are my native parts, and I be at ease here. I could make myself useful, so I could, and find employment while you fine gentlemen would starve. To be sure you could no more milk a cow than you could fly.'

'Would you not succour us?' cried Crocker. 'If you saw me wasted to a skeleton?'

Kitty haughtily tossed her head: 'I might zee fit to give 'ee a little bread and milk, if you was humble and begged it of me.'

Under the presiding eye of the tavern-keeper, maid-servants were bringing out food and wine. There could not have been a greater contrast with the crowded inn at Wapping where Pike and I had talked some days previously. We had a whole hill-side to ourselves, the wide vista before us seemingly provided for our private enjoyment. Our attendants were discreet almost to the point of invisibility. Pike had taken Trinculo from his cage and fastened him to a tree by a long silver chain. After some pert frisking, as though to attract our attention, the little creature settled on a branch and poked at its fur with probing fingers.

'Here on Richmond Hill,' said Crocker, 'we are at peace, far from mobs and Mohocks and impudent boatmen. Why did I quit the country for the town?'

'Because it can be damnably melancholy in winter,' I suggested.

'That is true. But London can be vicious at any season.' He turned to the ladies: 'Mr Fenwick here often wears a sword.'

Kitty affected a shudder: 'Have you killed many men?'

'Not one. I have drawn a little blood, and shed a little, too – but I lost more when a knife slipped as I was splitting a walnut. Mr Pike here could tell you about genuine combat.'

'Could you, Mr Pike?' cried Jane.

'By your leave, ma'am, I would prefer not to mention such things.'

'Mr Pike speaks wisely,' said Crocker. 'This is an enchanted space, far from all conflict.'

He was so cheerful that he smiled even as he ate. I noticed

again the understanding between him and Jane Page: there was a pleasant complicity in the glances they exchanged. Impressed by her discernment I tried to find out more about her, remarking that I had seen her on stage as Juno, as Ceres, and as Hermione.

'Such are my roles,' she said. 'I play the parts of queens and goddesses.'

'This is beyond coincidence,' said I. 'You must have innate qualities of majesty and divinity.'

'So I tell her,' cried Crocker. 'She draws upon her natural authority.'

Miss Page smiled: 'I thank you for your kind words, but you flatter me. I have but three aptitudes: I am tall, my voice is low, and I can be grave. Therefore on stage I cannot smile but must frequently kill myself. This habit fortunately discourages the gentlemen who try to take advantage of members of my profession.'

'I hope,' said Crocker, 'that you do not include myself or Mr Fenwick in that number.'

'By no means – otherwise I would have discouraged my innocent friend Miss Brindley from coming on such an expedition as this.'

'Have no fear,' replied Crocker. 'This is an idyll: no one can be disagreeable.'

'Methinks you have too much assurance, sir,' cried Kitty, in her rustic character. 'Though I am but a country wench I flatter myself that I can be as disagreeable as any fine lady in the town.'

'Then pray be merciful,' said I. 'We are gentlemen of delicacy, easily wounded.'

'As to that, sir, I will form my own judgement.'

Both women, happy and assured, exhibited a kind of brilliance of aspect. Crocker seemed to hint as much when he asked, a little later: 'Tell us now, ladies of the stage: do you not find it a relief to travel far from the theatre, free to be yourselves?'

Miss Page and Miss Brindley looked at one another, smiling.

'The truth is,' said Jane, 'that I am so accustomed to assuming a character that I scarcely know who I am. But I know if I am happy or not, and today I am happy.'

'Jane speaks for me also,' said Kitty, with unexpected seriousness. 'A young actress comes to town before she knows who she is, and must then make her living pretending to be other people. How could she not be confused?'

'Your case is the more extreme,' said I, 'but we are all obliged to perform.'

'Indeed we are,' said Crocker. 'Let me admit that there is a gap between the character I convey through words and the person I feel myself to be. Perhaps Mr Pike has the best of it: he says but little and shows his disposition through his actions.'

Suddenly the focus of attention, Pike looked up: 'Then today,' he said, 'I show my disposition by looking after your monkey.'

We smiled at this remark, although uncertain as to its bearing.

'In the boat,' said Kitty, 'I was wondering whether a monkey could swim.'

'I have never seen it done,' said Pike.

As though aware we were speaking of him, Trinculo sprang from his branch and ran to and fro, chattering shrilly, before suddenly stopping to regard us with a satirical eye.

'He jeers at us,' said Miss Page, 'but I hope he is enjoying our expedition.'

'Of course he is,' said Crocker. 'Like ourselves he is released for the day.'

'Unlike ourselves, however,' I objected, 'he is fastened to a long chain.'

'But so are we,' said Kitty, unexpectedly. 'The long chain that will pull us back into dirty London at the end of the afternoon.'

'Trinculo is held by a metal chain,' said I. 'What is ours made of?'

'Habit,' said Crocker. 'And sloth and money and timidity. Miss Brindley is in the right: we are all prisoners. But we must make the best of our plight. I will give Trinculo an apple and open another bottle of wine.'

We continued lively and talkative. Only Pike remained quiet, maintaining an alert reserve, like a sergeant dining among officers. Our table was in a shaded corner, but the sun shone so brightly on the scene before us that we could admire it only through half-closed eyes. That fact, combined with the peacefulness of the place, gradually conduced to sleepiness. We were pleasantly subdued into the larger scene. Although I saw that Kitty looked more appealing than I had ever previously known her I did so with no nagging of physical desire, lost as I was in a collective reverie.

In this shared contentment our conversation insensibly died away. Jane Page murmured idly: 'I am very happy – and very drowsy.' It would have taken little to ease all of us, save Pike, into a peaceful doze. We were roused when Kitty said, with sudden recollection: 'A year ago this very day I left Helmstone for London.'

'With high expectations?' asked Crocker.

'With very modest and fearful ones.'

'A year ago,' Crocker replied, 'I was planning my escape from Somerset.'

'I was in Rome,' said I.

'And I was Dido at Drury Lane,' said Miss Page.

'Yet here we sit,' mused Crocker, 'our four lives drawn together into a graceful knot.'

'Where were you, Mr Pike?' inquired Kitty.

'I cannot recall.' As though feeling his reply had been too curt he added: 'The truth is, ma'am, that I live as I find myself from day to day.'

Crocker nodded approvingly: 'Perhaps for that reason, if we were faced with sudden danger Mr Pike would be the quickest to respond.'

'I do not doubt it,' said Miss Page, and Pike acknowledged the compliments with one of his infrequent smiles.

After the meal we wandered down the green slope towards the river, the ladies proceeding most carefully, holding parasols aloft and lifting their skirts. Crocker was content to go at the same leisurely pace, since the hill was steep enough to have given him an awkward fall.

Our boat being moored up a little side creek, Pike was sent to procure it, leaving the monkey in our charge. It sat peacefully on Crocker's shoulder as we stood on the landing stage. The air was a little cooler by now, but the sky was still cloudless, and the Thames and the fields beyond it glowed in the early evening light. All was quiet save for the rippling of the river beneath the planks we stood upon. Miss Page suddenly furled her parasol.

'How artificial we have become,' she said. 'Here in the gentlest of country we are wary of the uneven turf under our feet and the hot sun above our head.'

'Not I,' cried Kitty. 'Like Phyllis I trip lightly o'er the mead.'

Crocker, still flushed with wine, smiled at her words.

'Miss Brindley,' said he, 'you return us to art.'

He threw back his head and sang:

See how the setting sun resists the night,
Adorning distant hills with golden light.

On an impulse I seconded him, and the ladies took up the measure, improvising sweet harmonies as we ran through the couplet several times. Our voices rang out across the smooth-flowing Thames. Trinculo remained on Crocker's shoulder throughout, at ease with the song. As seen from the river we must have made an odd sight; yet when our impromptu performance faded away we found ourselves applauded from a distance by the occupants of a passing pleasure boat. We waved to them and they waved a response as they sailed on.

We all fell quiet during the return journey to London, but at first ours was a silence of contented reflection rather than of weariness. Insensibly the mood changed when we drew nearer to Westminster, and the river traffic thickened as the air grew dirtier. By the time we alighted at the steps we were a little dazed, like people waking from an agreeable dream into intrusive realities. Our party soon divided because, as arranged, I was to take Kitty to the Full Moon, where we had first become lovers.

In the coach I took her hand, and she pressed against me, whispering in my ear, still in her droll vein: 'Pray take no liberties, sir. I am no such simpleton as to open the premises to an intruder. I could have tasted carnal pleasures long ago if Will Bumpkin had had his way, but I valued my virtue above such rustic fingerings.'

Later, in our bedroom, I gave her the necklace I had purchased in Knott's Market. It seemed that she was moved, because she gazed at it for some little time saying nothing. When she did speak, it was again in character: 'Sure, sir, you would not take advantage of a poor country girl? A full purse, a frilled shirt and a lusty member are all very fine; but what if the man has no heart? I scarce know what to think. But I must like you, sir, for you do buy me a beautiful necklace, and make me laugh and squeak.'

She embraced me and hid her face in my shoulder. When I made to kiss her I found that there were tears on her cheeks.

'Why should you weep?' I asked her.

'I cannot say. I will not say.'

She stepped away from me, smiling now, and began to remove her clothes, all the time looking me in the eyes. When she was completely undressed she put on the necklace for the first time. I raised a candle to look at her, and the red jewels blinked warmly above the pure white skin of her breast.

'I have not seen you more beautiful,' I said.

'We have passed a beautiful day. I will never know a better.'

For want of a reply I took her into my arms, suddenly moved by the thought that she was right: she could look for no more than this. Mr Gilbert would no doubt have seen such tears and blushes as incidental expressions of the breeding impulse, but I could not yet think as he did. I kissed my actress-lover with something more than animal lust, startled to find a minor player in my private drama presuming to take a major part.

16

The following day I retreated to Cathcart Street and sat brooding with a clouded mind. Having found the previous twenty-four hours sweetly pleasurable, I struggled to convince myself, as I had to, that they amounted to an interlude only, a distraction from my serious pursuits. I felt a new tenderness for Kitty – she had formed an attachment to me while knowing that there was no future for it: if I had had promises to make I would have made them by now. For my part I recognized that, given her growing fame, what I was able to offer her was sure to be outbid: I would have to endure the blow to my pride and pleasure of seeing her pass into the protection of another. I could not foresee this loss without a pang.

That disturbing thought prompted another. Although my love for Sarah had seemed to me to be of a different order from my affectionate lust for Kitty, would it not bring me to an identical conclusion? Beyond the physical seduction what could ensue? Would Sarah consent to be my occasional mistress? Might she puzzle her husband by producing a brown-eyed son? The possibilities were too squalid to be pursued. If I were blunt with myself it seemed that all I could offer was fornication followed by misery.

I concluded that I could not afford to be blunt with myself. My future was at stake. Whatever my misgivings, I was obliged to maintain my pursuit of Sarah and feed the story to my godfather. He would already be looking to receive a further chapter.

A day later I settled to the task of composing one. I wrote a humdrum account of my visit to Margaret Street before proceeding to an attempted justification:

You may feel that there is little here to suggest that progress has been made. But as a young lady fresh to London and its ways, and not yet comfortably established in her new station in life, Mrs Ogden will hardly yield to an abrupt avowal or assault – least of all in her own house. Your letter from Lord Downs opened the door for me, but it afforded a single opportunity that I could not afford to put at risk. Accordingly I seasoned our conversation with only the faintest trace of warmer recollections and intimations.

As I have told you, I first knew the lady in York, when we were children. By referring to shared memories from those days I engaged her interest, made her smile and, I hope, began to reinstate myself as a friend and confidant.

But I was also able to imply, through glancing allusions, that I had since travelled widely and made the acquaintance of certain distinguished individuals. Thanks to your generosity this is indeed the case. Given that her present way of life would seem to provide wealth without diversion and comfort without society, I hope she will come to associate me with possibilities of greater excitement.

Such encroachments may seem a long way from carnal temptation, but I am persuaded that they may offer the most promising route to opportunities of that kind. That hope gains strength from two considerations. The Sarah I knew was of warm disposition: impulsive and emotional, ready of apprehension and quick to laugh or blush. I have seen her show strong feelings on occasion, whether of enthusiasm, joy or justified indignation. I suspect that she is, or could become, a creature of Passion.

My second consideration is that her husband seems hardly a man to evoke or respond to, ardent feeling. I suspect that he has done no more than awaken his wife to the possibility of pleasures that he himself cannot provide – if not from physical incapacity, then from a deficiency of grace. What woman of delicacy could endure to have this porky nullity pawing at her body? I hope to turn to account an accumulating, but as yet, perhaps, unacknowledged disgust.

My allusions to seeds, hints or glimpses will not appear strange to you. They derive from your own claim that we are undertaking an experiment. Indeed we are – an experiment of an elusive kind, involving matters physical, emotional and intellectual, and the interplay between

them. We will understand what happens, perhaps, only in
retrospect.

Should Ogden accept Lord Downs' commission, and
therefore be away for a time, I will have an ideal space
in which to move forward. Achieving a resolution of
whatever kind will take weeks – even months; but I shall
scrupulously record every sign of progress.

In the meantime I remain,
Yours, &c.

On re-reading my letter I found it pallid and strained. I had
thought it necessary, however, to slow the story down. The
conquests of Kitty and Mrs Hurlock had been so summarily
achieved as to encourage false expectations. If I continued
to achieve amatory success at that rate my doings would
seem tediously predictable, and I might rut myself into
prostration. By adopting my godfather's language of experiment I could perhaps satisfy him, for some weeks ahead, as
Cullen had suggested, with morsels of insinuation as opposed
to full platters of venereal description.

If, for all his show of intellectual detachment, my godfather
was after all chiefly interested in the activities of the
bedchamber he would surely find this thinner diet unsatis-
fying. I awaited his response with some little apprehension.
As it happened, however, the next message I received from
Worcestershire came from a different source.

Dear Mr Fenwick,
You will no doubt be surprised to receive this letter
from me, the more so when I say that I cannot

communicate as directly as I would wish. I will leave you to interpret my words as you see fit, confident that you will do so with discretion and good sense, and will suspect no dishonourable motive.

The essential information you will no doubt already have heard from Mr Gilbert. About a fortnight ago Mr Quentin set out for what he told his wife would be a long walk. They had for some time been confined to their cottage by heavy rain. She became alarmed when he failed to return by nightfall. Search parties were sent out next day, but saw no sign of him. It was more than a week before his body was found, a mile or so from his home. He had drowned in the River Moule, which had burst its banks and spread over the surrounding fields. The assumption was that he had fallen from a broken footbridge into deep water. Mrs Quentin confirmed that he could not swim.

The mere fact of his death is disturbing enough, as I am sure you would agree; but two or three other considerations have caused me disquiet. One – which I have mentioned to no one else – is the possibility that the poor man may have taken his own life. It fell to me to break the news to Mrs Quentin. She was greatly distressed, as was only to be expected; but I was struck by the fact that her first words after I had stated the bare facts were: 'I knew it; I knew it.' Perhaps mistakenly I understood her to be saying not merely that she had guessed that her husband was dead but that she knew he had intended to die. She may have suspected, as I did myself, that he saw the flood as creating a situation in *which accidental death by drowning would seem more plausible. In later conversations Mrs Quentin has said enough to confirm what I had myself seemed to observe: that during what proved to be the last weeks of his life her husband had been lost in dark meditation.*

Since it appears that no one other than myself has mentioned the possibility of suicide you might think that it would have been more humane on my part to keep my suspicions to myself – and indeed I have done so prior to the writing of this letter. I mention them to you, in strict confidence, for delicate reasons which I must leave to inference.

It was my task also to tell Mr Gilbert what had happened. Having asked one or two questions, he was silent for some little time before observing, in a level voice: 'It was a predictable conclusion.' After a further pause he added, as though in response to my own silence: 'He was a man with no remaining interest in life.'

Our quiet parish has seen a strange summer, most obviously in respect of the weather – a parching drought followed by dramatic floods which caused no little damage to crops and cottages. There was also Yardley's unfortunate injury – from which he has by now largely recovered, although he limps still. More recently I have heard rumours that Mr Hurlock has been – I must choose my words – somewhat erratic in his behaviour. It would appear that he is concerned about his financial situation, a bequest he had hoped for having failed to materialize. I understand that he is heavily in debt – to Mr Gilbert among others.

The dead man was, of course, one of Mr Gilbert's pensioners. I hope that your godfather will offer to make some sort of provision for Mrs Quentin, who is in great distress, and apparently has few relatives to whom she could apply. Should he not do so the unfortunate widow must look upon her future with foreboding.

As I feared, this letter has become unsatisfactorily oblique. No immediate reply is expected: I would not for one moment wish to put you in a compromising position. I do hope, however, that at some future date it may prove possible to discuss with you the serious issues I have obscurely touched upon.

I remain your obedient servant,
Henry Thorpe

The letter alarmed me. I was sorry that Quentin had declined so far into misery as – perhaps – to have deliberately ended his life, but I could not pretend to any great grief. To me the man had been no more than a dull enigma. But I recalled his seemingly purposeless visit to Cathcart Street, and wondered whether it had had any bearing on his subsequent fate.

Of more immediate concern was Thorpe's motive for writing to me. He might have assumed that I had influence with my godfather and could intervene on Mrs Quentin's behalf; but in that case would he have written so warily? In expressing confidence that I would not give him away he seemed to be hoping to enlist me as a potential ally *against* my godfather. There was a hint that Mr Gilbert's growing contempt for Quentin might have contributed indirectly to his despair. Perhaps it was also suggested that he was in some sense persecuting Hurlock. If there was a general inference to be drawn it seemed to be that my godfather had been behaving oddly and aggressively. As another of his pensioners, Thorpe would have reason to feel anxious at any such manifestation.

I myself had reason, of course, to think that his fears might be justified. In his dealings with me my godfather had been broken free of a shell of caution apparently maintained throughout his previous life. A rich old man turned rogue could wreak a great deal of damage. Given the ways in which Mr Gilbert was manipulating my own life the immediate application of Thorpe's warning was to myself.

My dear Godfather,

Tonight Horn, Latimer and I were drinking in the Red Anchor, near Covent Garden. It was a rare privilege to have Latimer with us, since his closeness to Lord Ashton has raised him in society's estimation and in his own. Horn was soon taunting him on this very theme.

'Have you perceived,' he cried, 'how our former companion has changed? He dresses more expensively; he favours a new style of wig. Even his physiognomy has altered: his face has plumped up and become solemn. By the end of the year Mr Latimer will be a portly politician, unrecognizable as the young rake we knew at Oxford.'

Latimer listened to this half-serious tirade with the

*placidity of a man among boys. To keep the game alive
I took up the topic myself, remarking – truthfully – that
he now even moves more sleekly, gliding where once he
strode. To my surprise, Latimer assented to this
description, taking it as a compliment:*

*'I move differently because I have studied to do so, and
have heeded the words of my dancing-master. I shall soon
be mingling with statesmen and diplomats. In such
company the novice must be graceful and unobtrusive.
Diplomacy is itself a kind of dance: there is no place for
hobbledehoys.'*

*Horn's jeering response was interrupted by the arrival
of two more of our old acquaintances, Nicholson and
Moore. The conversation widened inconsequentially. As
more wine was drunk, however, it narrowed again. Horn,
a bottle ahead of the company, was both facetious and
emphatic:*

*'Consider copulation,' he declaimed. 'This activity,
essential to the future of the human race, is a madman's
gamble. Pleasure walks hand in hand with disease. The
fond insertion may bring a child into the world or take a
man out of it. Chance rolls the dice. I tell you again:
Chance rolls the dice!'*

*This declaration prompted loud agreement. By now it
was growing dark, candles had been lit and the air was
thick with tobacco smoke. Drink had reddened our faces
and confused our voices. Our end of the tavern resounded
with crude phrases: 'a great sow of a Cheapside whore',
'went to work like dog and bitch', 'their tails peppered
with the pox', 'off to the quack with a poisoned pintle',*

'*pissing molten glass*'. Amidst the babble one corner of my mind was sober enough to conclude that here was the polar opposite of the pastoral mode. A few bottles of wine had set us playing with grossness as children play with mud.

Horn led us in a new direction. Half weeping from wine and self-pity he stood on his chair to shout: 'Gentlemen! Gentlemen! Why do we do what disgusts us and endangers our lives? Why are we drawn to the fatal notch?'

'From need!' cried Nicholson, as a man making a great discovery. 'That is the tragedy: we are born with the need!'

There was vociferous agreement. Someone proposed a toast to The Need, which we drank with great solemnity.

Now that Death had entered our discussion along with Chance we were unable to get rid of either topic. Latimer, who had shed his dignity and become loquacious, commanded the table with the dismal tale of his cousin, who had gone for a stroll one evening, simply on a whim, had happened to meet a former acquaintance, had taken disproportionate offence at an incidental remark and absurdly challenged him to a duel which had cost him his life.

'Even in the duel,' insisted Latimer, 'Chance was at work. Had the wound been an inch to left or right it would not have proved fatal. As matters stood he might have lived had the flow of blood been staunched, but his second turned coward and ran away. It took a dozen mischances to condemn cousin Andrew to death: he went *from one to another like a man descending a flight of stairs.'*

Latimer's story reminded Moore of another, yet more grotesque. He knew of a man challenged to a duel concerning an affair in which he was manifestly in the right. On the morning of the encounter he was weak and feverish – so much so that friends advised him to seek a postponement. As a man of strict principle, however, he insisted on proceeding – and died from a thrust to the heart. Only after his death did physicians see the marks on his body that showed him to have been suffering from smallpox. His victorious opponent contracted the disease from him, and within a few days fell victim to the invisible weapon.

This grim anecdote led us back to the issue of fornication, Nicholson suggesting the parallel possibility of a rapist poxed by his victim. Moore took the hypothesis a stage further, positing an unfortunate offspring of the union, born with the moral failings of his father and the sickness of his mother. Latimer, stumbling over his words, put the case that there was a flaw in the very scheme of things. The moral confusion we were contemplating could have been averted had the Almighty but decreed that illness should be solely a consequence of sinful actions or intentions.

'Why should we blame ourselves,' he cried, 'for the failings of God?'

Our foolish conversation gradually subsided into incoherence. I have recorded this much of it because, in a confused way, it bears upon our own experiments.

We are exploring 'The Need', and what prompts it. Are Strephon and Chloe merely dog and bitch in fancy dress? And what are we to conclude if they will not couple <u>without</u> the fancy dress?

If Sarah and I could encounter in the animal state, with no rationality to complicate the matter, I am sure we would conjoin most readily. In the human world, however, there are constraints of circumstance, habit, morality, loyalty, timidity, propriety to be circumvented or overcome. The intellectual challenge whets my animal appetite.

I remain, still a little tipsily, &c.

In fact I wrote this (pretty accurate) account of our conversation two days after it took place, and in a state of total sobriety. I held the quill a little loosely, however, to give my handwriting an unsteady cast. It was a relief to me to communicate in general terms and have the excuse of being not quite myself.

To pursue such advantage as I had gained from my visit to Sarah I hoped to procure one further conversation with her before her husband waddled home. For obvious reasons it was desirable that any such meeting should seem to come about by accident. My best hope was to catch her once again in St James's Park, where, I had reason to believe, she often took exercise. The weather was favourable to my plan, being fine but not oppressively warm. Nevertheless I went to the Park on successive days without success. My third attempt was more fortunate: I caught sight of Sarah walking with her aunt and went to accost them. As before, Mrs Kinsey's garrulity made conversation easy: 'Why are you loitering here, Mr Fenwick?' she cried. 'We women have nothing better to do than to idle away our time: a young fellow of consequence should be consulting his lawyer, or quizzing a statesman.'

'I am of no such consequence,' said I. 'In any case I find myself more agreeably employed in talking with Mrs Kinsey and Mrs Ogden. But I admit, in my own defence, that I am on my way to see Lord Vincent.'

I was pleased with the falsehood, plucked from nowhere. It was easy and plausible, and offered Sarah an immediate opportunity for raillery: 'Then we are depriving the great man of your company and your advice. Is the business of state to be brought to a standstill by our chatter?'

'You mock me, Mrs Ogden, as many a time in the past.'

'Only by way of revenge. You have teased me since I was ten years old and you threw a worm at me.'

'I could never have done such a thing. I was always chivalrous to a fault. Let me appeal to Mrs Kinsey.'

'All I can remember,' said the old lady with spirit, 'is that you were both very naughty children who deserved to be whipped.'

'We stand rebuked,' said I. 'But tell me: has Mr Ogden safely returned?'

'Not yet,' said Sarah. 'He may be home tomorrow. I am sure he will be intrigued by the invitation from Lord Downs.'

'With the weather so fine you should celebrate his return by a diversion of some sort. I recently went by boat as far as Richmond, and can heartily recommend the experience.'

294

Mrs Kinsey laughed. 'Mr Ogden is not easily diverted.'

'Indeed not,' said Sarah: 'He must always be about his business.'

There was a brief pause, as at the end of a paragraph.

'Well,' said I, 'for once in a way I, too, must be about my business. Lord Vincent awaits me – although not, I am afraid, with any great impatience. But this chance encounter has been most agreeable.'

With that I kissed the hand, first of Mrs Kinsey, then of Mrs Ogden. Brief as these gestures were, they could not have differed more. The former was mere convention: I could as well have been kissing my own wrist, or an empty glove. Kissing Sarah's hand became instantly an amorous act: for a moment I was in contact with the warmth of her body, and could feel the soft pressure of her fingers. Not in the minutest respect had I exceeded formal custom, yet I was certain that she had experienced the same stab of intimacy as I had myself – a certainty that was confirmed as I raised my head and fleetingly caught her glance.

As I left them my heart was beating hard. I had perhaps deceived myself in fancying that Sarah's face fell at the mention of her husband's return, but I could not, *could* not, have misinterpreted that last contact. The meeting had yielded all I could have hoped for: a year after Sarah had closed the door upon me it remained, after all, unlocked.

This might have seemed ideal matter for a letter to my godfather; but I knew it was not. Who could describe a rainbow to a blind man? Worse, the very attempt at description would sully the thing described.

My dear Richard,

In my last letter I mentioned the unexplained disappearance of Quentin. His body has since been found in a river not far from the village. It is believed that the unfortunate man fell off a broken bridge and was drowned. When I first knew him he was a young fellow of some promise as a poet, and I gave him encouragement accordingly; but little came of his efforts. I suspect that in recent years he had become a disappointment to himself, and would not greatly have regretted the accident that put an end to his life.

His sudden death caused a stir in the parish, but occasioned little grief. He had no children and few friends. There was no great intimacy between him and his wife, to judge from their public appearances. Her future seems uncertain; I am advised that she has a sister in London to whom she might apply.

I was glad to receive your recent letters, providing further food for speculation. Your dealings with Miss Brindley suggest that although social refinements are said to touch female hearts, women are in fact more responsive to physical subjugation. On the other hand it may be that this particular female, like Mrs Hurlock, happens to be a creature of strong physical appetites, and therefore more susceptible to a direct approach. How could one find out, save by the attempt – which could go sadly awry?

For the majority, I would hazard, the raw animal instinct skulks as far below the surface of social convention as the pastoral tendency is pitched above it. It would seem likely, however, that while poetical delusions are intermittent and short-lived, the appetites of the body will lurk, gather and recurrently surge. If that is the case then marriage and domestic life are precariously perched on treacherous ground.

You and your drinking companions seem to have been debating a more disagreeable antithesis, one which made a strong impression upon me as a young man. John Pringle, an acquaintance of mine at Oxford, was envied for his good looks, and for the confident address derived from them. He seduced numerous women of all classes and sired several bastards. Within a few years, however, his beauty was eradicated. Disease destroyed his nose, deprived him of his teeth and his sight and diminished his mind. Like a figure in a morality tale the man once admired was shunned, and left to endure an early death.

My knowledge of Pringle, and others comparably situated, intensified my innate tendency to be over-nice. Even as a young man I was as physically fastidious as Dr Swift. Already disturbed by the knowledge that our final goal in the pursuit of love is a channel for urine and blood, I could not endure the thought that it might also transmit disease.

My collusion with you has caused me to relax a lifelong habit of secrecy. This reckless candour implies, of course, a confidence in your understanding and dependability. No one who knows me, or has ever known

*me, could guess at the nature of the correspondence into
which I have been drawn.*

*I have been a considerable reader in my time, but
novels at last proved unsatisfactory to me: they purport to
tell a true story, yet are too easily manipulated to produce
an edifying conclusion. By contrast I retain a certain
respect for Yardley, in that his speculations derive from
dispassionate study of a reality. Our own project would
seem to offer something like this rigour while also taking
into account the inconsistency of human motives, including
your own (and perhaps, indirectly, mine) and the
pressures of social constraint.*

*I fully understand that you will need time and
opportunity. It seems to me probable, however, that Ogden
will visit Lord Downs briefly in response to his inquiry,
and will later stay for some little time to carry out his
commission. You should therefore have several days, and
later some weeks, with the coast clear.*

*At the heart of this venture is surely the question of
motive. If Mrs Ogden yields, will it be for reasons of
'love', or of animal desire, or of fantasy, as in some
version of the pastoral conceit? Might she be negatively
driven (as you suggest) by resentment of an inept
husband? Or will all these factors play a part? Here is
an experiment by no means to be circumscribed to mere
physical conjunction. I will look to you for a diagnosis of
everything that it entails. This intrigue has taken on
peculiar significance in my eyes. You will find a successful
outcome to your advantage in more ways than one.*

I remain, &c.

17

A day or two after my meeting with Sarah I was indeed invited to attend a reception at Lord Vincent's. Again I found the venerable Lord upright, civil, and dry as a bone. We exchanged compliments and commonplaces to no great purpose. As we did so I saw on the far side of the room his antithetical cousin, Mrs Jennings, laughing and gesturing. She soon contrived to draw me into a quiet corner, where she confided that the invitation had been sent at her suggestion:

'I was eager for another gossip with you, young man. Last week I was in Worcestershire, visiting my nephew – Henry, the man of God. He spoke warmly of you.'

'I can speak as warmly of him,' said I.

'And well you may, for his heart is good, and responsibility has matured him. But for me the great event was dinner with Mr Gilbert: the first time I have set eyes upon him these twenty years. He also spoke well of you: he said you had your father's power to please – a compliment I was happy to endorse.'

'I am obliged to you. But you must tell me more. Was Mr Gilbert the man you remembered?'

'I must consider.' Mrs Jennings pursed her painted lips in thought. 'He was, yet he was not. In appearance he seemed to me little altered. I was quite mortified to see the fellow so well preserved. He is lean, scarcely wrinkled – even his teeth appear to be in good order. This is monstrously unfair. On the other hand I had borne three children since our previous meeting.'

'While he had borne none?'

'Pray do not be facetious, Master Fenwick: he has fathered none, and so has lived for himself alone.'

'Was he pleased to see you?'

'I asked myself that very question. He was – coolly affable. But now comes my reservation: he seems isolated from life – like a fish in a bowl. Do I go too far?'

'Perhaps not.'

We exchanged smiles of understanding before she continued: 'I well remember James Gilbert when he was about your own age – and warmly disposed towards me. He affected confidence but was cautious, too concerned with what others might think. I may have mocked him a little – I have been guilty of such things – but I found the awkwardness engaging.'

'And now?'

'Now that diffidence has gone. But he seemed reluctant to speak of those former times. I attempted one or two sallies, but he is not to be teased. His defences are complete. He has made himself a man of authority.'

There was a playful irony in her tone that invited exploration.

'You are discreet, Mrs Jennings. I suspect that you do not find those changes wholly for the better?'

'I have not quite said so – but no, I do not: though the achievement is impressive. Will Mr Gilbert's godson permit me to be frank – in strictest confidence?'

'He will – in strictest confidence.'

'The gentleman seems to have suffered a cooling of the blood. I can hardly now believe that once, years ago, I felt his hand tremble in mine. Tell me: is there life in him? Does he ever shout, or cut a caper?' She lowered her voice: 'To be more particular: has he ever, do you think, done the deed of darkness?'

'Madam, your bluntness might shock a more timid youth. I have asked myself that very question, but have not yet been able to answer it.'

'You share my contempt for false delicacy. This is an intriguing topic. Consider my husband.' She gestured towards him as he stood alone on the other side of the room, glass in hand, sleepily abstracted.

'Although Colonel Jennings is of an age with Gilbert, he suffers by comparison. He has lost much of his vigour and most of his hearing. But, after all, the dear fellow has exhausted his substance in living out his life, performing manfully as breeder and provider. He has fulfilled himself, and so remains cheerful in his own way. By contrast the carefully preserved Mr Gilbert is like a parcel yet to be opened. Can he be happy?'

Her bright eyes scanned me shrewdly as I sought for a diplomatic reply: 'Perhaps he still cherishes a hope that the parcel may be unwrapped.'

'But how? Who would wish to do so? And whatever would be inside it? Perhaps something not very agreeable.' She gave a little shudder, but then smiled. 'Do not mind me: I am a mischievous old lady.' She leaned towards me: 'At dinner with Mr Gilbert I had half a mind to squeeze his thigh to see if he would jump.'

'I am sure he would have been flattered by your attentions.'

'Alas, the opportunity is gone. And truth to tell, young man, I had rather squeeze your own thigh: there is more meat on the bone.'

'Mrs Jennings, you are not only mischievous but dangerous,' I said. 'Little wonder that you frightened Mr Gilbert when he was young.'

'Well, well: you yourself are a mischievous young fellow, if rumour is to be believed. I hear that you have been seen with the celebrated Miss Brindley.'

I tried not to show that I was taken aback by this sudden thrust: 'She is an excellent actress. Have you seen her perform?'

'I have – and found her most entertaining. But you will have enjoyed a rather more intimate performance. Or so it has been said. Ah – a hit! I see you turn a little pink. But never fear: I will say nothing to Mr Gilbert.' She laughed. 'Young appetites must be appeased. My nephew hinted at an entanglement of his own, if of a more conventional kind. Do you know anything of the matter?'

'I do not. But he did confide to me that he would like to be married.'

'Of course he would. Country life is so oppressive. Henry spoke of a man in the parish who had recently drowned himself. I was not surprised. If I were compelled to live in the country I would do the same.'

Colonel Jennings hobbled over, as though feeling it was time to attempt conversation. Crimsoned by wine he was tipsy enough to defy his deafness.

'You come in good time, Ben,' shrilled his wife. 'I was saying that if we lived in the country I would drown myself.'

'Very good,' growled the old man. 'We shall move there tomorrow.'

Mrs Jennings gave a little shriek. 'Bear witness: I am married to a murderer.'

'Pay no heed to her,' cried Jennings, cheerfully. 'She grows hysterical. I remember you, Mr Fenwick. We have been visiting your godfather.'

'So your wife has been telling me,' I shouted.

'He's a grave fellow nowadays. But we knew him when he was your own age. He was nervous then – always on the edge of things, peering about. Peering about. Some said he came to London to look for preferment. He dined with Walpole. But I say he wanted a wife. He smiled on this lady here, did he not Bel? But in vain. She was a cold-hearted tease, as I could have told him.'

'You see how I suffer,' she cried: 'I must share a bed with my slanderer.'

'No matter,' continued Jennings, ignoring her. 'She did not detain him long once Charlotte Tyler took his eye.'

'Ben, Ben' – she prodded him with her fan – 'pray control your tongue. You are speaking of this young gentleman's mother.'

'Am I? So I am. Well, there is no harm in it: she was a fine woman. Gilbert chose well. But then along came your father and stole the girl away.'

'We must change the conversation,' said Mrs Jennings. 'You mortify me.'

'What have I said, Bel?' The old tippler was suddenly confused. 'It is no such matter. The young gentleman is not offended.'

'Indeed I am not,' said I, very calm. 'I scarcely remember my parents. Colonel Jennings could as well have been speaking of complete strangers.'

'You are kind to say so. But he is a foolish old fellow who has drunk too much wine and should be taken home before he disgraces me.'

She did indeed lead him away, still loudly protesting his innocence. I understood her embarrassment, but I had meant what I said: I was not in the least put out. If there was something amiss with my disposition, a failure of imagination, or of natural affection, it seemed a small price to pay for my independence.

❦

I saw at once that the note, delivered by a servant, was written in a familiar hand:

> *Dear Mr Fenwick,*
> *The proposal from Lord Downs proved most interesting to my husband. He is to travel to Newbridge on Tuesday next to learn more. The visit will be a short one, because*

he must return to work on Mr Crocker's masquerade,
but he thinks it may well be productive.

Since he is particularly busy in the short period
before he leaves he has asked me to pass on his
thanks for what would appear to be a promising
introduction.
Sarah Ogden

I studied the brief message with rapt attention. The great news was that Ogden was to be away for several days, and would later, if all went well, be absent again, and for a longer period. But more than that: Sarah had specified the date of his departure. Had he indeed asked her to write to me, and if he had would he have expected that detail to be mentioned? Was not this a hint from Sarah herself, a signal that it would be possible for us to meet again? I would have to show myself responsive to the insinuation.

It seemed strange to me that the bovine Ogden was apparently to help design a setting for a masquerade. Here was perhaps another unlikely talent. But for me the important inference was that Sarah would surely be attending Crocker's entertainment. It seemed that door after door was opening for me.

One afternoon Mrs Deacon tapped at my door and said that Mr Ward and Mrs Quentin had called, and wished to talk to me. Greatly surprised and a little apprehensive I asked her to show them up. They were a sombre pair. Both were dressed in black, Ward from invariable habit, Mrs Quentin because she was in mourning. His long face was as inscrutable as ever; her narrow one was pale and timid. Both declined my offer of refreshment. Mr Ward made what was clearly a prepared announcement:

'Mrs Quentin wished to talk to you. I have encouraged her to do so, and have escorted her here. Now, with your permission, I shall wait downstairs.'

Once he had gone I expressed my condolences. Mrs Quentin acknowledged them with a small inclination of her head, but remained silent, sitting straight and taut. When she at last spoke I realized that she did so only with effort, partly through grief, partly from a difficulty in speaking through her artificial teeth.

'I come at Mr Ward's suggestion,' she said – and then stopped.

'I lack the courage to say what I wish to. It may be misunderstood.'

'Have no fears, Mrs Quentin. I have no reason to think anything but well of you.'

'You have always been civil to me, Mr Fenwick. I will take you at your word.' She paused to compose herself. 'You will recall that my husband visited you some few weeks ago. You may have wondered why he did so.'

'I was a little puzzled.'

'There were two reasons. The first was that Mr Gilbert had asked him to do so. His instruction – his instruction was that my husband should encourage you to talk freely about your life in London and your feelings towards himself. Everything you said was to be passed on to Mr Gilbert.'

I felt a jolt of disquiet, but was at pains to respond impassively: 'This is surprising to me, Mrs Quentin.'

'He found the task distasteful – too distasteful to carry out. He planned to tell you all, and to warn – to warn you of something dangerous in your godfather's character.'

She paused as though to give me an opportunity to demur; but I said nothing.

'In the event he found himself unable to do either the one thing or the other. He left this house, as he told me, feeling that he was a fool and a failure.'

There was silence. At last I ventured, in a dispassionate voice: 'What am I to understand by "something dangerous"?'

'I must beware of presumption.' Her lisp made the word difficult for her, and that difficulty increased her embarrassment. 'You must know more of Mr Gilbert than we could know. But we have been acquainted with him for many years . . .'

She seemed suddenly exhausted, sinking back on her chair.

'Might I have a little water?'

I sent for some, and for brandy to mix with it. Mrs Quentin sipped, rested, then sipped again. I watched with pity. Of the people I had met through my godfather she was the frailest, a sad creature, drained of life.

Once she was a little recovered I addressed her with a smile, trying to offer her a fresh start.

'When did you yourself first meet Mr Gilbert?'

'Many years ago, when my family moved to Fork Hill.' She was more fluent as she took up a familiar narrative. 'My father became the organist at the church, and was sometimes invited to play at Fork Hill House. I would go with him. As I grew older I was also invited to perform, and – and Mr Gilbert seemed to take an interest in me . . .'

She broke off, and I saw that her face was positively twisted with some new distress. Clearing her throat she spoke out plainly: 'It is mortifying to say so – it sounds absurd – but I was led to think that he might propose marriage. I had no experience in such matters – none at all; but that was my impression. There were looks, hints, small touches . . . My parents were quite persuaded that he would ask for my hand. Of course I was flattered – flattered but terrified.'

'And then . . .?'

'And then he introduced me to Mr Quentin, whom he had taken up. I cannot well describe what happened, for I was altogether confused . . . There was a change in Mr Gilbert's manner. He almost ceased to speak to me. It gradually appeared that John and I were to be gently impelled into marriage under his patronage.'

Here was embarrassment at every turn. I tried to continue diplomatic: 'Did neither party object?'

'That was not how we saw the matter. Mr Quentin and I had neither prospects nor money. We did not know the world. We were assured that it was a sensible match, and we felt ourselves to be sufficiently – sufficiently fond. I would be provided for and could look after my husband as he wrote his verses. At first we were contented enough.'

She had recovered her self-possession. Sitting forward she said earnestly: 'Until you asked your question I had no thought of telling you this history. Your godfather arranged our marriage as he arranged so much else in the parish. Since he seemed to do so in a benevolent spirit who could complain? Certainly my husband and I did not: it was Mr Gilbert who provided our house and our income.'

'But you have seemed to imply that something went wrong?'

There was a longer hesitation. 'Mr Fenwick, I cannot forget that you are Mr Gilbert's godson. I must choose my words with care.'

'I say to you again, be as frank as you please. Trust my good will.'

'Very well. But I must condense into a few words the impressions of many years. I was young and ingenuous. It was a shock to me when my husband suggested that our marriage was but one of many experiments Mr Gilbert was conducting. But I saw that he was right. Everywhere Mr Gilbert sought to – to assume control. Many of his schemes were successful, particularly in agriculture. My husband was subject to a very different experiment. He was to produce poetry – translations of Homer, dedicated to the patron whose generosity had made them possible.'

Here she checked herself: 'I must be fair: Mr Quentin had been heartily grateful for this opportunity. Yet under the pressure of expectation he found that his inspiration faltered. It was not for want of endeavour: he would sit at his desk day after day with paper and quill, but to little purpose. What he did write he would often destroy in disgust. The harder he tried, the less satisfied he felt. Gradually he ceased to try.'

'Did he never think of seeking a different way of life?'

'Very often. But the prospect was daunting: we would have had to begin afresh, without patronage. Our situation was alleviated, in that Mr Gilbert's expectations lapsed.

Rather than expecting my husband to produce poetry he asked him to draft letters or copy documents. By degrees Mr Quentin was reduced to a clerical drudge.'

'A drudge? Did he find this work so humiliating?'

'No, no. It was not the nature of the work. He was humiliated to think that we held our cottage and our income on sufferance.'

'Did my godfather hint as much?'

'Mr Gilbert became more distant.' She paused. 'Both our children had died in infancy. Our lives seemed valueless.'

She raised her hand to hide her teeth as her face crumpled in misery. To give her time to regain composure I took charge of the conversation, speaking reflectively.

'Can the attempt to gain information about me have been part of an experiment?'

She nodded, still through tears, and drank a little more brandy and water.

'My husband told him that he had nothing to report. His position was very delicate. Mr Gilbert had recently advanced us money to pay for the treatment to my teeth. It was doubly painful to disoblige him. He apparently said little, but his disapproval was plain. My husband came home full of apprehension, and sat brooding all the evening.'

'I speak now with great diffidence, Mrs Quentin. Do you think there was a link of any sort between this matter and your husband's unfortunate death?'

She wiped her eyes, and replied with unexpected composure: 'I know what you would ask: I have put the question to myself. Did my husband take his own life? It may be so. My opinion is that he looked for a situation in which he could allow himself to die. Perhaps there is little difference between those alternatives.'

'That is a sad conclusion, Mrs Quentin.'

More concerned upon my own account than she could have guessed, I was by now running short of commiseration. I tried to shift the ground.

'You have talked with Mr Gilbert since then?'

'Yes. He expressed regret. Then he encouraged me to come to London to look into the possibility of living with my married sister.'

'Is that a possibility you would welcome?'

'It is not. My sister and I have never been close. I shall speak to her, since I have undertaken to do so, but merely as a matter of form.'

'Then your hope is to remain in your cottage in Fork Hill?'

I was taken aback when she broke out in sudden passion: 'There is little left in my life, Mr Fenwick – almost nothing. But what I have I would like to keep. People such as myself – humble people – cannot take charge of their lives. Their fate is determined by decisions outside their control. I long for one last decision that would determine my remaining years in an acceptable way.'

I nodded gravely, several times, hoping to imply thoughtful sympathy. But I wanted this sad, skinny old woman to take her misery away and leave me to absorb what I had heard about my godfather. Finally I said: 'You have sought to make me suspicious of Mr Gilbert. Would you nonetheless wish me to try to influence him on your behalf?'

'I was attempting to do you a favour and hope you may return it. You have been kind in the past. There is one circumstance that works for me. Mr Gilbert wishes people to think well of him. He would value your good opinion in particular.'

She had gathered strength in the course of our conversation, and was by now speaking in plain terms. I tried to respond appropriately, although uncomfortable in adopting an authoritative tone to someone old enough to be my mother.

'Mrs Quentin, I appreciate what you have told me and the risk you have taken in telling it. I will respect your confidence, and will do my best to support your cause.'

I smiled encouragingly by way of suggesting that it was time for her to thank me and go. Thank me she did; and as she rose to her feet I could see that, although still tremulous, she was suffused with relief at having survived her ordeal. It occurred to me that I might have done almost as much for her as I had for Mrs Hurlock. Perhaps I should make my services professionally available to faded ladies of every disposition.

We went down to the drawing-room where Mr Ward was taking tea with Mrs Deacon. For all his impassivity I saw him comprehend, at a glance, that my interview with Mrs Quentin had gone as he had hoped. I tried to exchange further hints with him.

'Thank you, Mr Ward, for your assistance in this matter. I have learned much that I did not know, and am sympathetic to Mrs Quentin's cause. Perhaps you and I might discuss these matters again sometime – in the strictest confidence, of course.'

He conceded no more than an inch: 'Perhaps – if circumstances permit.'

'Does your wife continue well?'

'I am glad to say that she does.'

❧

Mrs Quentin's revelations had quite confounded me. The final sentence of my godfather's latest letter had seemed to hint, or so I had thought, that he was ready to make me his heir. Now it appeared that he did not even trust me. My situation seemed suddenly precarious, and the old man yet more devious than I had believed.

Perhaps my visitor's most startling suggestion had been that Gilbert had once seen her as a possible wife. She had been convinced, against all probability and so, it seemed, had her parents. If I mentally repaired her complexion and teeth I could conceive that she might once have been comely. I was inclined to believe her claim which, after all, was in keeping with the rest of my godfather's odd romantic history. He had pursued Arabella Thorpe, but made no declaration, had warmed to the young Mrs Hurlock, but yielded her to an inferior rival. He had loved and lost, it seemed, my own mother. Yet in each case he had retreated before there could be a question of commitment or possible rejection.

Yet in each case, also, he had maintained some kind of contact or control. I had witnessed his glee at contriving the conquest of Mrs Hurlock. Now it appeared that he had supplied a partner also for Mrs Quentin. It seemed that having been intimidated at the animal level he had tried to restore his self-esteem by an exercise of power at second hand. Perhaps, having failed to win my mother, he had assisted me in the same spirit.

It was also disturbing that the morbidly discreet Mr Ward had stepped out of character to bring Mrs Quentin to see me. Perhaps, like Thorpe he feared that my godfather was behaving erratically. If they were concerned by his treatment of the Quentins, what would they have made of his complicity in the assault on Mrs Hurlock? Perhaps he was breaking free of all restraint.

There was reassurance in the fact that I was after all his chosen partner, his proxy pintle. Having bred me for the task over many years, and at great expense, he could not easily replace me. Yet where would my duties lead? Would I have to entertain him into his dotage, rogering the nurse who tended his death-bed? Or might he repent at the last and discard me as a reprobate?

How far was he aware of his own inconsistencies? Plainly his interest in my doings had been far from detached and philosophical. It would be absurd for him to affect contempt for desire which he found exciting even at one remove. Yet obvious as that seemed to me I would have no way of enforcing the argument if my godfather refused to accept it. The power was all in his hands.

It seemed that all I could do was pursue my existing course, while remaining vigilant. Perhaps also I should try to lure this prudent intriguer into further indiscretion. If I induced more flagrant confessions I could threaten him with his own correspondence as with a loaded pistol. Here an immediate possibility occurred to me. It seemed the young Gilbert had been intimidated by his male rivals. By dramatizing my distaste – real enough – for Ogden, I might draw him out on a topic potentially humiliating to him.

❧

I rose early next day and devoted the morning to the composition of letters. My strange course of life, comfortable though it was, could sometimes keep me as busily occupied as a bricklayer or drayman. Newly cautious I made several false starts.

> *Dear Mr Thorpe,*
>
> *My thanks to you for your recent letter. I am flattered that you had sufficient confidence in me to send it. You may rest assured that this confidence will be respected. If I did not reply at once it was because I needed time to digest what you had said and implied. As it happens, that delay has provided me with further clarification, in that I have been visited by Mrs Quentin herself, and had a very frank conversation with her.*
>
> *She was naturally distressed: her husband's death, however interpreted, was a tragic happening. It casts a further shadow over her life in creating the possibility that she might have to leave her cottage in Fork Hill. She spoke emphatically of her unwillingness to move to London.*
>
> *This is a delicate business. I have written a carefully worded letter to my godfather strongly implying the desirability of her being allowed to remain, as his pensioner, in the village where she has spent most of her*

315

life. I use the word 'implying' advisedly. My godfather has shown that he can be a generous man, but he has earned the right to feel confident in his own judgement. He will take heed of suggestions, but is likely to resist importunity. I am optimistic in this particular case. If it becomes clear to him that Mrs Quentin wishes to stay where she is, and that the parish at large would approve such an outcome, I am confident that he will enable it.

I infer from your letter that you have been troubled not only by this sad affair but by the possibility that certain other local problems may emerge in the near future. I shall be glad to discuss such matters with you when occasion permits, and will in the meantime welcome any further hints of this kind. We both stand to gain by such mutual confidence.

I recently had the pleasure of meeting your aunt again. Both she and the colonel said how much they had appreciated your hospitality during their visit to Fork Hill.

I remain, &c.

My dear Godfather,

I was shocked to hear of the death of Mr Quentin. He seemed to me, for all his taciturnity, a man of force and intelligence. His poor widow must be sadly distressed. In these circumstances it is a relief to me – as it must be to Mrs Quentin herself and to her friends in the village – that she has your benevolence to depend upon.

As chance would have it I heard the story mentioned at the house of Lord Vincent a few days ago. I was once again in conversation with Mrs Jennings and her husband, who had learned something of the matter from Mr Thorpe on their recent visit to Fork Hill. They had much to say concerning their meeting with you, which I understand was the first for many years. Both were impressed by what they described as your youthful vigour, and seemed envious of it. It is difficult to credit that Colonel Jennings can hardly be more than a few years older than yourself.

Lately I have found myself insensibly adopting some of your own habits of thought. In particular I revert to the essential question: what the devil is one to make of the ceaseless reciprocal traffic between the intellectual and the animal self, between what a man tries to think and what stirs into life, unbidden, in his breeches? Your mention of Dr Swift reminded me of a third factor, that of perception. When Gulliver visits the land of giants, and becomes a plaything of the ladies at court, he is sickened by their smell, and repelled by the sight of a monstrous breast. But these ladies are twelve times his size. Surely it is self-evident that if our bodies were twelve times as large as they are their imperfections and their odours would be disagreeably magnified? By definition we are not so situated. I understand Dr Swift to be saying rather that if a man happened to view his fellow-beings with a hyperbolic eye he would be seriously disabled – and also to be insinuating that he himself has suffered from such an exaggerated sensibility.

I would diffidently infer, from my own limited experience, that we are all, at times, discommoded in this way. King Lear denounces women in his frenzy:

> But to the girdle do the gods inherit,
> Beneath is all the fiend's: there's hell, there's darkness,
> There is the sulphurous pit . . .

Yet Shakespeare the sonneteer can celebrate his lover in very different images:

> Shall I compare thee to a summer's day?
> Thou art more lovely and more temperate.

I admit, my dear Godfather, that I myself am capable of perceptions of either kind. I make this confession the more readily in that antithetical reactions, if of a different order, are vividly in play in my pursuit of Sarah Ogden. I am so drawn to that lady as to be ready to eulogize her in the most rarefied terms, spiritual or pastoral; for her husband, however, I have conceived an animal antipathy so strong as scarcely to be rational. I am dismayed by the strength of my hostility.

I find him physically offensive. He is sluggish and impenetrable, without a spark of wit. So far from contributing to conversation he seems to suck all energy from it. He is heavy and pasty-faced, with a waist as wide as his hips. Several inches shorter than myself he would surely outweigh me. It would be a keen pleasure to make this weighty gentleman cut a caper with a touch of a rapier to his rump.

Yet the graceless clod nightly shares the bed of my Sarah. How can she endure it? How can she bear the thought of his seed inside herself? Or does he sheathe *his unsavoury member in pig's gut to postpone conception?*

I must cure her of him. I must exorcize him. I can introduce her to sensations she has never known in the fat arms of her husband. For all these reasons my desire for her has a double edge: as I pleasure the graceful Sarah I shall be treading this lumpish creature under foot. Having written these gross words I know that I should apologize for them and mock their absurdity. Nevertheless I cannot but feel – and I suspect that you may agree – that at one time or another any man's amorous desires may be drawn towards feelings as ugly and foolish as these.

I am encouraged by my belief that Sarah is disposed to physical pleasure. On one occasion before I left for France there was a moment of intimacy, created and then cut short largely by chance, which seemed to imply a warm temperament. The challenge to me is not to start a fire but to fan an existing flame.

This letter may be too coarse in its candour. Your own directness has encouraged me to emulation. I have been lured further into the open by the news that Ogden is indeed to visit Newbridge and that he is assisting Crocker in designing his masquerade. Mrs Ogden will surely be present at what promises to be an intriguing entertainment.

I remain, &c.

18

Since the expedition to Richmond, I had seen Kitty but once, and that briefly. Although we conversed warmly enough I detected some hint of reproach at what she must rightly have seen as a retreat on my side. She had heard, as had I, that our intrigue was now a subject for gossip. I could have declared myself as her protector, but had not done so. Neither had I suggested that our dalliance should come to an end. She was in a false position, and would have been entitled to complain outright. In the few months that I had known her she had shown herself loyal and sweet-natured, even while making remarkable progress as a performer. If I had been an independent young gentleman I would have been preening myself on this association with an actress so celebrated.

However I was far from independent. Self-interest compelled me to concentrate my attention on Sarah; and certain predispositions and vanities confirmed me in that course. The transition was eased by my habit of forgetting those not of immediate concern to me: Sarah alone had survived this propensity. Fond of Kitty as I still was, I sensed her dwindling in my mind like a person waving goodbye from the harbour as your ship heads out to sea.

But it was awkwardly the case that Kitty was an intimate of Jane Page, now so close to Crocker. If I seemed to behave badly towards her I would surely lose a valued friend. A particular problem would be posed by the coming masquerade. She would naturally expect me to seek her out, yet my over-riding concern at that entertainment would be to advance my cause with Sarah. It promised to be a difficult evening.

A visit from Nick Horn chanced to touch on the matter. He urged me to join him that night at the theatre, to see *Love at a Distance*. When I told him that I had attended it already he brushed my words aside.

'What is that to the purpose?' he cried. 'I have seen it myself. You are damned ungallant, for of course we go for the sake of the divine Miss Brindley, with whom your name, at the very least, has been linked. I look for an introduction.'

About to renew my excuses I suddenly saw how to turn the situation to account, and allowed myself to be persuaded. Horn and I would meet at the theatre half an hour before the performance. In the intervening time I visited a jeweller in Holborn, and purchased a silver bangle of distinctive design. I packaged it in a small leather purse, enclosing a note that read: *R.F. hopes his country lass will wear this at the masquerade.*

Kitty performed charmingly and to great applause; but given my new preoccupations I found that I could watch her with something close to detachment. Afterwards I made shift to speak to her and to introduce Nick as a devoted admirer. As I had anticipated, our conversation was but brief, since many were vying for her attention. I had time, nonetheless, to slip my gift into her hand and to murmur, with what I hoped would pass for suppressed ardour, that I would be looking for her at Mr Crocker's masquerade. She seemed pleased.

Later, over wine, Nick declared himself ravished by this encounter, and bitterly envious of a conquest that he claimed to find inexplicable. I could smile at his jibes, since I was pleased by what had passed. My short conversation with Kitty seemed to have restored my credit with her. If she wore the bangle at the masquerade I could hope to identify her the more speedily, with a view to staying well away from her when making my approach to Sarah. I allowed myself the afterthought that I might return to the wearer of the bangle towards the end of the entertainment if so prompted by physical need.

❧

Given my diverse aims I found it hard to choose a costume for the masquerade. I wanted to pass unrecognized, but hoped my person would be seen to good advantage. Much would depend on the character of the occasion: an indoor masquerade would surely differ markedly from Vauxhall al fresco. To learn more I paid a visit to Wyvern Street.

Crocker proved ready not merely to talk about his entertainment but to hold forth.

'My friend,' he cried, 'it is to signal a great change. I like to overhaul my life from time to time. I came to London to indulge in a little city swaggering, but I have had enough of it. This house will enable me to preside. I look to become a notable London host.'

'Then are your tavern days at an end?' I asked, somewhat shocked.

'I plan to make but one further appearance on that stage, by way of farewell. You must be there to sing with me.'

'Will your comrades from the Seven Stars be attending the masquerade?'

'Some of them. But they will be intermingling with upright older citizens.'

'This all sounds strangely respectable, Mr Crocker.'

'Fear not. The unfathomable Mr Ogden has undertaken to create new worlds for my guests to inhabit. Formal invitations will be dispatched tomorrow and will declare a theme – Flesh and Spirit. I flatter myself that I am well provided in both categories.'

'But will not all the ladies appear as angels, and the gentlemen as satyrs?'

'The invitation will be so phrased as to discourage such simplicities. And who knows: in Ogden's strange domain a satyr may be sanctified or an angel debauched.'

'You have great faith in that gentleman's powers.'

'I have come to think him a remarkable fellow. You would have seen him working here now but for an unexpected professional engagement. He's as dull a man as you could meet, but he has strange pictures in his head. There could be alchemy at work.'

That evening I pored over the masquerade catalogues again, in doubt whether to aspire to the spiritual or to champion the flesh. At length I decided to become Hermes, the emissary of the gods, a licensed traveller between the upper and the nether worlds. The costume as illustrated seemed to promise both anonymity and freedom. Apart from winged sandals and winged hat my sole visible garment would be a loose white tunic. To confirm my identity it seemed that I would have to carry the Mercurial caduceus or wand, no doubt a tiresome accoutrement, but I was conveniently required to wear a short but dense black beard. Between that and my broad-brimmed hat little of my face would be available to the eye.

Ogden's absence in Worcestershire allowed me less than a week in which to contrive another meeting with Sarah. Having no plausible excuse for visiting her house I was once more reduced to haunting St James's Park. The weather was unpropitious – cool and intermittently wet. I visited the Park on successive days, to find it all but deserted. On the third morning, coming away despondent, I wandered towards Margaret Street with no clear plan in mind. As I neared Mrs Kinsey's house I glanced up to see Sarah approaching.

I had four or five seconds to devise a sufficiently innocuous greeting.

'A welcome encounter, Mrs Ogden. I come from the Park, where I was recollecting our last conversation there.'

'And that remembrance turned your feet in this direction?'

'Apparently so.'

'You might have seen me in the Park with my aunt, but unfortunately she is indisposed. I come from her house and am on my way home.'

'Then you have no particular engagement?'

'No.'

Her eye caught mine, and there was the slightest of pauses. I knew at once, and with a surge of hope, that we were united in wishing to prolong our conversation. But how to do so? Affecting easiness I found my voice a little unsteady: 'I would welcome an opportunity to talk with you . . .'

'Here in the street?' (This with a slight smile.)

'No.'

'Then where?'

I apprehended, of course, the unspoken words: 'The servants would talk if you came to the house again.' But did not that shared understanding immediately define us as conspirators? I took a risk: 'Having learned of your aunt's indisposition, might I not call upon her this afternoon with some small gift?'

Sarah considered the suggestion, and inclined her head: 'You might indeed – she was always fond of you. And might I not happen to be there and offer you tea?'

In this way the matter was speedily resolved. I went on my way with a fast-beating heart, exhilarated by this ready collusion. Three hours later, having sent up some fruit and established that Mrs Kinsey's ailment was nothing worse than a chill, I was seated in her drawing-room with Sarah.

'We can resume our conversation,' she said. 'Pray what do you wish to talk about?'

Her mood had changed since the morning: she was quickened, keen-eyed, slightly flushed, as though ready for argument. I tried to sound easy and affable.

'Anything at all. I want to learn about your doings. We have known one another extremely well, but lately there have been gaps in that knowledge.'

'Indeed there have,' said Sarah, smiling but sharp. 'The great gap opened after you left for France and ceased to answer my letters.'

Here was direct engagement. I found it encouraging rather than otherwise.

'I plead guilty to that charge. My only defence is a feeble one. I have an ingrained weakness that you may recall. It seems that, more than most people, I live in the moment, with only a diminished recollection of those not present to me.'

'You are right – it is a pitiful defence. Absorbed in foreign pleasures you forgot me.'

'At least I am properly remorseful. And such *meagre* pleasures as I enjoyed abroad are correspondingly forgotten now that I have returned.'

'If they are forgotten you are in no position to claim that they were meagre. Nothing you say can be trusted.'

Sarah spoke teasingly, but looked triumphant. Unsure of the balance between banter and reproach in her words I tried to regain the initiative: 'Meanwhile, however, you were marrying well.'

'Marrying *very* well. In at least two respects.'

'Money being one of them?'

'Most certainly. I had never dreamed of such wealth. I was transformed: suddenly I could speak with authority. Do you not detect it? Are you not a little in awe of me?'

'A little.'

'You never were before. This is the effect of wealth. Formerly you had money and I had not. Now you fear I may hit you on the head with a bag of guineas.'

'Surely you would do nothing so violent?'

'Not if I am treated with proper respect.'

The remark could have been a pleasantry or a warning, but was probably both. Although I smiled, my hopes were fading.

'You spoke of two great gains from your marriage. What was the other?'

'How can I express it? The experience of energy. Mr Ogden is a man of great force. You have seen that he is careless of convention. He cannot pretend. What he does not find interesting he ignores. If he wants something, he will set out to get it.'

'So you have told me before – instancing yourself as the thing wanted.'

I tried to speak lightly, but probably did not succeed. Sarah made no reply. At a loss, I sought for an observation neither jealous nor sneering: 'Are you allowed to participate in these forceful pursuits?'

'Almost never.'

'How do you entertain yourself when Mr Ogden is away? Do you pay calls?'

'Very few.'

'Is this not a somewhat – lonely life?'

'It is the life I have chosen. What of your own life, Mr Fenwick? Does it never grow wearisome to be a professional man of pleasure?'

I smiled before I had thought of anything to smile about: my last remaining hope was that I might somehow spin us into a lighter mode of discourse.

'You are hard on me, Sarah Ogden. Here we are, two old friends, all but quarrelling. You have squeezed our conversation into a tight corset; but I will cut the strings. The truth is that we are similarly placed, you and I. If your husband is a man of force, so is my godfather. I pursue my life of pleasure at his command, so that it has become a duty. Let me tell you, it is no easy matter to enjoy oneself to order. I cannot write to him and say: "I have duly tasted this or that pleasure, but to no effect." He is paying me to communicate sensations.'

Sarah was thawed sufficiently to be laughing at me in her old way.

'Poor Master Richard, I quite thought you would have found such duties congenial. How grievously you must have suffered. Have your sensations been altogether numbed?'

'I would not go quite so far.'

'It is a relief to hear you say so. I have credited you with strong susceptibilities.'

I maintained the light tone: 'Strong, perhaps, but also refined. You surely perceived the refinement?'

'I cannot recall doing so. But I accept your account of the matter. What I still do not understand is why your godfather should indulge you in this way.'

'I myself hardly know. Perhaps in an attempt to make sense of the world. He wishes to be better informed about experiences that he has missed.'

'Has he not left his inquiry rather late?'

'I think he has.'

She paused, and then struck out again: 'Where will this experiment end? When he is satiated with your pleasures, what will happen? Will you be withdrawn to the country to take charge of his estate?'

'I cannot say. I wish I could.'

'Then you do not know what you will be doing five years from now?'

'I do not know what I will be doing one year from now.'

'Then perhaps your situation is as strange as my own.'

She smiled, as though to herself, and the smile gave way to laughter. A little puzzled, I found myself laughing with her, if only from fellow-feeling.

'But how is your life strange?' I asked.

'That is something I am not at liberty to tell you. But strange it is.'

'You tantalize me.'

'So be it. Will you be attending Mr Crocker's masquerade?'

I welcomed the change of direction: 'Certainly. I take it that you will be there?'

'Oh yes. This will be the first masquerade I have seen. I like the idea that for an evening people can cease to be their customary selves.'

'I will be interested to see your unaccustomed self – if I can penetrate your disguise.'

'I shall expect to see *you*, Mr Fenwick, in the guise of a brigand or a pirate.'

'That is cruelly said, Mrs Ogden. I am a gentle spirit.'

'You are no such thing, as I well know. My friend Miss Martin told me that when she was but fifteen you forced your kisses upon her.'

'Can you believe me capable of such barbarism?'

'Readily. You were always a lawless fellow – as Mr Gilbert must have suspected.'

We continued in this easy vein, and I returned home with soaring hopes. If Sarah left her husband's side at the masquerade I could surely venture an advance of some sort.

But again I reminded myself that Kitty would also be present. Might it be that my two carefully separated narratives would close upon me like scissor-blades? Surely not, if I could retain my grip on the handles.

My dear Richard,

You show a proper sympathy for Mrs Quentin. I shall enable her to remain in her present residence if that is the course she prefers.

Your own story quickens in ways agreeable to my curiosity. You are steering a course towards the heart of that complication in human affairs which most strongly engages my interest. The lady in the case is but lately married. You are drawn to her, it would appear, for several distinct reasons. It seems likely that her motives, also, must be mixed. Desire and Morality, Illusion and

Passion are poised in a nice state of antagonism, and the outcome will not, as in a novel, be predetermined in favour of Virtue. It will be what it will.

We would all wish to be virtuous and rational: we are constantly urged to be so in prose and in verse. It has become clear to me, however, that these didactic works are riddled with contradictions, because the problems they pose are insoluble. In Mr Richardson's Clarissa *the heroine is presented as a paragon – yet she is fatally attracted to a notorious rake. This Lovelace, later to degenerate into a rapist, is the dominant figure throughout, the source of wit and energy. Hickman, the one wholly virtuous male character in the novel, is a timid booby, dismissed as a 'male-virgin' by Lovelace. Even his future wife, Anna Howe, calls him 'a dangler'. She repeatedly humiliates him, mocking his face, dress and manner. Indeed she praises Lovelace at Hickman's expense, arguing that 'turbulence must keep a woman's passion alive'. The author inadvertently discloses a belief fatal to his project: that Vice is exciting and arouses desire, while Virtue is dull and destroys it. Pious admirers of his novel, both male and female, have their interest maintained by the 'turbulence' of Lovelace, and laugh at the pitiable Hickman. I am reminded of Hunter's couplet:*

Lust stands condemned, yet potency is prized;
Virtue is lauded, but the prig despised.

I must wonder whether your feelings for Mrs Ogden will be altered if she submits to you. As we have agreed, there is something in us which seeks to elevate physical desire by idealizing the object of pursuit. To listen uncritically to that inner voice is to be self-deluded. Lovelace himself admits, after raping Clarissa: 'There is no difference to be found between the skull of King Philip and that of another man' – which is to say that in respect of the private parts one woman is hardly to be distinguished from another. To put the case crudely: in the very last resort what will Mrs Ogden have to offer that Mrs Hurlock did not?

Yet you are right to suggest that to lack the idealizing impulse is perhaps to be less than human. I myself, as a younger man, inclined too far in this direction. But I was a child of a divided age. It preached the virtues of the intellect, of clarity, of seeing the world as it is – yet in social life it feared physical facts. 'But to the girdle do the gods inherit': as though mindful of Lear's warning we buried the lower half of the female body beneath layer upon layer of fabric. The satirical Anna Howe hints that, for all poor Hickman knows, she may have three feet hidden beneath her skirts.

A woman's hair may be squashed beneath a wig, the face painted, the eyes chemically brightened, the breath artificially sweetened. Seen in this light Dr Swift's imaginings appear less hyperbolic. We seem to assume that the unadorned female form would fall far short of our ideals: it must be disguised and beautified to make good its deficiencies. Perhaps we similarly call in aid Jealousy, Vanity or Revenge as strong sauces to an insipid repast.

These ideas, or something like them, were in my mind recently during the visit of Mr and Mrs Jennings. You will perhaps hardly credit that many years ago I was strongly attracted to Arabella Thorpe, as she then was. In justice to her and to myself it should be said that she was then a beautiful and sprightly young woman. Perhaps too easily I submitted to what seemed her preference for Ben Jennings, a hearty buck. It was a strange business to see them again, half a lifetime later. Here was poor Ben, now an amiable buffoon. As for the lady, I found her lively enough; but if formerly I was tempted to picture what her dress concealed, I now felt no such curiosity. Yet so to my dilemma. Half my brain told me that I had done well to abstain from competing for so poor a prize; but the other half said that I had absurdly situated myself outside the natural range of human feeling.

More recently Mr Hurlock paid me an unexpected visit. I saw that he was the worse for drink: he moved unsteadily and his face was blotched. For a moment I wondered whether he had learned of the thorough plundering his wife had enjoyed at your hands. It quickly emerged, however, that he had called on financial business. His affairs now being in an even worse state than I had thought, he was asking for more time in which to pay the considerable sum he owes me. Having allowed him more than one such extension in the past, I said that I could not grant his request: he would have to yield to me the portion of his estate (adjacent to mine) which he had pledged against the debt. When his pleas proved vain he became heated and finally abusive. I rose and told him our conference was at an end. He hulked himself to his feet, turning towards the door, but then, in a fit of fury, lurched round and threw himself upon me, seizing me by the throat. Hector, who had been asleep in a corner, roused himself on the instant and fastened his teeth on Hurlock's leg. As the pitiful blockhead sprawled cursing on the floor two of my servants rushed in, disturbed by the commotion.

I was content to hush the matter up. The servants were sworn to secrecy. Hurlock's leg, by now bleeding profusely, was bandaged. The shock had sobered him: he blubbered abject apologies which, given that I had been left a little bruised, I accepted with good grace.

Years ago he was the principal bully of this part of the county. Now within weeks I had seen him first cuckolded and then routed – and he owes me a large tract of land. My triumph over him may be seen as a vindication of detachment and rationality. But I am no such hypocrite that I cannot see an inconsistency when I speak (or think) of 'triumph'. Perhaps I have not only transcended Hurlock's wretched standards, but stooped to them.

This transference of land can be carried through unobtrusively. I would not wish it to damage my reputation or even that of Hurlock. It is unfortunate for him that his essential pleasures, eating, drinking and hunting, are expensive ones. By contrast Yardley might live in a prison cell with equanimity, if he had but a mole or a magpie for company. With judicious retrenchment Hurlock can maintain his bottle and his horse, although he may soon need to be tied into the saddle.

I mention this episode to imply my sympathy for your instinctive, and physical, aversion to Ogden. After all the body has a voice of its own. In seducing his wife you will

334

enjoy the simultaneous pleasure of humbling a repellent antagonist.

Mr Crocker's masquerade would seem propitious to your hopes. So, too, does a letter I received this very morning. Lord Downs writes that he is to employ Ogden to assist in the renovation of his house. He found him 'a queer, glum devil', but thinks him a man of ability. I believe you would concur in both these opinions concerning the man you plan to cuckold.

I remain, &c.

My dear Godfather,

Do not the inconsistencies of Clarissa *run deeper than you allow? Richardson lauds the chastity of his heroine, yet plainly the true source of interest for him, as for his readers, is the prospect of her ravishment. As you suggest, no male reader of that novel will ever have felt drawn to emulate Hickman. But many will have wished themselves in Lovelace's position. It seems that, however lofty our doctrines, human kind has an irrepressible relish for fleshly dealings.*

Moving in London society as I do – thanks to your generosity – I can only concur with your observations concerning the extent to which the human body, both male and female, is presently bedecked and even deformed. Perfume may mask odour and paint hide dirt. Many a bedroom candle is hastily snuffed to forestall a disagreeable revelation before invisibly naked animals couple in darkness.

I hasten to add that Sarah Ogden's attractions are happily unambiguous. Her cheeks, her hair, her eyes are alive with their natural colours. Her waist requires no confinement from corsetry. Having known her as a girl I have been enabled, in contrast to Mr Hickman, to count her small feet, to the number of two, and even discern, through light skirts, the outlines of her graceful legs. At the animal level I have all the stimulus I could wish.

I was able to contrive a further conversation with Mrs Ogden while her husband was away. Let me give you an account of that meeting.

Here I transcribed the relevant parts of the narrative earlier provided, save only for a little judicious pruning, and in particular the omission of any of our references to Mr Gilbert.

I was at first dismayed by Sarah's asperity. However, I infer that this manner is adopted by conscious effort, as a kind of self-defence. Moreover she did not long sustain this mood: I was able to restore her to good humour. Because we conversed easily when children it comes naturally to us to do so once more. When in that vein she perhaps disclosed more than she was aware. I inferred that she feels an absence in her life, a need for novelty and excitement. I have reappeared at the right time.

You mentioned Mrs Jennings. When I met her again recently I found her often arch and provocative in manner, as she must have been when young. There is no harm, of course, in such jesting, as it now is: this is a conversational style, and to be taken as such. Yet I feel that, having been a lusty creature in her day, she makes such sallies through a survival of animal instinct. Perhaps in the same way some sagging female elephant or withered vixen will feebly parody the gestures of mating even till her dying day.

The immediate bearing of my observation is that I sense, in Sarah Ogden, a version of such an instinct. Our conversation came to have a tincture of unspoken dalliance. She does not deliberately provoke, as Mrs Jennings does, but she resorts to a rallying tone that is similar in effect and can tend towards indiscretion.

Any such process, of course, will depend upon time and opportunity. I am pleased to hear that Mr Ogden's services are to be required in Worcestershire. If all goes well his wife will not be lonely in his absence.

What you report of Mr Hurlock I find extraordinary. Drink, debt and stupidity must have undone the poor devil completely. He was fortunate not to have fared worse. Whatever occasional doubts you may have had about your own course of life you cannot for a moment have wished to be a Hurlock. Your thoughts easily encompass all he has done or wished for; his understanding could not begin to comprehend the workings of your own. In short, your habit of rationality can see, and can then make good, any suspected limitation; Hurlock's materialism is doomed to stupidity because it cannot see beyond itself.

This letter has been largely speculative. I hope that my next one will revert to actions. It will record the humours

of Crocker's masquerade, which will number both Sarah
and Kitty among the guests.
I remain, &c.

~

A note was delivered to Cathcart Street when I was away:

Mr Joseph Ward sends his compliments and hopes
that Mr Fenwick will be able to find time to visit
him at his office on a matter of personal concern.

I 'found time' the next morning, and was led into a small sanctum I had never entered before. It was impossible to judge the gravity of the occasion from Mr Ward's expression, since he never looks other than grave.

'Is this your confessional, Mr Ward?' I asked, to lighten the atmosphere.

He looked at me with a bleak eye.

'I have no such priestly powers, Mr Fenwick. The case is this: I have heard a report which caused me concern, and I would value your opinion on it, if you care to offer one.'

'Try me, Mr Ward.'

He drew a long breath through his nostrils.

'I learn from Mrs Quentin that Mr Hurlock attacked your godfather, and was in consequence savaged by his dog.'

'How did Mrs Quentin know this?'

'She was told by Mrs Hurlock.'

'I can confirm the story. My godfather described the episode in his latest letter. He did not want it noised abroad.'

'Nor will it be. Mr Hurlock can have no interest in repeating it, since he was plainly in the wrong. But he could not hide his injuries from his wife.'

'Did she know that her husband was in Mr Gilbert's debt?'

Ward gave me a hard glance. 'She did, and was naturally concerned. So Mr Gilbert has spoken to you of this transaction?'

'Only in the most general terms.'

Ward frowned, as though considering his position. I tried to help.

'I think you may wish to express a misgiving that might seem to reflect badly on Mr Gilbert. Let me say what I think is in your mind. If I am near the mark we can discuss my words without your having to commit yourself to an opinion.'

He took in the suggestion and nodded.

'Very well,' I said. 'Here is Mr Quentin, drowned in unfortunate circumstances, apparently in a state of desperation. And here is Mr Hurlock making a gross physical attack – seemingly again as a result of desperation. Is it possible, therefore, that Mr Gilbert has lately been showing an unaccustomed harshness? Have I come near your thoughts?'

The reply was characteristically indirect: 'Mr Gilbert is a gentleman of wealth and influence. Many lives are dependent on him.'

'Many – including my own. If it is indeed the case that he is becoming more capricious I have selfish reasons for concern. But I am by no means clear what can be done.'

Again Ward sat silent, digesting my words.

'No more am I, Mr Fenwick,' he said at length. 'But I hope I may continue to confide in you should further issues of this kind arise.'

We parted cordially, with a handshake. I was pleased with my show of judiciousness, given that I had been treading the thinnest of ice. Mr Ward could never have guessed that I had been vigorously abetting my godfather's degeneration.

❧

When my masquerade garb was delivered my first response was disappointment. Could these crudely concocted bits and pieces have any transformative effect? Having put them on, however, and posed before the mirror, I was on the whole pleased. As I had hoped, the proportion of my face visible between winged hat and beard seemed small enough to render me anonymous, unless to a few intimates. In general I appeared to good advantage, nimbler and lighter than my everyday self. My caduceus, although a tiresome encumbrance, obliged me to strike graceful attitudes, as of a being ready to walk upon air.

My one doubt concerned my sandals: the wing-tips trailed the ground in what appeared to me an insufficiently Mercurial fashion. In need of an observer's view of the matter I summoned Mrs Deacon and paraded myself before her. She was composed, as always, while she surveyed me, but I detected a stifled smile.

'Do I amuse you, Mrs Deacon?'

'Certainly not, Mr Fenwick. You are god-like. But you have the beard of a pirate.'

'And why not? There is much that we do not know about the shaving practices of the immortals. But what say you to these trailing wings on my feet?'

She examined them gravely.

'The wings are very well in themselves; but if you are not to trip yourself you must be able to fold them. I can alter them for you.'

I welcomed the offer, and had my sandals returned that night, expertly emended. Mrs Deacon smiled again when she delivered them. I was grateful for the service she had done me, and pleased that having seen me in celestial apparel she seemed to look on me with favour. Here was a good omen for the masquerade.

19

This uncertain account of Crocker's masquerade is set down the day after the event. My memories of it are clouded by drink and by the phantasmal character of the entertainment itself. I write with an aching head, in an effort to make sense of what I only half recall.

I began the evening in excellent spirits. Arrayed as Hermes – musician, traveller, friend to thieves and harlots – I felt my powers increased. The mirror showed me a figure that could have passed muster on a Greek vase.

I took a chair to Wyvern Street. Stowed in a malodorous box borne by two trotting oafs, the god of motion was free to review his plans. I would risk some new advance upon Sarah, almost at any cost, but my recklessness would have to be discreet. Much would depend on the disposition of the house: I would need privacy and shadows. Ogden and Kitty, in particular, would have to be safely occupied elsewhere. But I should find Kitty also, and perhaps even persuade her to supply a pleasant postscript to the evening.

I travelled bare-headed, but resumed hat and beard when my ignoble chariot arrived. Clutching my caduceus I looked about. Chairs had been directed to the front of the house, coaches to the courtyard at the rear. The August evening was warm and bright. A crowd of onlookers was being held at a distance while the guests, brightly-coloured as parrots, alighted and made their way to the front door. Pike was presiding there, in the guise of a footman, on watch for the uninvited.

The interior of the house was disappointingly plain at first glance, most of the furnishings having been removed. There was no evidence of Ogden's claimed artistry. The evening sunlight shone through high windows into the spacious rooms where the guests were mingling and circling very much as they might have done at Vauxhall. But these guests themselves offered a remarkable spectacle. I saw a great-bellied glutton, a Titania, an exotic Delilah with scissors in her hand and hair in her girdle. Some were garbed as at Vauxhall: a Cleopatra, a golden-haired angel, the ghost from *Hamlet*. A little Puck darted past me. Medusa, with twitching locks, was in conversation with Falstaff, while across the room stood a dramatic Diana with glittering head-dress and silver bow. Flesh made the livelier show, but Virtue could boast longer robes and more graceful postures. None of those I saw did I recognize at this first glance.

I went from room to room. All were similarly crowded and similarly unadorned. It seemed that colour and mood were to be provided by the guests alone. I saw none of the sensual enticements or shadowy nooks that I had hoped for as being favourable to my intentions. The mood was nevertheless lively. White-clad cherubs and black-faced imps were distributing generous quantities of a potent punch. I assuaged my disappointment by drinking as freely as I could through the strainer of my bristling beard. The guests were more decorous than their counterparts at Vauxhall. It was as though a fashionable assembly had had its elegant garb transformed by a mischievous fairy. There were few of the squeaked greetings common at a public masquerade. Instead I heard a parody of polite prattle: 'I know you, Mr Mars. I have met you before, in company with Miss Venus.'

'You mistake me, madam. I consort with no such trollops.'

A suave satyr, with his long tail slung over one arm, was attempting to wheedle a grey-robed, half-masked nun in white gloves: 'Might I tempt you, Sister, into a minor trans-gression – a little insobriety?'

'Indeed not, sir. A second glass of punch might numb my conscience.'

Yet after all she seized the proffered glass and took a hearty draught. I was glad to see that at least the level of drinking promised frolics as the night went on.

A short fellow was grinning at me through a purple beard.

'I not deceived,' said he, in a wretched attempt at a foreign accent. 'You Meester Fenwick.'

'Good God, Nick: who are you attempting to be?'

'Of course the great Meester Bluebeard.'

'But your beard is purple.'

'Never mind, Meester Fenwick. Women will come to me – many women.'

344

I felt a pang of condescending sympathy, having already two women in play.

But it was necessary to find them. I went from room to room, warily searching. The next individual I recognized, however, was Lord Vincent, a perpendicular St Peter, with keys at his waist and a glass in his hand. He looked at me blankly, and I did not greet him.

The evening light was fading by now. Some servants began to close the curtains, threatening total darkness, and the sound of a gong reverberated through the house. Voices called: 'Come this way, ladies and gentlemen. Pray come this way.'

We were led by footmen to the back of the house and out into the courtyard, which had somehow, since the departure of the carriages, been enclosed by an enormous tent, and set out with long dining tables. We were seated at random. I found myself between a lady of the night, gown tattered, cheeks aflame, and a Quaker gentleman, whose head was almost extinguished by his hat. I could do nothing about my designs for the time being, so contented myself with present company.

'Good evening, flying god,' hissed the harlot into my ear. 'Might I entertain you for an hour or so?'

'That would be a great pleasure, madam, but I fear you are beyond my purse.'

'Try me, sir. My rates are moderate, for I am fresh to the trade – all but a virgin. Or you, sir,' she called across to the Quaker: 'can I tempt you into my arms?'

Her offer was ignored, my virtuous neighbour not even turning his head.

Crocker's imps and cherubs served profuse quantities of food. For my part I was not hungry, and my beard was more amenable to drinking than to eating. The conversation of the assembled company grew louder and louder, trapped in the fabrics of our tent. My friendly harlot and I maintained indelicate badinage at the tops of our voices, but the Quaker remained resolutely silent, as though locked into religious contemplation. When he spoke at last it was merely to growl 'May I?' as he motioned for permission to hang his hat on the caduceus I had propped against my chair.

With that extinguisher removed I recognized at once both the gentleman himself and the reason for his taciturnity.

'Pardon me, sir,' I shouted. 'Are you not Colonel Jennings?'

He turned to me a puzzled face that gradually relaxed into a smile.

'You young devil – I know your voice. That damned beard deceived me.'

'Is Mrs Jennings here?'

'Of course. Why else would *I* be here? She's out there somewhere–' he waved a hand uncertainly, bawling: 'Bel grows lively as she drinks the more. God forbid she takes her clothes off.'

'Has that happened before?'

'So they tell me. She waits till I am drunk.'

Trapped in a corner of this packed pavilion I had had little opportunity to look about me. Nobody that I did see could have been mistaken for Kitty or for Crocker, or for either of the Ogdens. Becoming restless I was glad to hear again the crashing of gongs, followed by an invitation to us to leave our dining hall.

Since darkness had fallen the guests moved in noisy procession towards the one illuminated portion of the house, its main staircase, now lined with bright lamps. We crowded at the foot of it beneath a great ornamental clock. In a moment our babble was silenced by the flourish of a trumpet. At the top of the stairs appeared the unmistakable form of our host, arrayed as a Roman emperor. Flourishing a fiddle he screeched a few notes to establish himself as Nero. Another trumpet call. Then Nero spoke out, his voice resonant even in that large space.

'Welcome. You have not seen me before because I have been presiding over a transformation. Tonight this house invites Flesh and Spirit to mingle, whether in conflict or comradeship. Perhaps the Sensual may be redeemed from excess; perhaps the Spiritual may be seduced into Sin. All shall be as you decide.'

A third fanfare, in the course of which lights came alive, as though by magic, first behind Nero, from above, and then in the rooms around us. There was an astonished murmuring, because we saw that the house had been transformed while we sat at dinner.

Scores of assistants must have been at work. Everywhere chandeliers and candelabras had been covertly lighted and were now summarily unveiled. The bare walls were hidden behind colourful hangings, to which were attached an assortment of masks, some beatific, others sensual or grotesque.

When the crowd began to disperse I repeated my earlier exploration. Various entertainers were by now performing, in one room a wheedling fiddler, in another a fire-eater exhaling streams of flame. Imps and cherubs were again dispensing punch, the brew seeming, to my taste, more fiery than before.

Enlivened by food and liquor and this transfiguration the guests waxed far noisier. The rooms echoed with laughter, squeaked greetings and occasional shrieks. I was approached by the nun in white gloves, who pressed my hand and cried: 'If I pray to you, false god, what pleasures will you grant me?' She simpered beneath her half-mask and was gone. But in that moment I had recognized her as Bel Jennings, although of her whole physical being only a narrow strip of painted face was visible. I realized that the gloves were worn to hide the age of her hands. A moment later I passed Latimer, garbed as a bishop, with crozier in one hand and a glass in the other. He cried at random: 'I don't know you, sir, but you are a pagan dog and I condemn you to hell fire.'

Chance came to my aid. A squat, tonsured monk thrust past me as though bent on a serious errand. From his shape and manner I saw that he was Ogden. When he paused to exchange words with the silvery Diana who had earlier caught my attention I realized with a shock that the goddess was Sarah.

Here were two points simultaneously gained: I knew whom to avoid and whom to pursue. I hoped that my goddess would become increasingly susceptible as the evening wore on. Meanwhile I would explore the house to seek out secluded corners into which I might lure her. My other task would be to find Kitty Brindley.

I climbed the main stairs behind a butcher with a bloody apron, and perceived that the light from above was white and muted. This upper storey being far quieter I could detect faint music in the air. Turning a corner I found myself in Crocker's – or more probably Ogden's – rendering of Heaven. My first impression was of misty radiance, and of blanched hanging veils, threaded with wires of gold and silver. The general indistinctness was created by odorous steams, as of incense. The music came from a castrato singer, dimly visible through the vapours. Insipid as the scene was, coolly considered, it had a visible effect on those who entered: we lapsed into reverent silence, as though in church. The several saints, clerics and angels among us seemed to preen themselves, at ease in their natural element. Several clasped their hands in simulated prayer. I hoped that there would be other corners of the house similarly persuasive, but to more fleshly effect.

Descending a rear staircase I reached a closed door. I opened it with hesitation, suspecting that I had strayed into private territory. Ahead of me a line of small candles, so feeble as merely to render themselves visible, marked out a path through pitch-dark space. Again there was music in the air: the sound of a fiddle, faintly scraped. I stood motionless till my eyes could see further, but could make out no more than dark gauzes suspended from above. Walking cautiously forward I was soon bewildered, as though benighted in a forest. The gauzes assumed the character of clinging, confining webs. Pushing blindly through them I was relieved to reach another door, which opened to a room altogether different in character.

The prevailing colour was a deep and sumptuous blue. Several guests were already reclining on what appeared to be banks of cushions loosely covered by swathes of fabric. In a far corner the satyr was whispering into the ear of a shepherdess. The light was subdued and the air headily scented.

Another narrow stairway took me back to the main landing and the clock. There was loud music in the drawing-room, where dozens of guests were now engaged in dancing of a sort. Gods and monsters, saints and sinners, were mingling promiscuously, yet performing in character. A Minotaur dominated the rout, taller than the rest by the height of a bull's head and horns. As he spun I saw behind him Diana, standing very erect, her silver bow held upright before her.

I circled the room till I stood beside her. She turned as I did so, and I saw her expression alter as she guessed who I was. Even at close quarters the goddess was striking. Her silver half-mask was crowned by a crescent moon with a great diamond at the centre.

'I believe we have met, madam,' I cried, above the music.

'That is impossible, sir. I did not exist until tonight.'

'Perhaps before the evening is out we can converse in a quieter room.'

'I hope we may.'

Satisfied for now I passed through to a further chamber, at one end of which Nero was seated on a red velvet throne. At his side sat Medusa, whom I could now translate into Jane Page. I slipped behind the couple and spoke into Crocker's ear.

'Your highness, this is a degenerate entertainment. I have seen lewdness.'

'And you will see more,' growled Crocker.

He looked me over: 'I know you, sir, and know you for a false god.'

Before I could reply there was a commotion in the room. After some shouting the floor was cleared for a battle between St George and a dragon. Although on foot the saint brandished a formidable lance; his antagonist could offer only a long mouth, lined with pointed teeth. After some posturing and one or two tentative lunges, the dragon charged, and for his pains was skewered through the head. He rolled onto his back, legs waving, and expired amid applause.

Crocker leaned towards me, his face pink and sweating below the imperial wig.

'It's cursed hot,' he said, fanning himself with a languid hand.

'Never mind. This is a triumph. You have created a world of your own.'

'The credit must go to Mr Ogden, a man of imagination.'

Jane turned to me. Each of her locks had a spring within it to make it twitch.

'Have you found Miss Brindley?'

'Not as yet.'

'You must try harder, or I will turn you to stone.'

There was a ripple of movement as the castrato from the upper world made a formal entrance accompanied by an angel with a lyre. Mounting a low platform he struck a dramatic pose as prelude to a soaring performance of Nathan Tinsley's song, the angel accompanying him from below:

Alas for Man – how shall he choose
Betwixt extremes of frost and fire?
On this side Virtue dwells, on that Desire.
The saint, on Virtue's Arctic coast,
Forgets his dreams of Paradise:
Feeling and Faith alike are lost,
Benumbed by unrelenting ice.
The sinner seeks the Tropic zone,
Yet finds his dearest hopes are doomed;
His joys no sooner come than gone,
Dissolved to ashes, self-consumed.
Now having weighed what must be lost
We boldly still proclaim:
'We will not stifle in the frost,
But leap into the flame.'

As the song ended, a small army of gibbering devils charged in, brandishing their pitchforks. The masqueraders turned tail and were driven from the room.

'They are bound for Hell,' said Crocker. 'I inspected those regions while you were eating. That is exercise enough for one night. But the place is worth a visit.'

'I will sample my future fate,' said I, and set off after the crowd.

We were herded towards a region of red light. At the foot of some steps we emerged into a wide cellarage where saints and sinners, urged on by shrieking demons, were prancing wildly around a central pyre of fluttering flames. Without a thought I joined in, leaping like the rest. There was a whiff of madness about it all. I saw some lewd leering and groping as we spun together. The close air reeked of sweat.

When I at last withdrew I felt a tug at my sleeve.

'Give me your hand if we be friends,' said a voice.

I looked down, startled, to see that the speaker was the little Puck. On the wrist of his proffered arm was the bangle that revealed him as Kitty.

'With all my heart,' I cried, with an impulse of joy, and picked her up to kiss her and whirl her about.

'Fair sprite,' said I. 'Will you leave with me when the evening ends?'

'If you undertake to use me well.'

'On my honour as a god. Let us meet by the great clock at midnight.'

'By the clock at midnight,' cried Kitty, and danced away from me.

There was a sweet little bird in the hand – now for the other in the bush. It was time to find Sarah again. Hot and thirsty I refreshed myself with more punch before embarking on a second tour of the house.

Beyond that point the succession and duration of events are not clear to me. Only snatches remain. I recall that the white-gloved nun detained me for a moment: 'Mr Hermes,' she cried, 'we must end the evening in one another's arms.'

'Might not Colonel Jennings object?'

'Never fear: he will be unconscious by then.'

And she was away with a yelp of laughter.

I found Diana again, a little apart from the crowd. She received me with serene confidence, standing tall, her head-dress glittering.

'Are you pursuing me, Mr Mercury?'

'I confess that I am.'

'Then have a care. In this garb I find myself imperious.'

'I will be obedient to your commands.'

'Will you indeed? I am not convinced.' Her eyes were bright through the half-mask. 'I suspect you mean mischief.'

'What mischief could I possibly intend?'

She did not reply: her eyes strayed past me. Glancing around I saw that Brother Ogden had entered the room; but he was looking away, and perhaps had not seen us.

'I will find you later,' I murmured, and moved on.

My heart was beating hard. Sarah had been stirred by the unrealities of the night: before it was over I would stir her more – extract an admission, even a promise. There would be opportunity enough. The great clock told me that I had still an hour in hand. I took another glass of punch from a passing imp and drank it down.

Drunk as I was I sensed that the mood of the evening had changed. At Vauxhall the intensity was diffused into the open air: here, enclosed by walls, it impregnated the house. The air had surely been thickened by scented, intoxicating fumes. The masks on the wall seemed to leer and wink at me. There were cackling freaks and monsters on all sides. Some lurched aimlessly, others clung together.

I stumbled my way back to Heaven, on uncertain feet. The singer had returned, and was warbling ethereally; but his audience had degenerated: hands were straying. In the dark room I saw no one, but heard panting and groans. The sounds being suspended as I passed I cried: 'Do not mind me, friends – let the sport continue.'

Here was the place to bring Sarah, to tempt her to a touch, a kiss, a crucial concession. I advanced into the blue bower, hoping she might be there, but she was not. The burning of so many candles had made the room intolerably hot. More couples were embracing here. In two distinct stages of recognition I saw in a corner Latimer, in his Episcopal garb, pawing at a breast he had laid bare, and then perceived that his inamorata was the white-gloved nun, still wearing her mask. This rising young statesman was fondling a woman old enough to be his grandmother. The idea so tickled me that I left the room doubled over with laughter, laughed my way down the stairs and staggered away, still laughing, at the bottom.

'I see you are amused, sir.'

Sarah was beside me, regal but smiling. Drunk and dazzled I could not find words. Fortunately she spoke again:

'I am no longer sure who I am. Can you tell me?'

I made a great effort: 'Who do you think you might be?'

'Either the goddess of the moon or a girl you once knew in York.'

'You are both.'

My words were lost as those nearby sprang aside, shrieking, to avoid the fire-eater, once more breathing flame. When order was restored Sarah had gone.

Resuming my search I passed Crocker, solitary upon his throne.

'Will you dance, Tom?' I asked him. 'Will you sing?'

'No, sir,' said he, whey-faced and fuddled. 'I find myself languid. Also I am drunk, and from time to time unloose a great fart, to keep my subjects at bay.'

He waved a feeble hand. 'My entertainment becomes disgusting. We stink like a costumed cattle-market.'

Lurching uncomfortably on his throne he made an effort to sit upright. He drew one or two deep breaths and then shook his head, as though to clear it.

'You see me at a disadvantage, Dick. You see me vulgar. The night has been too much for me. Ears, eyes and nose – all besieged. The mind confused.'

The glimpses I recall become briefer. I was in Hell once more, where the dance around the flames had become more abandoned. Sarah was not among the revellers. Puck appeared from nowhere saying: 'Soon, Mr Mercury.'

'By the clock,' I cried. 'I shall be there.'

I was in one of the drawing-rooms, where I saw Ben Jennings snoring in a chair, his wig askew, his Quaker hat on the floor.

I was blundering up the stairs in pursuit of Diana, and caught up with her among the gauzes of Heaven.

'Winged messenger, what do you want of me?'

'I hardly dare to say.'

'Can a god fear to say what he feels?'

'Come with me.'

I led her down into the darkened chamber. Most of the candles being by now burnt out, the darkness was intense, but in her white garb Sarah was faintly luminous.

'What is this place? I cannot see.'

'But are you not Queen of the Night?'

There was a movement between us: she had drawn an arrow from her quiver and the point of it was at my breast. I heard a low laugh.

'You are in mortal danger, sir.'

'But I am a god.'

I clutched at the arrow and it collapsed in my grasp, being no more than rolled paper. Throwing it aside I pulled Sarah to me and kissed her mouth with a famished fury that she reciprocated.

How long we clung together I do not know, but we broke apart when there were exclamations around us. Something was leaping and bounding and scuttling about the room. Those within, Sarah among them, ran to the doors as my brain sluggishly comprehended that the intruder must be Trinculo.

When I had felt my own way out I found that the panic had spread from room to room. The screaming subsided only when Francis Pike appeared with Trinculo in his grasp and carried him off towards his cage.

The mood of the gathering had been changed by this alarm. A number of the guests took it as their cue to leave. Cursing the interruption I went to find Sarah again, to renew our moment of intimacy. She would have returned to the dark room, surely, in the expectation that I, too, would return. And so I would.

The steps had grown steeper. I took them one at a time, priding myself on my caution. Heaven, where the light appeared weaker than before, was occupied solely by a monk – who was Ogden. We did not look at one another as I went past.

In the dark chamber I floundered my way through the black gauzes, calling out 'Diana! Diana!' Reaching the blue room I saw with joy that Sarah was standing at the far end of it, facing me. But she was in conversation with Medusa.

She looked at me past the snaky locks of her companion but continued to talk to her as I stood and waited. At length she turned, and the two women left together. After a moment of blankness I set off after them, hobbling down the stairs.

In the hallway Sarah was standing apart from the chattering groups. I approached her with relief, but she spoke before I could: 'Mr Fenwick, I have breathed some night air, and am myself again. I am ashamed at what passed. It must never be repeated.'

'Why not?' I asked doltishly, but she was already walking away.

I stood on the spot hardly able to take in what had happened, beyond a puzzled sense of having clambered to a summit only to slither straight down the other side.

At this time, or perhaps later, I glanced at the clock and saw that midnight had long passed. I let out a cry that attracted some little attention. Was I to lose even my second prize? In a show of fatuous indignation I stood directly beneath the clock, and looked about as though Kitty might have been hidden in the vicinity.

'Mr Fenwick,' said a voice.

It took me a moment to get my eyes and my mind into order.

'Mr Pike?'

'Are you looking for Miss Brindley?'

'I am. I am looking for her. Where is she? She should be here.'

'She waited here for quite some little time, sir, and seemed to be expecting you to come. But at last she left with Mr Horn.'

'With Horn? With Nick Horn?'

I lurched out of the front door among other guests who were leaving.

'Nick Horn!' I shouted. 'Nick Horn!'

I was very angry and very bewildered. There was a bright moon in the sky. Of Kitty or Nick Horn there was no sign.

How I made my way back to Cathcart Street I cannot remember. My next recollection is of standing in my parlour and contriving, after several attempts, to light a candle. Seeing a strange reflection in the mirror I stripped off my helmet and black whiskers. I was in need of something. Tea – a dish of tea. I had to have a dish of tea.

'Mrs Deacon!' I called, then opened my door.

'Mrs Deacon!' I roared. 'Mrs Deacon!'

There were sounds on the stairs and my landlady entered in her nightgown. I had never seen her in a nightgown before. Nor had I seen her angry before.

'Mr Fenwick, what is this uproar? You will waken the whole street!'

I stared at her, struggling to make sense of the situation.

'Mrs Deacon,' I said at last, 'take off your nightgown.'

I took a step towards her.

'You are drunk,' she said. 'Go to bed.'

Not to be deterred I made to seize her in my arms, but she pushed me away.

'You are repulsive,' she cried.

As I reached for her again she snatched up my helmet and struck me a ringing blow on the head. I staggered back, half stunned.

'Go to bed!' she cried again.

359

'Mrs Deacon,' I said, with a hopeless attempt at dignity, 'there has been a misunderstanding.'

She left the room without speaking again.

After some moments I moved once more. Having blown out the candle at the third attempt I fumbled my way up to bed and was pitched into instant oblivion.

20

Half-awake I made to turn over, but found that I could not. My face was stuck fast to the pillow. In a panic I wrenched it free and sat up. I was giddy, and had an aching head. It seemed that my cheek had been glued down by dried blood, and that my movements had set the wound trickling again. I pressed my sleeve to it. As the events of the preceding night came back to me, one mortifying recollection succeeding another, I closed my eyes and groaned aloud. This was the worst morning of my life: everything I had played for I had lost.

When I forced myself to look about I could judge from the light that the day was well advanced. I got uncertainly to my feet and stumbled to the mirror. One side of my face was scabbed black, with fresh blood oozing down; the other was pasty. My eyes were small and bleared. Moving a dry tongue I became aware that my mouth was foul and that I was exceedingly thirsty.

I lowered myself into a chair, and struggled to think.

Somehow – yes – I had been rejected by three women in a single night. The worst of it – what *was* the worst of it? Yes – that I might be turned out of my lodgings and denounced for assault. I would have to make my peace with Mrs Deacon. But how to do so until I had washed and dressed myself and set my mind working once more? For all I knew Mrs Deacon might be already on her way to see Mr Ward and demand that I be removed from her house. After sitting for some time huddled in despair I tested fate by ringing the bell.

To my unspeakable relief Anna, the maid-servant, knocked on my door as usual and set off, obedient to my request, to fetch me tea and hot water. When these supplies were delivered I drank the tea thirstily before beginning to put myself to rights. I cleaned the blood from my face and hair: the wound was tender but not serious. I stripped off the Mercurial robe – soiled with sweat, blood and punch – in which I had fallen asleep, and steeped it in the water to wipe down my whole body. Having drunk more tea I opened the window and pushed my head out into a slight breeze and the noises of the street. I left it out there for some minutes to adjust to the conditions of normal life. A little revived, I put on a clean shirt and clean stockings, which restored me further. My head still throbbed, but less painfully. With a little adjustment I made my wig all but hide the damage Mrs Deacon had done to it. I felt hardly less wretched, but I was myself again.

One thought in particular came to my aid. This predicament was mine to deal with, as a ship's captain must deal with a storm at sea. Chance had led me into a strange career – living by pintle and pen. That being so I had now to exert myself to cope with the difficulties into which I had strayed. My first task must be to secure my home ground by making peace, if I could, with my landlady.

I summoned Anna once more and asked her to tell Mrs Deacon that I would be most grateful if she would spare me a few minutes, since there was something I needed to say to her. Anna went composedly about the business, conveying no sense that she had heard mention of an attempted ravishment.

Mrs Deacon came in, as calm as ever, and looked at me with an appraising eye. My defence had been hastily prepared. I would put on a show of abjection, and had in reserve two further cards to play.

'Mrs Deacon, I must apologize most humbly for my misconduct last night. I could not feel more ashamed.' I played my first card: 'You will not need to be told that what I did was the effect of drunkenness.'

She remained expressionless for a moment, but then I thought that I detected the merest glint of a smile.

'Are you suggesting, Mr Fenwick, that only a drunken man could covet my person?'

She had caught me off balance.

'By no means, Mrs Deacon,' I blustered. 'I meant only that I was free of the restraints that normally—' Finding myself about to add 'keep my hands from you' I abandoned the sentence and hastily played the second card, twisting my wig awry.

'I can but hope that this wound, which you quite properly inflicted will seem to you an adequate punishment for my wrong-doing.' I attempted a smile. 'I would never dare to re-offend.'

'I had no thought of punishment – only of self-defence. But it looks to be quite an ugly cut.'

'It was no more than I deserved.'

'And no less.'

I tried to appear suitably chastened, but no doubt simply looked a fool. I had run out of words.

'You are young, Mr Fenwick, and you do not alarm me. But I will not be bullied in my own house. I am a peaceable person: it offends me when I am forced to act out of character. The matter is closed. But if there is another such episode we must part company.'

'Thank you, Mrs Deacon. I shall not offend again.'

This interview left me both humiliated and relieved. I had not felt such embarrassment since I was twelve years old. But at least I had managed to dispose of one of my self-inflicted problems. What should my next task be? Soon – very soon – I would have to write to my godfather describing the masquerade, but as yet I had no idea what I should say. Plainly I could not mention my assault on Mrs Deacon without shrivelling from bold seducer to seedy bully. As for Sarah and Kitty, it seemed that both the bird in the hand and the bird in the bush had flown away, never to return. What had I to communicate that he would possibly want to know? I sent for more tea, and sat brooding as I sipped. It occurred to me that in Crocker's house a bevy of servants would now be employed in taking down screens and curtains, sweeping floors and clearing away empty glasses and burnt-out candles. The house would be its usual self by the end of the day. I should try to cleanse my own mind correspondingly.

I remembered the events of the previous evening as one remembers a dream. If I was to write a convincing letter to Mr Gilbert it was necessary that I should record what impressions I had before they faded to nothing. Already I felt in myself a powerful instinct to forget everything that had passed, and I could not permit myself that indulgence. Accordingly, 'with honest anguish and an aching head', I set down the account already recorded. Some few memories were revived as I wrote, but I was alarmed to realize how much of the evening, especially of its latter stages, now eluded me altogether.

By the time I had written out all that I could retrieve it was the middle of the afternoon. The relief I felt at having completed the task was outweighed by the renewal of some of my miseries. I winced to think of my jaunty little Puck waiting in vain by the clock, and mourned at the memory of my three minutes of passion with Sarah before Crocker's detestable monkey intervened. Was that to be the last and only time that I would kiss her?

Partly in order to escape from these disagreeable thoughts I summoned the energy to take a walk. It seemed to me that no more than half my brain was awake, and that exercise might begin to rouse the other half.

Needing quiet I headed north, past the Foundling Hospital, through Lamb's Conduit Fields and on towards open country. I walked listlessly, but by degrees the exercise and the cleaner air refreshed me a little. It came to me now that my impressions of the previous evening had been influenced by the demeanour of Crocker himself. He had seemed to recoil from the very entertainment he had been at pains to provide. It was as though a glutton had sickened himself by procuring too lavish a banquet. But his response had been just: there had been something more gross in the conduct of the evening than might have been anticipated. It was not merely that many of the guests had strayed beyond the normal boundaries of propriety – so much was implicit in the very nature of the occasion. What was less to have been expected was their failure to improvise any new boundaries of their own. In particular my thoughts reverted to Latimer. If this promising young politician had not crowned his evening by ploughing a sixty-year-old woman disguised as a nun it could only have been through physical incapacity. Such thoughts made me the more concerned about the parts of the evening I could not recollect. Might I myself have been seen in a compromising situation – perhaps by Jane Page, perhaps even by Ogden?

Whether I had or not, Kitty was now surely lost beyond recall. Even supposing her to be persuadable following this latest humiliation I did not think I had it in me to work up a fresh set of prevarications and promises; nor would it be fair to do so. Sarah was a different case: quite apart from my feelings towards her it was essential to my interests to maintain my pursuit of her if I could contrive an appropriate means. But that possibility now seemed remote.

I had found my way well out of town on a rising slope of pasture land. Beginning to be hungry I stopped at a roadside inn for a chop and a pint of ale. I sat outside alone, in country silence, looking at the smoke-wreathed towers of London a mile or two ahead. My mind seemed the clearer for the surrounding space. I drank some ale, and for the first time that day enjoyed a glimpse of hope concerning Sarah. My original thought, still a persuasive one, had been that now she was fully aware of my likely intentions she would cut off all communication with me and remain quite out of reach: even if our paths crossed in the Park I could expect to elicit no more than distant courtesies. Now it came to me that I could perhaps turn that conclusion on its head. If a time should come when I *could* once more converse with Sarah alone, then the fact that we had gone so far meant that she would know we were linked by mutual temptation: any concession she then made must therefore be a prelude to the *last* concession. How likely it was that I would ever be in that situation, or how soon it might come about, were less encouraging considerations.

Meanwhile I had a letter to write to Mr Gilbert. I put it to myself that I might tell him, in a humorously rueful spirit, more or less what had passed between Sarah and myself. Since he wished to taste, vicariously, the pleasure of a young rake, might he not find an interest in his tribulations? The possibility did not survive more than two minutes' consideration. However I told the story its outcome could not but appear what it was: a defeat – quite probably a final defeat. Should I lie? Should I invent?

As I pondered these questions I was shaken by a sudden surge of fury. It was my godfather who had plunged me into these miseries, yet the old schemer could sit back serenely and wait for me to translate my discomfiture into entertainment.

I chewed at my chop without tasting it, my mind as empty as the fields around me. As I did so my attention was caught by a movement nearby. Two butterflies fluttered towards me in haphazard flight. Perhaps intrigued by the odour of the chop they hovered nearby, circling one another as though in a dance. Mr Yardley would have known their species and their gender: I could see only that they were brownish in colour. It struck me that they must be dancing their way towards whatever miniature form of copulation butterflies might be supposed to enjoy. Although I watched them with no great interest the brief distraction must have done my brain a service, for as they departed I realized what sort of letter I should attempt to write to Mr Gilbert. I finished the ale and fell into a doze, sprawled across the table.

It was a full half-hour before I woke, with my headache renewed, and set out sleepily for London. Before reaching Cathcart Street I stopped at a bookshop to purchase *Clarissa* – all eight volumes of it, together with a bag to carry them in. The proprietor was a quiet-spoken old fellow with faded eyes. A touch of drollery in his expression led me to talk to him as he took my money.

'Have you read the work yourself?'

'I have, sir.'

'And did you find it morally improving?'

'I need no such improvement, sir. Temptation rarely comes my way. I am safe among my books, like a tortoise in his shell.'

'Do you never pine for the world outside it?'

'Oh no, sir – I hear that it can be dangerous. But you might know that better than I.'

'I will read Mr Richardson,' said I, 'and strive to be good.'

Bearing a million words of morality I walked on to my lodgings. Once in my parlour I rolled up the damp and disgusting garment I had worn the previous evening and gave it to the maid, with its accoutrements, to be thrown away. I unpacked *Clarissa* but had no appetite for reading. Putting the volumes aside I went to bed.

❧

The following morning I was likewise devoid of inspiration or energy – but not of will. I settled myself to my labours as staunchly as any carpenter or bricklayer – those labours in my case consisting of the preparation and composition of a letter to my godfather. It occurred to me that my plight was not unlike poor Quentin's: we had equally, if to different ends, been made slaves to the quill. As a preliminary I grazed here and there in the endless pastures of my newly-purchased *Clarissa*.

It came as a relief to me to be interrupted by a visit from Cullen.

'I allowed you a full day in which to recover,' said he, dropping into a chair and splaying his long legs. 'Tell me the story of the masquerade. Whom did you see? Whom did you swive? And how came you by that scar I see peeping from beneath your wig?'

I gave him a loose and partial account of the evening, pleading my increasing tipsiness and uncertainty.

Matt expressed surprise: 'You are a man of few virtues, Dick, but one of them has always been a hard head for liquor. You must surely have been drinking like a camel.'

'I enjoyed my share, as may be imagined; but as for quantity nothing remarkable. The *quality* was perhaps unusual. Crocker hinted that the punch was brewed stronger as the evening wore on.'

'Then he might have had a bacchanal on his premises by the end of the night?'

'And so perhaps he did. To say the truth I've given little thought to what may have taken place after I left. But I fancy that the antics of the monkey sobered many.'

'Including Mrs Ogden, by your own account. Good God, Dick: you fell from the masthead. Do you live to fight another day?'

'Indeed I do.'

'It seems that you injured your head in the fall.'

'No: that wound came from a later skirmish.'

Reluctantly I told him of my ill-advised attempt on Mrs Deacon. Matt laughed so hard that he all but toppled from his chair. I had to make him stifle his guffaws lest my landlady should hear them from below and guess what was passing.

'You may well laugh,' I said when he was sober again. 'But the whole venereal enterprise is an absurdity. How do you make shift yourself?'

Matt's face contracted into a rare frown and then relaxed again into a grin.

'If the truth must be told – which God forbid – my present remedy for the itch is a humble one: an informal contract with a maid-servant. I would have nothing to report to an inquisitive godfather but "Thursday evening: we did it again."'

'Then you should sympathize with me, who must have

a story to tell and a commentary to write, whether I have spilt or no.'

'You're well paid for your pains, Dick: you'll get no pity from me. But what do you plan to tell the old Spectator at this point?'

'Nothing about Mrs Deacon – you may be sure of that. As for the rest, I have a double strategy. Sarah's parting words will be rendered milder, so that it will still seem possible that I can advance my cause. And you will have seen that I have a great column of *Clarissa* here. I plan to divert the old weasel into the intricacies of deception and pursuit, and away from the crude pleasures of insertion.'

'But is not insertion his favourite theme?'

'I hope the case is not so simple. He is eager to put an eye to the bedroom keyhole, but he affects to despise what he sees. I must muse with him over the contradiction. And in the time thus gained I will try to resume the siege of Mrs Ogden.'

When Matt had gone I set about composing my letter. The attempt to describe my intentions had served to clarify them: soon I was writing quite briskly. I made my account of the masquerade fitful and dreamlike, with the emphasis almost wholly upon my pursuit of Sarah and Kitty Brindley. Generally speaking I was faithful to the facts up to, and including, the entry of Trinculo. It seemed necessary, however, to alter the terms of Sarah's eventual rebuff. After consideration I decided that she had said: *'Mr Fenwick*

– you threw me into confusion. I have gone too far – I have gone too far.'

Having finished the narrative I attempted a modulation into a breezier vein:

In short, at half past eleven your godson was very hopefully situated, with Miss Brindley reserved for his immediate pleasure and Mrs Ogden having heartily compromised herself. Then that confounded monkey was somehow set loose, and these gains were thrown away. But I must blame myself. If I had been less frantically concerned to find Mrs Ogden once more, I would have offered her no opportunity for second thoughts and would have enjoyed a night of pleasure with Kitty.

Kitty, I fear, is now lost to me – but perhaps her attractions were beginning to grow thin. Concerning Sarah I remain hopeful. Having thrown her into confusion once, I may hope to do so again; and if on this occasion she went 'too far', there must be a chance that she can be persuaded to go further. It may even be the case that I can resume my attempts during her husband's forthcoming absence.

Taking a hint from your observations I have been looking again at the letters of Mr Lovelace. I suspect there is a limitation in his general strategy. He sees his campaign solely as a series of advances or 'encroachments' – a term used repeatedly by both the lady and himself. In short, he is the active party, while Clarissa is passive, a fortress under siege. My own hypothesis is that in such cases the woman feels herself to be equally an active

*agent. If her resistance can be represented to her as
aggression she may, in contrition, instinctively falter. I
hope Mrs Ogden is now regretting her cruel change of
mind and may therefore be unwittingly ready to take the
half-step back that will allow me to advance once again.*

Lovelace's philosophy is open to question at several
points. He takes pride in his powers of contrivance, even
seeming to construe them as an aspect of his virility:

> 'What a matchless plotter thy friend! Stand by and
> let me swell! – I am already as big as an elephant:
> and ten times wiser! Mightier too by far! Have I
> not reason to snuff the moon with my proboscis?'

Yet for all this hyperbolical manliness his ingenuity is
exercised upon a victim whom he has imprisoned, and whom
he is eventually obliged to rape. His vaunted cunning has
been exhausted by persuading Clarissa to run away. The
rest is rant.

What is more remarkable is that he values this plotting
more than its object:

> 'More truly delightful to me the seduction process
> than the crowning act – for that's a vapour, a bubble.'

Later he puts the point yet more strongly:

> 'What is the enjoyment of the finest woman in
> the world to the contrivance, the bustle, the
> surprises, and at last the happy conclusion of a

373

well-laid plot. For all the rest, what is it? What but to find an angel in imagination dwindled down to a woman in fact?'

If the 'angel in imagination' did <u>not</u> prove to be 'a woman in fact', no 'happy conclusion' would be possible. But there is a further contradiction. Not merely does he, in Shakespeare's words, make the service greater than the god: he extols the service while denying the existence of the god. The close of each amorous campaign, a mere 'vapour' or 'bubble', will confirm, yet again, the senselessness of the endeavour. Yet I can after all see some perverse sense in his claims. The consummation which he so belittles serves to colour all the enabling circumstances that precede it, if only in terms of metaphor. He soliloquizes when writing to his friend, Belford:

'Lie still, villain, till the time comes – my heart, Jack, my heart! – It is always thumping away on the remotest prospects of this nature.'

Here, as often in Lovelace's letters, the heart is clearly a proxy for an external organ. More surprising is another metaphor in this kind:

'Thou hadst the two letters in thy hand. Had they been in mine, the seal would have yielded to the touch of my warm fingers, and folds, as other plications have done, opened of themselves to oblige my curiosity.'

We two have remarked on the way in which one
may elevate animal consummation by adducing images
from nature, from art, from the moon. Lovelace shows
us that process in reverse. Anticipation of the physical
act can touch with eroticism every step taken towards it.

I admit that a further fallacy remains. If pursuit and
conquest are validated reciprocally then the experience
itself is mysteriously annihilated.

After all, however, Lovelace's inconsistencies are
surely every man's inconsistencies. In the heat of
desire logical contradictions seem immaterial. If the
whole multifarious business must eventually be
compacted into a few moments of animal sensation,
a culmination absurdly incommensurate with the
emotions and activities that have brought it about,
then it may be that the Thing Itself is to be glimpsed
only indirectly, as by means of a series of mirrors,
mutually reflective.

Whether that is indeed the case may perhaps be
confirmed or refuted by the outcome of our present campaign,
concerning which you will shortly hear more from
Yours, &c.

By the time I was spinning out these latter paragraphs I
scarcely knew where I was heading or what I was talking
about. What mattered was that I should provide Mr Gilbert,
as he read my words in his distant country house, sufficient
material to exercise his mind and his imagination. My immediate ambition was simply to secure myself a respite. I
despatched the letter with relief.

The following morning I myself received both a package and a letter. In the former there was no message of any kind – only the bangle that I had bought for Kitty. I knew now, with a sudden sad rush of warm recollections, that my liaison with her was indeed at an end. The letter was a brief one in anonymous capital letters:

IF MR FENWICK WALKS ALONG MARGARET STREET ON TUESDAY NIGHT AT TEN O'CLOCK HE MAY LEARN SOMETHING OF INTEREST TO HIM.

21

That anonymous invitation I could not refuse. Whatever the outcome, here would be a tale of some sort for Mr Gilbert. In any case mere curiosity would have driven me to seek an answer to the puzzle. The most probable explanation was a joke of some kind. If that were so I would need to be wary of making a fool of myself. But what could be achieved by luring me to Margaret Street? A graver possibility had occurred to me: perhaps Ogden, guessing at my interest in his wife, had hired a couple of Bravoes to break my bones. But I had confidence in my own prowess. Margaret Street was a peaceable thoroughfare. I would arrive early, to spy out the territory, and I would wear steel.

Meanwhile I could use the intervening Monday to disentangle my affairs a little further. There was to be a carousal at the Black Lion: if I attended I was likely to meet Nick Horn, and could learn how matters stood with regard to Kitty Brindley.

In the short time since the masquerade I had more than

once felt hot rage against Nick. Had he not sneakingly spirited Kitty away, behind my back, knowing her to be my property? But it was a mood I could not sustain. If I was indeed Kitty's protector I had failed her. Nick had even done me a favour of sorts by coming to her aid. What might have passed between them since I scarcely wished to know; but felt it necessary to find out.

When I arrived at the tavern the entertainment was already well advanced, as evidenced by the loudness of the laughter. A grinning booby of a fellow was being roundly abused for having relieved himself from the window overlooking the street. It was Horn who came to his defence, scrambling onto a table to be better heard: 'Gentlemen! Gentlemen! Be reasonable. George Edgar has done no more than we have all done in time of need. If a man has to piss, then piss he must. The King pisses. Our Saviour Himself pissed many a time.'

The claim produced uproar. John Herbert mounted another table to bawl a rebuke: 'Horn, you are worse than Edgar! You have shamed us! We are disgusted.'

There was more cheering and jeering, but Nick, always in his element when attempting provocation, shouted down the shouters: 'Those who object profane our religion. They reject the Incarnation. God took residence in a human body: of course He pissed like the rest of us.'

'Animal!' roared Herbert. 'Such physical matters are not to be contemplated.'

'Not to be contemplated?' cried Nick. 'The scriptures demand that we contemplate blood and wounds and physical resurrection.'

A random voice shouted: 'But could He have changed his water into wine?'

Here the exchanges subsided into blasphemy, one sot suggesting that Christ could have wrought an internal miracle and filled the Apostles' cups direct from his pintle, while another claimed to be capable of performing this very miracle on his own account, and offered to provide a demonstration. Amid the tumult Horn caught sight of me, jumped from the table and pushed his way across the room.

'You may be looking for me,' he said, more sober than I would have guessed.

'I was.'

We went halfway down a flight of stairs, away from the din. Nick looked wary, as though he feared I might seize him by the throat.

'We have business to discuss, Mr Horn.'

'Not business, Dick – not business. Let me tell you what passed. I chanced upon Puck, weeping, and spoke to her from a kindly impulse. She said that you had promised to take her away long before, at midnight, but that she had seen you since, warmly engaged with another lady. So I stripped off my beard and escorted her chastely to her lodging.'

'Then you took no mean advantage of the situation?'

Nick looked at me with some hostility.

'You are hardly entitled to ask – but I did not. I have a high regard for Miss Brindley, and would do nothing to cause her unhappiness. But if you ask whether I hope to improve upon this encounter, the answer is yes. I infer that your own artillery is directed elsewhere.'

I had no ready reply, and could hardly stand upon my dignity since there was none to stand on. At last I said, stiffly and unwillingly: 'I behaved badly that night. Please convey my apologies to Miss Brindley. She had every right to feel wounded. I still think fondly of her, but I cannot claim the right to trouble her again.'

Horn stared at me as he took in my words.

'Are you suggesting . . .?'

'I am suggesting that you make the most of your chance. But be kind.'

'You need have no fear, Dick. I worship the lady.'

He shook my hand with an earnestness most unusual in him. Lacking words I nodded a response before slipping away in no very cheerful frame of mind.

On Tuesday night I approached Margaret Street by way of a dark alley, my hat-brim pulled down to my eyes. Though I moved like a thief my blood was up: it was a relief to be taking a physical risk after the many weeks of fabrication and pretence. I had not felt so fiery since leaving Rome the previous year.

Although no moon was visible it was one of those nights in which a certain luminosity seems to be suspended in the atmosphere. Turning the corner I could make out nearly the whole length of Margaret Street. Between small leakages of light from some of the houses there were patches of deeper shadow, but as I watched and waited I saw no sign of movement anywhere. Only when a distant clock struck the hour did I venture forward. I walked along the street at a steady pace, staying close to the centre to avoid ambush – but I heard no footsteps save my own. I reached the far end, near Mrs Kinsey's house, without seeing a soul.

Pausing there I heard a whisper: 'Mr Fenwick!'

I turned, with my hand on my sword-hilt, to see a cloaked figure emerge from the shadows. As it drew near me the hood was thrown back to reveal the face of Sarah.

Bewildered, I spoke in a low voice: 'Have you run away?'

'Of course not. I am staying with my aunt and have crept out.'

'You run a great risk–' I began, but was interrupted.

'We cannot talk here. Follow me.'

At the corner of the street was what seemed to be a rear entrance to Mrs Kinsey's property. Following Sarah through a gate, which she locked behind us, I realized that we were in a high-walled courtyard. She led me towards a shape I dimly discerned to be a landau, with the covers down. In a moment we had climbed inside and were sitting together in complete darkness. I pushed my hat and sword to one side of me: Sarah was on the other.

'I needed to talk to you,' she whispered. 'Here we will not be disturbed.'

'Is this your aunt's carriage?'

'No, no – my husband's. He leaves it here because it is rarely used.'

It smelt powerfully of musty leather. Seated beside Sarah I could have reached out and touched her, but made no move for fear of making a false one. The initiative was entirely hers. She spoke again, very low: 'This carriage is like a confessional. I can talk more freely when I cannot be seen.'

'I am listening.'

'My last words to you – at the masquerade – were foolish. Insincere. I find it hard to regulate my conduct. If I behave naturally I go too far in one direction; if I behave as I think I ought, I go too far in another.'

After a pause she resumed, whispering close to my ear: 'The masquerade was a wonder to me. It haunts my mind. You have travelled and attended great receptions. I have known only life with my aunt. That and my strange marriage. The masquerade was a new world. I could see a hundred lives.'

She broke off, panting slightly. I sat motionless, conscious of sounds alone.

'My life has been so cautious – one day like another. Some people – even some women – dare to take risks. Why should not I be one of them?

'Dressed as Diana I was a different person. In darkness I was a different person – I *am* a different person. When you kissed me I was a different person. Why should not these other selves be allowed to live? What stifles them? Nothing but habit and fear and propriety. Is not propriety a kind of murder?'

She was panting once more, from sheer force of feeling. By now I could apprehend her as a dark shape in a slightly thinner darkness. Her cloak had fallen against my thigh.

I whispered a question: 'You say your marriage is strange?'

'How can I be sure? It is the only marriage I have known. But I think it is strange.'

'Can you say why? Or will propriety prevent you?'

'Why should I not tell you? You can judge for yourself.'

She paused, creating a total silence: 'Mr Ogden is generous. He will buy me anything. But to him I am not a person: I am a possession. He married me – he told me as much – for my beauty. I do not boast: I speak only of his opinion. My person infatuates him.

'He has no conversation. He could never have found a wife if he had not met me by chance.'

She drew a long, tremulous breath.

'I shall shock myself by saying what I mean to say – and saying it to a man. But this is my life – my only life: why should I not talk about it?

'By day, in a drawing-room, I could not do it. Shut up in this box, in darkness, I shall say what I choose. I shall tell you about my wedding night.'

Another silence, then the whisper again, seemingly within my own head.

'I was timid, not knowing how things should be done. Walter and I had conversed but little during our courtship. When we were alone in the bedroom he was struck dumb.

'He sat me on a chair and stood staring at me. He shifted his position and stared again. He lifted the candle to alter the light. All this time, in great confusion, I sat motionless. I could see that he was greatly agitated. He began to make adjustments to my hair or to my clothes, each time stepping back to view the alteration. It was as though he were making preparations to paint my portrait. At last he unfastened my dress, with shaking hands, and then pulled me upright to strip away all my clothes. He gazed at me as I stood naked and turned me about, grunting to himself. Suddenly he lifted me and flung me on to the bed. I cried out, but he forced himself upon me with a kind of snarl.

'When he was done he rolled aside, still without a word, and fell into a profound sleep. I was left shocked and bleeding, bewildered by the secret practices of marriage.

'In the morning he was in excellent humour, more easy than I had ever seen him, but he made no reference to what had taken place the night before.'

Sarah stopped, as though she had concluded a chapter of her story. At that moment there came a clattering of hooves and a rattling of wheels the other side of the wall. As Sarah turned her head, startled, I inhaled her breath. I could have seized her, then and there, but had the self-command not to do so. When the sounds died away I ventured a question: 'Has that performance been repeated?'

'Night after night. It is the heart of our marriage. He views me, then he seizes me. I think he has no words for what he wants or what he feels.'

Then she was insisting again, as though to make her meaning clearer: 'You must understand: Walter is not cruel. He has some vision in his mind. Save for the final act I could as well be a statue. He will have me stand naked, raise an arm, turn this way or that. Sometimes he has me stand by a mirror, so that he sees two of me.'

'What goes through *your* mind?'

'Usually nothing. I am lifeless. But on occasion I feel – something. He is obsessed with beauty and thinks me beautiful. This is flattering. And he has an art to make me *more* beautiful, with a costume, a jewel, a posture.'

Somehow our positions had shifted slightly: I could feel the warmth of her body against my shoulder. We had reached an equilibrium of understanding that one false gesture could destroy. I spoke scarcely audibly, my lips touched her hair: 'You were beautiful as Diana.'

'So it seemed to me. I felt that I could have men kneeling at my feet.'

'You know that I, for one, was ready to kneel.'

Sarah breathed a stealthy laugh into the darkness.

'I think kneeling alone would not have satisfied you.'

'You indulged me very sweetly. But that damned monkey . . .'

'It was like waking from a dream. I was back in the real world, and trying to remember how to behave in it.'

'Here is the dream again. We could as well be in some mountain cave.'

I reached to take her hand, but attempted nothing further. We sat silent together in mutual invisibility. For the moment I was calmly replete in this strange medium, my senses alert to the slightest of sounds or sensations. It was Sarah who spoke again: 'Walter showed me how a prism can transform light into a rainbow. For me the masquerade had that effect. I could hardly bear to return to colourless daily life.'

'Did Mr Ogden feel as you did?'

'The evening had a great effect upon him also. He said nothing as we went home – not a word, but I could sense his excitement. In the bedroom he tore off my costume, quite beside himself, and threw me to the floor. I have never seen him so frantic. He even bit me until the blood came.'

385

'The man is an animal.'

'He is not. I must do him justice. His inner fantasy is very vivid, and it seems that I inspire it. But he cannot put feelings into words. They overflow as physical excess.'

'You are too generous.'

'No. No longer. I have ceased to be generous. That is why I wrote to you.'

She clasped my hand more tightly, and pressed against me.

'He has made me rich. But if I fulfil his demands, am I not honouring my contract? Can he complain if I look beyond him?'

'In search of what?'

'Passion. Excitement. Joy. Why should I not be exceptional? Why should I not be an adventurer?'

'Would you risk wickedness?'

'With you – yes.'

I drew her to me, gently, very gently. When I kissed her on the mouth, as at the masquerade, she put her arms around me, her body trembling against mine, tense as a violin string.

I broke off to whisper: 'It seems that your experience has not given you an aversion to carnal love.'

'I have never known carnal love.'

'It is this.'

We kissed once more. I pushed off her cloak and felt for the softness of her breast. Her arms tightened around me and I winced as she bit my lip. Lost in darkness, caught up in a tangle of clothes, I was at once clutching her warm body, hearing her moan, feeling the wetness of her mouth and tasting my own blood. The landau rocked beneath us as I leaned above her and reached below her skirts for the smooth skin of her thighs. A compound of images and sensations had fired my body to the hottest lust it had ever known. My mind, too, was on fire, but some small chamber within it was thinking still. Should I complete the conquest there and then? Yes, yes – because we were ravenous. But no, because we were already forced into contortions in this wobbling box, hobbled by fabrics, struggling with skirts and buttons, a slipping wig, a sword. Inflamed as I was, to the very brink of discharge, I might mortify us both: in seconds our intensities could precipitate as a few hot spurts of animal seed spilt into darkness. Better to wait, if I could bear to, and appease this passion with the fullness it deserved.

As a timely distraction a second carriage rattled past a few feet away. Gently releasing Sarah I sat back and with a heroic effort stifled the sweet pang rising in my loins. I waited for the noise, and for my own panting, to subside before speaking.

'You must be loved as you deserve to be. Can we find somewhere else?'

There was an immediate answer: 'Not now. But very soon – if you are bold.'

'Try me.'

Sarah spoke as one summarizing a prepared stratagem.

'On Friday my husband leaves for Malvern. I shall sleep here at my aunt's. If I leave you a key you can enter through the back door, behind this coach, and steal up to my room.'

I forced myself to be cautious.

'Surely we will be heard?'

'My room is at the top of the rear staircase. No one sleeps near me.'

387

'You will be taking a great risk.'

'I have had enough of timidity. This will be my first adventure. But I swear that we will be safe.'

I kissed her again, long and warmly, but drew away as an idea struck me: 'Why not tonight? Why not now?'

'There are precautions I must take. And I will be seeing my husband in the morning.'

'I understand.'

Sarah sat forward and pulled on her cloak. As she climbed out I retrieved my hat and followed her. We clung to one another, weak and shaken. She motioned me to stoop so that I could hear her whisper: 'Come at midnight. I will hide two keys – one for the courtyard, one for the door just behind us. Leave your hat and sword in the landau. Once inside you climb the staircase to the left. Two flights. At the top you will see my door on your right. It will be ajar.'

'Where will I find the keys?'

'I will show you.'

We stole out by the gate through which we had entered. Sarah took my hand and drew it along the side of the square brick pillar to the left of that entrance. Halfway down was a recess in the mortar, deep enough for me to insert two fingers. Sarah was breathing into my ear again: 'I will leave the keys there. Should any difficulty arise I will leave a note instead – and you can leave a reply.'

'Have you no fears?'

'Of course. But I am drunk. I have been drunk since the masquerade.'

'On Friday night,' said I, 'we shall be drunk together.'

'At midnight,' she repeated. 'Then I shall enjoy the first hour of my new life.'

After one more kiss she slipped away and disappeared into the courtyard.

I let my feet find their way back to Cathcart Street while my mind seethed. I could scarcely take in what had passed. This hour in a dark box had engendered the most powerful joy of my entire life, blending love, lust, sympathy, memory – all conducing to a paroxysm of physical sensation that I had contrived to suppress as one stifles an impending sneeze. How wonderful it had been – and how absurd.

But all was now well. My black night at the masquerade could be forgotten. I had recaptured Sarah and would have a fine tale to tell Mr Gilbert. I would have earned the promised reward, whatever that proved to be.

Where would this lead? Here was certain joy for me, but possible ruin for Sarah. Could she return to the arms of her husband? Could she deceive him? For my part, could I ever bear to let her go?

Such questions were for the future. I turned my back on them, exalted to be lost in the moment. Sarah and I – and my godfather also – had longed for the same outcome. And it would be secured in three days' time.

As I reached my lodgings I was quickened afresh, this time by a twinge of delicious fear. For weeks – for months – in the attempt to please my godfather I had been compelled to devise small adventures for myself. Now, suddenly, there was no need for me to instigate. A single conversation had plunged me into a rapid and possibly perilous narrative quite beyond my control. I would need to have my wits about me. I would need luck.

My dear Godfather,

There is startling progress to report.

An anonymous letter, puzzling to me when it arrived, summoned me to a clandestine meeting with an unnamed party – who proved to be none other than Mrs Ogden herself. She confided, with some passion, that she is made wretched by certain features of her married life – which indeed sound oppressive – and is after all eager to engage with a different partner.

The upshot is an adventure which Mr Lovelace would have relished. While her husband is in Malvern – an absence I owe to your shrewd intervention – she will stay with her aunt, who lives nearby, and I will be granted access to her bed-chamber. To be specific: she will hide a key which will enable me to steal in through the back-door at midnight.

Now I can be at one with Lovelace in anticipatory elation. Although my proboscis does not quite reach the moon, I will attain my goal without resort to drugs or compulsion.

I learned that the inflaming images of the masquerade had had their influence on the lady. Given that Mr Ogden devised them it would appear that he has contributed handsomely to the debauching of his wife.

I am restive with anticipation. Were I a bull I would be tossing my head and pawing the ground. Is such a state of mind and body to be accounted happiness? Not quite, perhaps, since I long for the pleasure to be made complete. Will I find, as Lovelace apparently did, that when completed it has been concluded? You will very shortly, I hope, read my opinions on this matter.

I remain, &c.

22

The following morning, still bursting with elation, I felt compelled to visit Matt Cullen, my sole confidant, to describe what had passed and solicit his opinion. He grinned, as ever, but shook his head.

'This is folly, Dick. You will be seized and charged with robbery.'

'By my old friend Mrs Kinsey? Never. Besides which I trust Sarah's good sense. If she says that we are safe, then safe we shall be. At need she can hide me in a closet.'

'You will have a fine tale to tell – one to raise a protuberance even from Mr Gilbert.'

'I have not forgot my scruples,' said I, 'nor the advice that you yourself gave me. This is private business. I consider Sarah to be under my protection. My godfather will receive no more than the pips and the peelings of the encounter.'

&#8;

That same afternoon, to occupy myself, I went to the Park for a stroll in the early September sunshine. I was hailed by Colonel and Mrs Jennings and paused to chat. The conversation was perforce with Bel, her husband withdrawing into the abstracted affability that masked his deafness.

'Ben told me that he saw you at the masquerade,' said she. 'But I did not – or if I did I failed to penetrate your disguise.'

'You spoke to me, but my face was lost in a beard. Did you enjoy the evening?'

'To be candid my recollection of it is uncertain. But I have reason to think that I must have done.'

There being no more than a glint of drollery in her manner I acknowledged her words with no more than the hint of a smile – but we understood one another. When the two moved on I retired behind a tree to laugh aloud. How various and freakish were human-beings in their gratifications. Perhaps after all I could consider myself an ordinary, sensible fellow.

❦

On the morning when Ogden was due to depart my exhilaration was tempered by unease: there was still scope for mischance. The coach for Worcestershire left, as I had good reason to know, from the Dragon, in Fleet Street. Once again I took the precaution of making sure that Mr Ogden did indeed depart. Standing in an alley beside the inn I saw his thick calves stomp by and watched him haul his heavy body aboard. My distaste for him was instantly refreshed. As the coach set off I could have shouted aloud to think that in a few hours I would be pleasuring his wife.

$$\mathcal{O}$$

My dear Godfather,

I am afraid that the content of this letter will suffice merely to account for the failure that its brevity implies.

True to the arrangement that Sarah and I had made I went to Margaret Street at midnight last night. Having watched Mr Ogden take the coach for Worcestershire in the morning I was full of confidence. Once satisfied that the coast was clear I slipped around to the quiet corner behind Mrs Kinsey's house and fumbled in the crevice where the key was to have been hidden. All hope was instantly dashed as my fingers encountered, not a key, but a folded note. The message was as follows:

I cannot see you tonight. After all I am not yet ready to take this step. I am ashamed of my inconsistency, but my fear was that all might not have gone well between us now that I feel these doubts.

Can you forgive me for having brought you here, with high expectations, for nothing? I can hardly forgive myself. Yet I need only a little more time, a little more resolve, to bring about the meeting we planned. It will happen – I promise it will.

I am afraid that your godson, alone at midnight in a most respectable street, gave vent to a rousing volley of curses before turning on his heel and returning to his lodgings.

This morning finds me less sullen and more philosophical. I have observed in the past Mrs Ogden's extreme fluctuations of mood and motive. Being impulsive she is always likely to venture a promise somewhat bolder than she can fulfil, and later recoil from it, as on this occasion. I have no doubt that in a very short time her conduct will catch up with her desires. Already this morning she will be regretting her own timidity. I will leave in our hiding-place a cool acknowledgement that I hope may hasten such a reaction. If all goes as I wish and expect, last night's rebuff will come to seem no more than an incidental delay. I reserve the right, however, to exact some little retribution for the slight. Rest assured that you will hear the full story as it unfolds.

I remain, &c.

Having written this letter to my godfather I set down in my Journal a full account of what had actually taken place, trying to be as precise as possible, in case my memory later deceived me.

It was a cool night. There had been one or two sharp showers, and more seemed imminent: the streets were patched with puddles. I was dressed to pass unrecognized and to be ready to defend myself, at need, in the dangerous midnight darkness. I made my approach by the same alley as before, and on this occasion observed from the corner as the watch passed along the length of Margaret Street. When they were gone, all was still. I went swiftly to the back of Mrs Kinsey's house, reached in our hiding-place for a key – but found only a note, damp from the earlier rain. I tore it slightly as I drew it out.

Unable to read it in the dark I hurried back along Margaret Street, but soon became aware of footsteps behind me. Anxious to avoid even the slightest chance of being accosted I quickened my pace – but heard my follower quicken also. In response I began to run, as best I could in the dark, jumping over puddles and stumbling on the cobblestones. Feeling I would be more secure on known territory I turned into Wyvern Street, heading towards Tom Crocker's house. After fifty yards or so I checked my steps and now heard nothing. Here it was darker yet. I stood stock-still for a minute or two, glad to recover my breath.

Calm once more I moved on until I saw a light ahead. It proved to be attached to the great iron gates behind Crocker's courtyard: the house itself being in darkness. I took from my pocket Sarah's message, and with a little difficulty deciphered it:

I cannot see you tonight. After all I am not yet ready to take this step.

I am ashamed of my inconsistency, but my fear was that all might not have gone well between us now that I have felt these doubts.

Can you forgive me for having brought you here, with high expectations, for nothing? I can hardly forgive myself. Yet I need only a little more time, a little more

resolve, to bring about the meeting we planned. It will
happen – I promise it will.

The mere fact of lighting on a letter when I had looked for
a key had prepared me for disappointment, but I nonetheless
swore aloud at what I read. As I thrust the paper into my
pocket and turned away I heard footsteps once more, and
almost at once my pursuer emerged into the weak circle of
light. To my astonishment he proved to be Ogden – Ogden
sweating, hatless, and dishevelled, his stockings spattered
with mud.

He made directly for me till he stood within touching
distance, and addressed me in a kind of whispered scream:

'I saw you, Fenwick – I saw you at the Dragon! Damn
you! Damn you! You are after my wife! Give me that note!'

He lunged at me and I stepped back to elude him, my
mind in confusion. I think I said: 'Mr Ogden, contain yourself.
I know you are a man of strong passions.'

'You know nothing about me!' he yelped. 'Nothing! You
are after my wife, you devil! I will kill you!'

He threw himself upon me, clutching at my throat. I tried
to fend him off, but he was heavy and strong and brought
me to the ground. We rolled in the mud, but I broke away
and staggered upright. As he scrambled to his own feet,
panting, I stepped back and drew my sword.

Ogden's wig had fallen off, disclosing the bald head I had
seen at the masquerade. His face was twisted with rage. This
huffing, dripping, fat fellow my rival in love? It was an
absurdity. I made to take charge of the situation, pointing
my sword at him.

'Mr Ogden, I give you fair warning! Enough, sir! I say enough!'

With each exclamation I made a small jab in his direction, to prick him to a distance. But the mad booby suddenly pushed the blade aside and launched himself at me, landing a heavy blow on my jaws. Staggering backwards I raised my sword again, thinking merely to keep him off; but with the rage of a bull he threw himself forward again, and was impaled. In a panic I tried to twist the bending blade clear, but with a second lunge he impaled himself further, and fell sideways. I wrenched the sword away as he did so, but he dropped down and lay sprawled in a puddle.

I stood stock still for a moment. Some dogs were barking nearby and there was a shrill chattering coming from Trinculo's cage in the courtyard. It had begun to rain again. Throwing down the sword I made to lift Ogden, but found him weighty and inert. With great exertion I managed to turn him on to his back. There was blood on his coat, though not much. I could see no sign of life in him.

'Good evening, sir,' said a voice behind me.

I leaped around, to find that Pike had emerged from a side gate.

'I was disturbed by the monkey,' he added.

'I fear I have killed a man.'

'Mr Ogden?'

Pike stooped to examine him, touching and peering. He stood and drew a long breath before saying calmly: 'Yes, he's dead.'

'But there's very little blood.'

'He'll have bled internally.'

Fear and shock stupefied me. I managed to say something like: 'I did not mean to kill him. He ran on to my sword.'

'The gentleman seems to have been unarmed.'

'But he attacked me. I did not mean to kill him. I drew only to keep him at bay.'

'Why did he attack you, sir?'

'He thought I was after his wife.'

'An old friend of yours, as I recall.'

'I knew her when we were children.'

To my shame my voice was quavering from fear and shock.

'We must decide what to do, sir,' said Pike.

He stood beneath the lamp, frowning. I tried to regain command of myself, but my mind was numb. Trinculo and the dogs had fallen silent. The rain was steady.

'I thought Mr Ogden was in Malvern,' said Pike.

'He left for Malvern this morning. I saw him go.'

'Then he returned secretly. Did he see you with Mrs Ogden?'

'No!' I cried, 'I have not been with her.' Then added lamely: 'He saw me outside her aunt's house, where she is staying. He chased after me.'

Pike nodded as he took in what I had said, and then stood with folded arms, still brooding. At length he sighed.

'I'll try to help you, sir. We can have the body put where it will never be found. But I must pay those who do the business. Can you find thirty guineas by tomorrow?'

'Yes.'

'He may be seen by the lamplight. We must move him.'

Together we heaved and slithered the sodden body into a dark corner.

'The job must be done before dawn,' said Pike. 'I'll take care of it. You go home, sir. Don't let yourself be seen. Clean your sword and your clothes. Behave natural and say nothing. I'll get word to you.'

He hurried off into the darkness, and I was left shivering. I retained just sufficient self-command to wipe my sword on a handkerchief before sheathing it, and to retrieve my hat, which was lying in the road. Fearing to be seen I took a roundabout route to Cathcart Street through the continuing rain. My mind was with Ogden, lying in the wet mud.

Back in my rooms I cleaned the sword thoroughly, feeling sick as I did so. The handkerchief I had wiped it with I would throw away in the morning. My shoes and stockings were muddy, but that would not be a suspicious circumstance of itself. As far as I could see by candlelight there was no blood on my clothes. Even wearier than I was fearful I fell into bed, and was at once asleep.

23

I woke early, cold with terror but able to think. If Pike had been as good as his word I might yet be safe. No one but Pike had seen what had happened, and he was my ally. Who knew of the assignation? Only Sarah herself, Gilbert and Cullen. I should use the morning to clear myself with all three before any suspicions began to arise.

As I sat upright I became conscious of a painful lump inside my mouth. I climbed out of bed and took a small mirror to the window. Peering into it I saw that I had badly bitten my tongue – no doubt when the frantic Ogden punched me. Somehow, in the confusion that followed, the hurt had gone unnoticed. Here was yet another concern: I would need to keep this ignoble wound hidden from others.

By the grey morning light from the window I wrote a brief message to Sarah:

I returned home last night, sadly disappointed, after reading your unexpected dismissal. You had so encouraged my expectations that the rebuff hit me hard. I know you too well to suspect mere fickleness or provocation; but where we now stand I cannot tell. For the present I am utterly discouraged, but I must hope that at some future time there will be further communication between us.

I left the house to deliver the message immediately. Early as it was the streets were already busy. I hurried along with bowed head. The rain had stopped, but the cobbles were still wet and the kennels were flowing freely. I contrived, unremarked, to drop my bloodied handkerchief into a workman's brazier, and saw it flare up. On reaching the quieter district near Margaret Street I trod warily, but saw no face that I recognized and attracted no attention. From outward appearances it seemed that nobody in Mrs Kinsey's house was as yet awake. I hid my message with shaking fingers and hurried on. A morbid impulse almost took me on to Crocker's house to see whether Ogden's carcase had been removed, but I resisted it and returned to my lodgings.

When the servants had risen I breakfasted as usual, although the tea sorely burnt my damaged tongue. All the time I was telling myself: 'I must think – I must think: everything must be calculated.' It was in this spirit that I wrote to Mr Gilbert the letter already recorded, and then set down a true account of what had taken place. Aware that my memory was already wilfully clouding over certain details I wanted to preserve the facts while I still could. It had occurred to me that should the worst come to the worst I might one day need such a statement to assist me in constructing a defence. I also felt that capturing the wretched episode on paper might help me to stop thinking about it.

The hope was partly fulfilled. Having completed my account and locked it safely in a drawer I found myself less concerned with the events themselves than with their likely causes and consequences. Ogden had been made suspicious by seeing me at the Dragon – what a fool I had been to allow myself to be noticed. Perhaps his suspicions had already been stirred by something in Sarah's manner – or had he even seen something at the masquerade? But I had certainly seen him depart. It seemed that he had become increasingly agitated as the journey proceeded and had therefore left the coach at one of the earlier stopping points to return to London. If he had gone to his house he would have been missed in the morning, and a search would be in prospect; but he might have stayed away from it in his determination to take his wife by surprise.

Sarah must have found my note by now, and her sole anxiety would be the rift between us. If Pike had succeeded in his task she would have no further cause for concern or suspicion until word came from Malvern that Ogden had failed to arrive.

Thinking back, I did not know what I would have done had Pike not appeared – surely nothing sensible or honourable. I had been stunned. Ogden was dead and beyond help. To confess to what had happened would have been to incriminate Sarah as well as myself. If I had simply run away the body would have been found soon after daybreak, Sarah would have been questioned and I would now be sitting in panic waiting for a knock at the door.

All my hopes rested with Pike. I respected his resourceful-ness and knowledge of the city's underworld, but I did not know how far I could depend on him. It seemed that he had elected to help me merely upon a whim. How far would that impulse take him? If he had encountered unforeseen difficulties would he not have given up? I was impatient to hear from him. Had he been successful his task would have been completed in the hours of darkness. Unfortunately I could not wait in the house for a message: I had to obtain the thirty guineas I had promised – a substantial sum, but no doubt a fair reward for disposing of a rich man's corpse.

Reluctantly I went out again into the crowded streets. As I walked towards Charing Cross I became aware of a tall fellow alongside me and in step with me. When his arm distinctly brushed my own I noticed a piece of paper held loosely in his hand. I took it from him and he was gone. We had not exchanged a word, nor had I seen his face.

At the first opportunity I stepped into a side alley to read the note: 'St Gregory's church, Trent Square, tomorrow morning at 10'. Here was Pike's message. Why not simply 'All well'? There was to be a further night of suspense, which would be hard to bear – but I might have been reading 'Escape while you can!' I walked on to procure the money.

By the time I had done so I was seriously fatigued, confounded by the shocks of the previous eighteen hours. If I had returned to Cathcart Street I would surely have fallen into a deep sleep. Instead I went doggedly in search of Matt Cullen, knowing that it was vital for me to see him before the day was out, if I was to secure him as a potential witness. He was not in his lodging, but I found him soon enough in a nearby tavern, where we withdrew to a quiet table. For all my weariness I was primed to perform.

'I bring black news,' said I, and showed him Sarah's note, torn and smudged. 'This was what awaited me.'

Matt shook his head as he read it. 'A grave disappointment. What did you do?'

'What could I do? I stalked back home in a damned ill humour.'

'How do you account for the change of mind?'

'By weakness of purpose. This is not the first time she has taken three steps forward and one step back. Perhaps her great toad of a husband somehow touched her heart when he bade her goodbye.'

I was relieved to hear my voice speaking out in a convincingly careless style even as my mind saw an image of the toad laid low.

'You speak with a lisp, Dick.'

'I know. Last night in a damned bad dream I threshed about and bit my tongue. I blame Mrs Ogden for that, too.'

'You are a wronged man, my friend. What will you do?'

'Nothing for the moment. I shall give Sarah time to regret her change of mind, and later I shall give her cause to regret it still more.'

'What a business it is!' cried Matt. 'Head and tail forever at odds. Thank God my little servant maid has no mind to speak of.'

When I was once more in my rooms I sat with my head in my hands, giddy with anxiety. The future was lost in dark cloud. I should have been racked by guilt for having killed a man – but I was not. Not for a moment had I intended any such drastic consequence. It had been Ogden who had attacked *me*. I had drawn my sword solely to keep him at bay. In a manner he had killed himself, throwing his body upon the blade, and in so blundering a manner as to suffer a fatal wound rather than a trivial one. Only by a chance in a hundred had the steel released soul from flesh. True I had excited his rage by trying to cuckold him – but I had failed in my attempt. The intended harm had not been done. At every turn I had been unlucky. So I excused myself.

I had to acknowledge to myself, with reluctant respect, that Ogden, in his crazed way, had shown determination and courage. But I could make sense neither of his life nor his death: he had been driven by forces of ambition, desire, and pride, of a kind unknown to me. He was an animal of a different and alien species.

❧

When I ventured into the silence of St Gregory's next morning there were no more than half a dozen worshippers at prayer. Among them, incongruously on his knees, was Pike, who rose when he saw me and went out through a side door. I followed, and found that we were alone together in a small graveyard enclosed by bushes. He motioned me close and spoke in a low voice: 'The goods were safely disposed of.'

'Thank God. Where?'

'Bottom of the Thames, with a thousand ships overhead.'

'I've brought the money.'

Pike nodded and took the purse. 'A large sum; but we needed dependable men.'

'Will they not blab?'

'It would be a death-warrant.'

'Mr Ogden should have arrived in Malvern last night. Word will get back. There will surely be a search . . .'

'There will be a search, but it can lead nowhere. Say nothing. Be yourself. Go about your business.'

I nodded.

'You've hurt your mouth, sir. Don't let it be noticed.'

I looked him in the eye. 'Why did you help me?'

'It was the spin of a coin. There was no time to think. As I say: sit this out. If I hear of trouble I'll send word.'

He was gone before I could express my thanks, leaving me alone in the graveyard. I wandered around it for a few minutes, thinking of Ogden's body lodged in mud below fathoms of black water.

The following morning I spent indoors. I tried to read, but could not. Imprisoned by my predicament I could think of nothing outside it. It was impossible to tell when and how the unavoidable threat would take form. If Ogden had simply failed to arrive there might be a prompt inquiry from Lord Downs. If he had forwarded a message to plead an unexpected delay then days might pass before there was any cause for concern. Would Lord Downs communicate with Ogden's home, or with his office? I could not tell. At what point would Sarah be consulted? I was a little reassured by the reflection that, whatever she was told, she could have no reason to suspect me of foul play. In my rivalry with her husband the advantage had been entirely on my side. What reason could I have had for attacking him?

Hungry as I was for news I even thought of hovering in the vicinity of Margaret Street, to look out for any unusual activity there. I needed repeatedly to remind myself that such a venture would be folly. Pike had been right: I could do nothing but wait. In the course of the afternoon, however, a chance recollection so disturbed me that I could stay indoors no longer, but hurried out to the bookshop where I had purchased *Clarissa*. Affecting to look about at random I sought out an account of famous trials at the Old Bailey. In five minutes I hit on the passage that had come to my mind, a quoted 'Statute of stabbing': '*If any one stabs another, who hath not at that time a weapon drawn, or hath not first struck the party who stabs, he is deemed guilty of murder, if the person stabbed dies within six months afterwards.*' Should rumours somehow emerge of an encounter between myself and Ogden this statute could prove fatal to me: my opponent had never carried a sword. It was true that he had 'struck' me, but only with his fist; and in the case described the unfortunate defendant, a Mrs Churchill, had been sentenced to death even though the slain man had drawn his sword and she herself had had no weapon. She had merely pushed him back, so that he was off guard when suffering the fatal wound, inflicted by her lover – who promptly fled the country and escaped scot free. This history disposed of my lingering hopes that a fair account of what had passed between myself and Ogden might see me acquitted. Everything would depend upon silence, luck and dissimulation.

When more news came it was from an unexpected quarter:

My dear Richard,

You had every right to be exasperated by Mrs Ogden's second change of mind. It exemplifies the feminine changeability which confused me as a younger man. I then assumed that what a woman said, she meant – only to be puzzled by subsequent amendments or contradictions. It was as though I should have been making allowance for a simultaneous language of glance and gesture which modified the spoken word. If that was indeed the case I was doomed to bewilderment, being wholly deficient in this mode of communication. It is clear that you labour under no such disadvantage. This rebuff postpones the resolution you seek, but may at the same time add zest to it, as offering a resistance to be overcome.

I have every confidence that, despite the setback you report, I shall soon be reading a further chapter in your pursuit of Mrs Ogden. The contest has so engaged my attention that I have written to Lord Downs with a view to visiting Holbrook Hall while Mr Ogden is at work there. I would be intrigued to form my own opinion of the rival for whom you have conceived so lively a distaste.

Yours, &c.

The sequel followed soon afterwards:

My dear Richard,

A singular development, which will surprise you as it surprised me. I hear from Lord Downs that Ogden failed to arrive at Holbrook Hall on the appointed evening. His trunk was delivered, together with a note of apology, to the effect that in the course of his journey he had found himself obliged, for pressing reasons, to turn back to London. He expected, however, to be in Malvern within two or three days.

Have you heard anything of this matter? Might there be a connection with Mrs Ogden's unexpected change of mind?

Yours, &c.

Anticipating some such letter I was already resolved not to reply for several days. I would always be able to plead that I had used the time in fruitless inquiries. The very next morning, however, this expedient was cast into doubt. Matt Cullen burst in upon me and paced the floor in his excitement at what he had to tell.

'I bring you strange news, Dick – exceeding strange. I have this moment come from a chance encounter with my acquaintance, Mr Gow, who is employed, you will remember, by Mr Ogden. He tells me that he was surprised to see Ogden in his office in Duke Street on the evening of the day he left for Malvern. That is to say on the very night that you were purposing to pleasure his wife. What say you to that?'

In the circumstances I was commendably cool.

'You surprise me – but less than you might think,' I said, and passed him Gilbert's latest letter, which he eagerly read.

'His questions are my questions,' said he, 'and they must surely be yours also. Did Ogden come back because he had suspicions? Did his wife shut you out because she knew of his return?'

I improvised as readily as I could have hoped: 'The last question is easily answered: no. Why should she have written what she did when she might simply have said "Not tonight"? Ogden's return was no more than a coincidence — but it was certainly a grim one. There could have been awkward consequences. Did your friend Mr Gow speak to him?'

'He said that he tried to, but that Ogden pushed past him without a word. Apparently Ogden would occasionally spend a night at the office after working late, and for that reason he was not unduly surprised to see him. He assumed that there had been a change of plan.'

'Has he seen him since?'

'Apparently not.'

I made a show of ruminating on the situation.

'After all I see little in the matter. Even if Ogden had suspicions they must have come to nothing. By now he is presumably at work in Holbrook Hall.'

'Unless he found his wife looking flushed and shifty.'

We speculated about the mystery for another half-hour, all to no purpose. I found it surprisingly easy to improvise possible explanations, serious or facetious. Ogden had been racked by sudden giddiness or failure of vision, and therefore hastened back to London to see his physician. He had realized that some optical equipment, vital to his mysterious trade, had been left behind. An angel had appeared to him in a dream and told him to postpone his visit. Amid this frivolity I did manage to suggest that, since I myself was clearly in no position to pursue the matter, Matt could do me a favour by maintaining contact with Mr Gow in the hope of gleaning further information.

When I was alone again the anxious thoughts flocked like ravens. Cullen's news had been far more disturbing than he could have known. My hope had been that when Ogden's disappearance was eventually acknowledged – as it soon must be – he might be thought to have vanished anywhere in south-eastern England. Now the search would be narrowed to known London territory. Perhaps others had seen Ogden, or even spoken to him. Moreover Sarah herself would surely associate his return – and in time perhaps even his subsequent fate – with our planned assignation. Greatly agitated I found comfort only in Pike's assertion that any possible search was doomed to lead nowhere. There was no evidence of crime. Suspicion would have nothing to feed on. Thus I reassured myself.

As I dressed the following morning I recalled Pike's advice that I should comport myself as normally as possible. It might prove awkward if someone later observed that I had been particularly elusive around the time of Ogden's disappearance. This disagreeable thought gave rise to another: that I had been left solitary. With whom could I comfortably pass the time? On no account could I see Sarah. Kitty was lost to me. For related reasons I could not comfortably seek out Crocker or Horn. I was condemned to the loneliness of a criminal, and far from happy in that predicament.

It was nonetheless essential to preserve appearances. The day being fine, if windy, I took a turn in the Park, bowing to several acquaintances and pausing to make conversation with one or two others. All the time I kept a wary look-out for Sarah or her aunt, but there was no sign of them. Later I ate a chop at Keeble's, where I contributed to the general talk easily enough.

By the time I returned to my lodgings it was already dark, but I was soon to be surprised by another visit from Matt Cullen.

'More news,' he said, 'direct from an agitated Mr Gow, whom I have just left. Ogden's hat has been handed in to his home. Apparently it was found in the mud in Margaret Street the morning after he was seen in his office.'

'Can they be certain it was Ogden's?'

'Mrs Ogden has apparently confirmed it, although expressing astonishment.'

Here was a double blow. I was at once reminded that Ogden had indeed been hatless when he caught up with me outside Crocker's courtyard. It would now be suspected that he had come to grief in or near Margaret Street. Moreover Sarah had learned of her husband's return and would have sudden cause for surmise and misgivings. I asked eager questions to hide my dismay.

'When did all this come out?'

'This very morning. Gow was sent for.'

'And then he spoke of having seen Ogden?'

'Of course.'

'What does he make of it all?'

'The poor devil is in dire confusion. He's a retiring fellow who finds himself suddenly obliged to assume responsibilities. Acting on advice he is sending post-haste to Holbrook Hall to find out whether Ogden has yet arrived. I could have told him, of course, but only by involving you and Gilbert.'

I summoned up some spirit: 'You bring strange tidings, Master Cullen. There may have been dark deeds in Margaret Street.' I made a show of reflecting. 'And I myself might have been nearby at the time.'

'What time were you there?'

'I can tell you exactly: at midnight.'

'Did you linger after reading the lady's message?'

'Certainly not. It was a dismal night.'

'You noticed nothing untoward?'

'There was nothing to notice but darkness and rain.'

We stood in silence for a moment till Cullen grinned: 'This will all prove to be nothing – much ado about a hat.'

'Meanwhile,' said I, 'let us go and drink some wine.'

And this we did. I had never felt less convivial, but it seemed necessary to put on a show of careless good cheer. I contrived a passable imitation, but it left me empty. The worst of it was that as we drank and chattered I had no space to think. Only when I returned home two hours later, with my head none too clear, could I attempt to review the changing situation.

Sarah must now be in a state of bewilderment and suspense. On the very night of our planned assignation, and perhaps when I was still in the vicinity, her husband had been unaccountably lurking nearby. Then, as would soon emerge, he had vanished forever. She could not but look for meaning in this coincidence. Whatever she felt or suspected, however, she could surely say nothing. To implicate me would be to implicate herself. Yet there would surely be an inquiry of some kind, and it could come close to me: I might have to nerve myself to feel its breath on the back of my neck. But still my one reassurance remained a strong one: that Ogden's body, already decomposing, would never be found.

In any case, nothing further could happen until a succession of horses had relayed from Malvern the news that Ogden had never arrived. There would be two or three more days of suspense through which I would have to perform the part of my usual self as persuasively as I could manage. Perhaps fortunately for me the weather proved poor, with gusty winds and a good deal of rain. It seemed reasonable that I should choose to stay within doors, and perhaps understandable, given the dark skies, that my manner should be a little subdued.

My dealings with Mrs Deacon, though civil enough, had yet to return to their former cordiality. Partly to occupy the time, and partly as a small step towards regaining her confidence, I ventured on another game of chess with her daughter, Charlotte, in the parlour downstairs. To stiffen my sinews for the encounter I pretended to myself that here was a model of my present predicament: I would safely survive it if I could win this game. Perhaps as a consequence I captured more pieces, and held out somewhat longer than on previous occasions, but I was still comfortably defeated by this quiet child.

As I was congratulating her afterwards I found myself saying, on impulse: 'Wait here a moment. I have something to give you as a reward for your prowess.'

I went upstairs and fetched the bangle that had been intended for Kitty.

'Please accept this gift,' I said. 'It is too old for you now, but one day you can wear it. I value it because it belonged to my mother.'

Charlotte, though tongue-tied, was blushingly grateful. Mrs Deacon, who had been present throughout, sewing while we played, smiled warmly and said: 'You are a generous man, Mr Fenwick.'

I returned to my rooms ashamed of myself. Why had I told that silly lie about my mother? Could I do nothing now that was not tainted by deviousness? I sat alone as the evening darkened, my spirits darkening with it.

24

The story soon came to public attention. In the *London Chronicle* was a prominent item:

Mr Walter Ogden, a prosperous dealer in diamonds and ornamental glass, has disappeared in mysterious circumstances. It is feared that he may have come to harm. On the morning of 4th September Mr Ogden, who has an office in Duke Street, set out by stage coach for Malvern, to fulfil a professional engagement at the home of Lord Downs. For reasons as yet unknown it seems that he broke off his journey at Aylesbury and returned to London: he was seen entering his office that same night. Since then there has been no word from him; but his hat was picked up in Margaret Street, close to the house in which he lives. His affairs were in good order, and it appears that he had intended to resume his journey to Malvern. Mr Ogden is thirty-eight years of age. He is of medium height and stocky build. A reward will be given, with no questions asked, to any member of the public producing information that might bear on this matter. Application should be made to Mr Gow, at Mr Ogden's Duke Street office.

I read the announcement repeatedly, trying to guess what dangers it might pose, but it did not take me far. I was sure that on that dark wet night there had been nobody to see Ogden chasing after me, or the skirmish that ensued. Pike and I had hidden the body where no passer-by, even had there been one, would have noticed it. What left me still in doubt and some fear was my ignorance of what came next. I could only guess that the corpse had been thrown into a covered cart of some sort to be taken away. The task would never have been attempted until the street was empty. When it came to the work to be done at the river, those concerned would know what they were about: after all, their own lives would be at risk. I clung to my hope that Pike was right, that there was no trail to follow.

As I anticipated, Matt Cullen called that very morning, ready to show me the *Chronicle* if I had missed it. Apparently he had had no further chance to talk with Gow, but had paid a visit to Margaret Street and seen reward notices, worded very much like the newspaper reports, pasted up on posts and walls.

'Surely they will come to nothing,' said I. 'If the watch had seen anything suspicious they would have reported it already. This is a prosperous district: who would be abroad so late at night?'

'Other than yourself,' said Matt. 'But you miss the point. The tell-tale phrase, as always in such cases, is "with no questions asked". There is the hope that one robber might inform upon another.'

'Assuming that a robbery took place . . .'

'What else could have happened?'

'For example,' I said, forcing myself to improvise, 'Ogden broke his journey to spend a night with his mistress, but died in her bed of an apoplexy.'

'And the hat?'

'It was blown away by the wind as Ogden trotted to his lady's door.'

'Perhaps she poisoned him for the money in his pockets,' said Cullen, pleased with this new fancy.

'Or stabbed him with a kitchen knife,' I suggested. 'In either case she would drag his body down to her cellar, and will be safe from detection.'

'Unless a neighbour heard his dying squeal,' concluded Matt, with satisfaction.

I laughed as best I could.

That very afternoon I sent my godfather a copy of the report in the *Chronicle*. It would no doubt soon have come to his attention in any case, and I wished to show my readiness to correspond on the Ogden mystery.

⌒

At about this time I was sent a printed invitation that distracted me from my preoccupation but then led me back to it:

> *MR THOMAS CROCKER is proposing to renounce,*
> *in great measure, his previous indulgence in tavern*
> *hospitality and mischief (although the pleasures of talk*
> *and song will not be forsworn).*
> *ACCORDINGLY he is to host a species of farewell*
> *entertainment which he hereby invites you to attend.*
> *It will be held, as tradition dictates, at the Seven Stars,*
> *in Coventry Street, as from eight o'clock on the night*
> *of Friday next.*

Crocker had written below, in his own hand: 'I hope to see you there. It has been some little time since we talked.'

I immediately resolved to attend. Crocker's hint of reproach was justified: the length of time that had elapsed since I had contacted him might soon begin to seem a suspicious circumstance in its own right. It would be convenient to see him again in a convivial gathering with only limited opportunity for private conversation. There could be awkward questions about my abandonment of Kitty and possibly about my interest in Mrs Ogden.

❦

Time had slowed to a crawl, and the period of suspense was the more oppressive to me in that I was denied my habitual distractions. When waking in the morning I would wonder how to occupy myself. Two or three times I hid myself under greatcoat and hat and walked along the river or out into the country. But I had lost my taste for such expeditions, and nothing I saw could distract me for long.

My efforts to avoid thinking about the danger I was in had so constricted my mind that it was almost lifeless.

Jaded by this nullity I went out late one night, with a fast-beating heart, and made my way to Margaret Street. It was as calm and quiet as ever: I was no doubt the only person who had ever killed a man in that vicinity. Glancing about to be sure I was unseen I walked directly past Mrs Kinsey's house, and even slipped stealthy fingers into the empty crevice where Sarah and I had hidden our messages. Would she be asleep at this moment, some few feet above my head, or would she have returned to her home? I thought of her with pity, but without desire. In a shadowy corner the other side of the street I could make out the archway where Ogden must have been lurking, frantic with jealousy, on the night of his death.

The nocturnal placidity of these prosperous streets proved unexpectedly reassuring. It confirmed my sense that the skirmish with Ogden had been a freak of chance, scarcely to be credited. Now it was over, leaving no trace, surviving solely in my own memory. With each passing day the recollection would fade and dwindle. When I had erased it altogether – and I had always had a gift for forgetting – all that would remain would be a disappearance, a nothingness.

The following morning, as a further gesture of unconcern, I paid a brief call on Mr Ward. To my surprise he mentioned Ogden immediately, saying that my godfather had shown a particular interest in his story. He had written to Ward about the matter as soon as he learned of Ogden's failure to arrive in Malvern. Having effected the introduction that had led to the planned visit to Malvern he claimed to feel a certain responsibility for what had ensued. Following his instructions Ward had sent him any newspaper reports that bore on the matter. I was relieved that I had done the same thing, and could not, therefore, be suspected of any failure of openness.

The sight of Ward immersed in his day's work, black-clad and sober as ever, seemed almost a rebuke. Here was a life slow and steady, all of a piece with that of Thorpe or Mrs Deacon. Meanwhile I had become a creature of another kind, living at a different rate. I could be swept away at any time by helter-skelter intrigue or accident. I recalled the highwayman, Jack Gardiner, who had looked me in the eye so familiarly on his way to the gallows. Perhaps he and I and Pike were three of a kind, foxes among sheep, hungry, free and dangerous, compelled always to be on our guard against those who would hunt us down.

I delayed my arrival at the Seven Stars until after ten o'clock. The chamber in which Crocker's friends were assembled was noisy and hot, the air heavy with the vapours of punch and the smoke of candles. So much I could have anticipated. Yet somehow the disposition and mood of the gathering were unfamiliar. There was not the sense, as in the past, that Crocker was the central and presiding figure: indeed at first I did not so much as notice him. My own business was to be seen and to appear to be my habitual self. Fortunately for these purposes most of the guests were standing rather than sitting. I moved briskly about the throng, initiating exchanges here and there, but avoiding longer conversation. Among those I spoke to were Latimer and Talbot. Neither Pike nor Horn appeared to be present. Crocker was seated in a far corner engaged, as it seemed, in serious conversation. Catching sight of me he motioned me to approach. I pushed my way across and seated myself close to him, so that we could hear one another amid the chatter and laughter.

'I am glad to see you here,' said Crocker, without warmth.

'I am delighted to be here.' Then, trying to find a tone of easy banter: 'So your resolution has not changed: you are still minded to withdraw from the world?'

'I am,' said Crocker, still unsmiling. 'I own a large town house. I have somehow acquired a consort. And as a result I now find myself a little sickened by excess. I told you, I think, that my masquerade went further than I had intended. There were outcomes I had not foreseen.'

I tried to steer away from this dangerous ground: 'Will you be offering more decorous entertainments in future?'

'Possibly,' said Crocker. He continued in a sharper voice: 'You know that Kitty Brindley is now under the protection of Mr Horn?'

'I do. The blame is all mine: I behaved badly at your masquerade. I had drunk too much to be sure how badly. But Nick is a good fellow in his way.'

Regretful as I was, my attempt to appear so sounded hollow to my own ears.

'On a topic perhaps related: have you read the strange reports concerning our acquaintance, Mr Ogden?'

Ready for some such a question I responded with

animation: 'Most certainly. I have taken a particular interest in the matter, since it was my godfather who first spoke of him to Lord Downs.'

Crocker continued grave: 'It is disturbing to hear of a man vanishing so close to his own house. Have you an opinion as to what may have happened?'

'I have not. As you yourself have said, Ogden was a strange fellow. Perhaps he was caught up in dangerous dealings we knew nothing of.'

'Perhaps . . .' After a pause, uncomfortable to me, Crocker added: 'His wife was a childhood friend of yours, as I recall. Jane saw you with her at the masquerade. But there are questions one does not ask. Have you visited her?'

I tried, unconvincingly to myself, to offer an easy answer: 'Not as yet. I felt a delicacy about intruding – most particularly about seeming to offer condolences where perhaps none are needed.'

Crocker nodded absently, and seemed to dismiss the topic: 'Ogden's disappearance found an echo. A few nights ago Trinculo somehow made his escape.'

'I am sorry to hear it.'

'I had become attached to the creature. The poor wretch is either dead or scavenging a lonely life in the streets of London.'

He fell silent and looked gloomy.

'Will you sing tonight?' I asked, by way of diversion.

'No. I am not in the vein. But I should speak. Indeed I will speak *now*.'

He leaned forward, heaved himself upright, and clapped

his hands. Quickly hushed into silence the crowd drew back to leave their host the centre of attention. He spoke out with his usual force: 'Gentlemen, I thank you for your presence here tonight, in response to my uninviting invitation. The valedictory tone should not be interpreted too solemnly. In truth I hope I will see many of you again – but in gatherings a little more formal. My way of life is to change: I have resolved to attempt respectability.'

From somewhere came a cry of 'Shame!' followed by laughter; but Crocker resumed imperturbably.

'I was born thirty-five years ago today. If I live as long as my father – an achievement I hope to exceed – I shall have three or four more years of activity. It is my ambition to pass them a little more soberly – perhaps even a little more usefully.'

There was embarrassed silence. The great majority of those present, who had never heard their host speak in a serious vein, were at a loss as to how to respond. Crocker looked about with a magisterial air, but then lapsed into a laugh.

'However, these admirable changes, gentlemen, will not begin until tomorrow. Tomorrow I will become a serious man. For tonight I say to you "Drink about and be merry!" And to set the mood I will ask Mr Fenwick to join me in song.'

In apparent relief the guests cheered heartily. Bewildered by the sudden change of heart, but willing enough, I stepped up alongside Crocker, and in a moment we were singing together as some months before:

Come, friends, and bear me company:
I dare not go to bed.
I've drunk too little or drunk too much,
And my heart is heavy as lead.

My tongue, still a little swollen, hurt as I sang. We performed well enough but, as it seemed to me, without zest, avoiding one another's eyes. The assumed melancholy carried too much conviction. When the company joined the chorus they somehow caught our mood by contagion, and performed rather as though singing a mournful hymn:

In an hour, in a week, in a month, in a year,
Where shall we be? No man can say.
If we drink, if we fight, if we whore while we're here,
Then later or sooner the devil's to pay.
So sing through the night,
Sing while we may,
Till a new dawn reminds us to live for the day.

The last line, though bellowed forth, sounded empty to me – and perhaps to others, for the applause that followed was flat, and there were no further offers to sing. Crocker turned away from me as we concluded, almost as though to snub me.

Discomfited and distressed by what had passed I made half-hearted conversation with one or two more acquaintances and was then ready to take my leave. In courtesy I motioned a farewell to Crocker, who was at the centre of a small group, and to my surprise he broke away and came heavily towards me.

426

'You will have thought me cursed gloomy tonight,' he said.

'You seemed a little subdued.'

'I have several causes for concern.' He paused. 'The latest is that Francis Pike has quit my service. Perhaps you knew that?'

'I did not. When did he go? And why?'

'This very day. The cause was personal and private,' he said. He had been happy to be employed by me, but he was compelled to go.'

'What does he intend to do?'

'He said nothing on that score, either. I offered him a farewell gift in appreciation of his service, but he would not take it.'

I managed to talk on, mechanically: 'You will miss him.'

'More than I can say. I had come to depend on him. Here is another mystery – but I must not cloud my mind with suspicions.'

We talked a little more, but in my agitation I scarcely took in what was said. When I made to leave Crocker took my hand almost formally.

'I am sorry to see you go,' he said. 'You were my best singing partner.'

His use of the past tense grieved me: it meant that I had lost the trust and the friendship of a man I admired. But my sadness was dwarfed by the alarm I felt at the news concerning Pike. His abrupt departure suggested fresh developments concerning Ogden.

The *London Chronicle* confirmed my fears the very next morning:

There is disturbing further news concerning Mr Walter Ogden, whose strange disappearance we recently reported. It seems that a coat and a watch belonging to him have been found on sale at the disreputable Knott's Market, in Wapping, often called the Thieves' Market. How the articles came to be there is not yet clear. Mrs Ogden has identified the coat as the one her husband was wearing on the morning of the day on which he was last seen. It is suspected that certain marks upon it may be bloodstains. There are now grave fears for Mr Ogden's safety.

It will be recalled that Mr Ogden is a dealer in diamonds, with an office in Duke Street. He seems to have disappeared on the night of 4th September. Having that morning set out for Worcestershire, to see Lord Downs, he broke off his journey, for what he described, in a note sent on to Lord Downs, as 'pressing reasons'. He returned to London, where he was seen in his office. His hat was later found in Margaret Street, close to his home, but other than that there had been no further trace of him until this latest discovery.

Mr Ogden is thirty-eight years of age, a stout man of medium height. A reward of **one hundred guincas** will be paid, with **no questions asked**, to any member of the public who can give information that sheds light on this mystery. Application should be made to Mr Gow, at Mr Ogden's Duke Street office.

I grew cold as I read the report. It surely meant that Pike's plan had failed. Those asked to dispose of Ogden could now be traced – and no doubt would be when an informer claimed the reward. It must have been advance notice of this announcement that had led to Pike's abrupt departure. For one hundred guineas someone would say how the body had been disposed of, and just when and where it had first been found. With Pike gone I was left alone to face any questions that might arise. I had been in Margaret Street at that time. I had been trying to seduce Ogden's wife. What would my godfather think when he learned this news? What would Matt Cullen make of it? Above all, what thoughts would be running through Sarah's mind, now that it seemed certain that her husband was dead?

I read the *Chronicle* in my lodgings, around the middle of the morning, and at once decided to leave the house. Matt Cullen would certainly call to discuss the news, and I was not confident that I could seem easy and composed. I needed to find a quiet place where I could think over my situation.

I was so apprehensive that I left the house by the back door lest Matt should already be coming along Cathcart Street. Heading randomly northwards out of town I found myself on the road I had taken the day after Crocker's masquerade. My feet led me to the quiet inn where I had lingered to eat a chop on that occasion. Now I had no appetite, but I chose to sit outside once more, with a pint of ale for company. It was a grey, windless day, the surrounding fields were quiet, and ahead of me, as before, London lay half hidden in its own foul smoke.

My thoughts were dark. Ogden's bloodied coat would be seen as evidence of a probable murder. The huge promised reward would tempt informers. Pike himself had surely thought so or he would not have left Crocker's service. His flight might now be seen to incriminate him. How likely was it that I myself would be drawn in to the inquiry? Who knew of my interest in Mrs Ogden? Crocker's words returned to me: 'Jane saw you with her at the masquerade'. I inferred that Kitty had seen us too. How much might they have seen? How much might others have seen? I had been too drunk to know. Crocker's coolness the previous night told me that he suspected something. If an informant did indeed testify, I would quickly be incriminated. The case, prima facie, was an easy one to make. At midnight I had been seeking access to the bed of Ogden's wife: a short time later his dead body had been taken up a few hundred yards away by agents paid to dispose of it.

At this rate should I not emulate Pike and escape while I had the chance – going abroad with the money I had to hand? Such a course might be taken as an admission of guilt. But if I stayed, how likely was it that I could sustain a show of resolution and innocence under interrogation?

Tormented by indecision, I sat cursing, cursing, cursing the corrupt old villain who had manipulated me into this predicament. If I had to face trial, I thought, I would first throttle my godfather in revenge.

Finishing the ale I sat back, closing my eyes to shut out the view, across open fields, of filthy London. I could see nothing, hear nothing, smell nothing. Perhaps I drifted into a doze, but I do not think so. Rather I was in a kind of stupor. Whatever the case, I was roused by a movement of the bench on which I sat. I opened my eyes to find a shabbily clad figure sitting beside me – perhaps a workman of some sort. He had two glasses of ale, one of which he pushed in front of me. It was only as he turned to do so that I recognized him.

'I was waiting at the end of your street in hopes to talk to you,' said Pike, 'and I saw you slip out of an alley. I took the liberty of following you at a distance.'

He spoke so calmly that, with an effort, I tried to speak calmly in return: 'I'm told you have left Mr Crocker's service.'

'I had no choice. You'll have seen today's newspaper?'

'I did. What went amiss?'

'I came to tell you. The assistants I hired, handsomely paid, broke the rules in hope of an extra guinea. Before sinking Ogden they took his coat and his watch.'

'Have they been found? Will they talk?'

'They'll never be found, and no one will talk. There were two men did the job, and they're both gone.'

'You mean they're dead?'

Pike stared into the distance, and raised his glass.

'Your good health, sir,' he said, and drank some ale. 'The rules in such matters are strict, and they were broken. There's no one to talk.' He drank again. 'The truth may be that they've done you a favour. A coat with blood on it and a watch, for sale in Knott's Market. Everyone knows what

431

that means: a street robbery that met with resistance, and a body at the bottom of the river. That's the end of the story – nothing more to be said.'

I drank some ale myself, to wet my dry mouth, as I took in what I had been told. A question came to me: 'But if that's the case you had nothing to fear?'

'Concerning Ogden, no. But when I had advance warning from Knott's Market I had to take strong action at once. I'll have made enemies in Wapping. I had to move before they found me.'

We fell silent. I needed time to reflect on what Pike had told me, but I already felt that his reassurances made sense. After all I should be safe. Relieved, or half relieved, of fears for myself I was suddenly free to look out, as through a window, at the strange landscape of Pike's life.

'You leave me deeply in your debt, Mr Pike. I must give you money.'

'No thank you, sir: I have all I need.'

'But thanks to me you have lost your employment.'

'That's the turn fortune took. But I rarely stay long in one place.'

'Mr Crocker treated you well.'

'He treated me very well. But he has a new life with Miss Page. He won't be in need of my services.'

'Where will you go?'

'I've yet to decide, sir. Having no family I go as I please.'

'Is it not a lonely life?'

Pike scratched his chin as he considered the question.

'It suits me, sir, that's all I can say. I don't care to be too comfortable. Like that monkey. Mr Crocker thought he was tame, but he was only half tame: he made off.'

He drank the rest of his ale and got to his feet.

'If you'll excuse me, sir, I'll leave you now. It's as well we're not seen together.'

I stood and shook his hand.

'Thank you once more, Mr Pike. I wish you well. Perhaps our paths will cross again.'

'That may be, sir – but not for some time.'

I watched his retreating form as he went back along the road towards Islington. He was a mystery to me, a man who could live wild and kill at need, yet who had been unaccountably kind to me. There seemed to be something in his disposition that diminished both his pleasures and his pains. I envied his calmness. He would never have panicked and cowered as I had done.

The impression he had made upon me was so strong that it was some little time before I reverted to my own affairs. It seemed that my quarrel with Ogden had now proved the indirect cause of two further deaths. I should have felt appalled, but again I did not. These were men I knew nothing of, river-rats who had paid the price of treachery. I trusted Pike's account. The potential informers had been disposed of: the offered reward would never be claimed. Equally I trusted Pike's capacity to disappear without trace. There was nowhere for potential inquirers to turn.

The obvious hypothesis would prevail – that Ogden had been the victim of an attempted robbery that had gone too far. The one circumstance left unexplained would be his abrupt decision, in mid-journey, to go back to London. If it could be assumed that he had returned for some professional reason, then it was natural enough that having visited his office he should have been making his way home when he was set upon.

The narrative I was inferring seemed to me very persuasive – more plausible than the events that had actually occurred. Ogden's business acquaintances and the readers of the *London Chronicle* would no doubt be content with some such explanation.

But, but, but – there were several potential sceptics, including Sarah, Crocker, Matt Cullen and no doubt my godfather, who had reason to suspect, at least, that Ogden's return was not professionally motivated. Matt I was least concerned with, for I felt sure that my earlier show of frankness had sufficiently convinced him. There might be awkward exchanges ahead with Gilbert, by letter or in person; but my more immediate concern was with Sarah, whose thoughts and emotions I could not guess.

In my revived mood I was soon confident, after all, of surmounting such difficulties. Twenty minutes previously I had been half dead with despair: now I was fully alive again.

As on that same spot, not so many days previously, I ordered a chop and sat thinking, determined to be methodical. Cullen I would see that very evening, taking a high, boisterous line and hoping to laugh the whole story away. As for my godfather, I would need to write to him that day or the next, cool and meditative, but perhaps admitting to feeling somewhat shaken by the tragic coincidence of events.

Sarah would be less easy to deal with. Only by talking to her could I gauge her feelings and hope to influence them.

But I could not yet visit her, so much was certain, having no idea how she would receive me, or even whether she would admit me. In any case she was no doubt compelled to spend much time with Mr Gow, with lawyers, perhaps with John Fielding, the Bow Street magistrate. I should wait until these activities abated.

Whatever Sarah's sentiments I was the only individual in the world to whom she could now speak with full candour. Sooner or later it would be a relief to her to see me. In the meantime the *London Chronicle* report at least gave me an excuse to write her a letter – a sympathetic but circumspect letter – which might open up further opportunities for communication.

Back in Cathcart Street I learned that Cullen had indeed called in my absence. Here was the expected cue. As I strode towards his lodgings I tried, like an actor, to adapt myself in advance to the role I was to play. I had taken a glass or two of wine to elevate my spirits, and when I met Cullen I was pleased to find that he was similarly primed. He broached another bottle, and in no time we were reading the *Chronicle* story aloud in jocose vein. I had some lines of jest prepared, and was able to risk them sooner than I had thought possible. Might the missing man be buried *in absentia*, I wondered. What could be inscribed on his tombstone? Perhaps 'Here lies the jacket of Walter Ogden.' Matt suggested that the watch should be placed in a jacket pocket, and wound up immediately before burial, so that it would tick for some time under-ground, like a clockwork heart.

'To my shame,' said I, affecting seriousness, 'I can't but be facetious about the poor devil. When I think otherwise I am seized with guilt. It might have come about that I was cuckolding Ogden at the very moment that he was being killed. No man should have to suffer that double outrage.'

'For the same reason,' said Cullen, 'his wife must be grateful for her own change of heart.'

'Most certainly,' I concurred, and dragged us into the depths of imagining wife and husband simultaneously pene-trated. Matt went further still, having them simultaneously exclamatory: 'Too deep, cruel man – I cannot bear it!'

'Cullen,' said I, 'we have become disgusting.'

The two of us were laughing helplessly, as only drunken friends can.

'You are now free,' cried Matt, 'to resume your pursuit of the lady.'

'That is a gross observation,' said I. 'I must let a decent interval elapse – perhaps a full week.'

'Your delicacy does you credit. And perhaps the grieving widow will put black sheets on the bed.'

I left him at midnight, pleased with my night's work. For Matt the mystery of Ogden's disappearance had been resolved into a shared joke. One potential questioner had been disarmed: there were two more to appease.

25

My dear Godfather,

It may be that you have already seen the enclosed report from the London Chronicle. *I waited a day or two before sending it in case it elicited further information from members of the public, but as yet there has been nothing. It seems now to have been accepted that Ogden fell victim to a robbery that went too far – perhaps because he resisted too boldly. The guilty man, or men, may yet be identified, but it appears unlikely. I am assured by one well acquainted with the ways of Knott's Market that the proceeds of a robbery are never put on sale there until the former owner has been securely lodged at the bottom of the Thames. Nor, apparently, is any member of the riverside fraternity likely to come forward with evidence, no matter how large the reward. There is a strict understanding that the price of such betrayal must be death. So there, most unsatisfactorily, the story seems certain to conclude.*

It could be argued that the identity of the assassins matters little. If they were caught they would surely prove to be commonplace thieves altogether unknown to the public until condemned and hanged. Ogden presumably fell prey to them as a matter of chance, rather as a man may be unluckily laid low by fire or flood or illness. Perhaps street banditry of this sort should be seen as a moral infection lurking among the poorer citizenry at large, claiming victims as randomly as smallpox or the stone.

Why did Ogden turn back? I can conceive of several possible explanations, but my surmises are unlikely to be wiser than your own. He was a secretive man driven by passions and ambitions that he did not choose to disclose, even to his wife. More extraordinary than that change of mind, perhaps, is the fact of his returning to his home so late at night, and falling among thieves so very close to it. I walked that street again a few days ago, and could hardly believe that there had been a fatal encounter in so sedate a district.

In the wake of this tragedy, as we must now call it, I find myself puzzled and perturbed by conflicting feelings. Although I will not pretend to any great grief at the death of a man whom (as you know) I heartily disliked, I cannot but pity him for his wretched and premature demise. I must confess to you my profound relief that, thanks to Sarah's sudden change of heart – which caused me so much vexation – I was not in her bed, as I otherwise could have been, at the very time when her husband was losing his life in the next street.

438

She herself will surely have felt a similar relief. Her other emotions I scarcely dare guess at. Mingled with shock and confusion there will perhaps, after all, be some traces of love.

For me the intimidating reflection is that, as the events of the fatal evening took shape, our project and Ogden's miserable fate were ultimately but a hair's breadth apart. I could have stumbled into deep waters indeed.

I need hardly say that the proposed escapade with Sarah is now at an end. Keenly as I compassionate her predicament, I have made no attempt to contact her – although I may shortly venture to do so. You can conceive how difficult it will be for me to find appropriate terms in which to condole with this unfortunate widow. Still less have I any thought of renewing my advances over a coffin, in the spirit of Richard III.

I veer towards frivolity, for all that these are serious matters. In such painful circumstances jesting becomes a kind of defence, holding disagreeable realities at a safe distance. An intrigue that I was pursuing, as you know, with great fervour, has been abruptly and harshly closed off. I am left bewildered, wary and temporarily becalmed. It will surely take me some little time to recover my spirits.

I remain, &c.

Dear Mrs Ogden,

You will know just how difficult I find it to write this letter, and will understand, I think, why I have waited until now to venture an approach to you, even though you have been constantly in my thoughts.

439

When I saw in the London Chronicle *the first account of Mr Ogden's disappearance I was startled indeed, but also half incredulous, having good reason to think that there must be some mistake in the matter. When succeeding rumours darkened the picture further I still thought it my best course to postpone writing to you as long as there was any uncertainty in the case. If I rightly interpret the latest reports, however, it seems that a tragic outcome to the story is now considered almost certain. I can no longer withhold an expression of sympathy and renewed friendship.*

This would seem to have been not only a tragic but a doubly unaccountable happening. I cannot understand why Mr Ogden should have so suddenly decided to return to London: perhaps you have information on that score which has not been made public. Then, if the report in the Chronicle *is to be trusted, it seems that, with equal improbability, he was set upon near his own home, in placid Margaret Street. Certain circumstances brought me to the district a little earlier on that same night, and I saw no sign of anything untoward.*

Having known you since our childhood, and known you well, I think I can guess at some of the particular misgivings and emotions that will have been haunting you during these difficult weeks. Given that state of mind your dealings with inquiries and practical problems of all kinds must have been painful in the extreme. Hardly daring to imagine your situation from day to day I can only hope that you were able to find appropriate advice

and help. You will certainly have needed all your
habitual strength and clarity of judgement.

In these difficult circumstances I urge you – though
with a diffidence I am sure you will understand – to
turn to me if you come to think that I can help you, or
relieve your situation in any way. It may be that at some
point you will find it a comfort simply to talk with me as
a friend. After all, we are <u>old</u> friends, and I have a
particularly close knowledge of some aspects of your
present sad situation.

I remain &c.

I spent far more time on the composition of these letters than their comparative brevity might suggest. Repeatedly I hesitated over hints to be dropped, issues to be skirted, doubts and questions that should be anticipated. These were crucial communications. My prospects would be far clearer, for better or for worse, when I received replies to them.

After this solitary day of dogged composition I again made my way, for the sake of fresh air and a meal, to Keeble's steakhouse. I had forgotten that this was one of the nights when the Conversation Club dined there. Being by now regarded as a friendly acquaintance I was left free to join in their talk or to hold my peace as I chose. Their initial exchanges were of little interest to me, but I pricked up my ears as they drifted into a discussion concerning the disappearance of Mr Ogden, a story now widely known from newspaper reports.

'Where was the watch?' cried one. 'Here, it seems, was murder in the open street in a thriving neighbourhood. If the watch provides no protection, which of us will be safe?'

'None of us,' said another. 'I for one have had my purse taken.'

'I have had my wig snatched,' said a third.

To whip the top I spoke up for the first time that evening, describing how I myself had been the victim of an attempted robbery earlier in the year when returning from that very steakhouse. The company listened attentively and responded with interest. Someone said that assaults of this kind might be common enough in St Giles, a notoriously dangerous area – but that it was a different matter when they took place in Margaret Street. Another observed that I had been able to defend myself because I was a well-made young fellow. What hope would there be for an older man? I hazarded a comment to the effect that Ogden, so near his own home, had been the victim of an unlucky chance.

The bony man who commonly dominated the Club's proceedings responded to this mild suggestion with unexpected vigour: 'Pardon me, young gentleman, but I think otherwise. I have lived my life in this town and believe I can claim to know something of its ways. I say there was more than chance at work in the attack on Mr Ogden.'

This bold claim having secured respectful silence the bony one proceeded, in weighty, deliberative style: 'Here we have a wealthy man, a diamond merchant, who does dealings abroad. On the day he disappears he breaks off a journey to return to London. Why, unless to keep an appointment? Instead of going to his home he is seen at his office. Why, if not to pick up some diamonds? And that very night he is done away with. There are sinister figures at work here. It is all too easy to lay the blame on some unknown ruffian. I smell an intended business transaction that ended in robbery and cost Mr Ogden his life.'

The fool concluded with a triumphant air that clearly impressed most of his audience: there were knowing nods all round. However a thin gentleman with a yellow face intervened more knowingly still: 'Our friend here states his opinion, based on speculation. I can do a little better than that. I have talked with someone who once worked with this Ogden and could claim to know his tastes. It appears'– he lowered his voice – 'that here was a man who preferred the company of men. For all that he was married he was regularly seen at the Fountain, not two hundred yards from here, where such as he are known to foregather. To put the matter plainly, gentlemen, this Ogden was a backgammon player – a sodomite. He came back secretly to London for a night of pleasure with his own kind – but these companions did away with him for the sake of his money.'

Since no evidence was produced in support of this imaginative hypothesis it provided no grounds for dispute. It had additional authority as implying familiarity with the workings of a sinister underworld. The bony man was eclipsed, and the sodomitical solution carried the day. Heads that had previously nodded were now shaken in moral deprecation. There was a feeling that, after all, the goatish Ogden had fared no worse than his sins deserved.

As I walked home I felt unexpectedly reassured by all this nonsense. It seemed to confirm that Ogden's death was now securely accepted, explained and done with, digested by public discourse. The fanciful conjectures I had heard were like so many leaves beginning to cover his non-existent grave.

Perhaps because warmed with wine I was seized by a sudden sense of superiority. The members of the Conversation Club, complacently prattling, were pitiful bystanders, the idle chorus of a play. Fittingly enough none of them had for a moment supposed that they were in the presence of a protagonist.

⟋⟍

Dear Mr Fenwick,

I do not know in what terms to reply to your letter. My predicament is so singular and so distressing that perhaps no appropriate terms exist. I inhabit a dark dream, the normal pleasures and processes of life having been all at once suspended. A month ago, although beset by certain problems, I could be confidently myself: I occupied a certain position; I had it in my power to choose my course. Who or what am I today? I scarcely know. Probably, as it has lately come to appear, a widow. What is my future life to be? I cannot see so much as a week ahead, but grope forward from one day to another, hearing scraps of news, answering questions, receiving advice, signing documents.

Of the circumstances leading to my husband's death I know nothing, or almost nothing, that you do not. His doings on that day and night remain a mystery to me. I have reflected upon them again and yet again, but to no purpose. Why Mr Ogden should have cut short his journey, and why he should have been walking the London streets so late, on that night of all nights, I cannot guess. Such surmises as have come to my mind have served only to confuse and unsettle me further. I do know that my husband was a determined, fearless man. If threatened by a robber he would not lightly submit. It may be that this courage proved to be his undoing.

Fortunately for me all his business responsibilities would seem to have been assumed very capably by his associate, Mr Gow, a quiet gentleman who has risen to this difficult occasion with resourcefulness and calm. He has been assiduous in looking after my interests, shielding me from importunate inquirers and keeping me informed. At his suggestion I have also sought advice from a lawyer, Mr Semple. He took me to see John Fielding, the magistrate who explained the probabilities of the case with kindness and wisdom. You may rest assured that I have not been without assistance and protection during this difficult time. But I have nevertheless been subdued to a timorous half-life, passing nearly all my days within doors, in the company of my aunt.

After all, and for reasons you will understand, I have not been able to talk to any of these kind helpers with complete freedom. Largely for those same reasons I feel that I cannot speak with you as yet. There may come a time, however – perhaps at no distant date – when I will find it a relief to do so. In that case I will write to you again.

I remain, &c.

My dear Richard,

*I have read your letter concerning the unfortunate
Ogden with close attention, as also a number of newspaper
reports. This is a strange tale indeed, much talked about
even in these parts because of the incidental involvement
of Lord Downs. (The gentleman is faintly gratified, I
fancy, by the temporary notoriety.)*

*My responses to the gradually unfolding news have
resembled your own in being curiously compounded.
Only in the past few days has the essential truth seemed
to emerge: that an honest citizen was murdered for his
money in a London street. A pitiful fate. One cannot
but feel at the very least a formal sympathy for this
unfortunate man. Yet certain aspects of the matter
remain puzzling. Here, at a distance of more than a
hundred miles from the events I have heard fanciful
explanations concerning Ogden's return to London and
his subsequent fate.*

*You and I, of course, have a peculiar and oblique
interest in the matter of which others can know nothing.
It is surely the case, as you suggest, that if you had been
seen in Margaret Street on the night concerned
some embarrassing questions might have arisen. The
uncomfortable truth is that we were plotting to do this
gentleman a major disservice at the very moment when
fate intervened to inflict a far greater one. Having
contributed to bringing about Ogden's proposed visit to*

Malvern I feel disagreeably close to the events of that unfortunate night. The partly exculpatory consideration, as far as I am concerned, is that if Mr Ogden had completed his journey to Malvern he would today be alive and well.

I confess to finding the story disturbing in another sense, which could be accounted trivial, but to me is not. You will be aware of my interest in the workings of cause and effect. I am positively ill at ease with the unpredictable and the accidental. In the case of Ogden we began and developed a story only to lose control of it through what seems to have been sheer chance. The narrative turned in our hands and became another tale altogether.

It is absurd in me, of course, to feel put out by the failure of people and events to conform with my plans. Moreover, as Yardley has more than once pointed out to me, the experiments of the Royal Society itself often go amiss and yet by the very fact of doing so can provide valuable findings. In this case, however, I see no such potential gains: it seems simply that there were considerations in play of which I knew nothing. I still look for elucidation.

I would therefore welcome an opportunity to talk with you, reviewing what has happened and why, and considering what should next be done. I would be greatly obliged if you could pay another visit to Fork Hill, perhaps arriving by Saturday next.

I remain, &c.

26

Of all my journeys to Fork Hill this proved the most exhausting, for my mind was ceaselessly active. At first I was plagued with recollections of Ogden. He had travelled these very roads not long previously, perhaps in this same coach, with no notion that he would be dead before the following dawn. Only when we were well clear of London was I able to banish those images and return to my own situation. I was soon suffused by anxious excitement. Within days, for better or worse, my prospects would be dramatically altered. Mr Gilbert and I could not continue in our previous course because it had come to an end. We would need a fresh start, on fresh terms.

I would first have to put the Ogden misadventure completely behind us; but I felt that this would not be difficult. Mr Gilbert would know only what I myself had told him, and any questions he asked I could readily dispose of. The received version of what had taken place occupied so exactly the space of the actual events that by now I half believed it myself.

The next challenge would be to decide upon a new project, a new way for me to earn my godfather's money. An advantage I now held, I flattered myself, was that I had surely earned his confidence. Everything he had so far asked of me I had duly performed – save only in the case of Sarah, where the matter had been taken out of my hands. Our partnership being now firmly established it was time – and more than time – for a parley about terms.

As the coach bumped and swung through the autumnal countryside I spoke out boldly, within my own head, addressing my godfather with a frankness and underlying indignation that I certainly would not be able to display to his face: 'Since we are to review the future, sir, I must ask whether you think it reasonable that I should be expected to continue on the same footing as before? For six months, as you have tacitly acknowledged, I have been a discreet, dutiful and active agent on your behalf, responding to your secret wishes, feeding your curiosity with regular reports. Yet I have been living in the dark, with no hint as to what might come next.

'You are after all my godfather, and have otherwise no living relatives. I think you would concede, sir, that as the weeks have passed, our communications have taken on an increasingly confidential, even intimate, tone. We have become close. Is it not now time for that affinity to be publicly declared? I put the question with diffidence, because I could have hoped that you would be before me in this matter, but have I not earned the right to be recognized as your heir?'

Unfortunately I could hear with equal clarity a cool rebuttal: 'I have listened to your reproaches with some little surprise. I do not think I can convict myself of a lack of generosity towards you. Have I not paid for your education, for your travels abroad, and for your comfortable life in London? I have yet to learn that one who gives on this scale – even a godfather – incurs an obligation to give more. And is it not also the case that in March you accepted the present arrangement with some alacrity?'

The debate was played out repeatedly in my mind, with various additions and shifts of emphasis. At one point I fell asleep and even in my dreams found myself angrily proclaiming: 'You presume too far, sir. Do you know where you have led me?'

I was woken painfully when the coach thumped into a deep rut, and my jaws were banged together. Unluckily I had bitten hard into the lump in my tongue, which had never fully healed. The coach came to a halt, and had to be emptied before the horses could haul it clear of the miniature trench in which it had lodged. My fellow-passengers saw me dabbing blood from my mouth and kindly commiserated with me. It struck me as curious that they should at once have noticed this slight physical hurt yet could not have guessed my mental turmoil through hour upon hour of the journey.

❧

When I met Mr Gilbert the following morning I saw at once that he was unwell. His face was flushed and his breathing shallow. He had just enough energy to dismiss, in a diminished voice, my attempt at sympathetic inquiry: 'Since writing to you I have contracted a slight fever. I hope it will prove no great inconvenience. But I must ask you to entertain yourself for a day or two.'

That afternoon I took the now familiar walk down to the furthest edge of the estate, where the surrounding woods, soon to be the property of my godfather, were already taking on their autumn colours. There were birds squawking loudly above, and squirrels frisking in the trees, nimble as Trinculo. It was a bright day, warm for October, but a lively breeze sprang intermittently to life, whirling yellow and orange leaves high into the air.

I strode along as buoyant as the wind – the more so in contrast to the enfeebled old fellow I had seen that morning. Could this be the man whose secret desires had regulated my conduct, and had even put me in danger of death, whether at the hands of Ogden or of the public executioner? He was ailing, he was dwindling. I was in the ascendancy, and could at last bend him to my will.

On my fourth evening at Fork Hill, greatly to my bewilderment and somewhat to my disgust, the familiar guests were yet again invited to dinner. Everything was against such a gathering. My godfather, whom I had scarcely seen since our interview, was plainly no better. I could tell, moreover, that his condition was hateful to him, at odds with his innate fastidiousness. He could not be himself, could not preside as he would wish, with his body hot, his face perspiring and his throat sore. Yet here he was, insisting on playing host to a group of dullards, themselves variously damaged by the doings of the previous half year. It was impossible to believe that the occasion could give pleasure to any of the company.

I contrived a few words with the local visitors before the meal began, but most of the words were mine. When I told the limping Yardley that I was glad to see him out and about again he vouchsafed me no more than a nod. Hurlock harrumphed a greeting while his wife, with lowered eyes, ventured a smile. I was luckier with Mrs Quentin, who told me that after all she had been permitted to remain in the home she had shared with her husband. She thanked me for the kindness I had shown her, and I found myself pleased to be thought kind. Thorpe greeted me as affably as ever, and observed in a low voice that since he had last written to me the threatened hostilities seemed to have subsided.

'But the conversation tonight is likely to be muted,' he added. 'You and I may have to exert ourselves.'

He proved to be right. The seven of us could barely keep silence at bay. Hurlock seemed morose and ill at ease, and his wife correspondingly subdued. Mrs Quentin, although more composed than I had previously seen her, rarely ventured to open her mouth. Fortunately Mr Thorpe spoke up cheerfully about parish matters, my godfather croaked out a few responses, and I managed many more. Hurlock had at last a little to say about the harvest – which had apparently been less than good – and in the course of subsequent exchanges remarked to me abruptly: 'I see you have something wrong with your tongue, sir.' I explained that I had come to bite upon it in the course of my journey from London.

'Stage coaches are damnable!' cried Hurlock, as if glad to have an excuse for venting fury. 'They swing and they bump. It's a mercy you didn't bite your tongue clean off.'

Since he chuckled at his own hyperbole I was able to smile and steer the conversation in a new direction, with a remark upon the fine autumn weather. Thorpe took up the topic, and Mrs Hurlock unexpectedly observed that she had enjoyed taking walks across a carpet of golden leaves. For a second or third time that evening I caught a collusive glance from her, seeming to suggest that she was still warmly disposed towards me. Recent excitements having driven her from my mind she was now of no more interest to me than a sack of potatoes, but I fatuously contrived a glint of collusive response for the sake of good manners. Fortunately no one suggested that we should sing.

As on previous occasions Yardley was at first taciturn, but found his voice after consuming two or three glasses of wine. By the time the ladies left the table he was jauntier than I had ever seen him, as he waxed eloquent about extremes in nature. He likened me, as a young man about town, to the swift, apparently a bird of boundless energy that does everything on the wing. By contrast, he said, he himself resembled the tortoise, looking to achieve longevity through slowness and stasis.

'It has been claimed,' he said, '– and I apologize to Mr Thorpe for recalling so coarse a pronouncement – that the tortoise can devote an entire month to a single act of copulation. I confess that I myself have never enjoyed a pleasure so prolonged.'

'Human life could hardly accommodate such prowess,' I observed.

My godfather had been roused from his exhaustion by Yardley's remarks.

'I believe I have heard you say,' he ventured, huskily, 'that there may be strange affinities between creatures seemingly antithetical.'

Yardley assented, instancing a friendship he claimed to have observed between a bull and a goose who shared a field.

'But,' said he, 'there are antipathies equally as strange. Dr Smollett remarks in his *Travels* that the silkworm is so delicately constituted that it may actually die if approached by a woman – Heh! Heh! – who is menstruating. You must excuse me, Vicar.'

Mr Gilbert nodded, without a smile: 'Perhaps one day we shall comprehend this commerce between bull and goose and woman and worm.'

❧

So feverish and fatigued had my godfather seemed during the dinner that I was hardly surprised when he took to his bed for the two following days. The weather having deteriorated I stayed within doors, rehearsing again and again in my mind the conversation I hoped soon to be having. I was beginning to fear that Mr Gilbert's indisposition might postpone it indefinitely. It also occurred to me to wonder whether it might not carry him off altogether – but I concluded that this was not yet desirable, given the uncertainty of my prospects.

By my seventh morning at Fork Hill a strong wind was slapping rain against the window panes. To my surprise I received word that Mr Gilbert was somewhat recovered, and wished to speak with me in his study. I found him sitting in an arm-chair with a blanket around him and a large handkerchief in his hand. He looked weary, but his voice was clearer.

'You have come a long way to visit me,' he said, 'and it is time that we talked. Mr Hurlock remarked upon your tongue. How is it?'

'Somewhat better, sir, I thank you.'

'How did you come to injure it?'

I told him again about the jolting coach, not sure whether the lapse of recollection was a good or a bad omen for our interview.

He heard my explanation absently, and asked if I had enjoyed the dinner.

I remarked that I had been surprised to see Hurlock there.

'A sign of subjection,' said my godfather. 'A tame bear.'

I waited for further prompting. Mr Gilbert closed his eyes for a moment or two, before asking: 'How, in your opinion, did Mrs Ogden feel towards her husband?'

Taken by surprise, I paused to consider.

'I would surmise that she had a measure of respect for him. And there was gratitude – certainly gratitude. But little warmth, little fondness.'

'Did they quarrel, do you suppose?'

'I cannot say with any certainty, but I would think not. He was a taciturn fellow.'

That damned lump on my tongue made it difficult for me to say 'taciturn'. I was wondering where these questions might be leading, but it seemed that they were to lead nowhere. My godfather clapped his handkerchief to his

455

face as a sudden fit of coughing took his breath away. When he recovered and could speak again it was on a fresh theme.

'Your letters have been empty of incident since those unfortunate events. How have you been passing the time?'

I explained that I had thought it advisable to remain inconspicuous, but that I would shortly be looking for a fresh start, for a new adventure of some kind.

'You have not seen Miss Brindley again?'

'I have not. I believe that she has passed to the patronage of my friend Mr Horn.'

'And you still have no thought of resuming your pursuit of Mrs Ogden?'

'None at all, sir.'

'I understand you. I understand you.'

Clearing his throat painfully the old invalid said: 'It would be interesting to know what passed between her and her husband on that morning – on that last morning.'

'Perhaps nothing, sir. He left very early.'

My godfather nodded, and then closed his eyes again, as though he would gladly have dozed. He roused himself to say: 'There is one aspect of this affair that seems not to have come to public attention.'

I was at once alert. 'And what is that?'

'Mr Ogden wrote to Lord Downs that he was returning to London for pressing domestic reasons.'

I kept my voice steady: 'The word "domestic" did not, I think, appear in the newspaper reports.'

'Exactly.' Mr Gilbert huddled the blanket around himself and sat up. 'It was not quoted because although

Ogden wrote the word he then scored it through. Lord Downs showed me the original. The wording had been plain: ". . . for pressing domestic reasons."'

Thinking frenziedly, I managed a response: 'Given that circumstance it seems remarkable that Mr Ogden went to his office rather than to his house.'

'But it appears that in his office he did and said nothing. When Mr Gow spoke to him he simply walked past him.'

'I believe Mr Ogden was never talkative.'

My godfather discharged a great sneeze into his handkerchief. I think that no man could have hated more the indignity of having the cavities of his skull filled with mucus. He sat for some moments breathing heavily before making an effort to speak: 'Let us suppose that his wife had said something to give him cause for suspicion . . . Might he not have chosen to lurk in his office before going on to Margaret Street to have an eye to her doings?'

I met the challenge directly: 'Are you suggesting that he might have suspected *me*?'

'Not you, perhaps. But a lover.'

'Could he have thought that this lover would invade Mrs Kinsey's house? Or that his wife would creep out?'

'It sounds improbable. Yet it is said that jealous men may harbour the most unlikely suspicions. And of course in this case the suspicion would have been justified.'

Increasingly uncomfortable I made an effort to speak thoughtfully: 'But this suggestion implies an unlikely circumstance: the poor wretch felt confident enough to take the coach, yet was sufficiently concerned to change his mind on the journey.'

Mr Gilbert made to reply, but was seized by a fit of coughing that left him scarlet in the face. As he recovered he wiped his eyes and sank back into his chair.

'I find myself a little languid,' he said. 'I must ring for some brandy. Will you take some yourself?'

'Gladly.'

I was by now in full need of the brandy, but I welcomed equally the interruption as the servant was summoned and the errand carried out. It gave me a few moments to collect my thoughts. By the time we were settled again I was ready to take the initiative: 'If Ogden did return to spy on his lady he must have come too late or given up too soon. I saw no sign of him in Margaret Street.'

My godfather reached out from his blanket to some papers on his desk, and produced what I recognized as a letter I had sent him. It disturbed me to see it here, produced as though in evidence. Mr Gilbert donned spectacles to consult it.

'You were there at midnight?'

'Exactly at midnight.'

'But you did not stay long?'

'By no means. Having read Mrs Ogden's note I went briskly home.'

'Was there light enough to read?'

'There was not. It was a wretched night.'

'And you had a torn paper with writing smudged by the rain?'

'Exactly so. I had to walk some little distance before I could find a lamp bright enough to tell me the bad news.'

It was as though I were on trial in a court of law. I sipped some brandy to help me keep up appearances. Fortunately Mr Gilbert seemed to weary of the topic, shaking his head and lapsing into silence.

I felt a sudden surge of anger. Here was this old wretch assuming authority, and asking impudent questions, as though a detached inquirer, when he had been the one to lure me into danger. I had suffered weeks of fear in his service yet now found myself seemingly distrusted and reproached. Before I had time to think I found myself blurting: 'I cannot but wonder what the promised reward would have been had I concluded the business with Mrs Ogden.'

I felt a qualm even before my sentence was concluded. This was the first time I had ever presumed to question my godfather. There was astonished hostility in his face as he stared at me with bloodshot eyes, appraising my words.

At last he said: 'You have declared that possibility closed.'

Uncertain whether to advance or to retreat, I said: 'Indeed.'

'Then that situation no longer obtains and is no longer to be discussed.'

Hoarse though Mr Gilbert was, his statement was a challenge. I held his gaze and said nothing, still hot with rage, sucking on the lump in my mouth. One misplaced word and we would be quarrelling, perhaps fatally. My godfather drank some brandy, and paused to feel its effects before, in a gentler voice, offering a fresh start.

'I invited you here for two reasons. One was to hear more about Ogden's disappearance. It sounded to me a strange affair – and still does. The other was to consider future possibilities.'

This was more promising. I tried to sound conciliatory: 'As to Mr Ogden, sir, I do not think I have anything left to say. I know little more than I have read in the newspapers.'

'But that "little more" – it seemed to include some knowledge of the criminal underworld?'

I was inwardly cursing again: 'A very little knowledge. Acquired at second hand.'

'You mentioned an individual who was familiar with Knott's Market.'

There was no time for invention: 'That was Francis Pike, Mr Crocker's man.'

Thanks to that damned swelling I could barely pronounce the name 'Francis'. My godfather coughed hoarsely once more, but then smiled.

'This is a queer business,' he said, in a cracked voice. 'We both have our difficulties in speaking.'

He dabbed the handkerchief to his watering eyes. 'Did that swollen tongue discommode you in the London salons?'

'No, sir. The damage was done on the journey to Fork Hill.'

'Of course, of course.' He shook his head as though irritated with himself, and succumbed to a shuddering sigh. 'I have been anxious to talk with you, Richard, but our conversation comes too soon. This illness clouds my thinking. I am not myself. It is unspeakably vexing. I find I am speaking thoughtlessly.'

'Let me leave you to rest, sir,' I said, rising.

Mr Gilbert raised a hand, but lowered it again, too weary to shape a gesture.

'You are kind,' he said. 'A day or two more, and perhaps

we will try again. But perhaps—' he broke off, panting '—perhaps we both need a respite. It may be too soon to discuss new projects before this affair of the Ogdens has been fully digested.'

'I will be guided by your wishes, sir.'

Bowing, I turned away, but could see that he had settled back under his blanket even before I left the room.

I passed the rest of that day in the library, sometimes idly glancing at a book, sometimes staring out at the wet garden, but with my mind always occupied with what had passed between me and my godfather. My thoughts were as cheerless as the weather. Plainly Gilbert entertained doubts and suspicions concerning Ogden's fate. How serious were they? How far would he pursue them? After all, he knew more about the affair – even if it was but a single word more – than had been reported in the *London Chronicle*. If he picked and picked away at the matter might he uncover the truth of it?

I tried to reassure myself that he could not. I alone knew the full truth: as long as I kept my nerve and my counsel I would be safe. There was Pike – and I cursed myself for having let slip his name – but he would remain silent and invisible, having his own skin to save. What had caused my godfather's qualms? Two circumstances only: the mighty coincidence that Ogden should have died on the very night when I had planned an assignation with his wife, and the single, and obliterated, word 'domestic'. As to the latter I could, at need, suggest that Ogden had originally included it almost at random – for example because he had not wished to imply that he considered some other professional task more important than his appointment with Lord Downs. As to the former: well, coincidences were a matter of common experience. It occurred to me also that I could mention the hypotheses advanced at the Conversation Club. Fanciful though they were, either should seem a more persuasive possibility than that the urbane young man who quoted them had committed manslaughter.

With such arguments I gradually calmed myself, but it remained true that I had done a bad morning's work. My hopes of reaching some new settlement with my godfather now seemed remote. I had been guilty of misjudgement, been too aggressive. Rather than challenge him I should now further ingratiate myself, become a still closer confidant. When my godfather showed signs of recovery I might attempt overtures of this sort; but I could not tell how long I might have to wait. The following morning I learned that he was once more confined to his room. I resolved to allow him three further days before leaving for London.

Meanwhile there was empty time to fill. The rain had ceased and the skies were clear. I thought of riding into the village to chat with Thorpe, but decided that I felt a little too vulnerable at present. Once more I lingered in the library, restless and discontented, running again and yet again through the whole sequence of thoughts that had troubled me the previous day, and getting no more satisfaction from them.

In the afternoon the sun began to shine quite brightly, drawing a faintly visible steam from the moist ground. I went out across the wet grass on my habitual walk to the edge of my godfather's estate. Its aspect was quite changed.

In the few days since I had arrived at Fork Hill autumn had conclusively supplanted the last of the summer. The echoing bird-calls sounded melancholy now. There was a scent of vegetable decomposition in the air. When I reached the woods I perceived how the fallen leaves, flattened by rain, had formed a dank carpet, soon to become an earth-like substance. This was the season of decay and change. In my imagination I saw Ogden's body, deep beneath foul water, resolving itself similarly into mud. Yet, after all, my mood was tranquil: such transformations were the way of the world. One day my own turn would come, but not yet, not yet . . .

As I walked on through the trees, musing in this vein, my foot slithered on a stone, almost throwing me over. Again I bit my swollen tongue, and again I swore. I sat down on a fallen trunk till the bitter pang should have passed.

It was exactly in that moment, as I was squatting on damp bark, with my face caught in a grimace, that a chance recollection, and then a chance connection, showed me, with the clarity of a lightning-flash, the truth of my situation. In that single second I knew conclusively that I had been deceived, that my high hopes had been the merest delusion. The shock was so sudden, and so great, as to resemble a physical blow. I stood again, and gasped for air. In a few seconds of further thought I had interpreted my past afresh and expunged my imagined future.

The new understanding seemed to disconnect me from my surroundings. I looked about me, quite at a loss. It seemed that I had no reason to be where I was, or to be anywhere else – no reason to go forward or to go back.

Mere instinct led me to plunge deeper into the wet woodland, my movements mechanical, my mind empty. I came confusedly to myself as I saw someone standing in front of me and heard a voice saying: 'Mr Fenwick, you look pale. Are you unwell?'

It was Mrs Hurlock. Of course it was Mrs Hurlock. This was where we had met before: she must have been looking for me.

I could think of nothing to say. Here we stood amid misty autumn woods, two pitiable creatures. She was looking at me, concerned. Something was expected of me, but my mind was empty. Without a word, without a thought, I seized this plump lady and threw her down upon the wet leaves. I was kissing her throat, laying bare her big breasts, throwing back her clothes, forcing apart her thighs. In a moment I was thrusting myself again and again into her body, as I would have done at that moment had she been a child, a grandmother or a sheep. I think I must have shocked or hurt her, for she scratched my face as I spent with a long animal howl that reverberated among the dripping trees.

I do not recollect quite how it came about, but afterwards I burst into tears, sobbing on and on, like a child. My breeches, smeared with mud, were still unfastened and my wig had fallen off. Mrs Hurlock, whose dress had been torn aside, held me to her naked bosom, kissing my face, stroking my hair, and murmuring endearments. She seemed to interpret my wild grief as relating to herself, a wordless outburst of impassioned feeling. Having despised and abused and deceived her I could hardly begrudge her the mistake.

After some few minutes, when I had snivelled myself to silence I pulled away with some incoherent mumblings and a last peck upon her cheek, and stumbled off towards Fork Hill House. As I entered, mud-stained and distracted, I encountered the physician who was leaving. I cannot think what he made of my red eyes or the damp leaves clinging to my clothes. He told me, with professional decorum, that Mr Gilbert was still seriously, though not dangerously, unwell, and should keep to his bed for several days.

༄

The following morning I wrote my godfather a brief message of sympathy and farewell, and set out once more for London.

27

The latter half of my return journey was obscured by autumn mist. In London, where these vapours were thickened with city smoke, the streets through which we clattered were so many dusky caverns. The circumstance was apt: I felt suffocated by uncertainty, unable to discern what the future might hold.

Arriving at Cathcart Street chilled and stiff, I found some comfort in the friendly greeting from Mrs Deacon and more from the fire that had been lit in my parlour. I sat beside it sipping tea and wondering how to pass the days ahead. There was now no intrigue to pursue, nor had I any incentive to seek out odd sights. My single plan was to talk with Matt Cullen, find out from him whether there had been further news concerning Ogden, and discuss my changed situation.

Lingering discomfort from the journey caused me to retire early and to wake late. The house was as thickly muffled by mist as on the previous day. I sat by the fire once more, scarcely capable of thought – still less of useful action. There came relief of a sort when the maid brought a letter, newly delivered:

> *Dear Mr Fenwick,*
>
> *My aunt and I have decided to withdraw to York for a time. I am in need of respite, since I remain greatly distressed and confused by recent events. Mr Gow and Mr Semple have been empowered to take charge of all business and legal matters during my absence, and will keep me informed concerning them.*
>
> *You will yet again think me inconsistent, but I have concluded that, after all, I would like to see you before I go, should that be possible. There are certain topics which I can discuss with you alone. We leave very shortly. If you are free to call today or tomorrow I will be most grateful. You will find me at my aunt's house.*
>
> *Yours, &c.*

Blank as I was feeling I stirred myself and went that very afternoon – went on foot, wearing a low hat and a long kersey coat to hold off the wetness in the air. The gloom of the weather had subdued the life of the streets: I strode along unhindered. As I neared Mrs Kinsey's house I felt a renewed tingling of nervous recollection. I took a deep breath before knocking at the door.

It was Mrs Kinsey whom I first encountered. As ever she greeted me warmly, but she looked weary, and to my discomfiture I saw a tear on her cheek. She brushed it aside and recovered herself, saying: 'I know you will excuse me, Mr Fenwick. I have a heavy heart. How sadly things fall out.'

'I hear you are to travel to York.'

'It was my suggestion. Sarah has been very sorely tried. We can stay with the Martins, very quietly, away from the questions and the gossip.'

'This has been a hard time for you both.'

'A very hard time. Poor Mr Ogden. I used to laugh at him, but he was a generous man. He bought me this house.'

As she spoke I followed her glance and saw on the wall to one side of me a portrait of Ogden that I had not previously noticed. It was an unwelcome shock to confront again the heavy, inexpressive face of the man I had last seen lying dead in the mud. I looked away, but remained conscious of his gaze.

Mrs Kinsey retired, with a few murmured words, when her niece entered. Dressed in black, finely erect, her face pale, Sarah could have been a tragic heroine.

'I see you are in mourning,' I said, awkwardly.

'I have been for several days – since I was assured that there could be no hope.'

We sat facing one another, and I waited for her to speak. A week or two earlier such a meeting would have filled me with trepidation. I had imagined being stricken with a guilt that would make it hard for me to speak – let alone to lie. But in my new frame of mind I felt detached almost to the point of indifference.

'You wanted to see me?'

'I did. Before leaving London I wished to know what you could tell me about that – that fatal night.'

'There is little to tell.' I made a show of recollection: 'It was a dark night – and cloudy. I reached Margaret Street about midnight, and saw the watch pass by. When they had gone I came to the house and found your note. I read it under a lamp nearby. Having no means of immediate reply I made my way home. I recall that it began to rain.'

'You saw no one else?'

'No one.'

Perhaps my new-found unconcern helped me to speak with conviction. In my mind I saw the scenes I was describing more clearly than I had ever cared to remember the actuality. Sarah sat silent, taking in what she had heard. At last she said: 'It seems that there is nothing more for me to learn. I can hardly bear to think of that night, still less to talk about it; but it seems so strange that Mr Ogden should have returned as he did unless – unless he had some suspicion of a plan known only to you and me.'

I asked the question that had long been in my mind: 'What passed between you before he left for Malvern?'

'Almost nothing. But one moment I remember well. When about to go he returned to the bedroom – I think to say goodbye – and saw me smiling into a mirror. He said "You look happy" and turned away. Those were his last words to me.'

I was once more aware of Ogden's face looking down at us.

'Was that why you wrote to me as you did?'

'Perhaps. Partly.'

'It was as well that you did so.'

'It was. Otherwise my plight would have been insupportable.'

Her sadness would have saddened me at any time. In the light of my new understanding it stirred in me a sense of utter dreariness and futility. I could think of nothing to say that seemed worth saying. It was left to Sarah to speak again, looking me in the eyes as she did so: 'You and I can be candid with one another – and with no one else. Our lives have been linked.'

'They have. What do you now feel concerning your husband?'

Sarah spoke in a low voice: 'What I feel is guilt and pity, rather than grief. And therefore further guilt. I respected him, and was grateful to him. But he was hard to love. Perhaps no one ever loved him. Then he was killed. That was a sad life.'

I bowed my head in sober assent, but my thoughts were drifting elsewhere. I had been reminded of my interview with Mrs Quentin.

'What will you do in York?'

'I hardly know. Read and sleep and walk and think.'

'A quiet life.'

'A very quiet life. It is all I am fit for at present.'

She sat with clasped hands and lowered eyes. As I looked at her I could sense Ogden's painted eyes staring at my profile. I wondered whether she would take the portrait with her to York or whether it would stay here presiding over an empty house.

Sarah rallied a little: 'But you will be in town still, merry-making on your godfather's behalf?'

'I think not.'

'Why?'

'The link between us has been severed.'

Sarah looked up, surprised into attention.

'Can you tell me more?'

'Not at this time.'

'But what will you do?'

'I must seek employment of some kind.'

There was a further silence. We had each made a statement that led to a closed door. It remained only for us to exchange formal farewells. I glanced again at the woman I had widowed and saw that her cheeks were now faintly flushed. As when clasping Mrs Hurlock a few days previously, I could have wept from pure desolation. Getting to my feet I said: 'I must take my leave. When do you depart for York?'

'On Monday next.'

'Will you write to me?'

'Perhaps. I cannot promise.'

I kissed her cool fingers and left.

Matt Cullen called the following day. He entered with the large grin that meant that he had something entertaining to impart.

'I bring you news that will surprise you.'

'Will it please me?'

'Not necessarily. But it may amuse you. Miss Kitty Brindley is now Mrs Horn. Not content with being her protector Nick quietly married her last week. What do you say, Dick? Your face is a study.'

'I was fond of the girl. Nick is a mad young dog, but sentimental. They may both have made a lucky choice. Will she continue on the stage?'

'Most certainly. Nick will be luminous with reflected glory.'

'Perhaps that is better than none. Nick is the first of our band to tie the knot. Will you be asking for the hand of your servant-girl?'

'That is not the part I covet. Besides, she saves the money I give her towards marriage with a young lobcock named Barnabas. We are adjuncts, Dick, you and I. We promote the nuptials of others.'

We both laughed, he the more heartily of the two. I broached a bottle of wine and asked if there had been further reports of any kind concerning Ogden. He told me there had not. He had it from Gow that two men had come forward claiming to have vital knowledge, but had proved to be chuckle-head reward-seekers who knew nothing at all. The affair was as good as closed.

In turn he asked about my visit to Fork Hill, and listened with his usual smiling attention as I spoke of my godfather's illness and the frustration it had caused him.

'That does not surprise me,' said Matt. 'There is a man who cannot bear to feel the clarity of his mind clouded by the weakness of his body.'

I described Gilbert's keen interest in the disappearance of Ogden, and predicted that even Gow's latest pronouncements would not persuade him that the story had reached its end.

'In that connection,' said I, 'a question occurred to me.

How did you first come to make the acquaintance of Mr Gow?'

Matt scratched his chin.

'I scarcely recall. It was a matter of chance. We happened to strike up a conversation at the Pear Tree.'

'Well dissembled, Matt,' I said approvingly. 'What seasoned liars we have both become. So it was not that Mr Gilbert asked you to seek him out?'

Cullen's face lost all expression as I spoke. For some moments he sat still as a statue. When at length he replied it was in altered voice: 'So the old devil has given me away?'

'Not that he knows. Being unwell he let fall some careless words which made me see our past transactions in a new light.'

Cullen nodded slowly, two or three times, but said nothing. It was strange to see his face incongruously dejected, the wig perched above it like a hairy lid. I felt pity for him, and thought what sad creatures all human-beings were. To put an end to the stillness I poured more wine, and addressed him conversationally.

'When did this begin?'

'In March, after you had left Fork Hill.' Cullen spoke in a lifeless voice. 'I was at home in Malvern, with nothing to do. Mr Gilbert sent word that he would like to see me.'

'Had you met him before?'

'Once or twice, briefly – when you were abroad. He saw me again later, when my father had the gout.'

'The gout was true?'

'Yes.'

'And are you indeed related to the Duke?'

'Yes, but I scarcely know him, and have no hopes of him.'

'So you lived on my godfather's money?'

'Yes: as you do. As you do. He gave me a small allowance.'

'To do what?'

'To report to him about you – about what you had been doing and saying.'

'You were to be Rosencrantz to his Claudius?'

Cullen hesitated as he took in the reference.

'Mr Gilbert did not speak like Claudius. He used the language of experiment. He wished to oversee your doings, he said, but your letters to him might be so many inventions to beguile him. My accounts would confirm them.'

'Or otherwise.'

'Or otherwise. But far more often confirm them.' Cullen's voice became pleading: 'Dick, I was your ally. I was your guarantor. I could confirm that there *was* a Kitty, there *was* a Sarah.'

'Did you tell him of my attempt on Mrs Deacon?'

A pause. 'Yes. But with *humour*. He knew your disposition. He invested in it.'

'You told him that I had hurt my tongue?'

'I think I did.'

'Would your letters describe our conversations?'

'Some of them.'

I drew breath and drank some wine.

'Then he knew that I distrusted him, knew that I disparaged him, knew that I mocked him – and knew that I hoped to be his heir?'

'In general terms – only in general terms. And *tone*, Dick – the tone was all. I wrote in a spirit of humour.'

'Mr Gilbert is a merry old gentleman. He must have been greatly diverted. And through all these months you flattered my high hopes?'

'Why not, Dick? Why not? What did I know of your prospects? I was a mere agent.'

'So you did not know whether I was a potential heir or a specimen in an experiment?'

'I was told nothing of such matters. My letters received only the briefest of replies.'

'Save when you were asked to find out more about Mr Ogden.'

'That was an exception.'

I had exhausted my questions and exhausted myself. By now I should have been flaring into violence, but the fire within me seemed to have burnt itself out, leaving black vacancy. Listlessly I rose, took a turn across the room, and then stood staring out of the window across the narrow street.

'What are you thinking?' asked Cullen, hoarsely.

'I hardly know. I hardly care.'

He clattered abruptly to his feet and came to my side.

'Did you tell Gilbert that you had seen through him?'

'I did not.'

'As far as he knows, things stand between you as before?'

'For the moment.'

'Then do you not see—' he was suddenly eager '—we could outwit him. Invent any story you choose, and I will confirm it. His experiment will be turned on its head.'

I saw the hope fade from his face as I made no response.

'You are angry,' he said. 'I can understand it. But think about what I have said. We both stand to gain.'

Suddenly weary I had to exert myself to make a reply.

'I am not angry. I felt disgust – but it became self-disgust. We are neither of us to be trusted. We have both been bought.'

'What if we have?' cried Cullen. 'What if we have?' He was in a sort of passion. 'It is the way of the world. We could be bought because we were in need. If I deceived you, you were already deceiving Gilbert. You have deceived many a woman with those brown eyes. Have I behaved worse than that? We are liars both, but can we not still be friends?'

'You are not capable of friendship. Nor am I, perhaps. Our allegiance is to ourselves – and to money.'

I slopped out more wine, and ironically raised my glass: 'We have had some fine times together, Matt, but they were all worthless.'

Cullen emptied his own glass as though taking bitter medicine.

He spoke flatly: 'What are we now to do?'

'I shall do nothing. Your task is to write one last letter to Mr Gilbert, recording this conversation – faithfully recording it. Tell him that he will not hear from me again. With that letter your employment and my own will come simultaneously to an end. And then we must live by our wits.'

Cullen made to go, but turned back at the door.

'You have known me in happier times, Dick, and now you see me wretched. I am ashamed. But if you saw what I had written to Mr Gilbert you might think that I had not greatly harmed you. There was some deception, but I was always your friend.'

'And I was yours,' I said. 'But we can be friends no more.'

I lay abed next morning, feeling no inclination to stir. What was I to do? Where was I to go? All my reflections concluded in nothing. I had no plans and no engagements. Cullen had perhaps already written the letter that would estrange my godfather and leave me with nothing. I could confide in no one save, perhaps, Sarah, who would be by now on her journey north.

I hoped that Gilbert had not yet written to me – and would not before hearing from Cullen. It was possible, of course, that he would not now write at all, but silently stop my allowance. I would become a fish out of water – a gentleman without money. In this plight I envied Pike his freedom. There was a man who found it easy to move on, to step from one life into another – a man who could sleep in a haystack or a barn, and find employment anywhere.

The thought of Pike did something to stiffen my sinews. After all it was something to be oneself, to be indomitable. If I was condemned to be solitary and penniless I would at any rate have ceased to be a dependant, a cat's-paw, a dupe – the passive subject of a heartless experiment. Like Pike, like Jack Gardiner at Tyburn – even like Ogden – I could show myself unpredictable and defiant.

I rose from my bed and sullenly stretched my limbs. Peering in the mirror I thought that my face had hardened since the spring: there was no trace of charm or humour in it. I could expect to please no one. But merely for the sake of self-respect, I would don the uniform again: the breeches, the clean shirt, the fresh stockings, the wig. Through this final chapter of my gentlemanly career I would perform my duties in style.

And so through several succeeding days I tried to live as I had lived before. I walked in the Park, and bowed to a few acquaintances; I attended a reception or two. One night I set out for the Black Lion, but hearing the tumult within turned away, unable to rise to the occasion.

On another occasion, driven by a recurring and uncomfortable impulse, I walked along Duke Street and glanced through the window into what had been Ogden's office. I glimpsed within a grey fellow I took to be Mr Gow, the gentleman who had taken charge following Ogden's death, and had unknowingly provided one of the clues to Cullen's treachery. Still in this vein of disturbing recollection I walked on past Mrs Kinsey's home, along Margaret Street and past the Ogden house. With an effort of will I continued to Wyvern Street, and the spot where Ogden had confronted me. My recollections of that night now seemed no more substantial than a dream. How long had the episode lasted? Three minutes, perhaps? I was thankful to be forgetting so readily. The small, deep wound was healing, if over an embedded fragment of thorn or grit.

Each time I returned to Cathcart Street I expected, with fear, to see that a letter had arrived for me. But day followed day and there was nothing. It became clear that at least there would be no redundant message from Mr Gilbert, written before Cullen had intervened. I tried to revive my former hope that illness would carry the man off and leave his estate in my hands, but I now knew it to be a puerile fancy.

From this short period only one or two episodes stand out in my recollection. One stemmed from a visit I made to the theatre, alone and inconspicuous. Jane Page and Kitty Brindley were both performing, the latter in a minor role only. It was curious to see them from my new perspective: they shone and were applauded to the echo; I was nobody. When I left London they would still be here, and would still be celebrated. Kitty seemed to my eyes more charming, more vivacious, than ever. How foolish I had been to let her go – and how fortunate for her that I had done so.

Outside the theatre after the performance I felt a tap on my shoulder and turned to see Nick Horn. For a second I was at a loss, but Nick's expression so comically mingled embarrassment and triumph that for the first time in days I began to laugh.

'You have heard the news?' he said, laughing himself.

'I have heard that you are a married man.'

'I am.'

'Then I congratulate you.' I shook his hand, feeling a sudden warmth towards him. 'Does this mean that your pig-wrestling days are at an end?'

'I have not wrestled with a pig this fortnight.' He hesitated. 'Dick, I am here to meet my wife: would you care to speak to her?'

I recognized this for a gracious gesture, and tried to respond in kind: 'I would feel honoured to do so.'

So it came about that I shared supper with this married

pair. Kitty greeted me demurely, but with the smallest spark of irony in her glance.

'I am pleased to make the acquaintance of Mrs Horn,' said I.

Over the meal we conversed a little haltingly. Perhaps we could do no more than act out our friendly feelings, but that very attempt was a demonstration of goodwill. I was touched to see Nick so obviously infatuated with his bride. Having felt at a disadvantage I suddenly decided to venture a direct apology.

'This has been a most agreeable occasion,' I said. 'Let me take the chance to express deep regret for a past episode of unkindness to Mrs Horn. I can offer but two submissions in mitigation. The first is that I was disgracefully drunk; the second is that my failings accidentally promoted your shared happiness – to which I raise my glass.'

Both took the gesture kindly: there was even the glint of a tear in Kitty's eye. While the wind was in the right quarter I added boldly: 'You will know that the Diana who distracted my attention that night has been unfortunate since.'

'We have read the story,' said Nick, a little uncertainly.

'She was a friend when we were children together in York. I have not seen her since that night of the masquerade, but she wrote last week to tell me that she had retreated to York again to help her recover from the ordeal.'

Little more was said on the subject, but I felt sure that Kitty would pass on what I had said to her friend Jane, thereby perhaps retrieving for me a little undeserved credit in the Crocker household.

Later in the evening, when we were briefly alone together, she thanked me for my kind words to her.

'I meant what I said. I am pleased to see you look so happy.'

'I am happy – very happy.' She smiled at me, and put on her rustic voice: 'I do sorely miss 'ee, young Master Fenwick, but times do change.'

I went home in melancholy mood, but more cheerful than I had been. After all, these were friends worth having.

A day or two later I went, in a fit of bravado, to visit Mr Ward. I was watchful to see whether his expression changed as I approached. It did not.

'Mr Ward,' said I, 'when I last saw my godfather, more than a fortnight ago, he was somewhat unwell. I have heard nothing since. Have you any news of him?'

'No direct news. But he has sent me signed documents lately – after an interval. I infer that he is recovering.'

I hazarded one further question: 'Mr Ward, tell me, if you feel it permissible: have you had dealings on my godfather's behalf with a Mr Matthew Cullen?'

The brain inside Ward's big skull seemed to labour like the workings of a town clock about to strike the hour. At last he said: 'If the answer was to be the affirmative I would not feel free to give it. But I have had no dealings with a gentleman of that name.'

'I am pleased to hear it,' said I, and meant what I said.

❧

I tried to calculate how much money I could scrape together when my allowance ceased. I found it a hateful task. Without being a prodigal spender I was by now accustomed to living comfortably. This attempt to number my available guineas on paper twisted my face with discomfort. By the end of the year what would I be doing? Would it be the army, after all? Might I run a bookshop like the one I had recently patronized? I shrank from such possibilities. It came to me that my father, at about my own age, had moved to York to run a school. Could I endure a life such as his – or such as Thorpe's? Unwilling to answer the question I pushed aside pen and paper and poured myself some wine.

Another walk in the Park proved slightly more productive, in that I was greeted, with polite condescension, by Latimer, and briefly conversed with him.

'You will have heard that Nicholas has married? I believe that you once had dealings with the lady in question?'

'One might say so.'

'This is an indiscreet affair – a very indiscreet affair. Master Horn will live to regret it. Marriage can make or mar a career.'

He lowered his voice, as though there might be eaves-droppers in the bushes. 'I myself am in distant negotiation with one of Lord Ashton's nieces. It would be a most advantageous match.'

'Latimer,' I said, 'you are wise in the ways of the world.'

When I returned to Cathcart Street I chanced to see Mrs Deacon in the hall.

'A letter came for you,' she said. 'I have left it on your desk.'

The words set my heart thumping. At last the blow was to fall. To postpone the moment I began to practise the coolness I knew I would now need to show: 'Mrs Deacon, I am afraid that I may soon have to leave these lodgings.'

'I am sorry to hear it, Mr Fenwick.' She seemed to mean what she was saying. 'You have been very kind to Charlotte. And I shall miss your singing.'

As I opened my door the letter at once caught my eye. I drew a deep breath and paused to calm myself before picking it up.

But the handwriting was Sarah's.

Dear Mr Fenwick,

You may be surprised to hear from me so soon; and the content of this letter will surprise you still more. It may surprise me, too, since I know what I would say but not how I will contrive to say it.

Since Mr Ogden disappeared my thoughts have been sorely confined, my mind imprisoned within that one theme. The creeping journey north, hour after hour and day after day, the gradually changing scene, served somehow to extricate me from the worst of this despondency. By the time I alighted in the familiar streets of York I was halfway returned to a former self, able to consider more freely what I had been and what I would now become.

These reflections were greatly influenced by a long talk I had with Mr Semple on the day preceding my departure. It seems that my future prospects must be a matter for the courts, who will adjudicate on the delicate issue of Presumption of Death. Mr Semple is confident, however, that in this case the balance of probabilities is so clear that at no distant date I will inherit my husband's possessions and become a very

*wealthy woman. (Once again I am grateful that, if only
by chance, I did not quite betray this generous,
awkward benefactor.) I will be inevitably translated into
a very different person, with a very different mode of
life.*

*If I rightly understood what you said to me when we
parted in London your own fortunes have taken, or are
about to take, a very different turn. You are cut adrift
and may be left penniless.*

*Given these circumstances I am ready to put to you a
bold plan. If I write with audacious bluntness it is
because I am confident that I will not be misunderstood:
you and I have spoken together very frankly on some past
occasions.*

*The plan I am proposing is this. I will remain in York
for some few weeks, or even months. When I return to
London I shall invite you to visit me – more than that: I
will be so forward as slyly to encourage you to pay court
to me. I will respond to your overtures with bashful
warmth. In course of time – it can hardly be sooner than
two years from now – we shall be married. In the
intervening time I shall take steps to ensure that you are
discreetly enabled to continue living in London in the
style to which your godfather enabled you to aspire.*

*How rash my letter is! How outrageous to propriety!
Yet I am proud to be writing it: I exult in being so blunt
and taking such risks. Sustaining me in my intrepidity
are two mighty considerations.*

*First, you and I are matched in mind. I have known
you all my thinking life. We share memories, of course,*

but also beliefs and tastes. We understand one another very well. We can communicate not only through words, but through the language of eyes, expression, tone and gesture.

And we are attuned in passion. I need say nothing further on that score: you know as I know how we have caught fire when we have so much as touched.

I write this letter hastily in the heat of a compelling mood, but I mean every word that I have said. I long for an answer – a declaration of ardent acceptance. But do not answer yet. Consider my plan to be no more than hypothetical. I know, and so do you, that in matters of moment I have weakly changed my mind before now. So wait: ponder what I have said. Do not reply until I have written once more, probably in a very few weeks. If I then confirm, as I am sure I will, that my intention holds, I will hope for an answer from you which will seal the compact between us.

Yours, &c.

I had to read the letter twice before I could fully comprehend what it meant for me. Having just been transformed, my life was to be transformed once more. Curiously my first response was one of disinterested mental relief, as though at a difficult mathematical calculation producing a neat answer, or a philosophical speculation resolving itself into a compact proposition. All was clear, all was well. But this abstract satisfaction was almost immediately overwhelmed by a rush of exultation. I was like a man fallen from a tower and alighting safely on his feet – with his pockets stuffed with gold.

I sat savouring the elegance of what had happened. My godfather had unknowingly cajoled and bribed me into the very predicament that was to free me from his clutches. Mr Ogden, in his anxiety to avoid cuckoldom, had kindly bequeathed me not only his wife but his fortune.

My life, which I had hitherto improvised, now took on shape and sequence. Two years previously I had been in France; two years hence I would be living in London, a wealthy married man, ready to become a respectable citizen. I was not, after all, condemned to be an outcast like Francis Pike: I had been born under a lucky star. As one cornucopia was snatched from my grasp another was proffered. After weeks of despair and guilt I was bubbling with facetious glee.

It was true that I would have a tiresome secret to hide from my wife – the fact that I had – if unintentionally – killed her first husband. Perhaps I could all but forget the matter. Or on some mischievous night when we had both drunk more than we should, perhaps I might tell her the truth, and we would giggle with horror at the enormity of it.

The thoughts that energized my mind began to activate my body. I threw aside coat and wig and paced the room, pausing at the mirror to grin at my grinning reflection. I poured myself a glass of wine and drank it in a single draught. I burst into song, aware that Mrs Deacon would hear me down below:

> Pray fill up my glass: I must drink again.
> A beggar I may be – what then? What then?
> My credit is good, though my coat may be poor:

Old Nick will come later to settle the score.
Pour me some more, pour me some more:
Old Nick will come later to settle the score.

Rejoicing to be frivolous again, for the first time in weeks, I reached for pen and paper and composed some burlesque couplets to celebrate the occasion:

Thus random deeds sequentially connect:
Effects breed causes, cause begets effect.
The plan which fails to achieve what we intend
Perchance conduces to some unseen end.
Today's confusion may, in time to be,
Revert to pattern and to symmetry.
So monstrous billows, that convulse the deep,
Subside at last, and rock themselves to sleep.
The sapling rises as the old tree dies,
And one man's fall procures another man's rise.

I was half sorry that I no longer had my godfather as a correspondent. He might have been intrigued to see how neatly the old hackney maxims applied to my situation. Perhaps he would even have been blackly amused by the turn his experiment had taken.

I drank more wine and read Sarah's letter yet again. For weeks I had all but exiled her from my mind. What a fool I had been. Here was an exceptional woman. How fearlessly she spoke out, heedless of caution or convention. How generously she offered me everything she possessed. Together we would forge a remarkable partnership, shining together in London society as solitary Mr Gilbert withered towards death at Fork Hill.

She was once more fully alive to my imagination. I remembered her as she had been in the landau, in darkness, all warmth, all longing, her breath mingling with mine. Closing my eyes to lose myself in the memory I was at once swelling with lust. Not since the nonsense with Mrs Hurlock had I known venereal relief of any sort. Now body displaced mind, my whore-pipe was once more in my hand, and in moments, with a joyful roar, I was spending exultantly, snatching up my poem to protect my breeches.

28

My dear Richard,

   After my recent illness I was for some time a little
weak, but I recovered sufficiently to compose a letter to
you. Before it was posted, however, I myself received a
letter from Matthew Cullen, the content of which you can
guess. In the light of what he said I discarded what I
had written. Subsequently I made a number of attempts
to start afresh. However, each time I attempted to set
down my thoughts the emphases shifted: something had
been omitted or exaggerated. I conclude that there can be
no perfect version of what I wish to say; what seems true
in the evening may appear doubtful next morning. This
letter will fall short of my intentions, but will be as
complete as I can make it. I admit to certain inconsistencies
in my character: it follows that in trying to speak the
truth from day to day I will prove guilty of
self-contradiction.

   I gather from Cullen (who has now received a final

payment, and is out of the account) that you are resentful and wish to sever all contact with me. It irritates me to know that, through ill health, I myself let slip the clues that aroused your suspicions. On the whole, however, I do not regret what has happened. The time had come for clarification. This letter is intended as a step in that direction, and is an attempt to reconcile us.

Where to begin? As a boy I never learned to swim. I knew the strokes, and practised them on land, but to no practical effect. I could never yield myself to the water and trust that I would float. When I grew older I experienced what seemed to me to be comparable difficulties elsewhere. Brought up to value self-command I shrank from drunkenness: repeatedly I found myself the one sober man at a carousal. In the company of women my social self was rendered clumsily incapable by my observing self. I was deeply envious of those such as your father, who freely and easily followed their instincts. Lacking such confidence I would flinch from a courtship on the pretext of some physical reservation rather than risk rejection. I affected fastidiousness as a cover for my fears, and the affectation hardened into a habit. Rather than repine at my lack of animal vitality I preferred to pride myself on discrimination, and clarity of thought.

When I inherited the Fork Hill estate, as a young man, I therefore seized eagerly on the excuse to preside over the lives of others rather than take the risk of living my own life to the full. At the practical level I enjoyed some little success: my estate flourished and my tenants prospered. Some of my more ambitious ventures, however, fell short of my hopes. I sought to nurture a second Pope, a second Newton, but engendered merely a Quentin and a Yardley. Several doubtful marriages, including that of the Hurlocks, took place at my instigation, as I found husbands for those I had feared to embrace.

Over the years I became increasingly dissatisfied with the detached existence to which I had condemned myself. At Fork Hill House I had everything I needed to gratify eye and ear and palate. I was considered a man of taste – but what had become of my appetite? Where were my Passions? My contempt for Hurlock could be transmuted into contempt for myself. I feared I had become his fleshless obverse, an elegant shell, merely.

It was no doubt for this reason that I acquired a relish for tales in which an author assumes an alien personality. Thus Defoe can write as sea-farer, whore or pickpocket. Through an imaginary traveller Swift exposes his own obsession with the odours and what he sees as the ugliness of the human body. Fantastically he seats himself, as Gulliver, astride the jutting nipple of a stinking giantess and the self-denunciation is lauded as satire. Yet more revealing has been Richardson's immersion in his fictional works. Why is Clarissa *so grotesquely long? Because the author could not bear to let it end. It gave him freedom to dress and to undress his heroine, to observe and to assault her – and all in the name of morality. Does he not display a self-deception indistinguishable from hypocrisy? Of course he does. But it enabled him to write, through Lovelace, with a wit and iconoclasm that he could never have achieved in his own voice. By indulging*

a moral weakness he discovered an artistic strength,
and a hidden dimension of his own personality.

It was in this spirit that I myself looked to
experiment. For better or worse I wished to know
myself. The possibility of involving you in the project
emerged only by degrees. Although your godfather I saw
you but rarely in your early years. When I assumed
responsibility for your upbringing you were a child. At
this stage I did not think to make plans for you. I was
already conscious, however, of a small seed of curiosity.
As you know, your father was a friend of mine at
university. He charmed me, dominated me, and in
certain activities surpassed me. I found myself
wondering – rather in the spirit of Yardley – whether
as you grew older you would recapitulate the Fenwick I
had once known. As the years passed you did indeed
prove to resemble your father, both in appearance and
in disposition. I came to be intrigued by the possibility
that you could become both a reincarnation of your
father and a substitute self for me. You could be my
Roderick Random, my Lovelace, but a flesh and blood
instigator rather than a verbal figment.

It seemed to me that our partnership promised
well. We have enjoyed a happy division of moral
responsibility. My excuse can be that it is you, not I,
who have been the active performer. But you have had
available the disclaimer, equally specious, that you
indulged yourself only at my insistence. Setting aside
such casuistry I confess to having learned a great deal
about myself, much of it discreditable. The human body

*still disgusts me, but I enjoy that disgust. I have
succeeded in vindicating my detachment, scepticism and
fastidiousness, but through the very process of
participating greedily, if vicariously, in their antitheses.
Your awareness of the duplicity of my position cannot
be keener than my own. I confess that my pleasure at
Hurlock's humiliation was exquisite, and that my
conduct with regard to his wife was essentially more
gross than yours. But it is in just this respect that my
experiments have been bolder than Richardson's. He
escapes the implications of his tale by the arbitrary
imposition of a 'moral' conclusion in which the good
are lauded and the wicked condemned. In any case he
purports to stand to one side as a mere narrator. I
have been denied recourse to any such crude evasion. I
cannot tell how the stories I initiate will conclude –
and it is that very uncertainty which most particularly
solicits my attention. Moreover I cannot anticipate just
how deeply I will prove to be immersed in them and
perhaps deformed by them. I have been as much a
subject of these experiments as have you.*

*The disappearance and apparent murder of Ogden
was the extreme instance of a story taking an unexpected
turn. As I told you, I was intrigued by the fact that, far
away in Fork Hill, I perhaps knew more of what had
happened, and what might have happened, in that case
than any of those on the spot. I knew of your hostility to
Mr Ogden and your intended tryst with his wife, knew
that you had previously pursued her at a masquerade
which her husband also attended. I knew that you visited*

the coach station on the morning of his departure; I knew of his altered note to Lord Downs, and (through Cullen) of his strange demeanour as observed by Mr Gow. I even knew of the seemingly coincidental injury to your tongue. Now I learn, from Cullen's last letter, that by a strange chance your informant, Francis Pike, unexpectedly left the service of Mr Crocker at this very time . . .

I think you would share my view that it would be a pity if more should come to be written on this subject.

You cannot have regretted the opportunities that I put in your way: to go to Oxford, to travel and study abroad, to enjoy a life of leisure in London. How would you have preferred to spend those years? You are offended because I employed Cullen to report on your doings. Is that not a little squeamish? It would neither surprise nor disturb me to learn that you had compared your impressions of my character with those of Thorpe or Mrs Jennings. Cullen provided an additional perspective on my experiment. In the main he usefully corroborated your own account. He reported certain slights and jests at my expense; but I was never such a simpleton as to think that you would always speak of me with grateful reverence. Through him I was reassured that you were faithfully keeping your side of the bargain. In respect of episodes and characters his accounts and yours were at one.

Since that last unfortunate meeting between us some little time has now elapsed – sufficient, I hope, for your original indignation to have subsided. In a cooler spirit think back once more over your experiences of the past half year, and reflect also what you have learned about me in that time. You may find reassurance in noting that I have shown loyalty to those I have chosen to patronize. Mrs Deacon, whom you apparently admire, continues to live at ease. Quentin was not discarded when his muse failed – indeed his widow remains in the house I provided for them. Even Hurlock has been allowed to retain much of his estate.

You have lived comfortably enough, I think, since returning to London. Do you really wish to relinquish this way of life – to exchange the constraints of experiment for the constraints of poverty? Why end an arrangement that we have found mutually beneficial? Your anger with regard to Cullen confirms that you are what I already knew you to be: a young man of spirit – and I have enabled you to exercise that spirit.

We have need of one another, you and I. It would be an embarrassment to me if it appeared that my godson had been disowned, but an embarrassment I could sustain. More significant is the fact that, to some extent, we are in one another's power. I have revealed more of myself, and of my secret self, to you than to anyone else. Let me go further: I have come to depend upon you as an external projection of my Passions. You are a necessary prop to me, and one that is irreplaceable. On the other side of the question this letter may have suggested to you that I have acquired a comparably close insight into your own character and certain of your doings. Mere prudence suggests that we should remain allies.

I urge you to stay with me, to experiment again, to continue to take risks and to deal in compromise and ambiguity. What will your ultimate reward be? I am averse to making promises. But you are a young man who enjoys a wager. Will you not take your chance?

Yours, &c.

Dear Mr Fenwick,

In my last letter I said that I would soon write again, whether to confirm or to retract the forthright offer I made in it. Am I still of the same mind? Yes, yes, and again yes. I endorse, in this cooler frame of mind, everything that I so precipitately set down. I wholeheartedly renew my offer, and long for you to accept it.

I am compelled to admit, however, that in the intervening time a circumstance has arisen which you may see as an obstacle, although I hope you will not. I will say more on that subject below.

I am now both calmer and happier. The people here know something of my story from the newspapers, or from gossip, and of course they see that I am in mourning. On the whole they have been kind and tactful. Their good feeling perhaps comes easier because London seems so far away. What is said to have happened there can seem as insubstantial here as a fairy-tale. I am real to those I encounter, but my recent past in London is not.

During these further weeks in York I have become habituated once more to the life within which I was brought up. I have walked familiar streets and met former friends and acquaintances. I have talked with shopkeepers who have worked on through the past three years – years which have so radically altered you and me – exactly as they had done through the previous ten or twenty. To come from London to York is to step back half a century and enter a different world. It is one that seems to suit me: I am happy here.

Miss Martin professes to consider me greatly changed, and even says that she finds me intimidating – a claim I do not believe. I find her just as she was, still warm, lively and entertaining. Yet against my will I feel myself somehow wiser and more mature. Is this because I have seen a little of London, merely? Or, still worse, because I am richer? No – rather, I think, because I have lived more fully, have known stronger emotions and temptations, and the sharp taste of guilt.

You are still remembered here: there have been several inquiries about you. I say that I have met you since your return from your foreign travels and that you are now a fine gentleman. Some speak of you as you were when you were fifteen years old, and if they saw you now could hardly credit what you have become. But I think that if you visited York you could find refreshment here, as I do.

With regard to the possible 'obstacle' mentioned above I will speak out plainly, since I more and more detest equivocation in all its forms. The truth is that I find I am with child. I would no doubt have perceived the indications a little sooner if my last weeks in London had been less taxing.

I cannot think that this news will be anything but unwelcome to you. What can I say to make it more acceptable? Let me continue in my candid vein. It so happens that I can calculate exactly when the child was conceived. It was in the early hours of the morning that followed the masquerade. I told you, I think, that my husband returned home with me apparently half frantic with angry lust. I did not add, although I could have done, that he found me physically more receptive than was customary because my embrace with you had fired me with desire. This poor orphan, when it is born, will truly be a child, not of Mr Ogden merely, but of the masquerade.

I can think of several other perceptions of this circumstance which might render it more tolerable to you. After all you were willing, you were eager, to be my lover although I was married to Mr Ogden. The birth of this baby could be seen as no more than a re-statement of that acknowledged fact. By the time it is socially acceptable for us to marry I shall have recovered, I hope, all my looks, and the baby will be a small child. Both still young, we can start afresh. For myself I feel a special tenderness towards an infant entering the world in such inauspicious circumstances. To be fair to my late husband I cannot think that a child of his will lack character or intelligence. This oddly compounded little being should make an interesting companion for the children that you and I will have.

I could moralize, and suggest that as it was the arrangement between us that led Mr Ogden to return to London and so to meet his death, we owe it to him to take responsibility for his child. But I do not

think I need to do so. I know you to have a kind
disposition. As a boy you were always good-natured. I
cannot believe that you will be found lacking in charity
where an obligation seems to be owed, and where our
own love is in the case.

That last consideration is to me the greatest. I have
always loved you. It was possible for me to marry another
only because you had disappeared from my life. If I now
rejoice to be wealthy it is solely because at last I have
something to give to <u>you</u> – a person who, to my eyes, has
been so animated, so sparkling.

It pleases me to think that you and I, as a pair, may
be out of the common run, capable not only of strong
passion but of large views and generous imaginings. If
you can find it in your heart to accept this unlooked-for
situation it will be one more guarantee that our future
together will be happy.

I await your answer with trepidation – but with
confidence.

I remain, &c.

∽

My dear Godfather,
I mentally rehearsed what I wished to say to you, but
could not bring myself to write this difficult letter until I
was under the influence of wine. In consequence I feel
distanced from my task, and now find it indistinct, even
unreal. I watch my hand as it moves the quill. It is
directed by my mind. The mind is swayed by animal

tides within. These in turn may be influenced by the wine I have drunk or the weather beyond my window. (It is raining.) We do well to communicate at all.

I have lost my thread already. Perhaps if I set down some paragraphs as they come to me you will discern the sequence that I have forgotten.

I had not expected to write to you again, and do so only because you have written to me. I was offended that you had spied upon me and that our comradeship was proved false. But there is more to the matter. I am no longer swayed by your arguments: I reject the cynicism that I have affected to share. Of course we are inescapably physical beings. Repeatedly I have acknowledged the fact. But the argument cannot end there. If we are mere animals, what is it within us that deplores the fact? And why does it do so?

Man must endlessly struggle to reconcile those three irreconcilables, body, mind and spirit, as they vie for control. Mr Swift needed no great penetration to mock our inability to achieve the impossible. His position is a shallow one – and literally a barren one: he has left no descendants.

Can we not laugh without bitterness at our equivocations? They need not be ascribed to hypocrisy or self-deception: there is an instinctive wisdom in our willingness to compromise, to recoil from certain apparently logical conclusions. It enables us to live in affection and companionship. Gulliver's claimed wisdom leaves him banished to a stable.

I am glad to learn that you are recovered. We have seen much physical misadventure this past six months:

Yardley's injury, the loss of Quentin, your own indisposition, Hurlock attacked by a dog, the accidental death of Mr Ogden – for a kind of accident it surely was.

Perhaps such loss or damage should be set against the potential advance to be glimpsed in hopeful alliances. My friend Nick Horn marries Kitty Brindley, Crocker sets up house with Jane Page, and Mr Thorpe, I hear, plans to take a wife. Through some disinclination you have never made such a move and nor, as yet, have I. Perhaps we have both been more interested in using people than in relating to them. Neither of us belongs to a family – ours has been an alliance of the solitary.

As you all but admit, we are invalids of a sort, affecting detached curiosity to hide fear of engagement. It is safer to be an historian of war than a soldier. In your letters to me you have more than once implied the contradiction in your philosophy: it is as though an ant should withdraw from the marching line, foregoing his identity in order to reflect upon it.

In performing on your behalf over the past six months I have, like you, learned a great deal about myself. It has been dismaying to me to see how readily I have made excuses for behaving badly. When I at last learned how my friend Matt Cullen had deceived me I perversely felt some slight relief at finding a foothold: here at last was an action I could never have been guilty of. I could not betray a true friend. Perhaps from this recognition I may begin to improvise a morality of some sort.

I cannot but be grateful for the opportunities you have given me. I have lived very comfortably, and it is too late

501

now for me to find work as a shepherd, a bricklayer or a coachman. You seem to propose a continuance of that previous arrangement. Your letter arrives, however, at the very time when I have an opportunity of a different kind – one that would sever my links with you and set me free. In short it is suddenly open to me to marry an amiable, beautiful and wealthy lady.

There is no uncertainty in this fresh prospect – no coercion or obliquity. There is but one small stumbling block, which demands from me no more than a certain generosity of imagination and conduct, of a kind that should be readily afforded and which the lady in question effortlessly displays. But—

. . . But I have had to confess to myself that I am no longer sure that I can muster that generosity, even if I could once have done so. Perhaps I am not made for domestic dependability: my energies are fed by the excitements of the town. Perhaps I always was, or have now become irredeemably self-concerned, incapable of selfless love. Perhaps, after all, you and I are two of a kind.

Such admissions take me as far as I can go as a moralist. I will never attain dignity, but I can try to be honest. The excellent lady concerned will be grieved by my decision, but she deserves far more than I can give, and will not lack for suitors.

I will accept your offer and take my chance.

I have read your letter narrowly. It seems that I must be wary. So, believe me, must you. To an extent you have put yourself in my hands. The past few months have hardened me. You will be at risk equally with myself.

In making my choice I feel I am under compulsion from within: I am obliged to be the man it seems that I have become, even at the price of loneliness. In this perhaps I am at one with the times. Despite some ignominious misadventures Gulliver accepted that he was inescapably condemned to 'an active and restless life'. After twenty-six years on his lonely island Crusoe rested at home but briefly before once more setting out to sea.

Finis

Acknowledgements

I owe too much to too many secondary sources to be able to offer a bibliography, but I would like to express my particular indebtedness to Jenny Uglow, for *Hogarth: A Life and a World*, to Liza Picard, for *Dr Johnson's London*, to G.E. Mingay, for *Georgian London*, and to Jeremy Barlow, for his recorded reconstruction of the complete *Beggar's Opera*.